To Katie,
Caleb's Irrepressible Woman of Wit.
Thanks for the smiles and the inspiration.
Hugs to your little Caleb
with his bright grin and adorable ways.
May laughter and joy find you
and your family every day.

"Few writers can match the skill of Sarah McCarty when it comes to providing her audience with an intelligent, exhilarating Western romance starring two likable protagonists. The fast-paced story line hooks the audience." —*Midwest Book Review*

"Entertaining and kept this reader turning the pages. I've got a soft spot for Western historicals, with their hard times and smooth-talking cowboys. Ms. McCarty delivers on both of those fronts."
—*Romance Reader at Heart*

"I absolutely adored the chemistry and witty banter between these two spicy characters, and the sex, as always, was titillating, sizzling, and realistic . . . I don't know how she does it, but I want more and more and more. You will, too, once you read this fantastic tale."
—*Night Owl Romance*

"A must read . . . Enticing and erotic . . . I am already craving more!"
—*Romance Junkies*

"Highly entertaining . . . Plenty steamy . . . and a great compliment to the series." —*A Romance Review*

"A delightful tale with lots of intense passion . . . Outstanding! Not to be missed by fans of historical Westerns who enjoy a strong dose of erotic fiction." —*The Romance Readers Connection*

Praise for *Running Wild*

"[Sarah McCarty's] captivating characters, scorching love scenes, and dramatic plot twists kept me on the edge. I could not put it down."
—*Night Owl Romance*

"McCarty . . . skillfully brings out her characters' deepest emotions. Three strong heroines and three mouthwatering heroes . . . will tug at your heartstrings, and the well-written sex scenes will not disappoint."
—*Romantic Times*

continued . . .

THE SHADOW WRANGLERS

CALEB

Sarah McCarty

BERKLEY SENSATION, NEW YORK

McCarty,
Sarah

THE BERKLEY PUBLISHING GROUP
Published by the Penguin Group
Penguin Group (USA) Inc.
375 Hudson Street, New York, New York 10014, USA
Penguin Group (Canada), 90 Eglinton Avenue East, Suite 700, Toronto, Ontario M4P 2Y3, Canada
(a division of Pearson Penguin Canada Inc.)
Penguin Books Ltd., 80 Strand, London WC2R 0RL, England
Penguin Group Ireland, 25 St. Stephen's Green, Dublin 2, Ireland (a division of Penguin Books Ltd.)
Penguin Group (Australia), 250 Camberwell Road, Camberwell, Victoria 3124, Australia
(a division of Pearson Australia Group Pty. Ltd.)
Penguin Books India Pvt. Ltd., 11 Community Centre, Panchsheel Park, New Delhi—110 017, India
Penguin Group (NZ), 67 Apollo Drive, Rosedale, North Shore 0632, New Zealand
(a division of Pearson New Zealand Ltd.)
Penguin Books (South Africa) (Pty.) Ltd., 24 Sturdee Avenue, Rosebank, Johannesburg 2196,
South Africa

Penguin Books Ltd., Registered Offices: 80 Strand, London WC2R 0RL, England

This book is an original publication of The Berkley Publishing Group.

This is a work of fiction. Names, characters, places, and incidents either are the product of the author's imagination or are used fictitiously, and any resemblance to actual persons, living or dead, business establishments, events, or locales is entirely coincidental. The publisher does not have any control over and does not assume any responsibility for author or third-party websites or their content.

Copyright © 2009 by Sarah McCarty.
Cover illustration by Phil Heffernan.
Cover design by George Long.
Interior text design by Tiffany Estreicher.

PRINTING HISTORY
Berkley Sensation trade paperback edition / October 2009

Library of Congress Cataloging-in-Publication Data

McCarty, Sarah.
  Caleb : the shadow wranglers / Sarah McCarty.—1st ed.
      p. cm.
  ISBN 978-0-425-23057-2
1. Vampires—Fiction.   2. Werewolves—Fiction.   I. Title.
  PS3613.C3568C35   2009
  813'.6—dc22   2009024269

PRINTED IN THE UNITED STATES OF AMERICA

10 9 8 7 6 5 4 3 2

❧ 1 ❧

SEDUCING a man wasn't supposed to be this hard. Allie glanced at the clock on the wall, grabbed the tray of muffins from the cooling rack, and moved them to the display case. If she were to believe the women's magazines, a few strategic double entendres slipped into the conversation, a couple pouty smiles flashed at carefully chosen moments quickly backed by some searing come-hither glances, and she should be in gravy with any man of her choosing. Except—she dropped the aluminum tray onto the shelf where it landed with a satisfying clatter—she wasn't. Which was why she'd gone a bit more hard-core in her advice seeking, and shelled out some serious bucks investing in her catch-a-man arsenal. All because one devastatingly sexy, infuriatingly never-anything-but-polite rancher could throw her second chakra into overdrive with nothing more than one of those unfathomable glances from under the brim of his battered black Stetson.

Allie closed the bakery case door, wincing as the underwire of her bra cut into her chest. A Thanksgiving turkey couldn't be trussed up any tighter than she was, but if there was any truth in advertising, Caleb Johnson was finally about to perk up and take notice, because thanks to one carefully selected push-up bra, she magically had the blessing of cleavage. Seductive, dark, mysterious, drool-your-heart-out cleavage. Now, if she could just get the man to look when he got here, she just might have the satisfaction of watching his jaw drop. She glanced down at her display. Things looked impressive from this angle, but maybe she should undo another button just in case . . .

"You should lock the door."

That low drawl rolled over her like a first kiss—sweet, hot, and tempting, catching on her nerve endings. She took an extra second arranging the yin-yang doilies on the counter, indulging in a few soothing tantric breaths, seeking calm with the same intensity she sought that addictive scent she associated only with Caleb. "Why? I knew you were coming."

He arrived every morning promptly at 5:30 a.m., just before she opened.

"You didn't hear me come in?"

"I never do." She straightened and turned, keeping her back to him under the guise of getting his coffee. No sense diminishing the impact of the "grand display" by bestowing sneak peeks.

Behind her, the stool squeaked as he slid onto it. "Which proves my point. I could be anyone."

She grabbed a deep black cup emblazoned with the Chinese characters for peace off the stack and reached for the coffeepot. "But you're not."

She flashed him a smile over her shoulder, her peripheral vision gifting her with a brief image of broad shoulders, deep green eyes, and a simmering energy that tempted her inner slut to howl with anticipation. "And one of these days you're going to have to tell me how you get past the bell without making it ring."

The heavy leather of his coat whispered a protest as he shrugged. "That bell's annoying."

Which didn't answer her question. The man never answered questions. Just showed up like clockwork to wreak havoc on her equilibrium. She put the pot back on the warmer and brought his cup over to the counter where he sat, front and center, casually overwhelming the small space with the sheer force of his presence.

"Thank you."

"You're welcome." With his hat brim blocking her view, she couldn't tell if he'd looked up, but as there were no physical signs of male interest, no stiffening, no catching of breath, she was going to assume he hadn't.

She opened the case and took out the two bear claws, heavy with extra icing, that she'd prepared earlier and passed them to Caleb, making sure to lean in as she did, treating him to a nice view of her button-popping cleavage. This close she couldn't miss his scent as it mingled with odors of cinnamon and sweet dough. He smelled of the forest, of wildness. Of heaven.

Good grief, was there anything about the man that didn't make her mouth water?

Caleb hooked a finger on the edge of the plate and pulled the offering toward him, the creases beside his mouth deepening just a touch. With amusement or irritation?

"Thank you."

His deep baritone stroked along her senses, adding an excited flutter to her already jangled nerves. "You're welcome."

He didn't look up, just nodded and wrapped his lean fingers around the coffee cup and took a drink. This close she could count the dust particles clinging to the brim of his black Stetson but could see absolutely nothing of his expression. Not that she needed to see it to know the man obviously wasn't impressed. Nothing in his body language said he registered a half-naked, slightly-curvier-than-was-stylish brunette standing before him. Which was more than a little insulting. She wasn't fashion-model pretty, but she also wasn't hag-of-death ugly. And honestly, from her observations of her brothers, when it came to breasts, men simply didn't have standards.

"Can I get you anything else?" she asked, bending unnecessarily to align another tray under the glass countertop just in case he truly hadn't noticed.

"No, thank you."

She blew her bangs off her brow as she straightened. This was not encouraging. They'd had this same conversation for a month now, and the lack of variety was seriously making her question the wisdom of her interest in Caleb Johnson. After all, a body to die for, high cheekbones, forest green eyes, and more testosterone than one woman should have to endure without a tranquilizer could only carry a man so far. And Caleb had about maxed out the mileage on his assets as far as she was concerned. To the point that there was absolutely no reason for her to have this interest in him. Except she did. Way down deep where it wouldn't be denied.

She suppressed a sigh. She really should give up and accept that the big rancher just didn't have the hots for her the way she did for him. She should, but she wouldn't for the simple reason that her gut instinct indicated otherwise. And her instincts were never wrong.

The bear claws disappeared with smooth efficiency. So did the coffee. Caleb wiped his mouth, the white of the paper napkin startling against the darkness of his skin. He placed a ten on the counter, then tilted his battered hat back and met her gaze dead-on, the darker green flecks of his eyes somehow blending into shadows that shifted and moved, beckoned.

The impact of that look ripped through her like a bolt of lightning, immobilizing her muscles and trapping her breath in her lungs.

"Enjoy your day."

If she'd had to say anything but another knee-jerk "thank you," she wouldn't have been able to manage it. Thank goodness for the manners her mother always said could carry a woman through any stressful situation, because trying to maintain a civilized conversation while suppressing the urge to melt into a puddle at a man's feet had a way of taking a woman's stress factor from zero to ten in less than six seconds.

Allie smothered a sigh as Caleb headed toward the door the same way he'd done every day for the last month—head up, shoulders back, with that rolling stride that made her knees weak. Oh heck, everything about the man made her knees weak, and he treated her with the utmost courtesy and respect. She grabbed his plate and coffee cup off the counter and dumped them in the rubber tub. Damn his hide!

The bell jingling over the door startled her into looking up. Caleb stood in the opening, shoulders filling the expanse, one hand on the door, a ghost of a smile hovering around his wide mouth as he touched the brim of his hat with the side of his finger in an amused salute. "See you tomorrow."

She stood there grinning like a fool as his richly textured drawl wrapped around her in a seductive pulse of sound. Such a simple thing, but the man ringing her bell was the most she'd had in the way of overt encouragement to date. Well, that and the fact he kept showing up like clockwork.

The door closed behind him. As the last jingle of the bell faded, so did her smile. She was pathetic. Just because the man deigned to let the bell on her door ring as he passed through did not mean he was interested in ringing *her* bell. With a disgusted grunt, she reached behind her and unfastened the clips of her push-up bra. With three deft twists, she slid it free of her arms and out from under her white baker's smock. A flick of her wrist sent the instrument of torture into the trash.

Damn it, she'd paid good money for that bra and the implied promises that came with it, endured two hours of painful constraint in the hope that someone—specifically Caleb Johnson—would at least flick an eyebrow in appreciation at her newly blossomed cleavage. But all she'd gotten for her money and her effort were breasts that ached and quarter-inch depressions in her sides from the band.

Tossing today's hopes into the trash alongside the discarded bra, she buttoned up her smock, flipped the closed sign to open, and set another pot of coffee on to brew. Today had been a bust, but tomorrow was still there, as always, just brimming with opportunities. And maybe over the course of the day, she'd think of a new way to exploit them.

OPTIMISM and her feet were shot by the end of the day. Her stomach was gnawing on her spine, she had a mother of a headache, and it was getting dark. She wanted nothing more than to go home, scarf down a low-carb frozen dinner, and crawl into bed. But first she had to get there. Which meant she had to walk, thanks to her I'm-turning-thirty-and-I-can't-afford-to-ignore-my-cardiovascular-fitness-anymore birthday gift of health to herself. Ordinarily, the walk wouldn't bother her. She closed the bakery at four o'clock, and it was an easy mile to her home. But today the dishwasher threw a hissy fit, and she lost track of time while coaxing it back into a cooperative mood. So now she was going to walk home in the dark. Damn. Some days it didn't pay to get out of bed.

She hit the lights and shrugged into her wool coat. Moonlight illuminated the street with a bright glow. At least she wouldn't have to walk in complete darkness. She grabbed her keys out of her pocket. Just as she reached for the door, a swirl of leaves flew into the glass pane. She shrieked and jumped back, bumping into a chair and toppling it over, feeling foolish as the chaotic swarm rustled their way to the ground before meandering off down the street. She needed to get a grip and get it now. She was too darn old to be afraid of the dark.

She locked the door and stepped out into the crisp evening air. No boogeyman jumped out of the shadows to attack her. No monster leapt onto her back as she turned the key in the lock. Still, if Dunnesville, Montana, had taxi service she would have called it. And if her only friend in town hadn't left town to attend a wedding, she would have called her. Nighttime always gave her the creeps. Even in a tiny, friendly town with an ongoing crime rate of zero.

Tucking her hands into her pockets, Allie headed west. All she had to do was clear one town block, pass one happy, innocent playground, stroll along a quarter mile of pretty woods, and she'd be home. Not much to that. Fifteen easy minutes of beneficial exercise and the soothing opportunity to absorb the beauty of nature all dressed up to impress.

It definitely was a beautiful evening. The moon, just clear of the trees, shone white light on the stretch of road, turning the packed dirt at the end of the asphalt into a path of soft amber, and the bare trees to a glowing silver gilt. The shadows wove through it all, providing contrast and depth, pulling the elements together into a landscape of otherworldly beauty.

She took a deep cleansing breath of the cold air as she strolled along, enjoying the peace. She'd been so busy this last month getting the bakery established that she hadn't done anything more than work or sleep. These few moments of relaxation made her realize all she was missing.

She passed the playground, feeling like she was walking down a mystical path into a magical landscape, drawn forward by the impulse to be part of the moment. If every night was like this, she might just get over her fear of the dark. Tension disappeared as she strolled along, and the pall that had been hanging over her day since Caleb had withstood the allure of her suddenly D-cup breasts faded away.

Ah, Caleb. It'd been such a long time since she'd met a man who'd piqued her interest, she wasn't sure certain parts of her hadn't atrophied. She'd even debated whether she was hormonally deficient, but one second in Caleb's presence, one brief connection with his energy, and suddenly more hormones than she could contain were running amok, making demands and taking over her thought processes. It was as lovely a surprise as his feigned indifference was irritating.

Like he was fooling anyone. Allie huddled deeper into her coat and blew out a breath. Mr. Studly-but-silent wanted her. He was just, for some reason, resisting doing anything about it. Well, if he thought he could out stubborn her, he was in for a shock. She'd once perched in a tree for three rainy, wet miserable days, drawing crowds and newscasters until the city had agreed to hold off cutting down a tree until the baby raccoons who lived there were old enough to move on. Momma raccoon hadn't been any more thrilled with her sit-in than her butt, which sported a bruised imprint of that branch for a week, but she'd stuck it out because there were some things worth fighting for. The lives of innocents being one of them.

Nope, no one, but no one, could out stubborn her. Sooner or later, she'd have Caleb talking, and once they dealt with whatever issue he felt kept them apart, the man was going to stop hiding his attraction and start doing something about it. And when he did, he damn well better not turn out to be a dud. She absolutely wouldn't forgive him for that. Not after making her work so hard.

The growl, coming from the right, stopped her in her tracks. Low and threatening, it rumbled along her nerves, bringing every childhood nightmare to the fore. She searched the shadows for the source, but it was too deep to see anything. And truth be told, since it didn't sound like she was facing a Chihuahua with an attitude problem, she wasn't too anxious to get up close and personal with whatever she'd disturbed. The growl came again. Deeper. Louder.

She scouted the side of the road for a weapon. The most she came up with was one rotted twig and a handful of loose gravel. None of which looked substantial enough to take on what suddenly stepped out of the gloom.

It wasn't a Chihuahua, or even a dog. It was a wolf. She'd never seen one before, but that didn't diminish her conviction. And it was huge. Its back stood as tall as her chest. Its head was massive and so were its fangs—dear God—she could have used those last Halloween when she was trying to scare off the rambunctious teenagers egging her house. She backed up another step. The wolf took two forward, coming into the light, its coat glowing as eerily white as its eyes blazed a ghastly yellow.

Lowering its head, it stepped closer, the hackles on its ruff raised in a clear threat.

Three emotions ripped through her at once. Fear, disbelief, and anger. Of the three, the last took root. She was so sick of this. Every time she got a new life started, something came along and yanked the rug out from under her. First it had been her father, then her fiancé, and lastly the pompous head chef at the plush Empire Hotel.

Maybe she didn't have a thick ruff to puff up and make her look bigger, but she had a ton of pent-up resentment and plenty of attitude to bring to the discussion.

"Back off," she warned with a growl of her own, trying to project aggression rather than fear, throwing some mental force behind the effort. Just in case animals really were naturally telepathic.

To her surprise, the animal paused and tilted its head, almost as if it were listening. She added more "back off" aggression to her mental litany. Reaching into her pocket, she worked her keys between her fingers. With a start, she felt the small penknife attached to the chain. She'd forgotten about that. Using her coat as a brace, she pried the blade open. It wasn't much of a weapon. At most she could take out the wolf's eye, while it could do a hell of a lot more damage to her, but if she was going to die here tonight, she was not going meekly.

She pulled the knife out of her pocket. The keys jangled obnoxiously. The wolf lifted its lip, displaying those vicious teeth. It was trying to intimidate her, and on many levels it succeeded, but on another level it was really pissing her off. At no time in her life plan had she written down to die as tabloid fodder under the teeth and nails of a killer wolf. She gripped her makeshift weapon and took a fortifying breath.

If it wasn't on her to-do list, it simply wasn't getting done.

Her bravado lasted right up until the huge wolf moved, more of a shifting of its weight than a real step, seeming to float over the frozen ground. Every survival instinct screamed *run*. She managed one panicked gasp and a step back before it caught her, shoving its nose into her crotch, snarling when she flinched.

If it was a warning, she was incapable of heeding it. Terror was a great motivator and having this thing so close scared her witless. Jabbing downward with the knife, she aimed for the wolf's right eye. At the last second, the animal jerked its head aside. The blade hit bone, deflected and sliced down the wolf's snout. The fur of its muzzle brushed the side of her hand as metal tore through flesh, the softness a shocking counterpoint to the violence of the act. The ferocity of the wolf's response was a raspy snarl that defined retribution.

Oh shit! She jumped back. Now she'd pissed it off.

The wolf reared up. Its huge paws slammed into her chest, driving the air from her lungs. Her keys went flying and so did she. There was a moment of disorientation, and then she was on her back on the ground, staring up at the gaping jaws of the wolf as shock waves from the hard landing reverberated through her body.

The wolf was in no hurry now that it had her pinned. It lowered its head with taunting slowness, jaws angling in, spreading wider as they got closer to her neck. Its claws stabbed through the padding of her coat into the ridge of her collarbone with equally agonizing slowness. She tore her gaze off those gleaming teeth, crashed into the barrier of the wolf's eyes . . . and paused.

If she didn't know this was an animal, didn't know it was incapable of human emotion, she'd swear the beast was laughing at her. Playing with her like a cat played with a mouse. Amusing itself on her fear.

As if sensing her thoughts, the wolf's grin broadened, wrinkling its snout into a savage grimace that hit squarely on that primal core of genetic fear every human possessed. A drop of blood dripped from its wound, slapping her cheek in a hot splash. She cringed and closed her eyes when the animal leaned in, its fetid breath hitting her face a split second before the equally repugnant roughness of its tongue touched the same spot. The chuff of air it emitted sounded too damned much like laughter. She opened her eyes, took in the wolf's expression, and just knew deep down in the only place that mattered, that the animal was getting off on her terror.

The sick son of a bitch.

Anger surged up behind her fear, swamping it in a torrent of backed-up rage. She glanced down between their bodies and found inspiration. Grabbing handfuls of the coarse fur on either side of the bloody muzzle, she braced her arms and added a snarl of her own to the mix. "Fuck you."

Before the last syllable ended, she drove the hard point of her mini boots up into the beast's groin, feeling a sense of satisfaction as they sank deep into the soft flesh before striking bone.

She'd never heard a sound like what came out of the wolf's mouth as it reared back and spun around snapping savagely, missing her foot by a breath. She didn't wonder at it or catalog it for future reference. She just scrambled to her feet and took off running, the hoarse howl that followed her raising the hairs on the back of her neck and sending a chilling surge of adrenaline through her body. One glance over her shoulder showed the wolf in pursuit, eyes glowing eerily bright, all illusions of laughter gone from its expression as it raced after her.

Oh God, she needed a miracle.

She didn't hear or see a thing, but one minute she was running for her life and the next something big and hard knocked her flat on her butt directly in the path of the oncoming wolf. *Oh God. Oh God.* She threw her hands over her head, curling herself into a ball, making herself as small a target as possible for those fangs.

Moonlight winked under shadow. There was a loud thump and then a vicious chorus of snarls punctuated the night, swiftly followed by the bone-chilling clash of sharp teeth. She lowered her arms in time to see two shadows blend into one hellish, writhing mass of primitive fury.

Another wolf, Allie realized as she rolled to her knees and panted for air. Her miracle was another wolf, black and as big as the first, and from the timbre of its growls, more than a little ticked off. Good. She hoped it killed the first. Though it was irrational, she couldn't help but attribute human characteristics to the first wolf, and if she'd had to analyze him, she'd have pegged him as a serial killer run amok. He just had that cold, disconnected feel to his energy.

She lurched back as the two wolves rolled toward her, barely missing a slash from the gray wolf's teeth as they whirled past. She needed to get out of here. She also needed her keys because without them she had nowhere to go and no defense at all. She cautiously edged to where they gleamed in the moonlight, swallowing back terror, reaching for the anger that got her through so many scrapes as she took another step. One more and she was within two feet of the wolves. One foot from her keys. Never taking her eyes off the fighting animals, she stretched for the leather key chain. The second wolf glanced her way, its deep green eyes glowing red around the edges. For one brief moment their gazes connected and in the fringes of her mind came an impression of fury, determination, and an imperative.

Run.

As she blinked in shock, her fingers an inch from the keys, the first wolf moved in, taking advantage of the second's distraction. His teeth flashed eerily in the moonlight as he dove for the black wolf's neck. With a twist of its body, it had her savior pinned.

The order to run echoing in her mind, every sensible instinct telling her to obey, she stood there, and knew—just knew—she was the stupidest woman alive because even though he wasn't human, and even though he probably planned on eating her, too, she couldn't just leave the black wolf to die. Not when it was her fault he'd been distracted in the first place. Not when he'd saved her life. She just wasn't made that way.

Grabbing the keys, she hustled to the left and took aim. With a quick prayer that God really did watch out for fools and idiots, she kicked the gray wolf as hard as she could, right in the testicles.

"Leave him alone!" she hollered, terror and anger pitching her voice to almost the same high tenor of the gray wolf's muffled howl.

It turned, its eyes glowing, fangs dripping blood, and came at her, one measured step at a time, looking no weaker from the fight, and none the worse for her kick. And that smile, that totally evil smile was back on its face as the powerful muscles in its shoulders bunched in preparation to take her down.

Oh God, she should have run when she'd had the chance.

This time the thought that pushed into her mind was more co-herent.

Goddamn it. Run!

She blinked. She'd recognize that deep baritone anywhere. That was Caleb's voice. The second wolf heaved to its feet, blood pour-ing in a dark river from its torn neck, and charged the first, collid-ing with the gray wolf's side in a violent crash. Air grunted from the gray wolf's lungs before momentum carried it and those gnashing teeth away.

Allie dragged a shuddering breath into her own lungs, assimi-lated the near miss, and then for once did as ordered. She ran. Straight down the road toward her house. As fast as she could, the sounds of the battle not fading from her mind with distance, actu-ally seeming to increase with each step she took until she wanted to cover her ears and scream from the primitive fury battering her sanity.

With a suddenness that made her stumble, the noise stopped. No grunts. No snarls. No snapping of teeth. Just a hollow aching void that hurt more than the rage. She stopped running, clutched her side against the searing stitch, and listened. The calm of the night enfolded her once again in an ethereal beauty, unfazed by the vio-lence she knew had occurred, revealing nothing of the outcome.

And then it came, that strange connection and along with it the

knowledge that *that* was what she'd been searching for. It wasn't as
strong, and it wobbled with an uneven tempo, but the voice came
to her again.

Run.

It was Caleb's voice. She knew it in her bones. She'd studied up
enough on psychic phenomenon to be convinced it was possible,
but she'd never thought to experience it. But she was. With Caleb
Johnson. And he was telling her to run in a mental voice so weak it
was barely audible. Instead of running, she hesitated.

She mentally tested the energy she could feel, grabbed it as best
she could with her thoughts, and asked, *Where are you?*

He didn't answer, but the sense of urgency increased as the
stitch in her side eased. It was only twenty more steps to the base of
her driveway. She took them in a lurching jog, the keys jangling
in her hands and her leg muscles shaking as they struggled to meet
her request. She stopped at her bright purple mailbox, starkly illuminated in the strange light. The long shadows reached out to her
from her tree-lined drive. The arced branches of the poplar trees
hovered over the entrance, looking like huge, clawed hands just
waiting for the unwary to step within reach.

Her heart raced from exertion and pure fear as she forced herself into that pit of darkness, the crunch of gravel scraping down
the raw edge of her terror as she took one step and then another.
If there were any more of those wolves in the shadows, she hoped
they didn't give any warning. She remembered the horrible gushing
wound on her savior's neck and shuddered. She'd rather not know
in advance if one of them was planning on ripping her throat out.
Her steps slowed as she reached the darkest part of the driveway. A
feeling of damned-if-she-did and damned-if-she-didn't froze her in
place.

What if there was a whole ton of those monster wolves between
her and the house?

There aren't. But they're coming.

Oh, shit! She glanced behind her. Nothing moved, but goose

bumps sprang over her skin, and the nape of her neck tingled with cold anticipation. "They're" implied more than one, and the one she'd tangled with had been bad enough. With no other option, trusting the voice because she had to trust something, she plunged into the gloom, a silent scream in her mind the only outlet she allowed the terror eating her alive.

Nothing pounced as she raced through the dense darkness toward the moonlight ahead. Nothing snapped at her heels or hit her back and brought her down, but the feeling that any second she was going to be wolf chow pounded harder and harder on her conviction that it was only a matter of time. She broke into the clearing of her yard, found an extra burst of speed, and headed for her front door, its bright red paint washed out to the color of dried blood in the harsh moonlight.

Her hands shook so badly she couldn't fit the key into the lock. The nerves all along her back prickled as if in response to invisible eyes. She shoved the key at the lock, swearing when it slid off. Oh God, she had to get inside.

A strange calm settled over her, soothing her, taking the terrible panic away. On the next pass, she got the key in. The dead bolt clanked open. She unlocked the handle, opened the door, and all but fell into the small foyer before slamming the door shut.

She immediately threw the dead bolt and leaned back against the cool metal, sliding to the floor. She wrapped her arms across her torso as she drew breath after needed breath into her starved lungs. The warm, familiar sugar cookie scent of her home enveloped her in a comforting hug. She was safe.

She dropped her sweaty forehead to her knees and let the knowledge seep in. She was in her home, and she was safe. But they were coming for her. If she was going to believe that telepathy was possible, she had to believe more of those monster wolves were coming for her. Which meant she wasn't safe. Panes of glass and dead-bolted doors wouldn't protect her for long. She had to get out of here. She sat up straight.

Stay.

The voice was more a stutter of sensation than a formed thought.

"Caleb?" she whispered.

There was no response, but a stroke of calm stilled her alarm.

It *was* Caleb Johnson who was giving her orders, and he was hurt. She didn't know how any more than she knew why he could talk to her like this, but he was hurt. She closed her eyes and concentrated on that strange feeling of calm, trying to follow it to the source. At first, she got nothing. Just the feeling of being ridiculous for even trying, but then there was a break in the wall, a sensation of expansion in her mind. Horrendous pain and weakness overwhelmed her before the door she'd opened slammed shut, and she was left alone to contend with the vivid memory.

Her hands went to her throat, surprised to find it intact.

There was only one thing she'd seen with its throat torn recently—the black wolf that had saved her life. It was connected to Caleb somehow. And now it was out there alone. Terribly wounded because of her. And more of the monster wolves were coming.

She did what any sensible woman would do in that situation. She went for her gun.

❧ 2 ❧

CALEB might be weakened. He might even be on the verge of dying, but he was still turning out to be a hell of a nag.

Go back.

Allie ignored this order the same way she'd ignored the last three, turning her compact hatchback out of the drive and down the dark road. The night wasn't nearly so scary when she was in the car with the weight of the gun in her lap. She didn't know where those monster wolves had come from, but she was pretty sure a bullet in the eye would take them down.

She slowed when she saw the dark mound in the road. Her heartbeat, which had never returned to normal, sped back up to impossible when the blob separated into two distinct bodies in the beams of her headlights. She pulled the car to the side of the road just past the bodies, turned off the ignition, and sat there, taking deep breaths, beating back the suddenly overwhelming fear through sheer force of will.

Stay in the car.

"Shut up," she muttered as she reached for the door handle. The fear that swamped her was unreasonable and beyond imagining. It was all she could do not to flee in terror.

Go home.

Those feelings were not coming from her, she realized as sweat soaked her palms and dripped into her eyes. She grabbed the flashlight and revolver, yanked the handle on the door, and kicked it open when the latch gave. "Get out of my head!"

She practically threw herself out of the car. As soon as the door slammed shut, the panic receded and she was left with just her own cowardice. That, she could handle.

She cautiously moved toward the bodies, keeping the revolver trained on the wolves. The gray wolf lay still, its head twisted at an awkward angle, tongue lolling, and eyes staring unseeingly, the malevolence surrounding it undiminished by death. About three feet away lay the black wolf. Hardly daring to breathe, she shone her flashlight on the animal. A huge pool of blood surrounded the body, seeping from the thick ruff, which glistened with the slow ebb of life.

"This can't be good," she muttered as the pool of blood crept outward. She gave the gray wolf a wide berth as she approached the black. Dead or alive, the beast gave her the creeps.

The black wolf merely gave her a sense of urgency, which didn't make any sense considering it had won the fight and was therefore the greater threat. But there she was, once again with her gut instincts overriding common sense. She stopped a foot away from the black wolf's side. She panned her light over the body. Its ribs heaved and jerked with every breath, but at least it was breathing.

"Easy, Big Boy," she murmured, shoving the revolver into the waistband of her jeans before she knelt just outside the ring of blood.

Big Boy's response was a lift of his lip. She didn't get any closer, but she also didn't move away. "Nice set of teeth."

She touched a slash by its hip. The wolf flinched, and the order came loud and clear. *LEAVE!*

"Just as soon as I take care of Big Boy, I'll do that very thing," she retorted. It was weird carrying on a conversation with a voice in her mind, but on a scale of one to ten of all the weird things she'd done in her life, it actually only rated a four.

She sat back on her heels. In the fury of battle, she hadn't really appreciated how big the wolf was. It was a good foot and a half taller than she, which wasn't saying much as she barely cleared five feet, but the sheer mass of the animal was awesome. It had to be over two hundred pounds, which was going to make getting it to the vet a major issue. There was room in her hatchback for him, but getting the wolf to the car could be a problem. For sure, she wasn't just picking him up.

They're coming.

"Don't pressure me," she muttered. "I don't work well under pressure." The fresh rush of adrenaline made her hands shake and her breath rasp in her throat. She really wasn't cut out for this kind of thing.

She stroked the wolf's side gingerly before getting to her feet. "I'll be right back."

Leave the wolf.

Everything inside of her rebelled at the thought. "Not an option."

Do as I say.

Like that was going to happen. She snorted as she grabbed a tarp out of the back of the car and slammed the hatch closed. She wasn't taking a chance with any surprises waiting for her when she got back. "I might be nuts, and I might even talk to the voices in my head, but even I know better than to take orders from them."

Caleb didn't respond verbally to her sarcasm, but what felt like a long-suffering sigh wafted through her mind.

You are one stubborn woman.

"It's one of my more endearing qualities," she said as she laid the tarp flat alongside the wolf's back, tucking a large fold underneath.

What's your plan?

"I'm going to roll the wolf onto this tarp and drag him to the car, and providing I manage that without having my own throat torn out, take him to a vet."

He won't harm you.

"Like you can guarantee that."

She looked at the wolf, especially at the teeth still exposed in its snarl, and shook her head. After this, she really was going to have to go see that psychiatrist her family kept recommending.

You're not crazy.

"So says the voice in my head."

Whether she was crazy or just on the verge of toppling over the edge was neither here nor there right now. She took a breath and reached over the wolf.

"I hope you're right about his friendly level," she muttered as she grabbed its front legs and pulled up and over. The wolf made a horribly wet gasping sound as she rolled its front half over. Midway, the weight of his body fought her, almost dragging her face-first into the road on the other side. She quickly straddled its torso, holding its legs upright with her inner thigh while she grabbed its back legs and dragged them along. There was a moment when she thought she wouldn't be able to do it, but then the wolf twitched just enough, and she rolled him onto the tarp.

Breathing hard with the effort, she tugged the fold out from under the wolf, shuddering when blood smeared her hands, pausing only to wipe them off on her jeans before continuing. Her gut was talking to her again, and it said she had to hurry.

Grabbing the end of the tarp, she tugged. The tarp slipped out of her hands.

"Son of a bitch." She wiped her hands again, and gathered the excess folds into a better grip. Leaning back against the resistance, she dug in her heels. The wolf moved a foot before she had to take a break, her muscles screaming in protest.

A bone-chilling howl pierced the night. It was immediately fol-

lowed by another. And another. All from the same direction. All
sounding too damn close for comfort.

Hurry.

Like she needed him to tell her that. "If you think you can do
better, do it yourself."

A feeling of extreme displeasure rolled over her. Great, just
what she needed. An inner voice with an attitude. She braced her
feet and pulled again. "What's got you upset?"

Your insistence on risking your life.

"That was an amazingly calm not to mention sweet thing to
say," she said as she panted through her next break. A quick glance
revealed two feet to go.

I'm not sweet.

She gritted her teeth and gathered her energy. The howling
came again. Closer. She glanced over her shoulder. It was tailgate
or bust.

"Sweet is all in the eyes of the beholder, darling, and that
sounded pretty darn sweet to me."

After that, she didn't have air for extras like speech. She needed
everything she had to move the wolf. She pulled until her arms
and legs ached. Inch by inch, she got the wolf over the ground, desperation giving her a bit more strength as the howls rose to an
obscene cacophony, ringing inside and outside her head. She was
profoundly grateful Caleb didn't add another "hurry" to her own
internal litany.

She didn't know if they were going to make it. Didn't know if
she could get them the last foot, but she closed her eyes and gave it
everything she had. When she opened her eyes, the wolf was just
clear of the rear bumper. She'd done it. Leaning against the side of
the car, she popped the hatch.

"Looks like we might make it after all."

Leave now!

She didn't have to ask why the order screamed through her

mind. She could hear the crashing in the bushes, hear the growls, literally feel death approaching.

She wrapped her arms around the massive torso. "Help me, Big Boy!"

To her shock, the wolf did, getting its feet under itself, exerting the last of its strength, heaving its torso up so they both fell into the cargo area. She didn't waste a second marveling at the miracle. She just grabbed its hind legs and shoved them into the small space before slamming the hatch.

A glance toward the woods revealed eight massive wolves of assorted colors spilling out of the shadows, closing in on her fast. She tore around the car, sobbing as her bloody hands slipped uselessly on the door handle, trying twice more before she got it open. In the time it took to get a prayer of thanks out, she had the door closed and the key in the ignition.

For once the car started without protest. As she slammed it into gear, something struck the windshield. She threw up her hands and screamed, the impression of fangs and glowing eyes striking terror through her. Another body hit the driver's door window so hard she expected the glass to crack. It held. Thank God for safety glass. *Drive, Allie.*

As before, calm soothed her panic and for once she didn't mind following an order. She stomped on the gas, yanked the wheel so the wolf slid off, and headed for town, glancing in the rearview mirror as her tires grabbed the blacktop. The wolves were in hot pursuit.

Turn around.

"And drive back into fang and company?" She shook her head. "I don't think so."

Another glance in the rearview had her blinking. The wolves were gaining. She checked her speedometer. She was doing thirty-five miles an hour and climbing. That wasn't possible.

"What in hell are those things?"

No answer, just more of that calm stroking of her nerves, and another statement of fact. *No one in town can help you.*

She stepped harder on the gas. "So Mr. Know-it-all, where would you suggest I go?"

She shouldn't have been surprised by the answer.

The Circle J.

The turnoff to the Circle J was a mile in the other direction. On the other side of her house. On the other side of that rabid pack of monster wolves.

She tightened her grip on the wheel. "Come up with another suggestion."

There isn't one.

She believed him.

"Shit!" She hit the brakes, spun the wheel, and accelerated out of the slide. Behind her there was a heavy thud. A glance in the rearview showed the black wolf in a heap on the other side of the cargo area. She winced. That had to have hurt.

The tires squealed a protest as she floored the accelerator, heading straight for the wolves. She expected them to separate, not form a solid wall across the road. She instinctively went for the brake.

Don't stop.

"Okay," she licked her lips, "but I hope you realize hitting one of those things is going to total my car."

Don't hit one.

Great advice from the amorphous voice in her head, but she wasn't sure she was going to be able to avoid it. They were a solid line of snarling determination spread across the narrow road. She fumbled with the gun in her lap until she found the safety. She flipped it to off.

On a "Here goes nothing," she tromped on the gas.

The wolves didn't move, just held their position slightly behind the one in the middle, the expression on his black-masked face both arrogant and vicious. In the second her gaze met his, his chin lifted. A challenge?

Keep going.

There was an edge of desperation in the weak order.

Why did everyone, from her family to voices in her head, think she was unreliable?

"Don't worry, I've never lost a game of chicken yet."

They're not playing.

"News flash." She ducked her chin and braced her arms. "Neither am I."

She hit the wall of flesh doing fifty, at the last minute swerving so the fender glanced off the lead wolf's shoulder rather than hitting it dead-on. Yanking the wheel to the left, she sent another wolf flying. In the interim, four more swarmed the car, their snarls bruising her ears while their claws screeched against the metal. One jumped up onto the hood, limiting her view to the gray-black of its chest and the white gleam of its huge teeth.

She pulled the gun from her lap, pressed the muzzle against the windshield, closed her eyes, and pulled the trigger. The roar was deafening in the small interior. The recoil slammed her forearm down into the wheel. Only her death grip on the revolver kept it in her hand.

When she opened her eyes, there was a huge spatter of blood on the windshield and open road in front of her.

"And stay off my car," she muttered in weak relief as she hit the windshield washer button. Most of the blood cleared, leaving an oily smear between the maze of cracks.

She looked in the rearview. The wolves were gone. For the first time in ten minutes she took a deep breath. She glanced at the unmoving wolf in her cargo area.

"We might just make it after all."

They're going to head you off.

"Gosh darn it!" She slapped the wheel in frustration. "Can't you even let me enjoy one stupid second of relief?"

The man was becoming quite the killjoy.

Listen.

The weakness in the faint order alarmed her.

Get to the Circle J. Stay on the road and keep going. Don't trust your eyes. No matter what you see. No matter how bad it gets, do not take your foot off the gas.

Call her a skeptic, but how much worse could it get? "What do you mean, 'no matter how bad it gets'?"

Get to Circle J. The wolves cannot go there.

She glanced longingly at her driveway as she passed by. "How do you know that? Do you have some sort of monster wolf fencing installed?"

Yes.

That might have been just a trace of mocking amusement she heard at the end of the soft affirmative. When she didn't answer, she felt the mental nudge again.

Damn persistent man. She just wanted to go home and pretend this never happened.

Promise me you won't stop. No matter what.

She turned right onto the entrance road to the Circle J ranch, feeling like she was heading down a path of no return. "I promise."

His *Good* was just a sigh in her head. It winked out on a whisper of energy, and then he was gone, leaving her alone on a strange road in a race with killer wolves that planned on cutting her off from a sanctuary she wasn't even sure existed. Son of a bitch. Wasn't that just like a man?

"Caleb?"

There wasn't an answer. And she wasn't really expecting one. There was an emptiness where his voice had been. A dead feeling void that scared the bejesus out of her.

She shook her head and drove as fast as she dared up the rutted, tree-lined road. Her car bottomed out in a deep hole, making her jump. The gun fell to the floor. She swore and fished around for it, not taking her eyes off the treacherous path.

Another bump had her abandoning the gun in favor of trying to stay on the road. Clenching the wheel tightly in her hands, she squinted through the smears and cracks into the night and cursed her luck. It just figured the first man to believe that she could keep a promise would be a fictitious voice in her head.

She wrestled the car around the corner against the series of ruts trying to bounce the vehicle off the road. By the time the car hit the next smooth patch, her teeth were vibrating in her head. Lord knows how her passenger felt. If he was even still alive.

"Sorry about that," she whispered, afraid to look, wrenching the wheel to the right, narrowly missing a big boulder sticking up in the middle of the road. Caleb had to be out of his mind to think her little car could handle this path masquerading as a road. She had half a mind to turn around.

The white wolf that leapt out of the trees put paid to that idea. She hit the gas and fishtailed to the other side of the path, narrowly avoiding the collision that would have taken out her car. More wolves appeared on both sides of the car, taking advantage of her slowing to swarm her. It scared her, how willing they were to sacrifice themselves to stop her. They had to be after either her or the wolf, but since they were a package deal at this point, she wasn't slowing for love or money.

The car leaned precariously into the next curve. She was driving too fast for the road, but it was impossible to slow down. Herded on by the wolves like a lamb to slaughter, she could only pray that the car held the road and that there weren't any unpleasant surprises between here and the Circle J. Sweat poured down her face, and her hands slipped on the wheel. The bumper scraped a tree before she got it back on the road. The wolves howled at the near miss, and then fell back into formation around her. The masked wolf paced alongside the driver's door, seemingly content to wait. For what? Were they waiting for her to crash?

She wiped the sweat off her brow with her coat sleeve. She wasn't going to crash. The only course she'd ever gotten an A in had been the defensive driving course in high school. She was damn proud of that A. She wasn't about to blow her perfect record tonight with a bunch of maniacal wolves as witnesses.

She looked up, and her heart sank to her toes. Even an A in defensive driving wasn't going to get her past that. The road dead-ended at the biggest boulder she'd ever seen. Just ended right at the base of it. With the thick growth of trees on either side, there was no way around. With no room to turn and no way back, she was out of options.

Beside her the masked wolf gave a victorious yip. She met its glare dead-on. Again the uncanny expressiveness of its face shocked her. And then pissed her off. There was nothing worse than a gloating wolf. She looked at the rock coming up fast. She was almost at the point of no return. The wolves around her picked up their leader's yip, their voices blending to a nerve-racking war cry.

Don't trust your eyes. No matter what you see. No matter how bad it gets, do not take your foot off the gas.

Caleb's words came back to her. She trusted Caleb, but more than that, she did not want to die as a wolf snack.

She caught the lead wolf's eye, flipped him the bird, and then jammed the accelerator to the floor. The little car shot forward. Her scream echoing all around the tiny interior, she closed her eyes and waited for the inevitable collision.

NO sudden impact. No grind of metal against stone. No shattered glass. And most of all, no horrendous pain.

She opened her eyes. There was nothing ahead of her. No gloom. No sense of foreboding and certainly no boulder the size of Mount Olympia. Just a straight rutted path dappled in moonlight. Allie depressed the brake and looked back. The wolves milled a hundred feet behind. She could see them through the shimmering mirage of the boulder. Freaky.

Caleb was right. For whatever reason, the wolves couldn't follow her here.

She slowed her speed to a manageable level, following the path for three more minutes before the ranch house came into view. It

was a huge, well-lit structure sprawled between two hills. Nothing
had ever looked more beautiful. She laid on the horn as she bounced
along the road. She wanted Caleb front and center as soon as she
stopped. She had a bone or two to pick with him.

A man came out of the house as she slid into the drive. He
was tall and from his silhouette, well muscled, but she knew instinctively he wasn't Caleb. He was down the steps and at the back of
the car before she completed her sideways skid. In the time it took
to open her door, he was speaking into a gizmo on his shoulder and
popping the hatch as if he knew exactly what she carried.

Which maybe he did. If Caleb could communicate with her
telepathically, he could most likely do so with others. She opened
the door and got out of the car, ignoring the stab of discomfort that
thought gave her. Slamming the car door shut, she asked, "Is the
wolf still alive?"

The answer was curt and slightly muffled as it came from the
depths of the compact "Yes. No thanks to you."

No thanks to her? "I saved his life!"

The man leaned out of the car, his expression drawn into one of
disgust as his cold gray eyes flicked over her with impatience. "You
would see it that way."

His gaze narrowed as he looked over her shoulder, the military
cut adding to his aggressive aura. "You two help me here."

A quick glance revealed three men right behind her, all big and
all looking at her with that same expression of dislike.

"Where's Caleb?" she asked the big blond, not liking the feeling
she was getting.

The blond didn't answer, just jerked his chin toward her. "Lock
her up."

She ducked, but it was too late. Her arms were unceremoniously
yanked behind her.

"What are we going to do with her?" a deep male voice asked
conversationally above her head as if she weren't kicking and twisting for all she was worth in his grip.

"That's for the brothers to decide."

The total disregard for her fate in the statement sent a chill down her spine.

She screamed for Caleb with every breath she could gather. He was here. She knew he was here. He'd told her to come here. She screamed again, loud enough to make two of the men flinch, but the blond who appeared to be in charge merely lifted a brow at her as the other man half carried, half dragged her away from the car and said with calm finality, "He can't help you now."

❋ 3 ❋

ALLIE sat in the dark, windowless barn for what seemed like forever. From the growl in her stomach and the ache of her bladder, it was probably only a few hours, but it felt like days since she'd been trapped in the pitch-black interior, kicking at the strange rustlings in the hay-strewn floor whenever they got near, trapped between hope and fear that the door would open soon.

"Damn it, Caleb, where are you?" Her voice, hoarse from calling for him, was hardly recognizable. Her brain felt equally strained from all her mental shouting. And it was all for nothing. None of her cries had resulted in a response. Had she been wrong to trust Caleb? Had it all been some sort of setup?

She yanked at her bonds again, gasping with the pain as fresh blood dripped over her wrists. Her hands slid more easily against each other with the slippery moisture, allowing her to jerk harder, the bonds to cut deeper, but not granting her a bit of freedom. In other words, she was hurting herself for nothing.

She slumped against the wall and blew her bangs off her forehead. How had her day gone from possibly landing a date with a hunky rancher to being tied up in a dark stall in his barn?

The metal bolt on the stall clanked and the door opened. Not a wink of light illuminated the interior.

"Who's there?" she asked, pushing to her feet.

Hands on her arms pulled her up the last foot.

She kicked out hard and fast. She struck only air. As if her struggles were nothing more than a pesky gnat buzzing around the man's purpose, she was turned around.

"You're bleeding," the man said.

"Like a stuck pig." With any luck he'd be a fancy dresser and she'd ruin his outfit.

"Good."

"Good?" she asked as he pulled her out of the stall into the slightly less dark of the barn corridor. "What are you, some sort of sadist?"

"What I am would shock you."

She highly doubted that. "After the night I've had, I think I'm pretty much past shock."

And way past caution. She might be terrified out of her wits, but she wasn't going to show it.

The stall door thunked shut. "Good."

Again with the "good." "Not much of a conversationalist, are you?"

Her comment didn't generate a response. She tripped over something on the floor. The hand on her arm didn't let her fall, but it didn't help her up either. She got the message. She either walked or was dragged. She scrambled to keep her feet.

"So, who are you?"

The man pulled her up short. She had a mental impression of something in front of her, but she couldn't see a thing.

"Jared."

"Caleb's brother Jared?"

He leaned forward, as if reaching for something. Damn it! She wished she could see.

"Yes."

All she needed was one moment of inattention to make a break for it. His grip on her arm didn't lessen as he slid the heavy barn door open.

As if he could read her mind, he said, "You can't escape."

She tossed her hair over her shoulder as the pale light of pre-dawn poured into the barn. "Who are you trying to convince, your-self or me?"

His eyes glittered beneath the brim of his hat as he looked down at her from his six-foot-plus vantage point.

"Would it be any use trying to convince you?" he asked, moving forward.

She had to skip every other step to keep up. "Not much."

"Then I guess I'm about done talking to myself."

Like Caleb, he had a unique way of stringing his words to-gether. Charming yet somehow old-fashioned. Well, charming if he wasn't holding her prisoner and dragging her across the yard at breakneck speed.

"I'm warning you right now, if you don't slow down, I'm going to have an accident."

"I won't let you fall."

"I'm not talking about that kind of accident."

His fingers tightened on her arm and just as quickly relaxed. He glanced at the eastern sky. His mouth, so like Caleb's generous one with the same well-defined totally masculine shape, flattened to a straight line of disapproval, but he slowed.

Well, that was one bit of useful information. They probably weren't planning on killing her, seeing as how they were worried about her peeing her pants.

"There are facilities inside," he finally said.

Her "Good to know" was a bit breathless. She really was going to have to get serious about getting into shape when she got home. She risked a glance up as they reached the wide porch. That might have been a smile on the man's mouth, but just that quick it was gone.

Jared didn't let her go as they climbed the steps, just kept that steady, uncompromising grip on her arm.

"Where are you taking me?" she asked as he half shoved, half escorted her through the front door.

"To the facilities." He leaned over her to open a door on the right. She never felt him touch her bonds, but her arms suddenly fell to her sides.

"Be quick."

Easier said than done. Her arms, so long confined, refused to listen to a thing her brain had to say.

Jared took his hat off, revealing a head of thick chestnut hair. The family resemblance to Caleb was even stronger without his hat. Same square face, well-defined cheekbones, large slightly slanted hazel eyes that leaned more toward green than blue, finished off by one stubborn-looking chin.

"What are you waiting for?"

"Feeling to return to my arms."

He frowned down at her and then brusquely started massaging her arms. When his fingers ran over her wrists through her shirt, raw pain made her cry out. She jerked out of his reach.

Something—regret maybe?—flashed in his hazel eyes as he looked at the blood on his fingers before his expression reverted to emotionless.

"Be quick."

He didn't have to worry. Her bladder wasn't going to let her be anything else. If she hadn't been in such a hurry, she might have paused before using what looked like an indoor outhouse from yesteryear, but bursting women could not be picky, and this was definitely an any-hole-in-a-pinch moment. It only took two seconds to determine there was no escape from the room. The door she'd entered was the only exit. The only light came from a small round window up high. There wasn't any toilet paper and only a crude basin for washing her hands. There also wasn't any water with which to fill the basin.

Her bladder relieved, tissue from her pocket substituted for toilet paper, she began to think of other things. Like how to get out of this mess. Clearly, she couldn't sneak out of the room. The tiny window wouldn't fit her foot, let alone her hips. Which meant she couldn't escape, but that didn't mean she couldn't stall. There was a bolt on the door. She carefully slid it home, wincing at the slight metallic grate as it worked into place.

"Hurry up," Jared called from the other side.

"Just trying to figure out how to flush this thing."

Which was only half a lie. She didn't have a clue as to how the monstrosity worked.

"Pull the chain."

She did, stalling for time. It snapped off its rusted hook and fell across her arm.

"Thanks," she called with false cheerfulness, dropping the thin chain in the basin. A quick glance at the walls revealed nothing in the way of a weapon. Getting down on her hands and knees, she checked under the cabinet. Maybe someone had lost a wrench or something over the years.

The door she'd locked swung open and two scuffed brown cowboy boots came into her line of vision a second before that familiar hand reattached itself to her arm and lifted her up.

"I told you there was no escape."

She shrugged. "Forgive me if I don't take your word for it."

She reached for the chain as he dragged her out. With a shake of his head, he removed it from her hand. "You won't need that."

"Why not?" she asked, arching a brow at him. "Because you don't mean me any harm?"

"Because it won't do you any good."

So much for that hope. She resisted as much as she could as he tugged her down the dark hall. Which wasn't much considering the strength in the man.

He stopped, his brows snapping down with impatience. "Would you prefer to be bound?"

"No."

"Then keep up."

He was a bossy son of a bitch. "Where are you taking me?"

He paused in front of another door. "To Caleb."

She stopped resisting immediately. She had more than a few things she wanted to say to that man. But before she said anything, she wanted an apology. Considering she'd kept her promise—getting here without stopping—that was the least he owed her.

SHE wasn't going to get an apology. Allie stared in horror at Caleb. He was pale. So very pale. And the life that usually hummed off him in waves was now just an occasional flicker she could barely feel. Half his throat was laid open. He wasn't bleeding anymore, and in truth his wound was like no other she'd ever seen. It almost looked as if it had started to heal and then had just stopped in some gross transitional phase.

She took a step forward, drawn to where he lay on the bed, his big-boned body dark against the white sheets.

"What happened to him?"

"The wolves." Jace practically spat the words.

She looked at the three men standing around her. She knew them by sight, all three clones of Caleb in one form or another. Indisputably brothers in looks and temperament—fists balled as if ready to fight at the drop of a hat, jaws set in preparation. The question was, for what?

"Why haven't you taken him to the hospital?"

"He doesn't need a hospital," Jared said, anger slicing through every word.

"He needs blood," Slade clarified.

Allie shook her head, touching Caleb's bare shoulder over the white sheet. He was so cold. So still.

"That's precisely why he needs to be in the hospital."

Jared stepped forward. "He doesn't need that kind of blood."

She looked at him, something in his tone alerting her. This wasn't going to be good. He grabbed her wrist, pulled back her shirt, and exposed her wounds. "He needs it straight from the source."

Blood flowed. His eyes glowed. Good God, his eyes glowed!

"No." She shook her head and stepped back as far as his grip on her arm let him.

"Jesus, Jared, I thought we were going to break it to her gently." Jace stepped forward as if to break his brother's grip.

"Why?" Jared asked, stepping between her and Jace. "So she'll understand why she's going to die? Do you think that makes it any more acceptable?"

"She's not going to die."

Slade's words might sound sure, but the expression on his face didn't do much for Allie's nerves.

"Caleb would never take too much," Jace argued.

Too much? Too much what? Blood ran down her arm in a hot stream, an unreal precursor to the incomprehensible.

"Can someone tell me what you're trying so hard to break to me gently?" Allie asked, her voice higher than normal as she fought the reality they were trying to force her to accept.

Jared stared at her for a moment, his fingers biting into her forearm, before he said flatly, "We're vampires."

"That's nuts!" She tugged her arm. Jared didn't let go. He caught and held her gaze with his and slowly spread his lips in an obscene parody of a smile. Fangs gleamed on either side of his mouth. Sharp, white, freak-a-girl-out fangs.

She yanked her arm free, clutching her wrist against the pain and took a step away, staring at those fangs, at what they implied. She shook her head.

"Are you telling me that the big, macho Johnson brothers went goth to the point of getting cosmetic dentistry?"

"Technically, I don't think goths are vamp imitators," Slade offered almost conversationally.

"We don't have time for this," Jared interrupted. "We need to get on with it."

"Get on with what?" she had to ask, even though she was reasonably sure she didn't want to know. The hairs on the back of her neck were prickling, and a sick feeling of dread settled in the pit of her stomach. First the monster wolves and now . . . this.

Jared grabbed her arm again. "Caleb needs a reason to live." He pulled her toward the bed. "You're going to give it to him."

She dug in her heels. It didn't do any good. The man was incredibly strong. "By giving him blood?"

His smile was cold and hard. "You'll give him a hell of a lot more than that."

He held her bloody wrist to Caleb's dry, cold lips. Caleb was so still, she couldn't even feel a breath against her skin.

"You're crazy," she breathed, staring, as everyone else was, at Caleb. Waiting in horror and a sick fascination for him to do something. As if he was capable of doing anything except dying right then. She shook her head. This was insane.

She braced her feet and pushed back against Jared's grip. "You don't have time to indulge in this mass delusion. You need to get Caleb to the hospital."

Jared merely held her wrist more firmly against Caleb's lips while the other brothers stood, tense with anticipation. Waiting. She didn't know what they expected of her, but she knew she didn't have whatever they thought it took to revive a dead man.

Caleb's eyes flew open with a suddenness that jarred a scream from her throat. She jerked back, met the barrier of Jared's strength, and went nowhere.

"Feed, Caleb," he whispered, for the first time showing the faintest hint of vulnerability as he scraped his nail across her raw wrist. The pain made her gasp. Fresh blood welled. Caleb's nostrils flared as his eyes changed from dead flat to a deep green lit with strange, swirling golden lights.

"Feed, damn you," Jace whispered as if terrified of disturbing the moment.

Caleb closed his strangely glowing eyes. Allie's knees went weak with relief. He wasn't going to do it.

"Son of a bitch!" Slade cursed. "He said he'd never do it again, and you know how he is."

Tension flooded the room.

"Oh no you don't," Jared muttered as he stared at Caleb. Allie dared a glance at his face. His lighter eyes began to glow in the dark room as the lines of his face settled into an expression of formidable determination. "You got us all into this. You don't just get to walk away."

Who or what were these people? Pain in her arm drew her eyes down. She could only stare in openmouthed shock as the nails on Jared's hand grew into talons that curved and pierced her skin. The scream that welled in her throat died as a presence pushed into her mind and quelled the instinct, holding her bound, paralyzing her in a cocoon of horror and pain.

We're vampires.

Jared's previous statement reverberated in her head, growing from a small black speck of knowledge to an ominous dark cloud of incomprehensible certainty that blocked all hope. With a calm slash of his thumb, Jared laid her wrist open. Blood sprayed over Caleb's mouth and face. Her horror exploded into terror. He'd severed her artery. She needed to clamp off the wound, but she couldn't move. Couldn't scream, couldn't do anything but watch as Caleb's eyes sprang open in his bloodstained face, the swirling golden light consuming his pupils, a vivid contrast to the crimson stain of her blood.

Everything in her recoiled. This wasn't her Caleb. She'd never buy a fancy bra to tempt something like this.

Could they really be vampires? Even witnessing what she was witnessing, she couldn't accept it. Vampires did not exist.

Feed Caleb. Take from me.

The thought welled in her mind, in her voice, and projected outward. But she wasn't thinking it. Would never think it.

She could feel the resistance in Caleb. She encouraged it. The presence in her mind doubled in strength and urgency. Her silent cries of *Don't do it* were snuffed out as easily as one extinguished a candle flame.

Her blood continued to gush, and Caleb continued to resist for precious seconds. The voice echoed in her mind again.

Feed. For me. Please.

Allie felt a moment of relief. Caleb would know it wasn't her by the pleading tone in the request. She wasn't one to beg.

Her relief evaporated to horror when Caleb's mouth opened and, with the speed of a striking snake, he sank his fangs into her wrist.

As the agony exploded through her body, she dropped to her knees, a chorus of yeses ringing in her head, three of them heavy with relief, one filled with a euphoric jubilation that scared her witless.

Every movie she'd ever seen, every book she'd ever read projected a vampire's bite as something seductive, but this wasn't seductive, this was pain. Pure white-hot agony. It felt like Caleb was devouring her arm whole, his teeth working harder in a constant demand for more, greedily sucking the blood from her body until all she could wonder was how long she had to endure before she passed out.

She glanced at his brothers, desperate for help. Her eyes met a wall of implacable resolve. They were playing a game in which only they knew the rules and in which her role was clearly one of sacrifice. They could block the pain if they wanted to. Common sense told her that. If they could hold her prisoner in her own mind, they could block her pain, but they wanted her to suffer for their own perverted reasons. Sick bastards.

She gathered every bit of energy she had left in her rapidly weakening body and met Jared's cold hazel gaze with her own. *Fuck you.*

Surprise flickered in his eyes, whether from her choice of words or the fact that she managed to communicate them telepathically, she didn't have the strength to debate. She laid her cheek on the side of the bed and followed the trail of weakness out of her body and sighed, "Caleb."

CALEB struggled with the lassitude holding him prisoner. Struggled against the weakness dragging him into the sweet, welcoming dark he didn't want to come back from.

Caleb.

The whisper echoed in his mind. Allie's voice, filled with an unbearable pain and hopelessness. His Allie, of the irrepressible optimism and incredible bravery. Someone had dared to hurt her.

He crashed into awareness on a surge of primitive rage and endless hunger. Immediately, he knew his brothers were in the room. He could feel their elation mixing with a wariness he didn't understand until he registered the other presence. Allie. Close and hurting.

He opened his eyes. She was slumped against the side of the bed, her hair a waterfall of silken brown on the white sheets, her arm stretched toward him, pale and insubstantial. Her body lifeless as the sweet taste of her blood filled his mouth.

Horror joined his rage. Jesus H. Christ, he was feeding on her. The woman he'd never meant to taint. He broke his brothers' mental hold on him, now strong enough to do so thanks to the infusion of her blood. He pushed up to his side. The wound on her wrist was a gaping testament to his hunger.

"Goddamn you," he swore at Jared, knowing who was behind this. "Did you even have the decency to block the pain?"

"You were leaving us, Caleb," Slade stated calmly. "We did what we had to."

As if anything gave them the right to use her. Hurt her. His Allie. His woman. The one he'd never intended to claim. He stroked his tongue over the wound, sealing off the sluggish spew of blood. He brushed the hair off her deathly white face, all that bursting life gone, leaving a waxen impression of her true self.

"She didn't ask for this."

"None of us did, but it didn't make a difference to you before," Jared inserted, his bitterness undiminished.

And it wasn't going to make a difference now, Caleb knew. Two hundred and fifty years ago he couldn't face eternity without his brothers, and today he couldn't face this. He slid down to the floor beside Allie, pulling her into his arms. She flopped like a rag doll against him.

"Goddamn you all to hell."

"We're already there."

The rage swirled again, primitive and nearly out of control as Caleb tilted Allie's head back. She was almost gone, the flicker of life in her barely detectable. All he had to do to let her pass over was to delay just a little longer, let the lack of blood starve her body of the oxygen it needed and she'd pass cleanly to the other side, untainted. The vampire in him howled at the thought, raged at the concept of losing his mate—primitive as always, thinking in terms of possession—while the human part of him, the part he struggled to keep alive, knew it was the right thing to do.

He positioned her body, placing her mouth against his chest. He whispered into her mind, to that small, terrified, huddled bundle of light that harbored her soul, "It'll be all right, Allie girl. I'll make it all right."

Slade came forward, reaching for her, "We'll feed her, Caleb. You're too weak."

For the first time in centuries, Caleb bared his fangs at his middle brother, ready to rip his throat out if he came an inch closer. "Don't touch her."

Jace caught Slade's arm and pulled him back. "Leave him be, Slade."

Slade jerked his arm free. "He can't afford the blood loss."

"We'll replace it," Jared said, as calmly confident as always.

"What if he refuses to take from us, like before? Caleb can be a damn stubborn bastard when he gets the bit between his teeth."

"Before he was protecting her."

"And now?"

"He'll feed."

"What makes you so sure?"

Jared's gaze stroked over Allie with something akin to satisfaction. "He won't leave *her*."

Jared was right, Caleb knew. As long as Allie lived, he'd stay in this world, doing what he had to in order to insure her happiness.

He elongated his pinkie nail to a razor sharp talon and slashed his chest. Blood gushed. He pressed Allie's mouth to it, blending his mind with hers, soothing her horror with calm, changing the scenario to one of a first date, changing the taste of blood to the effervescent bubble of champagne, ignoring the clenching in his body as her soft mouth moved erotically on him, each brush of her lips whipping through his body on a swelling wave of white-hot pleasure.

He looked at his brothers across the room as Allie fed, loving them, understanding their motivation. It had always been the Johnson brothers against the world. But no more. It had been their choice to change things. He stroked Allie's soft hair, better positioning her mouth against him, quelling her struggle for control with another touch of his mind to hers, biting back a moan as her lush hips shifted on his hungry cock. She was everything to him now. Joined to him forevermore. His hope and his reason for being.

He locked his mind to theirs and spoke very clearly so there would be no misunderstanding of Allie's importance to him. "If you ever endanger her again, brothers or not, I'll rip your throats out and leave you in the sun to burn."

❊ 4 ❊

ALLIE awoke to darkness, a scream tearing from her throat. One certainty beating at her mind. She had to get away. Now. Before they got her.

She couldn't remember who *they* were, but she knew they were bad. Very, very bad. She didn't need to know any more than that. She worked her elbows beneath her, trying to find up in the inky darkness.

A heavy weight settled over her, rupturing her scream into a gasp. She pushed off the mattress, twisting with the wild cadence inside her, but there was no moving the heavy mass. Pressure countered her every move. She was trapped. In a nightmare. This had to be a nightmare. Only nightmares left a person with this level of unsubstantiated panic.

"Easy, Allie girl. I've got you."

The murmur filtered out of the darkness, extending a thread of hope through her hysteria. Caleb. She was lying beneath Caleb. She tentatively reached up and bumped her knuckles on the flat of his chest. She opened her hand and slid it up over the hair-roughened surface until she found the solid curve of his shoulder. A naked Caleb?

Okay. Maybe this wasn't a nightmare. Maybe it was more of a fantasy. The heat of his skin seared her breasts, her stomach, and her legs. She wished she felt good enough to enjoy the intimacy, but the mother of all headaches was beating behind her eyes.

Caleb's sigh stirred the hair at her temple. She brushed the annoying tendril off her forehead, a tangled strand caught on her first knuckle. She closed her eyes briefly and worked at the knot. The damn thing held.

It figured. She finally had Caleb naked and horizontal and her hair was a tangled mass of knots, she felt like she'd been run over by a Mack truck, and instead of smelling like the expensive body powder she'd bought just for the occasion, she smelled distinctly unexotic and overworked. Allie put a question at the top of what she suspected was going to be a long list. How in heck had she managed to screw up landing naked with the man of her dreams so badly? There was only one way to find out.

"If you slipped me a roofie and had your way with my unconscious body," she warned him, "I'm going to geld you with a rusty knife."

"Why a rusty one?"

Nothing in Caleb's drawl indicated what he was thinking. She wished she could see his face. "Because that would hurt more and maybe lead to a life-altering infection, which you would so deserve for having fun without me."

Another pause and then his chuckle ruffled her hair. The mattress beneath her dipped as he shifted his weight. The fingers of his right hand worked between her skull and the mattress, cupping her head with infinite care as if she'd break with too much movement. The sheets rustled as he braced himself on his elbow. "You can rest easy. Neither of us has had a good time."

A shiver took her from head to toe, a faint prelude to the more violent one that followed. Her head ached, her stomach roiled, and she knew, just knew, she wasn't going to like the answers to the frantic questions humming in her mind.

"Should I be treating that as good news or bad news?"

His thumb rubbed her temple. She closed her eyes as the sickening panic receded. "You tell me."

"I asked first." It was very hard to lift her lids. "I need a bath."

Caleb's fingers pushed hers aside. "As soon as you feel up to it, you can have one."

Which probably meant no time soon, considering that working the snarl had tested the limits of her strength.

He demonstrated far more patience with the snarl than she did, untangling it with a few painless tugs. In her current state of mind that was more of an irritation than a plus. She didn't need anything making her feel more inferior. She batted his hand away. "How did I get here, Caleb?"

His hand dropped to her shoulder.

"I brought you."

"Why?" She jumped when his fingers touched her upper arm.

"Easy." Instead of withdrawing, his fingertips began slow distracting circles on her skin. "You were hurt."

"By what?"

"Something you weren't expecting."

No shit. She tried to remember and couldn't. "And what exactly was that something?"

"Me."

The answer lay between them like a living thing, writhing under the enormity of all it implied. She tried to shrug off his touch. All she succeeded in doing was stilling the movement of his fingers, but moving or not, Caleb's touch was deeply disturbing, creating a sense of connection between them, enhancing the certainty of the rightness of lying together like this. Which was crazy. It had to be. She couldn't have slept through the first time she'd had sex in the last two years.

Was she dreaming? A dream would explain everything. The

blankness in her memory, the surreal feel to the encounter, that overwhelming sense that something important hovered just out of her conscious reach. Those were all classic symptoms of a dream state. She dug her nails into Caleb's skin. He felt darned real for a figment of her imagination, all tough muscle stretched over hard bone. And warm. Blessedly warm.

Vampire. The warning whispered in her head. Images of fangs and blood sprinted across her mind in an indistinct blur, followed quickly by a flash of pain and betrayal. Her breath caught as she chased the illusion. Or reality. She couldn't tell.

The heavy darkness shifted as Caleb pulled her completely beneath him, the heat from his body settling over her like an electric blanket, alerting her to the fact that she was getting cold. In the dark. Naked. With a man she was in lust with but didn't really know. Allie braced her hands against his chest, taking in his warmth even as she attempted to hold him at bay. This was weird. Too weird. Figment of her imagination weird. "Are you real?"

"Don't I feel real?"

Lord help her, even her figments were contrary. She slapped at the fingers stroking her arm. "If I could tell that, I wouldn't be asking."

"I'm as real as you can take."

"Uh-huh." Like that told her anything. Allie wished she could see Caleb's face, but no matter how hard she squinted, she met that wall of darkness and the absolute certainty that she must be dreaming. Vampires didn't exist. And even if they did, they came with huge honking fangs, decaying flesh, and an accent that sounded more like Hungary in winter than Texas in the heat of summer. She felt with her leg over the side of the bed. Her toe didn't meet the pile of her clothes that she searched for. It didn't even meet the floor. She scooted over a little more, stretching farther.

"You're gonna fall off the bed."

"No I'm not." Dream or not, instinct said this was a good time to be making an exit.

Failing to touch the floor with her foot, she wiggled some more and let gravity aid her cause. Her curse followed in her wake as she dropped. Except the floor wasn't where she thought it should be. It was a good bit lower and landing on it hurt her butt almost as much as it hurt her insides.

"Shit!"

There was a rustle and a disturbance in the air around her. Caleb settled beside her with what could only be described as a long-suffering sigh.

"You don't listen well, do you?"

"I listen fine when people say something I want to hear."

She felt around the floor. There had to be clothes somewhere. Her hand caught on the trailing end of the sheet. She grabbed it and yanked it toward her. "You just haven't been saying what I want to hear."

The sheet only came so far. Had he nailed the thing to the bed? She used the resistance to pull herself more vertical. She got half-way there before blinding pain in her head dropped her back to the floor. Strong arms came around her. It was disgusting, the ease with which Caleb pulled her against him. Almost as disgusting as her natural relaxation into the hard planes of his chest. She was an independent woman, for heaven's sake! "As grateful as I am for your sparing my butt, I really need you to let me go."

"If I let you go, you'll fall."

She tightened her grip on the sheet. "Let's just give it a spin and see how I do."

From the little dots streaking behind her eyes, she didn't think she was going to do that well, but she had to try. Her gut said so. Caleb muttered something under his breath. She was reasonably sure it was another curse. Allie scooted to the side. His hand dropped, brushing her hip. She gave the sheet a big yank.

The damn thing gave as if it hadn't stood solid as a rock against her a minute before. She lurched sideways, hitting the wall with her shoulder and then her head. She fell to her knees. The two seconds it took to wrap the sheet around her were all her stomach gave her before it rebelled. Nausea rolled over her in a violent wave. Never, ever, had she thrown up this hard. It felt like her guts were turning inside out, but nothing came out. The next spasm sent her tumbling forward. Caleb caught her, his hand a welcome support against the violent heaves.

"I told you to stay put."

If she could have spared the energy to turn, and actually had something to throw up, she would have vomited on his toes. "Shut up."

"You need to lie down."

She knotted her fist into the sheet and pressed it against her stomach. "I just need a minute."

Dear God, please let this be a dream and do not let me be vomiting in front of the stud muffin of my dreams.

"A minute isn't going to do it."

If this was a dream, it was an annoying one. Not to mention embarrassing. "How do you know?"

"I've seen this before."

She caught his hand before he could move it off her hip. "What exactly is 'this'?"

"Your body's just getting shed of the poison in it."

The coldness of the next wave of nausea had nothing on the coldness of horror. "I was poisoned?"

One palm pressed into her forehead, the other into her stomach. It might have been her imagination, but the pain and sickness seemed to lessen beneath his touch. "In a manner of speaking."

In a manner of speaking? Had that brief image of her packing cleavage reduced his impression of her brain power to zero? "There's no 'manner of speaking' when it comes to poison. Either I was, or I wasn't."

"Come to bed, and I'll explain."

"Said the spider to the fly."

He ignored her mutter, just slipped his arm under her knees and behind her back and lifted her. The swirl of nausea kept her protest trapped in her throat.

"Easy."

Allie swallowed hard and gritted her teeth. She had about one intact nerve left and that "easy" was getting on it fast. "I'm not a horse."

"Things would be a hell of a lot easier if you were."

Well, that was a heck of a note. A shift in his grip and then the coolness of the bottom sheet met her spine. She felt along the expanse with both hands. "I know I came here with clothes."

"You did."

"So where are they?"

His hands came back to her head and stomach. "You lost your supper on them."

Again the pain and nausea seemed to recede. She should probably leave the horse comment alone, but damn it, she had to know. "Why a horse?"

"What?"

"Why would you rather I was a horse?"

"It's not a matter of a rather, but convenience. If you were a horse, you wouldn't ask so many questions."

The bed dipped as he sat beside her. She checked her body's tendency to roll with the flow. "And you wouldn't have to provide so many answers."

"Yeah."

Sick as she felt, the way he said that "yeah," all low and slow, made her pulse skip a beat. She grabbed his forearm. The rock-hard muscle didn't give a fraction under her frantic grip. "Caleb?"

His "Yes?" was distracted.

"I'm too tired and sick for word games."

"I know."

There was no doubt about it, she was feeling better. And the good feeling was spreading outward from his hands. Was he a healer? She'd read about healers. "Please, tell me what happened."

Beside her, there was sudden stillness. The hand on her forehead slipped down to her cheek, conforming to the curve as if he were memorizing the shape of her face. "I'd rather wait until you're stronger."

"And I'd rather know now."

His hand drifted down to her throat, the fingers curving around the base of her neck, his thumb lingering on the pulse point almost caressingly. She recognized that touch. She'd been on the receiving end of it too often to mistake it. It was something men did before they delivered very bad news, like tonight-was-fun-but-I-met-this-new-woman-and-I'd-like-to-see-her-instead-of-you kind of news. They always thought making a woman feel physically good a second before they delivered the crippling blow somehow made it better. Men were so clueless. She braced her shoulders into the mattress. "You might as well spit it out."

"What?"

"Whatever horrible thing you're going to say."

"You think that's going to make it better?"

"Can't make it worse." And maybe it would either get this dream over with or onto a better version. One that had him showing her how well he knew how to use the hard-on she could feel brushing her thigh.

"I'm not going to like what you have to say, am I?"

"No."

"It has to do with why I feel that I should be afraid of you, doesn't it?"

"Yes."

"Since I'm halfway there, don't you think you could throw me a bone and give me the whole thing?"

"I'll think on it."

He'd think on it. Huh! She'd give him something to think on. Her stomach churned on the rush of adrenaline. "I need to get to the bathroom."

His palm pressed on her stomach. The nausea subsided. He was definitely controlling her body's reactions. Her curiosity piqued. Years ago, during her journalist period, she'd searched the country for a real healer, chased down every tabloid rumor, hunted up every new age cult. She'd thought a piece on natural healers would make a great story for the magazines, but she never managed to find one whose talents she could verify. She'd come close at one cult, even believed the quack when he'd told her she had a special energy that needed nurturing, but when they'd started locking her door at night "for her own protection," she'd come to her senses. And now, she was laying next to a man who actually might possess real healing skills . . . Excitement bloomed. It was difficult to keep her voice even. "I'm pretty accepting of things, Caleb. I won't freak out if you have certain . . . abilities."

"I'm glad to hear it."

"I consider myself a very open-minded person." Nuts, if anyone asked her family, but he didn't need to know that.

His fingers massaged the aching muscles, relaxing them, soothing her body, her fears. She placed her hand over his. "I can take whatever it is you have to say."

"You really don't know what's good for you, do you?"

She bet if she could see him, he'd be staring at her with his head cocked to the side the way her brothers did whenever she'd confounded them with her brand of logic. "Just because I don't believe ignorance is bliss is no reason to get insulting."

"I'm not being insulting."

"No, you're stalling."

"Maybe."

"Well, cut it out. It's annoying and as this is my dream, I have a right not to be annoyed."

His fingers stilled. "You think this is a dream?"

"It's too bizarre to be anything other than a figment of my subconscious."

He resumed his stroking. "I can see you viewing it that way."

She stiffened. "Was that another insult?"

"You object to insults in your dreams, too?"

Was that a hint of a grin coloring the inflection in his deep drawl? "Absolutely."

"Then no, more of a statement of the obvious. It's logical you'd decide this is a dream."

"Thank you." Dream Caleb was much more accepting of the real her than most men of her acquaintance. Which was only fitting. Fiction should be stranger than truth. She placed her hand over his where it rested on her hip. "So what are you, and why am I afraid?"

The air between them thickened with tension.

"It's okay, Caleb. I can take it. Just tell me." The subconscious was very good at dealing with a lot of things the conscious shied away from. He cursed and then stilled. Tension built right along with her expectation. She felt his glare, heavier than the dark, scarier than the unknown. She clenched her fingers over his, but it didn't help with the truth he spit out on a hoarse growl.

"I'm a goddamn vampire and in a little while, you will be, too."

The shocking claim echoed around inside her head, veracity bleeding through each syllable, making everything she knew to be fact just jumbled bits of scattered reality. *Vampire?* Impossible to believe, horrifying to absorb, yet somehow, snapping into that empty place in her memory with irrefutable rightness. *Oh God. Oh God.*

"Is that answer enough for you?" he bit off.

She released his hand, pressed back into the bed, and inched to the far edge. "Absolutely."

✦ 5 ✦

So maybe she wasn't as open-minded as she'd thought she was, because she wasn't taking Caleb's announcement of vampirism with the same equanimity with which she would have taken a statement of homosexuality. And considering the hots she had for his body, a declaration that he was gay would have kicked up quite a ruckus with her hormones. "Turn on the light."

"You don't need light."

Like hell she didn't. "Turn on the light."

She wanted to see his face when she asked her questions.

His hand covered her eyes a split second before there was a click and then light flared. The burn to her eyes was incredible, even shielded. Tears poured down her cheeks. She pushed at his hand, wanting to see his face. Was he the same, or some monster caricature of himself? What in hell did a vampire look like anyway? What did she look like? Why did she even care if this was a dream?

His hand didn't budge and even though she didn't voice her question, he answered. "You're the same as always."

"I'll believe that when I see it." If she could see it. Weren't vampires supposed to be unable to produce a reflected image?

"You can see your reflection."

"Not if you don't take your hand off my eyes."

"Your eyes are still too sensitive for any light. You're going through the change."

She had an awful suspicion that the last phrase didn't mean for him what it meant for her. "I assume you're not talking menopause here."

"No."

Her breath came faster, harder. Allie quit trying to move his hand off her face. Breaks she didn't want him to hear peppered her order. "I think . . . you owe me a bit . . . more elaboration."

His hand twitched, and she froze. Any more light than the shadow she saw and she'd go out of her mind from the agony. In a lot of ways, this dream really sucked. She much preferred the ones where they were both naked and the only pain she experienced was from screaming herself hoarse as a result of multiple orgasms.

"Your ability to adjust to light will kick in when the change is over."

"Your optimistic side is showing again." She waved her hand in the air. "Turn off the light."

To his credit, Caleb didn't say "I told you so." He just flipped the switch and let the darkness roll over her in a soothing balm.

"How am I supposed to get around if I can't see in the dark and can't bear the light?"

"The halfway stage is not permanent."

Halfway, did that mean this could be reversed? "Can I go back?"

"The only out is death."

Great. So much for the easy way. "Do I have a choice?"

"No." The air around them filled with a relentless energy that felt like the edge of steel pressing into her mind. "I won't let you die."

She pushed back against that invisible force, gaining nothing but a return of the knifing pain in her head. "I might not give you a choice."

His hand returned to her throat, wrapping around it, the fingers pressing on her pulse point. The steel in his voice threaded his drawl. "You don't get to decide."

That was too much. "Are you threatening me?"

"I'm merely telling you how it's going to be."

With his hand on her throat, he was telling her he wouldn't let her die? Oh yeah, that made sense. She touched her fingertips to the back of the hand pinning her. "I hope you realize the hypocrisy in your position."

His thumb stroked along her neck. "I'm no threat to you."

A memory teased her consciousness. One of his eyes swirling with lights, a horrible wound, his fangs, the vicious bite. So vivid, yet somehow surreal, floating behind a veil she couldn't part. Fact or fiction or a blend of both? The memories danced through a distorted sense of time, her subconscious composing images to fit the reality it needed to create, rearranging the mental lies to make them seem real. A bit too real. She inched a little farther away, gaining a centimeter until that big chest came down over hers, pinning her. "You could have fooled me," she gasped.

"I wouldn't have converted you if I'd had a choice."

Images of male faces set in hard lines along with a memory of steely resolution in hazel eyes crashed into her brain. She continued her creep across the mattress. "That wasn't my impression."

Her head was firmly stuck in the middle of the bed, but she'd managed to find the edge with her foot.

"The blood loss weakened me."

Or what? He would have succeeded in resisting, or something else? "You were trying to die?"

"No." Something brushed over her forehead. She flinched, feeling foolish once she realized it was his fingers pushing her bangs out of her eyes. "Trying to resist converting you," he finished dryly.

The memory of three men's joint resolve overwhelming her opposition crept forward past her conviction that this was a dream. The memory disappeared as quickly as it came, leaving her fumbling with the remnants. "They forced you?"

It seemed the very air absorbed his sudden stillness. "I'm not sure how much force was involved."

Well, that was honest.

"Explain." She thought she understood, though. Because along with the pain and the fear, she remembered other things. Words filled with agony, hope, determination. Words that dragged her back from the darkness with the strength of the emotion contained within them. Words that had saved her because of the will of iron that had backed them. Caleb's will.

His shrug felt like an apology. "They knew as weakened as I was, they could influence me, make me do what they wanted."

"Which was?" Good grief, this was like pulling teeth.

"To take my mate."

"Mate? Who on Earth uses a word like that anymore?"

"Vampires."

He kept hammering that point, as if sheer repetition could make her believe it. He had a lot to learn about dreams. The mind only absorbed what it wanted in dreams, letting the rest drift around as unclaimed will-o'-the-wisps of illusion. "Uh-huh. Well, you had a life before you became a vampire, and I'm reasonably sure you remember it, so I think you can choose vocabulary to reflect it."

"You don't like the word 'mate'?"

She shook her head. "Way too caveman."

"Fine, they wanted me to take my woman."

"My woman." Like that was a step up from mate. "Why?"

The pause between her question and his answer was thick with emotion she couldn't define but felt she should. For her safety and her sanity, but, from one blink to the next, the strength to do so evaded her grasp.

"To keep me here."

"In this life?"

"Yes."

"Why didn't you want to stay?"

"It wasn't so much I wanted to leave as much as I was determined to do the right thing."

"By me?"

"Yes."

It was probably the sweetest thing anyone had ever said to her in or out of her dreams. "Is that why you came around my shop every morning? Because you liked me?"

"I couldn't resist you."

She was more the type of woman men had to get to know to appreciate than one who overwhelmed them with lust. "Right." She worked her other leg across the mattress. His fingers stroked her pulse with soft persuasion.

"You're the prettiest thing I've ever set eyes on."

"Thank you." She rubbed her forehead as the pressure beating behind her eyes increased in a slow, building threat. Thinking was definitely hurting her brain. "So, because you thought I was attractive, you thought it was okay to show up every day at my bakery tempting me?"

"Pretty much."

The weary note in his voice slammed her ego. Did he regret meeting her? "Well, no one asked you to strut your stuff in my store."

She was right about that, Caleb knew. Not one person had been happy with his fascination, least of all himself. But like a moth faced with the temptation of light, he'd needed to see her, and because he had, the D'Nally wolves had caught scent of his interest. And that had put her in danger. Because the renegade Dane had acted on it, seeing it as the perfect route to revenge for whatever the hell Jace had done to set the pack against them. The question was whether Ian D'Nally had sanctioned the attack. Caleb didn't particularly want to escalate the tension between the Johnsons and D'Nallys to outright feud, but a pack-sanctioned attack against his kin would do it. He caught Allie's hip in his hand as she inched toward the edge, his senses coming alive as the soft fullness shaped to his grip. "Didn't one tumble teach you that isn't going to work?"

"It taught me that I need a different approach."

He shook his head, the smile sneaking up on his blind side as she continued undeterred. She had to be the most determined, resilient person he'd ever met. He doubted she even had a passing acquaintance with the word "quit." "You need a guardian."

The shove she gave his arm spoke volumes. "I can take care of myself."

He slid his hand over her shoulder. His night vision was excellent. Not as versatile as day vision, though. It was more of a blend of intense black and white with startlingly accurate shading. It had taken him a while to get used to the lack of color, but after the first fifty years, he'd adjusted. Especially since the satin texture of Allie's skin glowed like the palest white against the surrounding dark. Like moon glow, calling for a longer touch. A lingering. He resisted the urge. She might think him a dream, but he was pretty sure she'd object to even his dream self taking liberties.

He settled for just making a bracelet of his fingers and sliding them down her arm. He turned her palm up and stroked the indent on her wrist that his bite had created. His fingertip slid along the groove that marked the change for them all. The deep indent would soon be invisible, obliterated as her conversion completed, but permanent nonetheless in the effect it would have on them all. In the change it would bring.

He had a wife now to protect, to answer to. A mate. A flicker of movement brought his gaze to her face just in time to catch the nervous pass of her tongue over her lips. A very scared and confused mate who needed his care. Beneath the translucent skin of her throat her pulse throbbed, a too-fast contradiction to the sass in her attitude. A sass he completely enjoyed. In his day, they'd have called Allie high-spirited. Forward. Hot-blooded. His eyes narrowed, concentrating on the pulse point, following the rich flow of blood as it raced along the artery. Very hot-blooded. A woman like her drew men like flies, many for the wrong reasons. A woman like her fed a man's sense of adventure, challenged his preconceptions, made him think, made him feel. A woman like her definitely needed a protector, because women like her were rare.

"You can let go of me."

He barely felt the tug on his grip. Another thing he'd forgotten in the last couple centuries: how much more delicate a human woman's strength was than a man's. He lifted his gaze to find her staring at him with wide eyes and parted lips, her expression a mixture of fear and fascination. As if she, too, were caught up in the chemistry between them. As if what was there was more than could be seen or felt. More than could be ignored.

"Am I making you nervous?"

"Yes."

He hadn't expected the truth. "It's a habit of mine."

"Staring?"

"How do you know I'm staring?"

"I can feel it."

"Ah."

Her tongue flicked over her lips again, leaving them glistening, revealing the uncertainty that didn't show in her voice. "So, do you think you could give it a rest tonight?"

"Your dream not going the way you planned?"

"If I'd planed it, we'd be having a lot more fun."

"Hmm, I bet we would."

"I can't be a vampire." Her free hand slid under his, rubbing at her stomach.

"It's not that bad."

"Vampires don't exist."

"Uh-huh." At least she was trying to absorb a little, even if she was approaching reality from the outskirts and working in. He squeezed her fingers. "You're going to need help with this, Allie. At least, initially."

"And here I thought it was all just going to come naturally."

He ignored the sarcasm. "Some of it will." Especially the need to feed. Primitive and violent. When it came upon her the first time, it would consume all of the humanity she clung to so hard. He pushed the bangs off her forehead. "Some of it, you'll have to work at."

"Like what?"

Regaining her humanity after that first feed, retaining it from there on, but he didn't say so. There was time enough for her to figure that out on her own. "Learning to sleep during the day, for one."

She didn't smile. Her hands pressed into her stomach. "I don't feel well."

Damn, he'd thought he had her nausea suppressed. He worked his palm between the sheet and her skull. Supporting her head, he turned her to her side. "Are you going to be sick?"

"It's not that kind of unwell."

"Then what?"

The eyes that strained to see him over her shoulder were wide, fearful, and oddly determined. "I just realized if this isn't a dream, I'm dead."

HER terror clawed at him, her cry for help unconsciously reaching along their connection. Help he didn't want to deny. It wasn't right that she hurt because of him, because of anything. Caleb followed the terror down the mental path, back to the seat of her fear and covered it with calm, sliding a tendril of energy out, feeding her shaky belief that this was a dream. Solidifying it. Adding a verbal push to his mental one as she rolled onto her back. "You're not dead. This is a dream, remember?"

It was wrong, but he wanted her to have the comfort of that illusion for as long as possible. Her nails sank into his forearm with the desperation lacking from her carefully modulated, "You're sure?"

"Baby, I'd notice if you needed to be put under."

Her big eyes narrowed with suspicion, "How?"

"I'd be the one digging the grave."

She blinked at that. "If I'm not dead, but I'm a vampire, how will I explain?"

"You won't."

"But I'll have to tell my family something."

Shit. This was the hard part. "Anybody looking for you will think you're dead."

The shock of that hit her like a blow. She jerked and then went absolutely still. The rapid blink of her eyes kept back the tears he could see shining there. "Why would they think that?"

He tucked her hair behind her ear, rubbing his knuckles on her cheek. Guilt flayed him with the deep cut of a whip as Allie lay there, looking into the darkness, trying to see his face, dreading what he was going to tell her, willing it to be different than what she suspected. "Probably because you disappeared and your car is in the river. When it's found, everyone will assume you drowned."

The truth burned like acid on his tongue, but he owed it to her.

"Damn you." Her fist slammed into his cheekbone, one knuckle wedging against his eyeball snapping his head back. "I have a family!"

He grabbed her hand, pressing it down into the mattress, blinking to clear his watering eye. She had a hell of a quick jab. Her body jerked as she snapped up her knee. He trapped it between his thighs, grunting when it grazed his balls. She bucked beneath him. She was no match for his strength. Within seconds he had her pinned. "I'm sorry. There wasn't any choice."

"You had a choice. Probably a hundred of them. All better than that." Allie turned her head and sank those small white teeth into his wrist. The bite burned through him like fire, a combination of heaven and hell. Blood scented the air. His vampire rose to the call. He threaded his free fingers into the soft silk of her hair and yanked her off.

"God damn it, Allie, think." A shake punctuated the statement. "There's no explaining the unexplainable."

The starkness of his night vision turned the glitter of her tears to a silver sheen.

"You don't know my family."

"Are they the open-minded type that can accept the thought of their daughter sucking their blood?"

She gasped and cringed into the mattress. "I would never touch them!"

"But they would always wonder if you would, would always speculate if you could."

"We'd work it out."

"About all you'd work out is mass hysteria when people found out vampires really do exist."

"You don't know that."

"Yes, I do." He let her struggle until exhaustion forced her to drop back against the mattress.

"Damn you."

He already was. "There's no going back. Just forward."

"Without my family?"

"Yes."

Waves of grief radiated off her. Every shudder in her breath rubbed salt into the open wound of his guilt. "I hate you."

"I'm sorry."

She took another breath, held it, and then her eyes narrowed and her chin came up. "If this wasn't a dream, I'd kill you for putting them through that hell."

They both knew this wasn't a dream, but if enabling her to pretend for a bit longer spared her pain, he wasn't going to stop any sooner than he had to. The reality was hard to take in small doses, let alone all at once. "Then I guess I'll be giving thanks to dreams."

He held her, absorbing her grief and tension as she wrestled with the loss. Silent tears slid down her cheeks into her hair, dripping onto the inside of his arm where they lay in a pool of hot accusation. Snippets of scenes with her brothers and her father raced through her mind along with the love she had for them. One by one, he muted the memories, creating a buffer to tuck the pain behind. Gradually, Allie relaxed. Her fingers unclenched and spread over his shoulders. Her chin came down and in a small, very un-Allie-like voice she asked, "So, I'm really not dead?"

"Not by a long shot."

He brushed his mind over hers again. He felt her hidden determination to reunite with her family along with the bundle of tension behind her eyes that indicated her headache worsening. He pushed it back out of her conscious reach and fed her belief that this was a dream. It wasn't as easy as it had been before. The woman's mind was going crazy muddling what had once been a clear path. He braced himself as she took a breath. Allie on a tear could lead to anything.

"When someone spots me drifting around at night, how are you going to explain that? Call me a ghost?"

She was still working on how to get past her immortality, using logic to make sense of the illogical. "No."

Her nails dug into his forearms. "My brothers won't stop looking for me."

He stroked her hair. He could understand that. He wouldn't either. "They won't find you."

"Why not?"

"I figured on changing your appearance."

"With plastic surgery?"

"No. Illusion."

"Welcome to the witness protection program for vamps," she muttered under her breath.

Her resilience made him smile. "Pretty much, though it was easier in my day. More space, less technology." In the last seventy years, hiding in plain sight had become more difficult; in the last twenty, almost impossible with people's love of cameras.

Her head canted to the side as she considered his statement. "The Internet must really screw with your lifestyle."

"Slade considers it his new best friend and digital cameras his mortal enemy."

"I can understand that. If you discount the Johnson hunk appeal, the man has geek written all over him."

His vampire stirred with a growl. "I'm the only Johnson whose hunk appeal you need to be noticing."

She waved his statement away like he was playing. He was glad she couldn't see the vampire's snarl at the thought of her with another man. One peek and she'd be running for cover. His desire to possess her completely was absolute.

"So if I'm not dead, what am I?"

"Stuck between a rock and a hard place."

She did not appreciate his sense of humor. That was clear. Her eyes narrowed and he got the impression she was just short of slapping him. She let go of his arm, depriving him of the sting of her claim, her hands bouncing off his shoulder, fingers grazing his neck, sending chills down his spine. Chills that bunched in his groin in pure anticipation as those same fingers wrapped in the hair just above his ears and yanked down.

"Right now, at this moment, what am I? Vampire or human?"

He let her pull him to within six inches of her face and then countered her tug with resistance. If he didn't, one of them was going to end up with a broken nose. "Human."

"You're sure?" She shifted beneath him, her toes brushing his legs, her hips moving against his. "You've checked?"

He lifted his torso, giving her more room to maneuver, savoring the hot slide of flesh on flesh. It didn't matter if she were only trying to get away. His body, so tuned to hers, took the rhythmic touching as an invitation and responded with hard impatience. "Not in the last five minutes."

"Check."

"Is that an order?" He did not take orders well, which was

something she'd better realize if they were going to spend eternity together.

Her impatiently rapped out "Please" wasn't much less of a demand but he could follow it a hell of a lot easier. He placed his hand on her stomach. Her insides were in turmoil. Gathering for the change, the invasion begun but not completed. In a bit she would feel like hell, no matter what he did to block her discomfort, but she still had time. "Human."

"Good."

He didn't like the sound of that. She was up to something. The hands in his hair slid to his shoulders. "You're not a bad guy, are you?"

He was a lot of things, but he wasn't a total goner. "I'm no saint."

"Have you ever killed anyone?"

"Not that didn't need it."

Her grip lessened and then, as if winning an inner argument, tightened again. "And if your brothers hadn't . . . influenced you, would you have attacked me?"

"No." But, he would have converted her eventually, he realized that now. Resisting her was a futile battle, but he would have made the conversion a pleasure, not pure hell. No way would she have described it, in the aftermath, as an attack. He slid his hand under her head, curving his fingers around as if he could protect her from the truth with a caress. "But now wouldn't be any different."

She frowned, tilting her skull into the cup of his palm. "What do you mean?"

"You'd still be lying in my arms, and I'd still be helping you through this."

"This being the physical transformation to vampire?"

"Yes."

Her lower lip slid between her teeth. Damn, of all the powers he had, at that moment the only one he wanted was the one he didn't have. He couldn't rewrite history.

"You would have given me a choice?"

He brushed the bangs from her eyes. "Yes. I never would have taken that from you."

"But you think I would have agreed?"

"Eventually."

She stretched her fingers, pressed with her palms. Embarrassment tinged her scent. Her eyes closed and then slowly reopened. "Because I made such a fool of myself over you?"

He shook his head. "You've never been a fool."

The roll of her eyes was pure Allie. "Puh-lease."

He touched his nose to hers. "You've been sweet, funny, incredibly brave, and tempting, but never a fool."

"That's one way of looking at it."

At the edges of her mind there was a fluttering. Was her memory coming back?

"You saved my life."

Her fingers skimmed his collarbone, searching and finding the healthy skin of his neck, moving over the surface in widening circles. "I remember the wolf . . . ripping out your throat?"

He leaned back. "Yes."

Her memory was definitely coming back.

She shuddered, squinting against the dark. "There was so much blood."

"But you saved me."

Her fingertips explored farther. "There's no scar."

"Vampires heal quickly if they can replenish."

Her frown deepened. "That psycho wolf was going to kill me."

Fear leapt with the knowledge. He hazed the vividness to a dream-like recall. "Yes."

"You didn't let him."

He stroked her cheek. "No."

Nothing would hurt her while he lived. There was too little laughter in the world and too few who knew how to nurture its light.

"He almost killed you."

"He gave it a good shot."

Her fingers stilled over his much slower pulse. "You risked your life for me."

"You risked yours for me."

"We would have made a good pair."

She said that as if her turning vampire negated everything good between them. He chose his words carefully, hating the haunting sadness in her eyes that spoke of good gone bad, hating he had been the one to kill the romance she'd envisioned between them. "We still could."

"No." She pushed him away. "It's impossible now."

"Why?"

"You're a vampire."

Caleb probed her mind, caught images of he and she together, naked in a tumble of bedclothes, the white of the sheets contrasting with the darkness of his skin. Candles surrounded the bed. A breeze blew in through the window, making the candles dance and the gauzy canopy billow. It was an incredibly soft, romantic image. His heart twisted in his chest and his cock went hard. "Ah baby, I can still give you what you want."

"You can?"

"Yes." At least the sex part. He wasn't sure about the romance.

Her fingertips caressed his shoulders in small hesitant strokes. "Sex wouldn't be enough."

He could feel the heat rise in her cheeks, see the darkening color. She was embarrassed. Damn, she wanted the romance, too. "I'd do my best."

"The same way you would if we were human?"

"Yes." And probably with about the same unlikelihood of success. He'd never romanced a woman.

He slid his right hand down her side, grazing her flesh with his nails as he did, noting the hitch in her breathing, feeling the hunger of desire rise between them, feeding it. As his fingers curled into the lushness of her buttock and pulled her under him. His cock slid between her thighs, nuzzling into her damp heat. She was aroused, and ready.

Allie caught her breath again and then burst out, "I want an orgasm."

It was his turn to blink.

She pressed her hips up in a silent plea that he didn't think she realized she was making. "I've never had one and I don't want to die, even in a dream, without connecting with y— someone that way."

He guessed he could understand that. If a body wanted a miracle to happen, a dream would be the place to make it occur. "And you've picked me to do something about it?"

Her "You owe me" made it sound as if he'd be reluctant. When every nerve ending in his body had just switched their full attention south.

"And you want repayment in the form of an orgasm?"

She shook her head, her jaw setting in that determined way it did when she wanted something. "Not just any orgasm. I want the screaming, lose-my-mind, lose-myself kind I read about in books."

She read about that in books? Jesus, Mary, and Joseph! "That's a tall order."

He inched his thumb in, brushing the sensitive crease between her thigh and groin. She shuddered. She was very sensitive there. She bit her lip, controlling the response. That, they were definitely going to have to work on. The one thing he didn't want from Allie in his bed was control.

He must have hedged too long because she went on in a desperate rush. "It doesn't have to be the real thing. I won't know the difference if you manipulate my mind. I just need to think it was real."

She wanted him to fake her orgasm for her?

He curled his fingers under her neck, pressing on the delicate vertebrae, arching her spine, presenting her breasts for his pleasure. "I don't have any problem making love to you, but Allie girl," he kissed the curve of her cheek, "there won't be anything fake about it."

She frowned. "I've only got the one shot. Once I turn, nothing will be the same."

"I'll still be here."

"But I won't."

She believed the conversion would change more than just her physical body. He placed the next kiss on the mutinous pout of her lips. "I've got the picture."

"Then you'll do it?"

His cock was so hard, so heated with his need to mark her, it could have been all over for him right there. His conscience insisted he put one truth out in the open. "You're asking to make love with a vampire."

"Your vampire powers are what make you the man for the job."

That and the fact that she clung to the hope that maybe he was a figment of her imagination. Son of a bitch, he'd never thought to be in such a position. Her hips tilted up, sliding her moist flesh against him in a blatant invitation.

"When are you going to get a better offer? Guilt-free, no-strings sex with full permission to go wild?"

Never. Because there'd never be another woman for him, and when this was over, when she couldn't fool herself anymore that reality was a dream, when he couldn't hold the illusion for her, there'd be hell to pay. But for right now, she was asking him for the one thing he knew he could give her. The one thing that would be all pleasure. He didn't have it in him to say no. "It'd be my pleasure."

She wrapped her arms around his neck and her legs around his thighs as if she, too, felt the nebulous uncertainty of the moment. "Then, please, hurry."

❖ 6 ❖

TWO minutes later Caleb had a damn good idea why Allie hadn't had the pleasure she'd sought in earlier relationships. "Hurry" seemed to be her defining word when it came to lovemaking. She chased every sensation like it was the last one coming, blocking any effort to increase it by her single-minded effort to capture it. The fourth time she tugged his mouth away from her nipple, he'd had enough. He grabbed her hands and placed them over her breasts. "Take over here for me for a minute."

Her hands sat where he'd placed them as if she couldn't divine his meaning.

"Squeeze those pretty nipples for me."

She gave a tentative twitch. He reached for the edge of the sheet, pulling it toward him until he could get a grip. "Did that make you feel good?"

"You can see me?"

"All vampires can see in the dark."

Shock, dismay, and then outrage chased across her face. "That's so unfair."

"And here I was thinking how nicely it was working out." He tore a strip off the sheet, the loud rip punctuating his statement.

Allie jumped, her head turning toward the sudden sound. "What was that?"

"The sheet tore."

"All by itself?"

"They don't make them like they used to." He pressed his finger to her nipple, creating the smallest of indents in the plump center. Her eyes drifted half closed. The tiny nub puckered. "Didn't I give you a job to do?"

"Yes."

"Then why aren't you doing it?"

"Sheer perversity."

As if his chuckle freed her inhibitions, her fingers tightened on the small peaks. Too hard, too fast, bringing nothing but discomfort. He sighed. For such an adventurous woman, she hadn't taken much time learning what pleased her. He took first one hand then the other in his, flicking her nipples with his fingertip in apology. He kissed her palms. "Put your hands above your head."

She did it too easily, as if she didn't connect his tearing up the sheet with anything happening now. He kissed her again for that innocence, and quickly tied the sheet around her wrists and then to the center post of the arched headboard.

Passion turned to alarm two heartbeats too late to do her any good.

He shook his head, a smile tugging at his lips when she tentatively tugged at her bonds as if unable to fathom how they'd gotten there. "Allie girl, for a modern woman you are amazingly trusting."

She twisted on the bed, neck arching in a vain effort to see how he'd tied her.

"I'm not into this, Caleb."

"You don't know what you're into." Of that he was absolutely positive.

"I am not into pain."

That pulled him up short. He paused, braced over her supine body, a good foot from the prize he sought. "What makes you think I'm going to hurt you?"

She tugged at her wrists. "This whole BDSM thing."

He checked the sheet to make sure there was enough play in the material for what he intended. There was. "I'm just aiming to slow you down so that orgasm you want has a chance to catch up."

That explanation just made her look put out. "I don't need to slow down."

"On that we differ, and since I can't control your pain and your hands, we're going this route."

Her head snapped around. "You said you weren't going to hurt me."

"I'm not. I'm talking about the pain of conversion."

She yanked at her wrists some more, frowned, and then added body movement into the effort to get free. "Stop harping on that!"

"Because you don't believe or don't want to be distracted?"

"Both." The mattress bounced with her efforts. "Untie me."

"Why?" He straddled her hips, catching himself as the mattress dipped. "I like you like this."

And he did. With her arms anchored above her head, her breasts were pressed up and out in a pink-tipped invitation that was enhanced by her twisting and turning that had them shimmying in a provocative display no red-blooded male could resist.

Her head cocked to the side and that irrepressible curiosity shone in her eyes. "Seriously?"

"Never been more serious about anything in my life." He balanced the edge of her cheekbone along the length of his finger. His thumb came to rest against her softly parted lips. "You're damn tempting stretched out for my pleasure."

"What about my pleasure?"

"That's not going to stop until you beg me." Caleb traced the delicate bone down to her temple, drawing her lower lip away from her teeth, testing the resiliency on the moist inner flesh with a gentle press. "And maybe not even then."

Allie sucked in a deep breath. He could feel her brain working on that possibility. Her next breath wasn't so deep, and when he leaned in, walking his hands up the mattress so he was propped over her, it fragmented to a gasp. Her lids lowered and speculation replaced protest. She curled her fingers over the strips of material and lifted her body in invitation as he braced his hands on either side of her head. "Talk is cheap, mister."

It was a little too obvious a ploy, a little too soon. "Don't worry, baby, I know what I'm doing."

"The proof is in the pudding."

The curve of her shoulder drew his lips. "If I answer that, are you going to throw out another cliché?"

"Maybe. I've got a million of them."

There was that sass he so admired. "Guess that means I'll have to work on a distraction."

"Better make it a good one."

Caleb brought his chest down over hers, enjoying the sinuous coil of her body against his, the prodding caress of her hard-tipped nipples as he delicately scraped his teeth along the line of feminine muscle, the tantalizing graze of her damp pubic hair across his groin. It only took a slight downward movement of his hips to bring his cock into play, letting her rub it all around in the moisture welling from her body, not giving her what she thought she needed, teasing her with light pressure. "How about I make you a deal?"

Her "What kind of deal?" was game. Very, very game. "How about you let me play for a bit like this and then if you want to be untied, I'll untie you."

"How long?"

"Ten minutes ought to do it."

"Ten minutes and you'll untie me? Just like that?"

He nodded, forgetting she couldn't see him before adding, "Just like that."

"And then I can touch you all I want?"

His body tightened at the anticipation loaded into that question. "If you want."

She ran her tongue slowly over her lips, and her eyes took on a dreamy cast. "Oh, I'll want."

"Not if I do this right. If I do this right you're just going to want to lie there and let me have at it."

She arched her back, pressing her soft breasts firmly into his hard chest. "If you knew how long I've thought about getting my hands on your body, you wouldn't say that with such confidence."

He slid down, tucking his head to the side so he could whisper in her ear. "If you knew how long I've waited to have you in my mouth, you wouldn't be wasting time with words."

Her "I wouldn't?" was a breathy gasp.

He bit down on her lobe, just hard enough to pluck a squeak from her reservoir of pleasure. "No. Do we have a deal?"

She turned her cheek farther into the bed, silently demanding another nip. "Yes."

"Good." He ignored the demand, choosing instead to stretch the syllable down the cord of her neck in a brush of his lips, controlling her body's instinctive shift away from the shivery sensation with a hand on her hip. "Shh, baby. Let it feel good."

She shook her head as he drew his hand up her stomach, over the ladder of her ribs to the fullness of her breast. He plumped it into the palm of his hand, wrapped his fingers around the base.

"I can't."

"Sure you can. Just focus on my hands, what I'm doing to you. Don't rush it, don't fight it, just lie there and let me make you feel good."

She raised her head off the mattress, a frown on her face. "Men don't like women to just lie there."

No way was he letting her think her way through this. "I'm old-fashioned, and I'd be thrilled if you did that very thing."

She blew her bangs off her forehead and dropped back onto the bed. "You've got nine minutes left."

It wasn't exactly the most encouraging statement he'd received while playing between the sheets, but it made him smile anyway. The woman just had fight in her bones.

"Thank you."

In a purely conversational tone, she suggested, "You might want to add some mental touching to turn up the heat."

Like hell. This was going to be all her and all him with no mental tricks involved. "Was that a moan of pleasure?"

She pressed her lips together but didn't offer any more input as he brought his hand back down the slope of her breast, separating his fingers as he went until he once again circled the base. After several slow caresses he detected a peak of interest, a catch in her breathing as he grazed her nipple. On the next pass, he increased the pressure slightly. The stillness in her body told him she detected the change. He nudged her chin with his, exposing her neck for his mouth. Her scent was stronger here, very feminine. Enticing. Addictive. He kissed the hollow of her throat, ignoring her stiffening, just keeping up his rhythm at her breast while he lapped at the tender nook, tasting her, savoring her. This was his woman. His mate. He sucked the soft flesh into his mouth. His.

She shifted beneath him, her request clear. He gave it to her, increasing the pressure and length of his stroke, squeezing the nipple just tightly enough to pull it away from her body. Just long enough to halt her breath in her lungs and center her attention, and then he was moving his hand back down the less sensitive sides, pausing longer at the bottom this time, letting her wait. Letting them both anticipate. Her legs shifted on the bed. She swallowed. Hard. Her throat worked against his lips, her pulse pounded in an enticing lure. He rubbed his mouth over the temptation and flexed his fingers before whispering, "This one's going to feel so good."

She didn't argue, just sucked in a deep breath and held it as his hand climbed the familiar path, her eyes closed, every thought, every fiber of her being centered exactly where he wanted it. On the sensation he was giving her. When he reached the nipple, he stopped and held her there, plumped and compressed for his touch, his mouth; whatever he wanted. "Watch, Allie."

Her lids lifted as if weighted; slowly, languorously. He tapped her nipple with his chin. "Watch me take your breast this first time."

"I can't see."

"Imagine it."

She strained upward as he curled his tongue around the needy nub. She was crying out before he made contact, her body arching in anticipation of the moist heat, struggling with the restraints and her need. He kept her pinned with his arm across her torso, kept her presented for his pleasure with his hand on her breasts, letting her helplessness feed her permission to do nothing but feel. Her pleasure flowed as he lapped and nudged the hard tip with his tongue. When she began to twist in frustration, the light touch no longer enough, he took her into his mouth and sucked.

She came off the bed, momentum propelling her breast into his mouth, against the point of his teeth. She moaned and sank back onto the head of his cock, granting him the sweetest, most intimate of kisses. Torturing them both with the hot friction, the promise of what was to come. He went with her as she collapsed onto the mattress, giving her more of the devastating passion that flowed to her from him, and then back again—harder, stronger, honed in feminine intensity, charged with her pleasure.

"Oh, God. Oh, God." The breathless chant echoed in his ears, catching in the edge of his desire, dragging it to the limit of his control. His fangs extended farther, reaching for her. Her nipple pulsed between the sharp points. His jaw muscles tightened. He wanted, needed to drink from her.

Too soon.

Though barely recognizable, the warning from his rational side filtered through his lust. He pulled his mouth away, moaning under the whip of unsatisfied desire. Sliding his hand up until he could capture the tight flesh of her nipple between his thumb and forefinger, he substituted a pinch for a bite, increasing the pressure until her voice broke on a guttural moan, holding it there for several seconds as she shook and gasped, her energy no longer spreading outward, but focusing inward, toward the building orgasm.

"That's it baby. Feel it." He wanted this orgasm for her, screams and all.

He stretched her nipple away from her breast, nice and easy, watching carefully to see how the new sensation struck her. She frowned. He shook his hand in rapid movements using the weight of her breast to deliver the unique sensation. Her eyes flew wide. Her mouth opened. Before she could voice her opinion, he pinched sharply. She flinched away with a startled gasp, but then just as quickly, returned, thrusting the taut peak back into his hand in a silent plea. He gave it to her slowly this time, increasing the pressure bit by bit, watching as her lip slipped between her teeth and she bit down, driving the blood from the soft flesh, leaving it white in the aftermath. A soft cry broke from her throat as he pinched the tiniest bit more.

"Right there, Allie girl? Is that where you like it?"

"Yes. No." Her head thrashed from side to side. "I don't know."

"Lets find out then." Caleb shifted to his knees. His cock left its warm nest with a protest of its own, catching on the side of her hip and bouncing up before bowing to gravity, the heavy head coming to rest on her pubic bone. He spread his left hand under her right breast. Using the same motion as before, he milked the flow of her desire. His reward was the immediate tightening of the small nipple. "Very good."

He didn't decrease the pressure as he reached the peak. Instead, he caught the puckered tip to leverage her breast up and out, stretching it away from her body, watching her expression as she battled conflicting impulses to twist into the stretch or to stay with the pinch. The scent of her arousal surrounded them now. A heady enticement to create more. More pleasure. More scent. More. Always more.

"Caleb!"

"Right here." Barely.

He lowered his left hand and shifted his grip until it matched his right. Caleb wanted more time, but the change wasn't willing to wait. It was growing stronger, taking more of his effort to subdue the symptoms so she could enjoy their play. If he dragged this out much longer, he would lose her and the feelings to the hell that was coming. He'd taken everything from her and she'd only asked for one thing in return. And she was right. Considering how knowing him had completely messed up her life, the least he owed her was a mind-blowing orgasm.

Releasing her nipples, he smoothed his fingers down the outsides of her delicate curves. Her whimper of disappointment echoed his own. She had the sweetest breasts.

"Soon, baby."

He followed the line of muscle down her stomach, fighting for control, shifting backward, almost losing it when his cock slipped between her legs and her gasp whispered past his ear as his groan tore past his control. Cupping her hips in his hands, he pressed his mouth to her stomach, breathing in her scent. Damn, he had to slow down. Get her ready. He'd shoot himself if he hurt her. He needed to prepare her.

He sucked in a deep breath, feeling almost drugged by the richness of her scent, the steady flow and rhythm of her desire. He worked his way down until he could drape her legs over his shoulders. He knew the protest was coming from the tensing of her thighs as he settled between them.

"Caleb? I don't think—"

"You're not supposed to be thinking." Was that guttural rasp his voice?

Her hips jerked in his hands as she pulled on the restraints.

"Why are you fighting? I like you like this, Allie. Open and available for whatever I want."

"Oh."

He hitched her back some. "Grab hold of the bedpost."

He liked that she immediately did so with white-knuckled intensity. It soothed something in his wild, primitive vampire core. "You just grab on to the good feelings I'm about to give you with the same gusto, and you'll have that screaming orgasm faster than you can say Jack Shit."

"Jack Sh—"

One swipe of his tongue wiped out the second part, but not his amusement. She was a sassy one. Very different from the women of his time. Different from the weres he'd slept with since turning, and damn, he found those differences to be a big part of her appeal. The rest of his thoughts died under the wave of lust that surged over him as that first intimate sampling spread through his being like wildfire fanned by a hard wind. His back arched and his fangs cut into his lip as the primitive roar of satisfaction bellowed from his soul.

At last.

The thought spun through his mind, picking up strength with every revolution, digging into his gut. At last, he had his mate. She was here, needing him. Nothing else mattered as he feasted on the delicately perfumed flesh so open to his hunger. Every whimper, every cry just encouraged him. There was only Allie and the drive to mark her, satisfy her, brand her as his. Caleb fought the primitive lust, fought for coherence, struggled to hold on to his humanity, but it was a losing battle. The vampire lust was upon him. Darker than bloodlust, stronger than could be imagined. A scream echoed above his head.

Allie. Dear God, Allie. He dropped his forehead against her, sucking in air, reaching for the little bit of coherence he had left that told him he was almost out of time. Definitely out of control. He pulled back.

In a move too fast to register, he switched positions, bracing her thighs apart with his, using his hand to align himself before coming down over her and pressing in. He rubbed his thumb on her most sensitive spot, kept his mouth at her breast, working both simultaneously, prolonging her orgasm, easing her through the power of his claiming because he couldn't stop. The beast was fully upon him.

Damn, she was tight. Too damn tight.

Through their mental connection he sent a command into the confusion that consumed her a split second before he thrust. *Relax.*

Either she couldn't or wouldn't. Confusion and passion warred. He slipped through that crevice, filling her mind with his pleasure, his need. The resistance gave, and he entered her in a slow, smooth glide. He held himself still within the tight fist of her channel, cries of victory screaming through his head. She was his now. Only his.

Beneath him Allie moaned and shifted. Her heel rode up his leg, opening herself to more of whatever he wanted. And suddenly what he had wasn't enough. He needed more. More of her cries, her passion, her taste.

Caleb pulled back. Allie twisted away. Another growl welled. It was too late to turn back. They were joined. In a few minutes it would be irrevocable. Had to be irrevocable.

He couldn't get close enough, deep enough. He lifted her thighs over his arms, spreading her wider, grinding his groin into hers on every downstroke, her joy at the contact spilling over him in a hot incentive. He bent over, drawing her nipple deeply into his mouth with every withdrawal, keeping her with him until the explosion burned up his spine. He pulled all the way out, releasing her nipple from his mouth, releasing the wild flare of emotion in her eyes with two words. "You're mine."

She shook her head. He thrust back in, letting her take what she could, easing her into the idea with his body seeking with his mind as well. He didn't just want to possess her, he wanted to bind her to him. Ensure her acceptance of him as her mate. Forever blend their lives.

He watched as she took a fraction of an inch, and then another, her body stretching to his need, her gasps sensual little punctuation marks to their passion.

"Mine." The claim sprang out of the deepest part of him. "Tell me you're mine."

Another inch disappeared. And then another. With every inch the urgency increased. He leaned in, bending over her, centering his thumb over her clitoris, rubbing in cadence with her gasps. Her energy pulled at him with the same desperation, drawing him into her with her strength of will, tendrils of her energy wrapping around his. She cried out and her hips bucked, sinking him deeper.

"Say it, Allie. Give me that much."

Her heel drew up his thigh, pulling him to her. Her inner muscles tightened, fluttered. Her back arched. Her lips parted, drawing his kiss. He changed his rhythm, capturing her cry, her gift, holding the declaration as close as he held her.

"Yours. I'm yours!"

Before the last syllable of her cry dissolved into the embracing darkness, he sank his fangs into her neck as cleanly as his cock sank those last vital inches into her body. Sealing himself against her, he took her scream—her climax as his, blending their minds, bodies, and souls, relaxing into the knowledge that she was his. At least for this moment. This time, he had her.

SHE was going to have to rethink her perception of herself as a lover. She was obviously much more into kink than she'd ever imagined. And Caleb had much more influence over her than she'd ever predicted. Allie shifted her position. He immediately pulled her against him, his hands spreading open on her back, sheltering her. Which immediately begged the question, from what?

She wiggled her fingers. My God, she'd let him tie her up. She tugged on her hands. "Could you untie me now?"

"In a minute." His chin nuzzled her temple. A brush of his lips over the rim of her ear shot a shiver down her spine. His chuckle sent goose bumps chasing behind.

"I'd prefer now." She had to get control of this situation. He reached up, his chest rubbing against hers. She sighed before she caught herself. His skin felt so good against her.

"I think you feel pretty good, too."

"How do you do that?"

The soft bonds on her wrists fell away on a soft *rip*. "You think very loudly."

"I do not."

"You'll get the hang of it."

"Hang of what?"

"Controlling your thoughts."

He brought her hands down, massaging her muscles. Her inner slut started to purr.

"I don't seem to be able to control much." Not the sickening clench in her stomach, not her reactions to this man, not what she was becoming. "And I'm not yours."

"Are, too. You said so."

"That was just the sex talking."

He pulled her into his side and draped her thigh over his.

"Damned good sex."

Her head fell naturally into the hollow of his shoulder. "That doesn't mean anything."

"I'm saying it does."

"Into self-delusion, are you?"

"Nope. I jut recognize the truth when it walks up and bites me on the neck."

"I'm not a possession. You can't just claim me."

He cupped her stomach. "But I can hold you. You need me."

Under his touch, the writhing pain abated. A reminder and salvation. "Until I'm converted."

She didn't expect him to agree, but the sheets rustled as he nodded, his biceps flexing under her head as he cupped her shoulder in his big hand. The warmth of his palm seeped into her skin, spreading beneath the surface, stretching deeper, feeding a hunger that had nothing to do with sexual desire. "But it does buy me time."

She tilted her head back, squinting against the darkness. It was no use. She couldn't see his face. "Do you ever give up?"

Short and sweet, his answer left no room for doubt. "Not if it's something I want."

And he wanted her. "And you want sex."

A flex of his shoulder muscles and her face was tipped up. "I want you."

Such a bald statement should have made her nervous, but it didn't. Not coming from Caleb. There were depths to the man. The kind that harbored deep emotion. There was also a strength that suggested stability. He was the kind of man in which a woman could put her faith. If she discounted the fact he was a vampire.

Pain coiled in her gut. She frowned, remembering something he'd said. "You said you'd been through this before."

He spread his fingers wide over her stomach. It didn't help this time.

"Yes. With my brothers."

She'd never heard so much said with so little emotion. She reached up, brushing the bristle on his chin, searching until she found his mouth. All the tension missing from his voice was in that tight line. She curled her fingers into a fist. "What happened?"

"I converted them."

"Why?"

"We've always been close-knit."

"They asked you to change them?"

Still that same flat monotone. "No. It just happened."

She pushed away from him, sitting up, clutching her stomach as nausea rolled through it. "How does something like that just happen?"

The darkness thickened. The hair on her arms rose as the very air stilled. "I got hungry."

"I don't understand."

His hand touched her cheek with infinite tenderness. "You will."

❧ 7 ❦

OH God, not another one. Allie clutched her stomach against the crippling pain and watched as Jared half dragged, half escorted a handsome young man into the study. Inside, the wild voice she didn't recognize screamed, *Yes!*

Elation and horror rose as the lust came over her. She shook her head, backing away, running smack up against Caleb's chest. His arm came around her, sure and strong, keeping her there. This wasn't a dream. It was a nightmare. And worse it was one from which she'd never wake up. There was no more fooling herself. Vampires were real and she was one of them. And if that wasn't bad enough, Caleb expected her to suck someone's blood. The shake of her head was as instinctive as pressing back against him. She wouldn't live like this.

"I can't do this, Caleb."

He wasn't pushing her at this one as he had the others, though there was no give in his drawled, "You have to feed, Allie."

"No." She shook her head harder as her fangs cut through her gums. "I can't."

"Pretend it's carrot juice."

Carrot juice never affected her like this. Jared pushed the young man closer. She heard his heartbeat, felt, with total repugnance, the lust for his blood that rose within her as his scent came to her. Clean and healthy. She clapped her hands over her mouth as her newly sprouted fangs ached, and again shook her head at Jared.

She would not do this. She didn't have to feed, didn't have to live. She had a choice.

"You can't possibly object to this one." Jared lifted the hypnotized man, front and center, by the back of his coat. "There isn't a speck of dirt on him."

Behind her Caleb growled as the man gazed at her through vacant gray eyes, smiled, and then presented his neck. A glance over her shoulder showed Caleb looking at the young man, an aggressive set to his jaw.

"Oh, for goodness sake." She waved her hand at the poor victim, grateful for the exasperation that helped her contain the wild hunger. "He's enthralled, and breakfast. How can you be jealous?"

Her comment was ignored. Caleb glared at Jared. "You couldn't find anyone else?"

Jared let go of the man, who immediately slumped to the floor. Allie yanked her foot out of reach of his hand. Yet another discovery. Enthralled people creeped her out.

"Who the hell else would you suggest? She won't touch women, the elderly, and no matter how vile the person, if there's a speck of dirt in sight, they're off the chow wagon. In an area this remote, this time of year, you're lucky I even found him."

"You're wasting your time." Maybe, if she said it often enough, someone would believe her.

With a disgusted prod of his boot, Caleb edged the man's groping hand away from her leg. "Well, she's not feeding on him."

"You worried she's going to want more, and you'll have competition?"

More? No one had told her about more. Allie looked between Caleb and his brother. "What more?"

"He didn't tell you about that?"

"Jared . . ."

That was definitely a warning in Caleb's voice, and it raised her suspicions nearly as much as the quirk at the edge of Jared's mouth. The man never smiled. She glanced up at Caleb, not liking the set of his jaw. "No."

"It's not something she needs to worry about."

"Not when you're bringing her derelicts for her first feed, that's for sure," Jace offered from the doorway, thankfully no offering in his hand. "I've got to believe, even in that kind of heat, a woman could have standards."

"Shouldn't you be hunting up something to eat?" Caleb asked, the edge in his drawl verging on a growl.

The young man moaned. The inner beast that had taken up residence last night within Allie howled, demanding the meal who lolled on the floor. With every minute that passed the demand grew. Soon, she knew, she wouldn't be able to resist. And now they were implying she had something more to worry about? Good God, who knew being a vampire would be so complicated?

"I'm not sucking anyone's blood." She included Jace in her glare this time.

He, in turn, leaned his shoulder against the worn wooden jamb. "You realize you soon won't have a choice?"

"There's always a choice."

"Not in this." The certainty in Jared's voice made her want to slap him.

"In the feeding or the other?" Whatever that was.

"I won't let anything go wrong." Caleb's hand shifted to her waist and pulled her back against him.

She looked at him over her shoulder. "Now something can go wrong?"

"There might be a concern if I wasn't here."

"What is this concern that you think you can control?"

The door to the back opened. The click of the latch sounded unnaturally loud to her ears.

Slade closed the door behind him with a decisive thud. "The lust for blood is often connected with the lust for intimacy."

"I'm going to fall in love with them?" She turned all the way in Caleb's arms and slapped his chest when he wouldn't let her step back. "You wanted me to fall in love with that smelly, lice-infested old man you tried to get me to maul?"

Caleb caught her hand, his expression more grimace than anger. "It's nothing as permanent as love, and it's feeding, not mauling."

Sex, they were talking sex. "I'd want to have sex with that derelict?"

Three yeses and one no. She didn't know who to believe, but she wasn't having any part of it, not the blood-sucking and not the indiscriminate sex. "I am so out of here."

With a twist, she broke free of Caleb's grip. As she stepped around the young man, he reached for her. The primitive, lusting voice inside her whispered how easy it would be to end both their pain. How simple it would be to sate the hunger. The voice grew stronger, the push to bend over and bite violently grew stronger. Too strong to be natural.

Feed.

She spun around. The command lingered in her mind. Faint and foreign, like nothing she'd ever felt before.

Who said that?

No answer came from the men around her. They were, however, all watching her with the same peculiar intensity as before, eyes glowing. Tendrils of invisible energy reached around her. Very recognizable, individual, and en masse. With a slash of her hand, she dismissed their influence. "Give it up already." She pushed past Jace. She needed to get out of there. "I'm a damn vegetarian. Blood is not on my diet."

She made it to the middle of the hallway before the dark wave of hunger rolled over her, impossibly forceful in its demand. Real this time, coming from within. A part of her. And according to Caleb, there to stay. Following the wave of hunger came the crushing pain. Harder. Longer. Building in intensity rather than diminishing. She fell back against the wall and closed her eyes. The moan she couldn't suppress ripped from her throat. She pressed her hands into her stomach, sliding down the wall. It didn't help. According to Caleb, nothing was going to help. She rode out the pain, panting as she'd seen women do on TV when they were in labor. As much as this hurt, it couldn't be worse than that.

"You're fighting a losing battle."

She didn't have to open her eyes to recognize Caleb. The sound of his voice, the whisper of his scent, the feel of his energy were as known to her as her own. Maybe that whole myth about whoever made a vampire owned that vampire was true, because she sure felt as if Caleb had stock in her. "So you keep telling me."

His knee grazed her arm as he bent down. "Probably because it's true."

His heat enveloped her like a comforting blanket. She had the incredible urge to turn to him and let him make this all go away. Except, she couldn't. He was the enemy. "Go away."

A cold wave of nausea swept over her, blending with the pain, making it more than it was and just slightly less than she could bear.

"I can't."

She believed him. Whatever bound her to him seemed to bind him, too. Making love with him had seen to that. At least the orgasm had been worth it. "You could try harder."

The hand he placed on her brow was calloused and warm. She leaned into the stroke of his thumb. "I don't want to."

"I won't feed on another human, Caleb."

"You don't have a choice if you want to live."

She didn't answer. The silence stretched, growing heavy with the implication. His thumb paused mid-stroke, pressed. Tension gathered within him and streamed to her through his touch. She opened her eyes to find him staring at her with those golden swirls gathering in his green gaze. Her hunger rose, swelled, and reasserted itself with the temptation he so beautifully presented. She brought out the compromise she'd mentioned before. "I could just munch on you."

The swirls flared to flames. He definitely liked the idea. "We discussed this. You need to know how to fend for yourself."

"I know how to fend for myself. Knowing isn't the problem."

"Now is the best time to get you around your distaste."

Because they felt she wouldn't be able to help herself, that her instincts would override her will. The naiveté of that almost made her smile. Almost.

"You just keep believing that."

This time, when the pain came, it wasn't a roll, it was a spear thrust through her gut. "Da-amn."

Swearing didn't help. The pain kept going deeper and deeper, riding its own momentum, burying itself in her abdomen. She knifed her knees into her chest in an effort to contain it. Caleb's hand kept her head from slamming into her knees, and she resented the hell out of it. She needed to control something, and if the best she could come up with was beating her skull against her knees, he needed to let her do it.

"Allie girl—"

"Don't say it." Choppy and weak, the warning lacked the strength she was going for. Cold flooded through her on the heels of the pain.

His knees spread and then she was between them, pulled up against the heat of his body, her shoulder pressing into the hardness of his groin, her cheek to the firmness of his stomach. "Don't say what? That you're hurting yourself for nothing, that in the end, you'll feed?"

He was so warm. So warm when she was so cold inside. Allie

wished she had the courage to tear his clothes from his back. She needed the heat he kept from her. "I'm not preying on people," she muttered through chattering teeth.

"It's no different than any other species in the food chain. Better even. You don't have to kill to live."

"It's not the same to me."

His fingers worked the tight muscles of her shoulder.

"In time you won't need to feed so often."

It was a measure of her desperation that she saw that as a good thing. "How much time?"

"Months. Maybe years."

"You don't sound sure."

"It's different for everyone."

"How often do *you* feed?"

"Once every few months."

That was a long time between meals, which might explain, along with their use of illusion, how the Johnson vampires had gone undetected by humans. "When you get hungry, do you go on binges and tear up the town?"

"No. With time you gain control." His fingers moved up the base of her neck as another bolt of agony shot through her. She bit her knee, forgetting about the fangs. The metallic taste of blood flooded her mouth. "Baby, how long do you think I'm going to let this continue?"

Allie tried to make her expression as serious as his, but the bolt of agony that shot to her core ruined the effect. His lips thinned at her whimper.

"As long as I want," she gasped with the remnant of her breath.

His thumb brushed her cheek. The molten lights in his eyes gathered as they pinpointed the smear of blood she could feel on her mouth.

"You're wrong. I could force you."

His other hand curved around her back and he pulled her up onto her knees and into his embrace. His scent flooded her senses, his heat reached into her cold center, and his blood—the sweet rhythm of his blood—drew her forward. Her belly cramped with devastating precision. Agony and hope. Why were both those emotions always part of what she felt for him?

"I don't think so." She placed her hand against his chest, maintaining the space between them. "Because if you could, you would have done it by now."

She felt the flinch of muscle that indicated his surprise. "I'm right, aren't I? You can't do a mental whammy to force this."

"Not now."

And that didn't please his bossiness at all, she could tell. "Because I'm too repulsed by the thought."

"Yes."

Allie let him cuddle her then, mainly because the next pain took every bit of strength from her. Her fangs ached and throbbed.

"The pain will eventually take the starch out of your conviction."

Caleb said that with a weariness that spoke volumes. "How long did you hold out?"

"Long enough to know you don't want to travel that path."

"I don't have a choice." She wouldn't, *couldn't*, feed on another human being.

"As you said, there's always a choice."

She absolutely hated having her own words thrown back at her.

"She could drink from me."

The suggestion came from her left, a voice she vaguely recognized over Caleb's snarl.

Allie looked up, way up, into the face of the blond muscle-bound bully who'd thrown her into the stall.

"*That* idea has merit." She'd love to suck the life right out of his high-handed ass.

"No," Caleb snapped.

Between one breath and the next she was shoved back against the wall, her view narrowing to Caleb's broad back. She didn't need to hear the growl to know he wasn't happy. The set of his shoulders conveyed that message quite clearly.

"A were is a good choice for her first feeding. She can't kill me."

"And she's not going to be fucking you either."

"I beg your pardon?" She had absolutely no intention of making love with the blond moron. Or anyone else. And then what the blond man said sank in. She cringed back against the wall, grateful for the way Caleb crowded her there.

"You're one of *them*," she gasped, clutching Caleb's shirt in her fingers. Where the hell was her gun when she needed it? "How can you have one of those monster wolves working here?"

"Derek is not one of the D'Nally weres."

Werewolves were werewolves in her book.

"And—" Pain jackknifed her into his back. His hand immediately came around to steady her. "This means what to me?" she finished in a barely audible rush, eyes closed, struggling to manage the rising tide within.

"It means you can trust him."

"But not as a food source?"

"No."

"He's worried you might just develop a taste for wolf."

Caleb's silence was unexpected, until, unbelievably, Derek laughed. The laugh took him from rugged to handsome so fast it left her staring.

"You can flash those fangs all you want, Caleb. The choice is hers."

Allie looked at Derek's neck. How could she not? He was tanned and strong and his pulse throbbed with a heady allure. Healthy. She took a breath, instinct guiding the search for more clues, recoiling instinctively from the knowledge that a hint of how he would taste was encased in his scent. Too late. The knowledge lodged deep within her subconscious. Again the savage wave of lust rose, both physical and sexual, so entwined there was no separating them. Dear God, what was she turning into?

"I'm sorry, but— Ah!" *Oh God, it hurt so bad!* "As prettily as you made the invitation, you're not my type."

Her rejection only instigated a lift of his brows.

"Do you have a type in mind? There are several weres who would be willing to aid the brothers."

Allie rubbed her head against Caleb's back. "Jesus, you make it sound like a scene from *The Godfather.*"

Caleb reached behind and caught her hand with his. She didn't have the strength to fight him as he drew it around his waist and pulled her into the solid strength of his back. Some of the pain faded, but not the hunger.

"There is a similarity in that we have a cooperative relationship."

"You might want to clue fang and company out there that vamps and werewolves can live in peace."

"They wouldn't listen."

"Why not?"

"It's a long story."

"I thought part of the perk of this vampire thing was that I wouldn't be short on time."

Against her cheek, Caleb's breath was erratic. She could only think of one reason. The pain she should be feeling was being redirected to him. "You can't shield me forever."

"I can do whatever I want."

"Then, want to explain?"

He grunted and then offered, "Weres are born. Vampires are made. The differences have caused issues over the years."

"Not for you and Derek."

"The McClarens are different."

Derek folded his arms across his chest. "Actually it's the Johnsons who are different."

The pain squeezed her entrails in a vise. "How so?"

The question was a high-pitched squeak.

"They think more like werewolves than vampires."

She cataloged the information for later.

Derek's icy gray eyes narrowed as they studied her expression. She had a feeling he saw everything she wanted hidden. "I was serious about the offer. I owe Caleb. It would be a pleasure to provide for your needs."

Again that surge of interest in his blood, followed immediately by revulsion. "No thank you."

"Too bad. I would have enjoyed your bite."

Caleb snarled and the rumble vibrated up her back. "You're pushing our friendship, Derek."

Derek cocked an eyebrow. "You have a mate. You can afford to be generous."

"And yet, I find myself feeling possessive instead."

Derek's smile returned. "No more than a wolf would." With a dip of his head, he took his leave.

Allie waited until Derek was ten feet away before glancing up at Caleb. "Am I going to turn into a slut, too?"

"What in hell makes you ask that?"

She watched Derek's progress down the hall, confidence and sexuality following him like the flow of a cape. "The way everyone looks at me."

Caleb's gaze followed hers. "They're just hungry."

"For me?" She grimaced. "I don't want you to be shocked, but that's not the thrill it's made out to be."

He shook his head. "No. Not you. For mates of their own. Weres mate for life, and if it's a true mating, only once."

"And vampires?"

"They're not as picky."

"Excuse me?"

His finger slid down her arm. "Fortunately for you, Johnsons are not only picky beyond belief, they're damn loyal."

She grimaced as the tension twisted. "You mean, lucky for you. I'm not the complacent type."

"No shit."

The tension wrenched into a hard and searing knot, consuming her with an agony so violent there was no hope of holding out. She dropped to the floor, curled into a ball around the pain, and struggled to contain it.

The dual thunks of Caleb's knees hitting the floor beside her blended with the thunder of her heart. "Goddamn, Allie."

She slapped at his hands as they slid beneath her. She couldn't bear his touch. Couldn't bear anything. He didn't leave her any choice as he swung her up into his arms and carried her as carefully as he could, swearing again when she screamed and strained against his hold, trapped in a prison of misery that wouldn't let up. Consumed by the horrible hunger to which she couldn't succumb.

Footsteps pounded through the house, coming at her from all directions. To her overly sensitive ears it sounded like an invading army. To her sensitive nose, it smelled like dinner on the hoof. She twisted in Caleb's arms, her mind rebelling at the thought. Caleb caught her before she could fall, letting her slide to the floor as the dry heaves racked her body.

"Son of a bitch, Caleb, if you don't do something, I will."

Caleb took the words out of her mouth when he said, "Shut up, Jared."

"She's just a woman. The hunger will kill her."

As soon as she finished vomiting up her guts, she was going to have a word with them about that "just a woman" crap.

"I know."

He knew. What in hell did Caleb know? The next heave brought up blood. A lot of it. Was she hemorrhaging internally? The thought wasn't as horrifying as it should have been.

She spit the last of the blood from her mouth, gasped a harsh breath between one pain and the next, and found a thread of her voice. "Caleb?"

His "What" was a brush of calm, belying the tension she could feel in his hands.

"Don't let me do it." She wrapped her fingers around his pinkie.

Too weak to lift her head to see his face. "No matter what, don't let me succumb."

"Jesus."

She didn't know which of the brothers breathed that harsh curse. They were all there, standing around in a circle of scuffed boots and badass attitude, watching her as if she were some side-show freak. She scrubbed at her mouth with the back of her hand, staring uncomprehendingly at the red smear across the formerly clean skin. She turned to her back, relying on Caleb to support her, crying out as her ribs compressed her abdomen, and blinked back tears as she met his gaze. "I couldn't live with myself."

The swirls in his green eyes tightened and then flared.

"Tough."

"She means it, Caleb."

Out of the corner of her eye, she met Slade's gaze. Thank God someone understood.

"I know." Caleb's hand cupped her chin, giving her additional support. "I understand your position, Allie. I just don't agree with it."

He had to. She wrapped her fingers around Caleb's forearm, holding on as the next wave bore deep into her gut. She'd never begged for anything in her life, but she needed this.

"I need you to." *Oh God!* "Promise," she gasped between pants.

Caleb stared at her, his will an impenetrable wall she couldn't hope to scale, until she saw it. The flicker in his gaze. Allie dug her nails into his wrist. She'd wrestled hope from less in the past. "Please." For a second, she thought she'd lost, that his resolve would outlast hers, but then he slowly inclined his head and gave her the words she need to hear.

"I promise."

She held on tighter, relief hovering on the brink of belief. "I can trust you to take care of me?"

His gaze didn't flinch from hers. His fingers pressed at the base of her neck, arching her head back. "Always."

The fight went out of her. She collapsed into the cradle of his arms, the support of his endless energy, holding on against the agony simply because he willed it. "Thank you."

"Leave us," Caleb ordered the others.

Yes. They needed to leave.

"No."

Jared. He was always causing trouble. She snapped her head around, her snarl echoing Caleb's much deeper one. Jared merely raised his brow at both of them as he took the towel Jace handed him. "She's too unpredictable." Jared tossed it over the pool of blood, hiding it from view. "And you, Caleb, are too vulnerable."

Caleb didn't take his eyes from her, as if he knew she couldn't hold on without the connection, and offered her the strength to endure for just one more minute, one more second. "Get out *now*."

He opened his shirt and brought her closer to the heat of his body, the lure of his blood.

"Caleb." The whisper tore from her throat. Was he offering himself?

"I've got you, Allie."

Jared's anger and frustration filled the air along with the acrid scent of . . . fear? "You don't have shit."

For one heartbeat Allie was without the sustaining grace of Caleb's stare as he shot a glare at his brother. "Leave, Jared."

"Make me."

She didn't hear Caleb's response, didn't hear anything beyond the rhythmic pound of his heart and the muted echo of the life-giving flow of blood in his veins. She knew how he'd taste. Heady. Like a rich wine, but better, fuller. She knew how she'd feel after she took that first drink. The heat of his skin burned her lips. Her fangs extended, aching with a hunger all their own.

"Feed, baby."

Yes! The salty tang of his scent stung her nostrils. This was what she needed, craved. She tucked her feet up underneath her hips and followed the directing force of his fingertips. He had plenty of blood, all she could want. All she needed. The touch of his skin on her fangs was an exquisite bliss. So good. The beast inside roared to life, revealing the level of its need, its all-consuming hunger, the depth of which scared the shit out of her. She had just enough presence of mind to extract another promise from Caleb before she went under.

"Don't let me hurt you."

❧ 8 ❧

*D*on't let me hurt you.

Allie's words echoed in Caleb's head as he rubbed her back. "A little bit of a thing like you couldn't hurt me."

She moved against him restlessly. Small, delicate, infinitely feminine. A frown pleated her brow as her teeth teased his skin. "Then why is Jared so worried?"

"He's just prone to it."

"Uh-huh." Her fangs scraped his collarbone before moving upward. His cock throbbed, and his breath caught. He cupped her head in his hand, pulling her mouth to his neck, pressing against her resistance.

"Goddamn it, Caleb, you know better than to let her feed from an artery," Jared growled.

But he wanted her to. He wanted to fill her need as fast as possible. He wanted it with a primal force that was almost impossible to resist.

"Why?" Low and husky, Allie's question slipped between them, along with her hand. The scent of fresh blood surrounded them. Her blood. He wrapped his fingers in her hair and pulled her head back. The gash on the back of her hand spoke of her sacrifice. She'd bitten herself to avoid biting him.

Allie repeated her question.

Caleb ignored it, pulling her hand away from his cheek, lapping the blood from her skin, closing his eyes at the taste, urging her silently to feed, unable to bear the echoes of her agony pounding through him. Jared had no such compunction.

"I'm prone to worry because you could drain him dry."

Allie's teeth left his flesh. He caught the back of her head in his hand, preventing further withdrawal. "Shut up, Jared!"

"Someone has to speak reason."

"Leave."

Jared leaned back against the wall, arms folded across his chest. "Make me."

"With pleasure."

"What happens if I drain him dry?" Allie asked again.

Jared's "He dies" coincided with Caleb's own "Nothing."

She looked between them, the gesture all the more wrenching for the slowness with which she did it. "I thought vampires were immortal."

"In the most common ways, yeah, but you suck 'em dry and they die like anyone else."

Allie's withdrawal was as much emotional as physical. Her fingers clenched on his thigh. If she were at full strength, he'd be flinching. As it was, he could barely feel the pressure. She needed blood, *now*. "Just ignore him, and he'll go away."

Jared snorted. "Hardly."

She looked at Jared. "I can't hurt him."

Every bit of her lingering humanity infused that soft whisper, which spoke more of hope than conviction.

Caleb rubbed his fingertips over her scalp. "You won't hurt me, baby."

"You're not going to be in control."

Leave it to Jared to lay logic over calm, regardless of the consequences.

Caleb cut his brother a glare. "You need to leave."

"I've already invited you to make me."

If he didn't have Allie to worry about he'd give Jared the knock-down-drag-out he was asking for. "I didn't know you were into watching."

All that got was the rise of Jared's brow. "There's a lot you don't know about me."

That was true. In the last two hundred fifty years Jared had gotten damn secretive about things. "She won't appreciate your presence."

"She's not my concern."

"She should be."

Beneath him, Allie twisted and said, "*She* is still here."

Caleb patted her cheek with his fingertips to let her know he'd heard, never taking his eyes from his brother. "If she goes, so do I."

"I know, which is why I'm not trusting your judgment in this."

"Caleb?"

He looked down. Allie's face was screwed up into a knot of pain and determination, her blue eyes dry and dark in her face. She was dehydrated. "Will you two stop fighting and come up with a compromise all of us can live with?"

"Caleb's the unreasonable one. He won't share."

"I don't understand."

"You're going to need more blood than one person can supply."

"Yuck!"

The twitch of Jared's mouth was the only indication of his lighter side. "Yuck or not, it's the truth. Combine that with the fact that Caleb's a possessive son of a bitch, and first blood is binding, and you have the fixings for a disaster."

Caleb tucked Allie against his chest. "Trust me, Allie."

Jared's "Don't" yanked her back faster than a lasso.

Her hands pressed against Caleb's ribs, small white indicators of her fragility. "You're smothering me."

He let her pull back an inch. With what he was beginning to understand was her customary inclination, she turned that inch into a mile, wedging her shoulder into his gut and wiggling until she could see Jared again. "I can't hold out much longer."

"I know."

"You have to work this out."

Jared's raised eyebrow was the only reaction to the order. "I'm willing."

Allie's nails sank into Caleb's forearm, spicing the air with a heavier scent as she looked up at him. All that incredible inner strength was reflected in her gaze as she begged for the impossible. "Please."

Caleb shook his head. It was more than he could stand, watching her give herself to another. Take from another. "I won't let you die."

Her hand opened over the five crescent cuts from her nails, closing the wounds from the sting of the air. "And I can't kill you."

"If you're done with the melodrama," Jared interrupted, "I've got a solution."

No sooner had he finished the statement than Allie crumpled under a new wave of pain. Caleb held her through the bone-wrenching spasm, his determination slipping its grip under the reality of the situation. She could die from this. He held her head to the side as she gagged, bringing up nothing, just enduring dry heave after dry heave until he couldn't take it anymore. He'd give her whatever it took to make this stop. He braced his palm over hers, supporting her through the next spasm as he asked his brother, "What's your plan?"

Jared stepped away from the door, coming closer, his eyes not straying from Allie. Though his expression was blank, Caleb knew her suffering tore at him. Jared had a soft spot for women and children.

"If her first and last blood is yours, your problems are solved."

"And in between?"

"She'll suck on me."

It was a compromise. He and Jared had always been close, sharing responsibility and retribution equally. This would be just one more thing in the bond they couldn't shake. Inside, his beast roared a protest. No man should know pleasure from Allie but him. With every bit of his sanity, he fought it back. It was a hard battle, the overwhelming possessiveness of his vampire side finding an ally in his human nature. Her next moan tipped the balance.

Promise me.

He'd given his word. He couldn't let her suffer anymore. And he couldn't give her any more future trauma. He'd learn to cope. Nothing, not his pride or his tenuous relationship with his brother, mattered more than Allie.

With a sharp nod, he gave his permission. Jared took that last step forward. Caleb ripped a gash in his right pectoral muscle, feeling his brother's mental strength join his, encouraging Allie to feed. Blood flowed like a river.

Allie gasped and lurched forward. The press of her lips to his skin set flame to his own lust. Her fangs grazed, pressed, and then entered. She fed tentatively at first, letting his blood merely flow over her tongue rather than actually drinking.

Caleb felt the exact moment the beast leapt to life within her. Every muscle in her body clenched and her mind sprang for his, wrestling his for control, her lust tapping into his, building it, relying on the primitive thrust of emotion to create a wedge she could utilize, more instinct than finesse in the maneuver, but that didn't diminish the power behind it. Allie wanted control.

He dropped his head back against the wall, passion consuming his determination. "She's strong."

"Hell, brother, I knew that going in."

Caleb shook his head, desire soaring with every lap of her tongue, every hot burst of suction. "Not like this."

Caleb pulled Allie's mouth tighter to his flesh, before yanking her thighs apart and pulling her down on him. He felt the hot bolt of elation shoot through her as they connected intimately, the denim of their jeans no barrier to the heat that bound them, centering them both on all that mattered; the passion between them, the emotion. The elemental exchange was as vital as breathing to their kind. Her bite grew ravenous, demanding, brooking no resistance as her body rocked violently on his. He gave her none, letting every pulse of her hips draw him toward completion. Allie could have whatever she wanted of him—his blood, his seed, his life.

"Fuck."

He ignored Jared's exhalation and shoved his arm aside when he would have pulled Allie off him. Arching his hips, he gave in to her demand, growing to her need, smiling with satisfaction when she whimpered as he countered her motion, snarling when Jared reached for her again. "Not yet, damn it."

"Now."

"No!" The order came too late, Jared had her out of his arms and up against his body. Her face glowed white against the black of Jared's shirt as her head fell back over his arm. The feral wail of disappointment that rose from her throat echoed his own loss. Caleb lunged into the space between them. Jared leapt back, his reflexes undiminished by blood or mate lust. His grip shifted to Allie's neck. Not with passion, but intent.

"Try it and I'll kill her."

Caleb pulled up short. One thing about Jared, he never bluffed. He would kill Allie if driven to it. Caleb closed his fists around the certainty, using it to hold at bay the driving instinct to reclaim his mate. Allie struggled in Jared's grip. Whether she was fighting to get away or to get to Jared's neck, he didn't know. It didn't really matter. "Let her go."

Jared shook his head. "Either it goes as we agreed, or I'll end it now."

Caleb believed him. His rational side even agreed with the plan, but that didn't stop the vampire's violent reaction to having Allie torn from his arms. Nor did it stop the near compulsion to see the man holding her gutted and dead. His brother. He buried his fangs in his lip, cauterizing the inner wound with physical pain as he said, "Get it over with."

"Turn around."

That was asking too much. "No."

"Jesus, Caleb, don't do this to yourself."

Blood dripped from his chin to his chest, joining the sluggish river already flowing from his wound. "Do it. Now."

On a harsh "Son of a bitch" Jared ripped his right wrist open. Blood spewed in an arc, splashing the side of Allie's face as she turned and capped the source. After an initial grimace of pain, Jared's expression went blank and his energy withdrew, hiding behind a wall of determination. Against his body, Allie writhed, bloodlust so mixed up with physical lust that Caleb knew the two were indistinguishable.

Mindless. Insatiable.

There was no way in hell that Jared was immune. Caleb had felt Allie's strength. Knew, even though he couldn't see or feel it, that Jared's body responded to the feminine lure of hers. The knowledge almost dropped him. She was his mate. No one else's—*his*. Jared looked up, his hazel eyes swirling with silver lights, the only indication of his distress. "Take her."

For vital seconds, Caleb couldn't move, bloodlust still rushing through his veins, every breath an agony, his vampire side screaming for justice, and then the fog cleared. He stepped forward, the relieved flicker of Jared's lids a bullet to his soul. After all they'd been through, Jared hadn't been sure he'd stop her.

Caleb wrapped his arm around Allie's waist. His other hand cupped her chin, applying pressure to her jaw, holding Jared's gaze as he did so. "Brothers to the end, remember?"

Jared grunted as Allie clung. "She's going to complicate that."

"Never that much." Caleb squeezed harder. Hell, was she going to make him break her jaw? "Give over, Allie." She shook her head and growled.

Jared, unbelievably, laughed. "Sounds like a kitten biting off more than she can chew."

The last syllable had a vagueness Caleb didn't like. Allie was taking too much. He leaned in against her back, cuddled her into the cradle of his thighs, and moaned as she rubbed that soft ass against him. Letting his blood drip over her shoulder in a potent lure, he whispered in her ear, "That's right, Allie girl. It's me. Come here, and I'll give you everything you want."

The slightest of relaxation in her jaw muscles was the sign he'd been waiting for. She looked at him from the corner of her eye.

Brushing his lips against her ear, he murmured, "Remember me, baby?" He pressed back against her, countering the movement of her hips with his own, seducing her with his mind, his body, his voice. "I'm ready to ride whenever you are."

She leapt for his chest, her arms going around his neck, her soft whisper of his name a balm to his soul.

"Hell, I'd be insulted if I had the strength to spare." Jared slumped against the wall, closing the wound on his wrist as he slid down.

Caleb ignored Jared, more focused on the miracle of Allie exerting her human side in the midst of bloodlust. Damn, she was strong.

"Come here, baby." He pressed her face to his chest, dropped his head until his cheek met hers, and felt her confusion, mixed with horror and lust. "It's all right, Allie girl. Whatever happens between us, I want it, and it's all right. Let yourself go."

"I'm sorry."

He lifted her against the wall. "Don't be sorry." He didn't want her sorry. "Just wrap your legs around my hips and let me see exactly how wild you can be."

"I'll be on the other side of the door if you need me."

Caleb didn't spare Jared a glance. He wouldn't need him. Allie was his only concern. Her fangs sank into his chest, her hips searching as her ankles locked behind his back. Wild, impetuous, and utterly feminine, she burned him to the core, made him angry, made him ache, made him long. Her hands slipped in the blood on his neck. She gasped and grabbed at his shoulders. He gave her a little bounce, switching his hands to her hips, sinking his fingers into the lush curve of her buttocks, granting her the support she needed. He slid one hand farther down, extended his talon, and slit the seam of her jeans before reaching for his zipper. "Now, sweetheart, let me see that wild side."

"YOU'RE not a dud."

It wasn't the most resounding accolade a man ever heard whispered in the afterglow, but it was pure Allie.

"That's good to hear." Caleb leaned his head back against the wall down which they'd slid during those last few frantic moments and drew a hard-won breath into his lungs. Against his side, Allie was breathing just as hard. He cracked his right eyelid. "Any particular reason you thought I would be?"

"It was a concern." Her shrug smoothed her breast up his sweat-slicked chest. His body tightened anew, too wrapped up in the previous pleasure to understand that he didn't have enough "oomph" to saddle up again. Allie was a demanding woman when she got going. He stroked his hand up her back. He'd have to get her going more often.

"It's just that you racked up a lot of 'I owe yous' over that last month and I wasn't sure you could make good on them."

"The other night didn't convince you?"

"The other night I was under the influence."

He cracked his other eyelid. "The hell you were."

Allie glanced up from where she was watching her finger create designs in his chest hair. He cupped her shoulder in his palm, smiling as she curled tighter against him. Her thigh rode up his in sweet invitation. "I wasn't?"

"No."

The tug she gave his hair stung. "Well, then . . . Wow!"

"I'll agree with wow." The smile came to him surprisingly easy. "You, Allie girl, are one demanding woman."

"Hey, I wasn't the one holding you up against the wall."

"Now that would be a sight, you holding me up."

There was a pause. "Could I? Now?"

He opened his eyes all the way. "Now that you're a vampire?"

"Yes."

"I don't know." He shrugged. "Men get a lot stronger, but I don't know about women."

"Aren't there female vampires?"

Oh yeah, there were. "At least one."

"Only one?"

"That's all I've ever seen."

Allie shook her head. He'd only seen one female vampire? As easily as he'd converted her, others had to have converted many more. "That doesn't make sense."

"That I can't help." The pad of his thumb touched the center of her lower lip. Despite the fact she felt sated to her bones, her pulse still quickened. What was he? Part magician?

His smile broadened.

"You are so not reading my mind."

"Just a little."

"There's no such thing as a little when it comes to that."

The pressure on her lip increased. "Yeah. There is."

Which brought up another point. "How come I can't read your mind?"

"You can't?"

She closed her eyes and tried. Nothing. "Nope. The only thing rattling around in there is me, myself, and I."

"Sounds like it's crowded enough."

She leaned into his big body. Despite the fact there was no give to the man, he was quite comfortable. "This is really going to suck,

Johnson, if I don't get some of the perks that go along with being a vampire."

His thumb pulled her lip down. Cool air wafted across the inner lining. "It's different for everyone."

"How so?"

"We all got strong, but each of us got different . . . perks, as you call it. Jared got the ability to control minds. Slade became smarter than a bedridden librarian. Jace is super strong and can go three times as long as the rest of us without feeding."

"And you?"

"I, my sweet Allie girl, got the best gift of all."

"Me?"

His smile was indulgent, the caress of his thumb a sultry promise. "That, too, but I can walk in sunlight."

A vampire who could walk in sunlight? "You realize that just totally trashes my whole early childhood education in paranormal science."

"You get educated in that?"

She nodded. "Every Saturday afternoon, and crash courses around Halloween."

His thumb slid between her teeth, riding the syllables. "You watch TV."

"Don't you?"

The smile at the corner of his mouth told more than his words. The man wasn't nearly as serious as he'd like her to believe. "Slade insists."

She snorted at the grudging note in his voice. He was such a liar. "And you just go along for the ride."

"That's about it."

"You are so full of crap."

"You don't believe me?"

She snuggled her head into his shoulder. She was so tired.

"I have yet to meet a man who isn't addicted to ESPN and the remote control."

His laugh bounced under her cheek. His thumb tucked under her chin and his fingers curved behind her skull. "No one gets the remote from Jace."

"And you?" She was definitely more interested in his habits.

"I like football and the rodeo."

She opened her palm over the curve of his pectoral, twining her fingers into the tight curls on his chest. "And music videos? Men always love the near-naked women strutting through those."

"How do you know so much about men's habits?"

Was that jealousy? "With six older brothers, a girl picks up a lot."

"Six?"

She opened her palm, rubbing it over the hair-roughened surface, savoring the tickle. "Yup."

"Damn, in my day those brothers would have kicked my ass from here to Cheyenne for even daring to look at a woman like you."

"Hmm, they still might."

"And I'd deserve it."

"You ever think, sometimes things work out the way they're supposed to?"

"No."

She guessed she shouldn't be so surprised by his disbelief in fate. It wasn't a widely held concept in the eighteen sixties. She smothered a yawn against the hard muscle of his arm. "So, what about the music videos? Do you watch them?"

"As long as the sound is off."

She smiled and gave him more of her weight, relaxing completely. "I like it that you don't lie to me."

"How do you know I'm not?"

How did she know? She didn't know for a fact, but she *was* sure. "Instinct."

"Ah."

Caleb pulled her into his lap, lifting her thighs and tucking her into his torso. "Tired?"

Allie smothered another yawn. "I don't know why."

His lips touched her ear. "You've had a hell of a day."

"What time is it?"

"About dawn."

She glanced around the barely lit interior. "How can you tell?"

"The air feels heavier."

"So that's why I'm tired?"

"The fact that you've just gone through conversion also might have something to do with it."

"I thought you said I'd be cured."

"You're cured, but your body still has to heal."

"But I don't get to read minds?"

"I'm not sure."

She snuggled down. "I was really looking forward to reading minds."

Again that chuckle that bounced her around. "I bet you were."

She patted his shoulder as the drowsiness descended upon her like an impenetrable cloud. "I really wanted to read your mind."

"Why?"

"So I'd know what you think of me."

"SHE'S a strange woman," Jared said, draping a blanket over Allie's sleeping form.

Caleb tucked it around her shoulders. "Definitely different."

"A body can't help but like her."

The possessive rage surged, ready, ever eager to defend his claim. He kept his voice civil with effort. "Not too much I hope."

Jared cocked his head, the only sign he'd felt the simmering rage, deflecting it with a sigh. "She's my sister-in-law, Caleb. It's good that I like her."

Rage faded beneath reason. No matter what the provocation, Jared would never violate their bond. But still, the niggling sense that Allie could be taken away hovered. "Sorry."

"No problem." Jared leaned back against the wall and folded his arms across his chest. "Heard she's got a hell of a temper."

"What makes you think that?"

"Word among the wolves is she kicked Dane's balls up between his teeth when he tried to take her out. Made quite an impression with the McClarens."

"She's not as impressed with them."

"They'll grow on her."

Caleb wasn't too sure of that. Allie had a lot to overcome, and the first impression the D'Nally weres had made on her would make any other weres' efforts to get into her good graces a tough row to hoe. Her lashes fluttered as her bangs tickled her eyes. He pushed the tendrils off her forehead, adding a mental command to go back to sleep. She settled back into his shoulder with a soft sigh. "That bastard Dane was going to rape her before he killed her."

"I wasn't criticizing." Jared motioned to Allie. "Do you think she had an inkling of his intentions?"

"No." He cut his brother a glance. "And that information stays between us." Dane had gotten off on inflicting terror. A real bad apple in a barrel of tough ones. He wouldn't give him the satisfaction of Allie's horror postmortem.

"A girl with the guts to take on a were with nothing more than a potato sticker and her bare hands can handle a bit of truth."

"Some things a woman doesn't need to know." He dipped his finger into the shadowed well atop her collarbone. "She's afraid enough."

Jared's smile was a rare thing. "Of what? Certainly not you and me."

"She's afraid."

"Then she does a damn good job of hiding it."

Caleb nodded. He shifted his grip on Allie and stood up. "Yes. She does. Sometimes even from herself."

"You don't sound happy about that."

Caleb headed down the hall. "Probably because I'm not."

Jared trailed in his wake, a deadly curious shadow. "Why?"

"Fear just makes her more determined not to quit."

"So?"

He headed down the stairs. "Think of it. All that curiosity, all those new powers, all that energy going anywhere it wants with no brakes."

"Shit."

Caleb laid her on the bed, "Yeah. I'm going to have my hands full keeping her busy while she adjusts."

❧ 9 ❦

CALEB lay back against the pillow and savored the warmth of Allie sleeping by his side, thinking of what she'd said before she'd succumbed to exhaustion.

So I'd know what you think of me.

She wanted to read his mind because she wanted to know what he thought of her. As if he'd ever kept it a secret. He kissed the top of her head, turning her a little, enjoying the full press of her breasts. He pretty much thought she was perfect, but Allie couldn't seem to grasp that.

For all her big talk, there was a hollow of insecurity within Allie that needed tending. She seemed to accept that he wanted her physically easily enough, but when it came to him wanting her as a person, she fought the knowledge tooth and nail. Sighing he tugged her closer. He'd have to work on that. A bruise on her shoulder caught his eye. He placed his thumb over the mark. A perfect fit. He blew out a breath. Another thing for his to-do list. He'd let her sleep a bit and then he'd show the softer side of lovemaking. She'd enjoy that. Assuming he got her to slow down. The woman was always in such a hurry.

A whisper in his mind pulled him away from his musings.

Caleb, we've got trouble.

Shit. Whenever Jared used the word "trouble," it was wiser to substitute bigger words like "disaster," or "hell on fire."

Coming.

Sliding out from under Allie's arm, Caleb caught her hand before it could fall to the mattress. He didn't need her awake right now. Not until the threat was taken care of.

His senses told him Jared wasn't in the house. Caleb grabbed his hat and rifle as he silently glided to the back door and just as soundlessly made his way out into the remnants of the night. It only took a few minutes to find Jared. He was down at the back gate, gun drawn, crouched over Jace. Jace wasn't moving but plenty was beyond the barrier. The hairs on the nape of Caleb's neck stood on end, tingling a warning. Danger.

"What the hell happened?" he asked as soon as he got close enough.

"Jace took one of his constitutionals."

Which meant he'd gone into D'Nally territory searching for whatever it was he always searched for. "Son of a bitch."

"That about sums it up."

Another step and the scent of blood surrounded him. Jace's blood. He scanned the darkness, sensing the prowling restlessness of D'Nally werewolves. "How many are out there?"

Jared looked up. "About ten."

Ten D'Nallys could do a hell of a lot of damage to an army. And as strong as Jace was, there were odds even he couldn't win against. Caleb knelt down beside Jace.

"Pissed off?"

Jared shrugged. "As always."

Caleb shook his head. "Damn it, Jace, why can't you leave them alone?"

The D'Nallys were a hell of a tight clan. Strong fighters with a code of honor that was black and white, and if they weren't trying to kill his brother, Caleb would probably like them.

"I don't think he can hear you," Jared interjected wryly.

Caleb glanced down at Jace, took in the slashes across his torso, the amount of blood soaking his clothes. No, he probably couldn't.

A twig snapped just beyond the illusion. Caleb chambered a round. If the D'Nallys figured out how to get past the illusion, he'd take them out the old-fashioned way. He liked the old-fashioned way. Clean and clear-cut, with none of the nebulous uncertainty that seemed so inherent in the technology Slade favored.

"They haven't figured out the illusion," Jared said, as always in tune with him.

"It's only a matter of time."

"Yeah, which means you should probably negotiate a peace with the hardheaded son of a bitches before it comes to full-out war."

"That would be a lot easier if Jace would stop provoking them."

"Not going to happen," Jace grated in a hoarse whisper.

He was pale, his lips dry and cracked, indicating the extent of his blood loss, but he still sat up.

"I've got news for you, it's going to happen." It had to happen. Their position was too precarious to call a war with a clan as strong as the D'Nallys. Caleb reached for Jace's rifle, to relieve him of the burden.

Jace lifted his lip, exposing his fangs in a clear warning.

"Hell, Jace, I was just going to hold it."

"When I'm dead and ash you can have it, not a second before."

Jared extended his hand, "Damn, you're touchy."

Jace took it, swaying as he reached his feet. "I'm having an off night."

"One in a series of several," Caleb pointed out holding on to his temper. "Whatever's eating you, you've got to get a handle on it before you start a war."

Jace smiled, a smile made all the colder for the blood obscuring one side of his face. "I wouldn't be adverse to kicking some D'Nally ass."

Caleb snorted. "Seems to me the only ass getting kicked lately is yours."

"That's just because they've gotten smarter and started throwing bigger numbers at me."

Caleb wanted to point out the illogic of the position— Jace might be incredibly strong, but even he couldn't take down a pack of fighting D'Nallys—but Caleb could already tell it wasn't going to do any good. Jace didn't want logic, he wanted a fight. "Well, if you keep bringing them around here they're also going to make it their job to figure out the illusion, and that's a threat to more than just you."

Jace grimaced. "Good point."

"So maybe you ought to leave them be," Jared offered.

"Or maybe I need to take the fight elsewhere."

Shots came from the dark, eerie howls broke the night.

"Who's out there?" Jace asked.

"Derek and nine of his favorites."

"Keeping the odds even?"

"You know Derek." Jared shrugged. "The ultimate negotiator."

Yes he was, and a hell of a good man whose friendship with the Johnsons had him walking a thin line between the werewolf world and the vampire one where the wrong decision could leave his pack condemned. And yet he refused to abandon the alliance.

"And a stubborn one," Caleb sighed, glancing into the darkness beyond the illusion. McClaren territory, which the McClarens were legally authorized by pack law to defend against intruders. To the death if they wished.

"Who we owe," Jared reminded Jace. "Which means you can't just go out kicking up a fuss whenever you get a burr under your saddle, and then walk away."

Jace's lip lifted again. "I can do whatever the hell I want."

Caleb hit his shoulder with the flat of his hand, knocking him back a step, gaining his attention. "No, you can't." He pointed behind Jace. "Those are our friends out there, fighting to save your ass for the simple reason, in their eyes, you're family and that's what family does. They'll defend you to the death if they have to, but son of a bitch, if you're going to demand that kind of sacrifice, you'd better have a damn good reason we can all understand."

Jace's jaw locked and he got that stubborn look with which Caleb was all too familiar. Blood still trickled from a cut under his eye, weaving down the well-worn path, reminding Caleb how often in the last year he'd seen his brother just like this.

Caleb spat, knowing he wasn't going to get an answer to his question, but compelled to ask it anyway. "What's riding you, Jace?"

Jace turned on his heel, heading toward the illusion and the battle raging beyond. The answer drifted behind him, more weary than angry. "Nothing I can put my finger on."

Caleb stared after him, guilt weighing him down. How long before what he'd done would stop affecting them all?

Jared cocked his gun. "Hell. Things were easier back in the good old days."

"The old days are gone."

"Someone needs to tell Jace that."

"I just did." Caleb motioned to the gun in Jared's hand. "You going after him?"

Jared pulled his hat down over his eyes. "If I don't, he'll get himself fried. In another five minutes the sun will be up."

The sounds of battle were fading. Weak and wounded, Jace would be chasing it, like he always did, the wildness in him forever seeking an outlet. "I'll go with you."

Jared held up his hand. "You've got a wife to get settled."

So he did. No matter how happy that made him, however, it didn't diminish the desire to go with his brothers, fight by their sides, cover their backs. Although they were all grown men and deadly vampires to boot, his first instinct was always to protect them as he'd promised he would when their parents died. Caleb watched Jared move as silent as a shadow along the path Jace had taken. Frustration gnawed at his soul. Another brother he was losing because they couldn't put that one irrevocable moment behind them.

Jared got to the edge of the illusion and turned back, standing as Caleb had seen him stand so many times before—tall, deadly. Determined. Caleb braced for the cut he knew was coming. What he got instead surprised him.

"Whatever this is with Jace, Caleb. It isn't because of you."

He disappeared from sight, leaving only the concession behind, the first one Caleb had received from him in a long time. On the surface, it wasn't much, but from Jared, it might as well be a statement of intent.

Jared was beginning to let go of the anger.

Now if he could only get Allie to do the same.

SHE'D finally found something to keep her busy.

Allie stood in the kitchen and smiled at her latest project.

It was a monster. Big, black, and ugly. She had absolutely no reason to be in love with it . . . but she was. Hopelessly and completely in love. Allie touched the newly blackened surface of the ancient woodstove and smiled again. Clothes didn't make the man and a new coat of paint wasn't going to make this stove, but the sheer challenge of baking the way her ancestors had, ah, that was seduction itself.

In the far corner of the room, the last ray of daylight disappeared from the crack she'd made in the curtains. She missed sunshine and autumn colors. Caleb was emphatic that she'd adjust, come to learn to love the beauty of the night. The man seemed to be convinced of a lot of things when it came to her. So much so, she didn't have the heart to tell him she wasn't really into adjusting. She much preferred to change her environment to suit herself rather than adjust to something she didn't like.

She stroked her finger over the stove again, tracing the pits in the iron honed by time, imagining the women before who had stared at this behemoth and had the same feelings of hope and inadequacy. Her hand tingled with the challenge of coaxing something edible out of the beast. Maybe even the bear claws Caleb liked. Of course, just getting the ingredients she needed might be a tall order, but that was a complication for tomorrow. Today she needed to reconnect the chimney and hope she could get enough draw to not burn down the entire house when she lit it.

The last of the sun faded from the room, plunging it into gloom. Her vision switched to the intense black-and-white night vision she hated. No matter how detailed, this was the one thing that pissed her off about being a vampire. She absolutely hated having to view the world differently, but she'd promised Caleb she would try to adjust. And he in turn promised she could try to bring this old kitchen back to life.

She went to open the heavy oven door. Faint rustling noises from inside had her immediately removing her hand from the latch and stepping back. She didn't want to find out the hard way that there were "were" mice. Just the thought sent a shudder down her spine.

"Problems?"

She turned, not sure which brother had found her now. She met Slade's hazel eyes and smiled. Things were looking up. The very intense, slightly wild intellectual. Exactly what she needed. "Nothing I'm sure you couldn't help me with."

He took a step back. "If you want help changing again, you're gonna have to wait for Caleb."

She arched her brow at him. "Chicken."

He didn't even bother to deny it. "Caleb about tore me a new one after that last fiasco. He was not fond of you running around with feathers sticking out of your fingers."

"I'll get the hang of it."

He pushed his hat back, his smile more relaxed. "I hope so because changing forms sure isn't coming naturally to you."

She crossed her arms over her chest. "I suppose none of you had any trouble shifting your first time?"

A frown replaced his smile. "Actually, no. If I recall it right, we kind of shifted without even thinking about it. Gave us a scare until we realized we could shift back."

She rolled her eyes. "Great. If all of this was so easy for you, why is it so darned hard for me?"

Instead of making fun, his expression grew serious, the inner intensity radiating outward. "Actually, that's an interesting question. I want you to come to the lab for some tests."

Scenes from *Young Frankenstein* flashed through her mind.

"Thanks, but no thanks."

He frowned, getting that scientist-in-search-of-answers expression on his face that scared her. "We need some answers. There could be multiple reasons for what you're experiencing."

Probably, and none of them good, which was why she wasn't exploring them. "That can wait."

"Actually the sooner—"

She cut him off. "Slade, I need your help."

Immediately, she had his full attention. "What's wrong?"

With a wave of her hand, she indicated the stove. "Do you know how to make this work?"

His gaze followed the direction of her wave. "Yes."

She rolled her eyes when he didn't elaborate. "Can you tell *me* how to make it work?"

Now she had his attention. Slade was a sucker for anything involving the word "how."

"Why? We've got a perfectly good kitchen in the front of the house."

"Because I want to cook in this kitchen."

His right eyebrow rose along with the side of his mouth. With a start, she realized he was as handsome as Caleb in his own way. She'd never thought of any of Caleb's brothers as men, but the brothers were actually very attractive. "That I figured, but for whom? Vampires have a limited diet."

She so did not need the reminder. Caleb was out "filling up" right now. Something he normally wouldn't have to do except for her higher need for blood. She seemed to require feeding on a daily basis.

"Caleb for one. He likes my bear claws."

"Caleb ate your bear claws?"

Okay. They could question her competency in a lot of areas but not when it came to her cooking. "Back off, Slade."

He held up his hands. "Hey, I'm not questioning your ability to cook, just Caleb's ability to eat."

"The man's been showing up at my bakery like clockwork for the last month. He had two bear claws and a cup of coffee every morning, which he ate with every appearance of enjoyment." Enjoyment she wouldn't believe was faked. "I think he can eat."

"Not unless he's been puking it back up as soon as he's out the door."

Now that was something she hadn't considered. "You think Caleb's bulimic?"

"Bull what?"

"Bulimic. As in throws up whatever he eats, a bad, sometimes fatal habit some women get into rather than gaining weight."

Slade first looked shocked and then amused. "Bullheaded maybe, but I don't think he's overly concerned with poundage."

"Then why is he throwing up?"

The look he gave her was long and considering before he shrugged and added cryptically, "Probably for the same reason you want to restore this old kitchen. A fondness for the past. And maybe a very strong attraction to the owner."

"He did mention something about that." A fact she was still having a tough time accepting.

"I bet he did." Slade knelt in front of the stove. "You checked the chimney yet?"

"No."

He looked at the freshly painted exterior. His glance clearly said she'd jumped the gun. "Why not?"

"I've been a little nervous about disturbing the inhabitants."

His head cocked to the side as he listened to the renewed rustling. "You're afraid of mice?"

"I'm not arguing they have a high 'ick' factor, but that wasn't why I was hesitating. Before I opened the door, I was going to ask . . ."

"What?"

"There's no such thing as were mice . . . is there?"

Her reward was a chuckle, completely natural and masculine, and sexy. Damn, were the Johnson brothers breast-fed testosterone? Slade opened the door. "No."

The sounds of a hasty departure echoed out of the interior. The pipe rising out of the back shook, and then all was quiet.

"Well, hell."

Allie looked down. Slade knelt and reached into the interior. When he pulled his hands out, he held what looked like a pile of debris, but there was no way that was just debris. He was holding it too carefully for that. And as it was moving of its own volition, probably alive. "Mr. and Mrs. Mouse have a family."

Her first instinct when he held them out to her was to scream bloody murder and demand an instant end to the rodent population explosion, but then Slade parted the top of the debris with his thumbs to reveal eight tiny, pale gray, helpless little babies. "Why in hell do they have to be cute?"

Again he cocked the eyebrow at her. She wondered if she knew how arrogant, and at the same time sexy, the gesture made him. Not as sexy as Caleb, but enough to tug at any woman's interest.

"You'd prefer them ugly?"

"Uh-huh. Then maybe I wouldn't find the thought of you smashing their skulls so repulsive."

He cradled the babies against his chest. "No one's smashing anyone's skull."

Well, she hadn't really been going to, but he didn't have to look like she'd just suggested offering up a blood sacrifice. "Then what are you going to do with them?"

"The parents won't come back, so I guess I'll just take care of them until it's time for them to find their way."

She shook her head. He was a vampire and a scientist. Some things he ought to just get without being told. "You do realize they're on the bottom of the food chain, and you're only saving their lives so something else can have a midnight snack later, right?"

He stood. "That doesn't mean they don't have worth."

No it didn't. "I guess I'm just surprised to hear you say that."

"Why? Because I'm a vampire?"

"Frankly, yes."

He shrugged. "That wasn't my doing."

"It wasn't mine either."

He cut her a knowing glance. "But we all have to learn to live with it."

Yes. They did. The little pile heaved and emitted high-pitched squeaks. She motioned to the mice. "Will they live?"

"I don't know, but at least they've got a shot."

"That's better than nothing."

"Yes." He paused. "Whenever the anger at what's been done to you rides you hard and you feel like lashing out, you might want to remember that you got a chance, too."

Did everyone know about the fight she'd had with Caleb before he left? She wrapped her arms across her chest. "It's not the same."

"The hell it's not."

"Okay. Maybe it's that it's not that easy then."

"Lady, nothing ever is." He jerked his chin in the direction of the stove. "The weres have a woodstove in their compound. I'll see if they have any piping for that flue."

"Thank you."

"You can install it, but don't light it until we have the chimney checked out."

Did he think she was a total idiot? "I wasn't going to."

"Caleb will be reassured to hear it."

"He knows I'm working on the stove?"

"The whole place does. That paint stinks to high heaven."

"Oh." Duh! "I guess he doesn't mind."

"Why should he?"

"I don't know."

"He wants you to be happy, Allie."

"I know." She just wasn't sure she could give him that, trapped as she was in a life-form that didn't agree with her, that didn't work the way it should. "I'm just not that good at adjusting."

"Let him help you."

She rubbed her hands up and down her arms as the familiar pain began again. She was going to need blood soon. Again. Instead of spacing farther apart, her need to feed was happening sooner. "That's another thing I'm not good at."

"What?"

"Being helpless."

This time the aura that surrounded him was one of strength and—she checked her inner radar—wisdom? "Sometimes you just have to accept what is, before you can move on."

ACCEPT what is. Allie lay on the floor in the kitchen, battling the crippling pain. How in hell was she supposed to accept this? Cold seared deeper than the fires of hell could hope to burn. And where the hell was Caleb?

I'm coming.

Faster. The mental retort shot out before she could contain it.

Hold on, baby.

The guilt in his mental path made her feel like an ass. Caleb was downright neurotic about keeping her happy. If he was delayed it wasn't by choice. *I'm sorry, this damned pain is making me into a bitch.*

You can apologize to me later.

How sick was it that even with her current level of distress, her body perked at the thought of making it up to Caleb.

Not sick at all.

The laugh shot out of her misery. *You would think that.*

Another pain slammed her head into her knees. She bit her lip through the spasm, trying to block the knowledge from Caleb of how bad it was. It was useless. He was in her head, too far away to take over, but there, sharing as best he could, mentally holding her hand. She clung to his presence, the sense of strength, riding it as the next wave swelled and swelled but never peaked, just sent the world into a realm of terrifying black.

She hated it here, this place created by agony where delusion reigned and she heard voices without faces, without words. Just voices, beckoning her to take the step over the invisible ledge she could sense but not feel, encouraging her to take the plunge. Every instinct said to step away, get back, but she couldn't. Not this time. She didn't have the strength. This time she kept falling deeper into the subconscious well, deeper into the cacophony. Deeper into hell.

"Come here, Allie girl."

The whisper slid between her and disaster. Caleb. The voices screamed a protest. She shook her head against the utter desolation of their plea. She couldn't help them.

"I've got you, baby." Another whisper, more welcome than the first. She leapt for the reassurance with everything she had, backing away from the ledge, away from that one cultured voice that rose above the rest, almost hypnotic in its rhythm.

Stay . . .

No. She wouldn't. Allie fought her way out of the void, struggling to get to the light that was Caleb, dragging herself up the trailing edges of his energy, feeling the pull of the void like a massive weight clinging to her legs. She fought harder, desperation lending her additional strength. She didn't want to be one of them. She didn't.

"Don't want to be one of whom?"

Oh God, was that Caleb's voice or was she imagining it? Was he finally here?

"I'm here." Firm hands on her shoulders confirmed the words filtering out of the dark. Normal dark. The kind that came from having your eyes closed.

"I'm not dreaming anymore, am I?"

"No." The broad support of his palm cupping her skull was welcome. "Feed, baby."

She was moving toward him before he even finished the sentence, awareness flooding her with his scent, the steady comfort of his heartbeat, the whisper of his life-giving blood flowing through his veins. Pressure from his pinky tipped her head to the right angle. Her mouth shaped to the firmness of his pectoral, letting the curve spread her lips as he pressed, taking his flesh into her mouth. She kissed him once. Twice. The third time inching higher, her muscles gathering for the push that would get her what she wanted. His artery. His free hand opened over her shoulder, pressing down.

"No."

The ravenous hunger moaned a protest, but surrendered to the learned knowledge that she couldn't win against his strength. She accepted his lead, rubbing her lips across his chest until she found the rhythm of his pulse, biting deep into the flesh above it, wanting it to be part of her.

"There you go. I've got what you need."

He did. Only he did. No other could satisfy the demands of her body. No other was right. The rich, unique taste of his blood spilled across her tongue. She held it there for a moment, not swallowing, letting the rightness of it, the bliss, settle the wildness before she drank.

He continued stroking her hair, adding calm to the hunger. "I'll always have what you need."

She waited until she could bear to part from him before asking, "Why?"

His hand rubbed her back as she stroked her tongue over his wound, closing it. "Why is it like this?"

His touch gentled as he pulled her up, ready for the second hunger that took her as hard as the first. "I don't know," he whispered, his face lowering to hers, "but we're handling it, so it's all right."

Yes the voice whispered up from her soul. They were. This was right. Caleb's blood in her veins. Caleb's mouth joined to hers, this was what she needed. But more. She twisted in his arms, yanking off her shirt, reaching for her pants only to find his hands already there. With a growl, he sliced them from her body. For a split second his hands left her and then his cock was there, as feral and ready as the rest of him as it slapped against her inner thigh.

She dropped her head back and closed her eyes at his heat, his strength. With an equal ferocity, she grabbed his shoulders and straddled his hips. She needed him in her. Needed him to come, to seal the bond between them, needed it with every fiber of her being. His palms caught her hips, preventing her descent. This time the snarl was hers.

"You can bare those pretty little fangs at me all you want, but we're slowing down."

"No." She opened her eyes. His features were so clear to her in the night, chiseled in planes of white, hollowed in valleys of black, the swirling glow of his eyes an incandescent statement of power. And she wanted it. Now. "Make love to me, Caleb."

"I'm working on it."

"Now."

"You're too soft for fast." He began a slow entry, one that teased her with the agonizing, promised stretch. She bent her knees, trying to force a faster union. He shook his head, his gaze holding hers as he steadily gave her what she craved. "I don't want you to tear."

She struggled with his restraint. "I don't care. I'm a vampire, I'll heal."

His "I care" was as resolute as his expression as he set the pace for the joining. "Damn, you feel so good, Allie girl."

He was in her, the broad head snuggling just inside the opening. A bit of the crazy wildness subsided with the knowledge, but not the need. "I need you to come."

"I'm working on it."

"Now." Oh God, why did she feel like this?

He lowered her as if she were the most fragile of treasures, as if she were breakable rather than immortal, letting her have more of what she wanted, answering her mental question. "I don't know, but I like it."

"I'm really beginning to hate that expression." And she was beginning to think the Johnson brothers didn't know a lot of things they should about being vampires.

The tension in his face spread to his drawl, roughening it. "I wish I had better answers. I'm asking Slade to look into it."

Another inch. Her body fluttered around his. His curse was music to her ears. As she looked up, she saw something primitive flash through his eyes

"You feel it, too."

He didn't answer directly, just dug his fingers into her buttocks and held her still while he teased her with sharp pulses of his hips, driving her wild.

"Caleb!"

"I've got you."

She knew that. "Damn it, I won't break."

"You feel damn fragile to me." This time he gave her more—

harder, a little deeper bringing an ecstatic gasp to her lips. Oh yes, that's what she wanted.

"Fragile and hot and wet."

She dug her nails into his shoulders, rubbing her breasts against his hair-rough chest, the sharp stab of pleasure making her clench around him. "You forgot eager."

The next clench was deliberate. His moan was not. She flexed her internal muscles again, coaxing him to the pace she wanted. Leaning in, she raised herself up until he barely breached her, teasing them both with the implication of what could come next, should come next. She whispered in his ear, "Very, very eager and if you don't come for me soon, I'll scream."

Against her, his big body shuddered. "Careful with that tempting, Allie girl. You have no idea how close I am to giving you what you're begging for."

Actually, she did. Streams of energy were pouring from him, leaking past his control, and along with them came random images of his desire. The one she liked best was where he had her on her back, her ankles over his shoulders, helpless before his desire, taking her as he wanted because she had no choice. Oh yeah, that had real possibilities.

She caught the image, focused it, and sent it back, knowing she succeeded by his harshly indrawn breath and the sudden stillness of his body. Beneath her fingers his muscles knotted. "Give me that, Caleb. That's what I want."

As if her whisper were what his demon was waiting for, he went animalistic. With a curse that sounded more like a plea, he flipped her. She braced herself for the impact with the floor, but his hand was there, cushioning her while he moved up between her thighs. His shaft prodded her intimately while his grip shifted. She lifted her rear, facilitating his efforts. Her reward was another of those curses that went through her in a shiver, and the erotic stretching of the tendons in the back of her knees as he hooked her ankles over his broad shoulders. He braced his hands on either side of her chest. His expression was a mix of desperation and lust as his gaze met hers. "Stop me."

She shook her head. "Not a chance. I want you like this." Bracing her hand over his, she held on. "Wild and mine."

"Then take me." He drove into her with merciless force, spearing deep, riding her shock and bliss to the core of her being where the rejoicing howl swelled, "Yes!"

His lips drew back from his teeth as he pulled back. "Son of a bitch." He lunged forward, filling her to the max, but not enough. Not completely. The unbearable pressure that bordered on pain grew. "All of me."

And she did. Opening more and more with each thrust, her desire ricocheting off his to that spot inside that wanted more. Needed more. Her nails raked the back of his hands as she shoved her hips into his, her need no less savage, no less consuming than his. Her cries of "yes" wrapped around his grunts of "mine," creating a pulsing, primitive rhythm that accelerated toward an ending she couldn't avoid but didn't know if she'd survive. "Caleb!"

"Right here."

She shook her head, the energy too consuming to bear. "I can't—"

His hand anchored in her hair, yanking her gaze up to his narrowed one. Nothing about his face or voice was soft. He was pure driven primitive male, staking his claim. "You will."

She almost didn't recognize his face as his body pounded into hers, his features distorted by vampire lust and determination, but the fire in his eyes, that she recognized. She clung to it as his body pounded into hers, demanding the response she feared. His energy worked deeper, forcing another opening. "Mine."

His grip on her hair tightened, drew her head back, the little stings joining in the conflagration consuming her. The tendons in her legs protested as her spine arched, lifting her breasts in an equally primitive offering. His head lowered. His "Always mine" was a feral prelude to the white-hot anticipation of his bite. Oh God, his bite. She shivered and held her breath, needing it.

He made her wait. One heartbeat, two, and then he was there, his teeth sinking into her flesh as his cock plunged deep, swelling and jerking within her as he gave her what she wanted, the dual possession more than she could take—burning, pleasuring, sending her senses careening off beyond her control as the whole world exploded in ecstasy.

❧ 10 ❧

"**T**ELL me about the dream."

Allie took her time putting the plate of bear claws in front of Caleb. This batch looked better than the last. Edible at least. "Which one?"

He leaned back in the chair, the powerful muscles in his arms and chest coming into stark relief beneath the black of his shirt. He caught her hand before she could get away. His green eyes focused knowingly on her as he pulled her front and center. "The one you've been dodging talking about for the last four days."

She tugged her hand free. "It's just a dream. What do you want me to say?"

He reached for one of the pastries. The laziness of the motion did nothing to mitigate the impact of those eyes. A bug under a microscope got more leeway than he was showing her. "I want you to describe it."

She shrugged. "I can't. It's a bunch of random flashes of images and stuff."

"Then maybe we can talk about that."

He took a healthy bite of the bear claw. She watched as he

chewed and swallowed. He didn't make a face, but he did grab his coffee.

"Too dry?"

With a shake of his head, he took another bite. "They're getting fair passable."

"Fair passable? What does that mean?"

His eyes crinkled at the corners. "Means I'm not planning on cocking up my toes on the next bite."

"Great." She'd really thought she had it this time. Maybe if she let the wood burn longer before putting the bear claws in . . . She sighed. "I'll keep trying."

He caught her hand again. His fingers, with their square tips and even nails, were as completely masculine as the rest of him, and just as strong.

His gaze flicked up to her face and his eyes narrowed. The feeling of being a bug under the microscope increased. "Feeling a bit contrary today?"

"Why limit it to today?"

Boredom and frustration had her just about jumping out of her skin.

"Want to talk about that?"

Still leaning back in the chair, long legs stretched out before him, one booted foot crossed over the other, Caleb was the total picture of nonchalance. If, and it was a big if, she discounted the intensity of his gaze and the tightness of his jaw muscles.

"Not particularly." She didn't know him well enough for that, which was weird, but true. Despite all that had happened, how much she depended on him, she didn't know him well enough to communicate how much that dependence made her crazy. Like she was trapped in a prison with no walls, no rules, and worst of all, no purpose.

"Why not?" He brought her palm to his mouth, pressing his lips to the center before flicking his tongue over the sensitive skin in erotic little passes that popped like sparks through her system.

This past week, desire had been enough to distract her from boredom, but today, edginess was winning out over potential pleasure. She tugged her hand. He didn't let go. She glared at him. "I don't want to make love either."

"What?" The right corner of his sexy mouth dented with the amusement she could hear in his drawl. "You've lost interest in me already?"

She rolled her eyes. Like any woman would get tired of all that single-minded intensity, all that masculinity, all that testosterone taking up residence in her bed. "Hardly."

"But?"

"I'm sick of you using sex to distract me like I'm some mindless bimbette."

His eyebrow rose and a smile started in his eyes, deepening slowly, as his gaze dipped to her hips where it lingered before rising to her breasts. His tongue eased over his lips, wetting them once, twice as his attention centered on the two peaks stretching the soft cotton of her shirt. "You are?"

She watched his tongue pass over his lips, felt the imagined touch against her breast, took a deep breath, and forgot to let it out. Beneath her shirt, her breasts swelled enticingly, offering themselves up like twin sacrifices to the pleasure of his kiss. Allie released the breath she'd been holding on a curse and took a step back. The man was positively lethal! "Yes. Truth is, I've only got one nerve left and it's fraying fast."

A frown replaced his smile. She wasn't surprised when his fingers tucked between hers, separating them, breaking the tension in her grip, breaking the tension in her. He was incredibly tuned to her, which was a change from her usual lovers, who always seemed to bumble along, only focusing when the urge hit them. His head tilted slightly, and his gaze zeroed in on hers, searching, she knew, for clues to what she was thinking. "I don't suppose there's any way to catch it and snub it down before it frays further?"

"Not unless you find me something to do."

He squeezed her hand. "Cooking and cleaning doesn't do it for you?"

He had to be kidding. "Did you sleep through the whole women's lib movement?"

He snorted, and the humor in him reached out and called to the laughter in her before a word passed his lips. "Not hardly. That bra burning thing was a real attention getter."

Allie rolled her eyes. "I'll bet."

As if he was that shallow. She knew him well enough to know that, which was an oasis of relief in the middle of havoc. Tears stung her eyes. Oh God, now she was going to cry?

Caleb sighed. This time she felt his concern. She needed to work on developing her barriers.

"I must be losing my touch. Used to be you'd lecture me until my ear fell off for trotting out a comment like that."

"Maybe I'm just losing my mind." These emotional extremes were going to drive her crazy. She didn't know if it was due to the change, boredom, or something else, but lately she wanted to scream and rage and at the same time, burst into tears. The last was not acceptable. The first two debatable.

His thumb stroked over the back of her hand. "Did you ever think you've just had to do a lot of adjusting and maybe you need more time than you're giving yourself?"

"No." She sniffed, forced a smile, took a slow deep breath, and pushed her bangs off her face. "I do, however, think being useless is definitely taking its toll."

Caleb went quiet, so quiet the very air around him stilled as he asked in a voice she'd never heard him use before, "Who told you you were useless?"

He was angry. The emotion hit her like a fist. Survival instinct sent her a step back before she realized what she'd done. She shook off the instinctive fear and stepped right back into the spot she'd just vacated. She cocked her head to the side. "That's a neat trick, projecting your anger. Does it work on everyone you try to intimidate?"

"More often than not." Not a bit of inflection colored his drawl as he asked again, "Now, who told you you were useless?"

"No one." She yanked a chair from the table, put it kitty-corner to his, and dropped into it. The table protested as she bumped the leg with her knee. She pulled it back into place. "I figured it out all by myself."

"Because you can't change?"

She dug her nail into a nick on the scarred wooden top. "Because I can't do anything. Heck, I can't even hack it as a vampire's bit of pampered feminine fluff."

His fingers caught her chin, balancing it on the edge of his knuckle, tilting her gaze up. "You're doing fine."

He just didn't get it. It didn't matter what he thought. She knocked his hand aside. "How can you say that? I'm no longer human, yet I can't do the simplest vampire things. I have to sleep all the time, and if I'm not sleeping, I have to feed." She threw up her hands. "Nearly twice a day now, and because I can't feed from anyone else, you have to feed three times a day, risking exposing yourself and your brothers."

Caleb caught her hands in his, bringing them to the table between them. "None of that matters."

The rage built in direct contrast to the restraint. The tighter he held her, the more she wanted to fight. "Of course it does. You've avoided detection for two hundred fifty years. Everyone around here thinks you're the offspring of yourselves." She wrenched away, the stab of pain in her shoulder welcome as she hit the resistance of his hold. "They think you're normal, for God's sake, and I'm endangering everything by being such a complete parasite."

He manacled her wrists in one of his, his grip like iron. "Look at me. You're not a parasite!"

The fingers that subsequently grabbed her chin tightened to

near pain. There was no looking away. No avoiding. Everything she felt was laid out between them, everything he felt just as visible. Her fear. His conviction. The emotional bond between them, appearing so solid, though it had formed so fast. Oh God, it was all there. And so very permanent looking when she didn't do permanent.

She found a fragment of her voice. "You need someone else."

This close she could see the lighter green flecks and the sparks of gold lighting within his eyes. She could also see his resolve.

"I've got what I want."

She closed her eyes against the strength of his will, trying to close her mind as well. Unable to, she felt his determination and his own fear. Only his worry wasn't fear of discovery. He was afraid she'd leave him. She wasn't sure she wouldn't. "I can't be what you want."

He didn't look away. "You already are."

"I'm not the type of person anyone should depend on. Just ask my parents, my brothers, my exes." She waved a hand, encompassing the whole damn world of people she'd disappointed. "Just ask anyone."

"I don't need to ask anyone."

She shook her head at the enormity of the responsibility he was placing on her. "I always screw up, always fail, no matter how good my intentions. And that's in the best of circumstances."

His grip didn't slacken and neither did the resolve with which he mentally surrounded her. "Allie, I know who you are, what you're capable of, and there isn't a damn thing about you that has me worried."

"Well, you should be!" He had no idea how badly she could screw things up without even trying.

Caleb's hand slid around to the back of her head. His expression blurred out of focus as he dragged her forehead to his. This close there was no avoiding his mental push.

"I'm not your father, not your brothers, not any other damn

man you've ever known. I don't want to pigeonhole you in a box that doesn't fit. I like you just the way you are."

And they called her strange. She tried again. "This is a mistake."

"No, it's not." There was no shake in his voice, as there had been in hers. "I've been in your mind. You've been in mine. You know as well as I do the strength of what we have."

His conviction smoothed over her anger, glided into her hope.

"Oh, God." Little more than an exhalation, the tiny prayer hung between them. He was asking too much of her.

His fingertips skated down her throat, spreading over the top of her shoulder. His thumb pressed against the pulse in her neck. "I know who you are, Allie. I've known since the first instant I saw you, when my vampire perked up."

A little of her willingness to believe slipped. "So it's your vampire who wants me?"

"Definitely, with my human side riding a hard double."

She hated the way he insisted there were two parts of him, and that the two didn't work in harmony. "They're one and the same, Caleb."

"Hardly."

For such a smart man, he could be so blind. She'd point it out to him if she wasn't having a contrary moment. One that didn't want to fight with him. "I'm still a burden."

"I hate to break this to you, baby, and I'm truly running the risk of you accusing me of going eighteen sixties again, but I like that you need me. That you depend on me. I like having a wife to take care of, someone of my own." His thumb rubbed her lips as he whispered against her cheek. "I like having you in my home, in my kitchen, and definitely in my bed."

All very normal things for a man who couldn't have normal anymore. "Caveman."

He smiled and kissed the tip of her nose. "Maybe, but it's who I am."

He was wrong. He was so much more than that. But he wasn't

responsible for her or her feelings, even if her breakdown had given him that impression. She scooted to the edge of her chair, spreading her thighs on either side of his, and rested her thumb over the tight corner of his mouth where his guilt wedged a constant tension. Guilt for converting her, and guilt for not being able to fix things for her once she had been converted. Guilt that she hated, because it was so senseless. He might believe he was the be-all and end-all of everything that happened to her, but she believed in a higher power and the workings of fate. Besides, she didn't want him feeling responsible for her. At least not that way.

Caleb tugged her off the chair to stand over his hard thighs. She blew her bangs off her forehead. Darn, could a relationship be any more complicated? "That still doesn't change the fact that I need to have a job, Caleb."

"Just give it time. You'll find your place."

He sounded a lot more confident than any man had a right to be. She flattened her palms on his shoulders and braced her arms as he widened his legs and caught her other hand in his. "Don't make me claw you."

The smile that grew as he kept pulling her between those strong thighs told her he didn't care. "I like your claws."

"I want answers, Caleb, not sex."

"Are you absolutely positive?" He slid his hands around her waist, his touch burning through the thin cotton of her T-shirt, arching her spine so her unconfined breasts swayed within inches of his face. She would have slapped him for taking her concerns so lightly except, this close, she could see that he wasn't. He was doing the best he could, relying on distraction because he really didn't know what was going on with her any more than she knew. However, eventually he'd have to understand that she was fine with him just admitting that. She caught his hand before it could slip down her hip, and replaced it on her waist. "You can't keep doing this."

The announcement drew his gaze up from her breasts. "What?"

"This whole chauvinistic, macho, protect-the-little-brainless-female routine you've been indulging in for the last week."

His fingers skated up her back and then down again, cruising the edge of her vertebrae, dual lines of temptation that hooked the corner of her interest. "Why not?"

"Because it's not eighteen sixty anymore."

He didn't respond immediately, just re-angled those fingers after arriving at the sensitive hollow at the base of her spine. Her skin prickled as it absorbed his intent. Her back arched ever so subtly, eager for the culmination of the journey, even if her mind was operating on a more intellectual plane.

"What if I said I'm only doing it because I know you're worried, and I can't think of any other way to get your mind redirected?"

She sucked in a breath as he accepted the invite, tracing the swell of her buttocks. Goose bumps immediately heralded the pleasure. His knowing smile, and the gold flecks in the depths of his darkened eyes, told her she wasn't alone in the rising tide of desire. "I'd say that was honest and you're very sweet, albeit misguided."

"I told you before, I'm not sweet."

If his fingers trailing over the curve of her butt were enticing, they were nothing compared to the shivery allure of their glide down the insides of her thighs. The man had more magic in his fingers than that rabbit toy, featured so prominently on *Sex in the City*. And that was saying something. "Yes, you are."

As a statement, it was way too breathy and airy to be convincing, so she wasn't surprised when Caleb ignored it. In an effortless move that thrilled her to the bottom of her feminine soul, he lifted her off her feet. Allie grabbed his shoulders so tightly she was in danger of clawing him. A squeeze on her right buttock had her lifting her thigh over his. A squeeze on the left had her repeating the move with the other. With that same easy strength, he brought her down on his lap, thighs straddling his, her most sensitive flesh cuddling the hardness of his. The heat of his body was such that the two layers of denim might not have existed. Her pulse took off under the whip of pleasure. So did his. It throbbed just inches away beneath the deep tan of his skin. The beat of his heart pounded in her ears in a seductive invitation. Her hunger rose. She pushed it back, staring at his throat. His tanned throat.

"How come you're not pasty white?" The question was more of a distraction for herself than a real seeking of knowledge.

"Because I choose not to be."

Now that was interesting. "You mean I can sprout a tan, too?"

"Probably."

It didn't take a genius to figure out what put the hesitation in his voice. She hadn't proven herself to be overly adept at learning vampire skills, but how hard could tanning herself be? "I think I'll give tanning a shot. Whatever goes wrong can't be worse than the orange I painted myself with self-tanners."

"You painted yourself orange?"

From his expression she could tell he couldn't picture it. "Not on purpose."

"Glad to hear it. But just in case this goes the way of the rest of your efforts, hold off on trying to tan yourself until I'm around."

He didn't have to be so skeptical. With the heels of her hands, she shoved him. "Don't you have to go puke or something?"

The only thing her shove dislodged was a frown. "Who told you about that?"

"Slade."

He sighed and resumed his stroking. "I'll have to talk to him about spilling secrets."

"Why is it a secret? Do you have a problem with it?"

"Nope." His hand glided back up her spine. His laugh, as deep and as sexy as always, brushed past her ear. "It's just not a spectator sport." A shiver traveled from the top of her head to the tip of her toes. God, he was too damn sexy.

"Why do you do it?"

He shrugged. "Because I like the taste of food even if it doesn't agree with me anymore."

"And there's nothing more to it than that?"

"Not a thing."

She didn't believe him. Slade was right. Caleb ate food for the same reason she cooked on that stupid stove. It made her feel connected to what she'd lost. It made her feel normal.

"Now that I've told you my secret," Caleb whispered in that deep drawl of his that was seduction itself, "why don't you tell me yours?"

"I don't have any secrets."

The stillness of his body should have been a warning, but she was so focused on the sparks of desire dancing in the wake of his touch, she never saw it coming.

"Tell me about the dream."

She dropped her head back into the cradle of his palm. He'd been distracting her all right, but not for sex. "Oh, you're good."

"Thank you." Beneath the lingering amusement in his gaze, there was an unmistakable seriousness.

She touched the indentation of his smile. "I suppose Slade put you up to this?"

"He's not pleased with you right now. He wants to run those tests."

She trailed her finger down over his chin to his neck, tracing the strong tendons under the collar of his shirt to the ridge of his collarbone. She didn't particularly care what Slade wanted. *She* did not want to be poked and prodded and maybe found deficient. "Which concerns me, how?"

He stared at her sternly. "His displeasure is mine."

She shook her head. Who did he think he was fooling, with that intimidation thingy? "I'm shaking in my shoes."

His hand shaped to the curve of her ribs. "If you're not careful, you're going to get that cute little ass paddled."

Only Caleb would describe her ass as cute. She kissed his chin, wiggling her rear on his thighs. "Promises, promises."

Beneath her, his muscles clenched along with the tightness of his grasp. The smile she loved mellowed his drawl. "You are a wild woman."

Other areas of their relationship might keep her up nights, but not this one. The sex between them was good. Very good. "You like it."

"I do, but it doesn't mean I won't take you in hand if you need it."

She rolled her eyes. "That is so archaic."

His fingers caught her chin and brought her gaze to his. "I'm not one of your modern men, Allie. I protect what's mine. However I have to."

She jerked her chin. Caleb didn't let her go. She knocked his hand away. She didn't need his support. Annoyance worked just fine. "How? By spanking me?"

"If necessary."

Good God, he meant it! "And when that doesn't work, what's plan B? Locking me in the tower with no food and water?"

"What makes you think it won't work?"

She grabbed his wrist, letting him into her mind, letting him see her reaction to just the thought. "Just a hunch."

His gaze sharpened to that razor intensity she felt deep inside. She let him read to his heart's content.

His grip tightened, then softened as he backed off mentally. "You are one damn stubborn woman, Allie Johnson."

She ignored the long-suffering sigh that punctuated the statement. "You like that, too."

His lips quirked. "Sometimes."

She shrugged, relaxing her own grip. "And it's Allie Sanders."

His body tightened in that way that was at once sexy and intimidating. "Like hell it is."

This probably wasn't the time to bring it up, but since the door had been opened, there was something Caleb needed to understand,

and sooner was better than later. "I do not consider a blood exchange as binding as marriage vows."

The squaring of his shoulders and the set of his chin spoke volumes. "We're married."

"No." She shook her head. "We're not. You're handsome, sexy, and you've got the best-tasting blood around, but I personally do not regard those as sound qualities around which to build a marriage."

"Then you'd better find something you do like and hold tight, baby, because you're well and truly hitched."

She sat up straighter. "We're not married until I consider us married. And I don't."

He pulled her in until her groin mated to his. He was aroused, angry, and determined, and her body reacted with an ecstatic, hopeful pulse. "Would you like me to prove it?"

She dismissed the reaction of her body with a wave of her hand. "That's just sex."

He pressed her hips down over his, drawing a moan past her lips. He felt so good. "This sexy little body reacts to me, and me alone."

"All that means is we're compatible in bed."

"In my day, two people who'd exercised that compatibility to the level we have were married."

She patted his cheek, feeling his frustration. "But your day has come and gone. Times have changed and women with it."

"Not that much."

"Oh yeah, that much."

His thumbnail sliced through the crotch of her jeans, the talon retracting as he slid his thumb into the wet folds pressed against him—rubbing, searching—until she gasped and jerked above him. "I disagree."

"I repeat—this is just sex, mindless chemistry."

But he was right. It did have uses. He was no longer hassling her about her dreams and Slade's experiments.

Caleb shook his head, his green eyes locked with hers, challenging her with the truth he obviously believed inviolate. She studied him more closely, remembering that fear she'd sensed in him. Maybe a truth he even needed to believe was inviolate.

"This is us together," Caleb growled. The rough pad of his thumb began a gentle massage that sparked an anything-but-gentle response. A whole chorus of yeses took off in her core, riding the timbre of his growl as well as the knowing stroke. "*This* is how I know you're mine."

No amount of deep breathing could control the surging passion, the drive for the magic moment he invariably delivered. She didn't even try, giving him this "win" because he needed it so much, letting him bring her to the orgasm he wanted. As her body jerked and contracted, his stroking slowed, but didn't stop, keeping her humming in the aftermath. He pulled her against his chest, enfolding her in his strength as if he knew what a lure it was to her. "This is how I know your protests to the contrary are just so much pride-puffing hot air."

"Why is it so hard for you to separate sex from love?"

"I'm not talking love."

He could have fooled her. "Then what are you talking about?"

"Commitment, and the fact that the primitive vampire in me is wild about the primitive vampire in you and, that being the case, neither of us has a choice on being together from here on out."

"You mean you didn't choose me?"

"No more than you chose me."

Oh hell, that hurt. She might not be up to marriage commitment but she'd definitely been leading with her heart. She shoved against his chest. Caleb didn't let go. She bared her talons. He just gazed at her, infuriatingly calm in the face of her threat. Allie dug the points into his chest. He winced, but instead of pulling away, he sat there, letting her do as she willed, strange lights swirling in his gaze. His thumb stroked her harder as blood seeped into his shirt. "Sheathe your claws."

"No." She wanted to hurt him the way he'd just hurt her. Deeply. Permanently.

"You're just making him happy."

"Who?"

"The vampire."

"You're the vampire."

"I'm not."

He was. "Let me go."

"Just as soon as you accept what's going on, I will."

She raked her nails down his torso, glad when he grunted in pain, furious when he wedged his hand farther between them, his thumb stroking as his fingers probed. Her body's immediate betrayal galled her pride. "Fuck you."

"If you keep this up, the only one who's going to be fucked is you."

"Go to hell."

"I'm already there."

"You are so clichéd." Despite her anger, her body opened for the thrust of his fingers and her mind opened for the intrusion of his.

"But you want me."

"No. I don't."

It was a lie. No matter how angry she was, it didn't matter to her body. It wanted him, and nothing she did dimmed that fire.

"But *she* does," he whispered in her ear as he lifted her. "And you can't fight her, can you?"

"Yes." She could. She was mistress of her body.

He held her still while he unzipped his jeans, then pulled her back against him until his hard cock pressed against the well of her vagina. A little pulse and jerk slid silky fluid across her flesh, burning hot as it imprinted his need into her skin.

"Prove it," he whispered in a hard, tight drawl. "Tell me to stop."

Stop.

The order never made it past her throat as her body wept and pleaded for the inch she needed to complete the union. The burn spread inside, burrowing deep into her need, amplifying it.

"C'mon, baby. Tell me to stop." Caleb lowered her a fraction more, just enough to tease her with the fulfillment she craved. "Before it's too late."

Oh God, she couldn't. She couldn't. Her entire body throbbed and ached, begged for the potential joining with mindless fervor. She wanted him, needed him, with a yearning that went so much deeper than anger or lust. Whether he felt the same or not. Whether he differentiated what part of him wanted what or not, she knew what she needed. Him. She wrapped her legs around his waist. The back of the chair bit into her calves. The sharp pain blended into the moment, driving her need higher.

He gave her a fraction more, the whimper that slipped past her lips a deeper betrayal than the internal need. There was compassion mixed with the lust in his drawl as he lowered her hard onto his erection. Her high-pitched cry wrapped around the truth as he said quietly, "In this, Allie girl, we're both fucked."

✴ 11 ✦

"**I** do not consider myself fucked."

"Your body hasn't even stopped pulsing around mine," Caleb said, his drawl sleepy and sensual, "and you're already arguing?"

She nodded against his bare chest, her muscles like Jell-O, unable to do more. "Yup."

His hand on her back stroked softly. "Fess up, you just like to argue."

"Not really, but I have a genetic incompatibility with lies."

"Meaning?"

"I can't just let something go if I don't believe in it."

He grunted. The chair creaked as he shifted her higher. The shiver that went through her as her body adjusted to his was echoed in his moan. "So what aren't you agreeing with?"

"I don't agree that I'm now schizophrenic. There isn't a vampire me and a 'me' me."

"Then what do you see?"

"Me with a slightly altered reality."

"Slightly?" She didn't need to look to know he arched his right eyebrow. His sleepy, dry tone said it all. "How do you figure that?"

She traced the ridge of his pectoral, pushing the edge of his shirt aside, noting the missing buttons as she did. She had a vague recollection of them popping off as she'd ripped it open, anxious to get to his skin. She really was a wild woman with him. "I'm still in this world, still in touch with who I am, and still in control."

"Except when you dream."

She pursed her lips in exasperation. "You're like a dog with a bone, Johnson."

He lifted her off him and settled her against his side. "It's important."

She clenched her thighs against the sense of loss. She felt so empty without him. So incomplete. She cuddled into his warmth, her hand dropping to the top of his stomach and then down to his washboard abs. She pressed. There was no give. The man was hard-headed and hard-bodied. "I don't see how. It's not even a dream, more like a delusion brought on by pain and chemical deprivation."

One arm curved around her shoulder. "So you hope."

He had her there. She was seriously hoping that's all it was. "It can't be more."

"Haven't you figured out by now that anything is possible?"

"Then, if anything is possible, it's possible the dream is just an illusion."

He looked at her from under his lashes. "So why aren't we talking about it?"

"Because you'll go all eighteen sixties on me and will want to wrap me tighter in cotton wool than you already have."

"It's that bad?"

"It's weird, the way all dreams are."

"In a way that has you worried."

"What makes you think that?"

"The way you cling to me when you come out of it."

With the sliver of strength that returned to her muscles, she pushed back. She reached the bend of his elbow before he put a stop to her retreat. Looking up, she realized he'd allowed her that much just so he could see her face. She poked her finger at his chest. "One of these days I'm going to perfect my poker face, and you are so going to be out of luck."

"Then I guess I'll just have to read your mind."

Not if she learned to block him first, he wouldn't. "An alternative would be to just allow me some space in which to work out my own problems."

The small smile faded. "There's no such thing as your problems. Everything that happens to you is my concern."

"Just because everyone else indulges your nosiness doesn't mean I have to."

His finger under her chin again had her looking him in the eye. "Keeping abreast of all potential threats has kept us alive for the last two centuries."

"The phrasing of that sentence would imply a threat exists."

"There's always something ready to come at what a man has."

He said that with the utter calm of a man used to conflict, who regarded it as a way of life. She didn't know whether to be comforted or be dismayed by that point of view. "War doesn't have to be a way of life."

"I'm not at war."

Allie blinked, checked his expression, and checked again, but nothing had changed. "You're serious."

"Don't I look it?"

He always looked serious. "If you're not at war, why do you hole up here with your army of weres behind a wall of illusion, guns always at the ready?" She shook her head. "Either you're at war with something or you're highly paranoid."

"Implying what?"

"Implying I don't think you're paranoid."

The corner of his mouth kicked up. "Some would argue with you on that."

"Then they would be wrong, but that just leaves the question, what are you?"

"Careful." A floorboard creaked as he adjusted their position. "Very careful."

Allie hitched herself higher. "Maybe too careful?"

Caleb laughed and kissed her lips. "There's no such thing."

She kissed him back before she realized what she was doing. "Statements like that will get you another argument."

He shrugged, unconcerned, his fingers ruffling her hair. "I can handle it."

Yes, he could. Allie was beginning to believe he could handle anything. Except her, because he had this idea that she needed peace. All the time.

"Caleb?"

"What?"

"You know this stress-free zone you're trying to set up around me?"

The ruffling stopped. "Yeah."

"It's one of the things that's fraying my nerves."

"I think you've had enough excitement for this year."

She opened her mouth to retort when a commotion in the hall redirected her energy. Allie grabbed her jeans and tugged them on, shooting Caleb a resentful glare when all he had to do was adjust and button. She wasn't going to fight with Caleb as his brothers bore witness. Not because she feared a public discussion, but one thing she'd learned over the last two weeks—the Johnson brothers stuck together. Didn't matter if they all agreed on the point under discussion, let an outsider disagree with one of them, and they all landed squarely on the same spot in an astounding display of loyalty. Something one rarely saw today in society's more "open" mentality. It was one of the things she really liked about the Johnsons. It was just a pain in the butt that they saw her as an absolute outsider when it came to disagreeing with Caleb.

She pushed Caleb's hands aside as he pulled her T-shirt down over her breasts. Jumping to her feet, she snapped her jeans just as the kitchen door opened. Jared tipped his hat as he strolled in. Jace wasn't far behind, their smiles letting her know they knew what she and Caleb had been doing. She smiled back. The werewolf who brought up the rear got a glare. She still hadn't forgiven Derek for imprisoning her that first night.

Derek reached for a bear claw as he cleared the door. Allie snatched the plate from beneath his hand. Caleb cocked an eyebrow at her as he rolled to his feet with lazy grace.

"They're not good enough for company yet."

Derek smiled. "I'm not picky."

She met his slate gray eyes squarely. "But I am."

She put the plate on the stove out of his reach. Behind her, she heard one of the men chuckle, and then Jace said, "Looks like you've got a bit of ground to make up, Derek, before you get baked goods."

A chair scraped across the floor. "Don't see why. It was Jared's order I was following."

Allie turned in time to see Derek settle his big frame into the chair, dwarfing it with nothing more than muscle and bone. "Next time you might consider exercising independent thought."

He leaned back and the ladder-back chair squeaked a protest. "Nah. Too much work."

She really wished the chair would break. He was so arrogant that he needed to be brought down a peg or two. "Then I guess you'll be doing without."

As one, the men broke into laughter. "What?"

Caleb shook his head and smiled, taking a seat beside Jace. "One thing a were never is, is without."

She rolled her eyes. "You just had to go to the sex factor, didn't you?"

Jared leaned back in his chair, rocking it to the edge of tipping over and snagged a bun. "You started it." He tossed the pastry to Derek who caught it deftly. "We're just playing along."

Derek took a bite. "They're a little dry."

Allie reached behind her. The handle of the rolling pin slipped into her palm. "You do have a compulsion to live dangerously."

Derek stretched and she blinked at the amount of muscle that bunched and flowed with the movement. "You can bury me six feet under when it goes away."

Caleb's swat on her butt had everyone looking at her; Derek smiling, the brothers frowning.

"What?" She raised her hands. "It's not like I'm interested."

Derek's smile broadened as he brought his arms down. His gaze dropped to her chest. "Are you sure, darling?"

The pulses of sexual energy coming off Derek made her vividly aware that she'd left her bra off that morning in deference to the heat of the stove. She crossed her arms over her chest. Dealing with Caleb was enough. She didn't need a wild card like the werewolf tossed into the mix. "I'm sure."

"If you change your mind in the future, you know where you can find me."

Good grief, along with long life, had the good Lord handed weres an excessive amount of ego and confidence? "Do me a favor, would you?"

"What?"

She smiled at him. "Hold your breath until I hunt you up."

Instead of taking the comment as an insult, Derek just laughed out loud and the interest she could sense in him increased. "How long are you planning on holding a grudge for that first night?"

"That depends."

"On what?"

She held his gaze. "Your life expectancy."

More laughter around the table. Caleb's hand cradled her hip, his fingers stroking along the full curve. "Stop flirting with the man, Allie."

"I'm not flirting, I'm aggravating him."

"With a were, that's one and the same," Jace cut in.

Derek chuckled. Displeasure whipped through Caleb's energy, blending with the antagonism she felt toward the big were. Heightening her need to irritate him.

Allie turned in Caleb's grasp to glare at him. "What is it with you paranormal men? When you got in line for long life, did you sneak back for a double dose of arrogance?"

Derek reached for another bear claw. "Yup."

Allie pushed his hand away from the treat. "I reserve those for friends."

The smile left his tanned face. "What makes you think I'm not your friend?"

"Something about the way you like to toss me into dirty stalls, leave me to the mercy of my bladder, and then use me as bait."

"I'll own up to the first, but the last was all Jared and the boys."

"You could have stopped it." It still irked her that no one had. Chairs creaked as weight shifted in them. Tension in the air increased.

"No. He couldn't."

Allie looked down into Caleb's eyes, drawn by the certainty in his voice. The uneasy feeling in the pit of her stomach wasn't completely due to the return of her insatiable hunger. "He could have tried."

"No." His hand slid up to wrap around her waist, his fingers warming the turbulence within. "No more than anyone here would let you die, they couldn't let me die."

"Your brothers don't even like me."

"That's not true," Jared cut in.

She wouldn't have questioned the statement from Slade or Jace, but Jared? "Oh, c'mon."

He looked at her with those eyes so like Caleb's, the strength of his personality hitting her like a blow, the lack of a smile on his face giving her nothing to hold on to. "You're one of us now. We can like you as much as we want."

Which told her nothing. Caleb pulled her fully into his embrace. Comfort flowed over her, soothing the fear wedged beneath her resolution to make the best of her situation. She stepped away. She wanted a good foot between them. She got an inch. She turned and pushed at his hand.

"You know I'm not interested in Derek, right?" She ignored the were's dry "Ouch." "It's just that I'm not used to all this freaking testosterone twenty-four seven. It's like being in the middle of a freak-fest."

"I know."

Derek laughed outright, his throat muscles rippling with the sound. At the base, his pulse throbbed. Her inner radar leapt to attention, reminding her that not only was the were big and handsome, he was breakfast on the hoof. "I've got a peace offering if you'll take it."

"What is it?"

He snagged another bear claw, his grab faster than her prevention. "My mother wrote a cookbook a while back. I've kept it."

"How long is a while back?

"A couple hundred years."

It was a measure of how much she'd been bombarded with in the last two weeks that Allie didn't even blink at the two-hundred-year reference. "Is it like 'ancient cooking devices for dummies'?"

"Yup. She wrote it for the new brides in the congregation."

A werewolf who wrote recipe books for the congregation? "You realize you are all just totally blowing my TV-induced conceptions of the paranormal?"

"They could use some shaking up," Slade cut in, tossing his hat toward the rack by the door. It hit the edge of the hook and fell to the floor. "You've got some dangerous notions when it comes to vampires."

Shut up. Caleb shot the mental order at Slade, but it was too late. Slade had Allie's full attention.

"Well, maybe you could provide me with some facts, and I could stop speculating."

Slade being Slade was happy to oblige. He picked up his hat, dusted some lint from the brim, and put it on the hook. "What do you want to know?"

"I want to know how you came to be. I want to know if there are others like Simon and the D'Nallys. I want to know why I can't—"

Slade came back to the table. "That's a heck of a lot to want to know."

"I've been saving up."

Caleb shook his head at Slade. "Now is not the time."

"She deserves answers."

Allie glared at Caleb. "Yes, I do."

Caleb sighed as Allie leaned away from him. Obviously, he wasn't going to get much work with that new gelding tonight. Not with the way Allie was chafing at her confinement. "She's got enough to deal with."

Jared took advantage of Allie's distraction to grab a bear claw. "Her change would probably be a lot easier to deal with if she had some background."

Of course, Allie was in agreement with that. "Absolutely."

The only security Caleb had to offer her was the illusion he knew what was happening to her and had it and everything else under control. If she knew they had no clue as to what was happening to her, if she knew how close the D'Nallys were to breaching the compound, she'd have no sense of safety at all. "No."

"Fine, if we can't talk about Allie, we'll talk about you."

"Jared."

Jared ignored the warning, tossed the bear claw to Derek, and turned to Allie. "Did you know Caleb was changed by a female?"

Allie perked up. "No, I didn't."

Shit, now they were going to have to relive this, and in doing so, bring up all Jared's festering anger. The day was definitely going from bad to worse.

"She found him after he'd been bushwhacked and jumped him when he was too weak from blood loss to fight."

"Damn it, Jared, when are you going to let it go?"

"When the devil starts making snowballs in hell."

Caleb ground his molars. The night of his conversion welled out of his memory. Weak, out of his head and in pain from a gut shot, worry for his brothers uppermost in his mind, he'd watched her step out of the twilight looking like an angel, long blonde hair flowing past her hips, highlighting the ethereal thinness of her build and her pale, perfect skin. She'd touched him, her brown eyes moist with sadness. Warmth had swamped the cold encasing him. He'd embraced it fully as she lowered her head. He'd taken her bite, thought the ecstasy a sign of God's deliverance and forgiveness for the shadier things he'd done to keep him and his brothers together and alive. When, in that last moment, she'd asked him if he was sure, he'd said, "Yes."

And so she'd changed him, giving him the second chance he'd asked for, even if it wasn't the one he'd anticipated. And he, in turn, had passed it on to his brothers. "The only person to blame for what we are is me."

"She manipulated your mind," Jared snapped.

"I don't need you telling me how it was," Caleb snapped right back. "I was there."

"When I find her, I'm going to put her out of her misery."

It was an oft-repeated refrain, and Caleb was sick of it. "If you want to blame someone for being a vampire, blame me."

Jared leaned back in his chair. "I'm comfortable with who I have pegged."

Caleb sighed. "She was very fragile, Jared. Converting me might have killed her."

"Obviously not, as we're all still vampires."

"You're clinging to a myth. Killing her won't change us back."

"Maybe." The hate in Jared's voice spilled into the room. God forgive him, he'd done this to Jared. To all of them. Not the woman. She'd been innocent. He'd bet his soul on that. He closed his eyes and remembered her face with its elfin piquancy, her weakness, the sadness in her eyes. And felt some sadness of his own. "She needed help."

Beside him, Allie stiffened. Too late he realized she'd tapped into his mind. Her snarl blended with Jared's "Bullshit." A mental touch revealed the primitive jealousy consuming her. Her vampire didn't like his thoughts on another woman.

"Relax, Allie. It was a long time ago."

She crossed her arms over her chest. Her nails dented her skin, driving the blood from the area, making deep valleys in the soft flesh. "You liked her."

He tightened his grip on her hip when she would have pulled away. "She saved my life, what wasn't to like?"

He ignored Jared's snort, focused on Allie's glare. He sighed. "She needed help, baby, and I didn't give it. It's guilt, not lust I feel."

"Heck, Allie, you can't blame a man for his thoughts," Derek cut in.

That stubborn chin came up. "Yes, I can."

The challenge stood. Around them, the other males stilled. Anticipation thickened the air. The soft scent of female anxiety drifted over the heavier scent of lust. His, the were's, and his brothers.

He didn't like the mix, the tension. He stood. Something wasn't right. "Allie?"

"What?"

He met the others' gazes. The way their eyes averted from his told him one thing. He wasn't imagining things. "We're all done with the questions."

"No." Anger, desire, and fear packed that one syllable.

He backed his first order with a mental one. It was rejected just as summarily. The longing of the other males reached out, touching the edges of his private line with Allie. Hungry, needing, wanting. Caleb bent, his instincts screaming a warning. He needed to get her out of here. Ignoring Allie's surprised cry, he tossed her over his shoulder and grabbed his hat. Her fists beat on his hips as he carried her from the room.

"YOU are a total ass."

Caleb followed Allie up the back staircase, settling his hat on his head. Every step reverberated with the anger radiating off her. Her lush ass swayed with every slam of her foot on the wood, each stomp ending with an inviting jiggle that had his palms itching to capture it. He could smell her blood from where she'd driven her talons into her palms. She was still having trouble with control. "A complete and total jerk," she reiterated.

"The situation with Derek was getting out of hand." He couldn't bring himself to mention his brothers. "I warned you not to go without a bra."

She stomped up three more steps. "It's hot in the kitchen."

"Adjust your body temperature."

"It doesn't work for me."

"Then wear a bra."

She spun on the landing. "You have no right to tell me what to wear."

His vampire reared in answer to the feminine challenge, his human pride right alongside. He took the next two stairs in one stride. Her eyes flew wide in alarm. She backed up, her feet shuffling in a rapid slide as she felt behind her for the wall. He followed. One step, two, until her back hit the sheetrock. He slammed his hands down on either side of her head, trapping her with his body. "And you have no right to drool over another man."

The tension within her changed and refocused with her thoughts. He searched her eyes, probed her mind, but she'd shut him out. When the hell had she learned to do that? "You think other men want me?"

"Derek did." And more disturbingly, so had his brothers.

She rolled her eyes. "He's just yanking your chain."

"If you gave him a glance, he'd be in your bed faster than I could slit his throat."

"And that worries you?"

"It's never going to happen." The mere thought of the wolf anywhere near Allie made him murderous. "And if you really want him dead, keep using him to tease me."

"Is that Caleb the vampire talking, or Caleb the man?"

The arch of her brows conveyed how she felt about his sense of duality. He ignored her sarcasm and answered with the truth. "Both."

Her fingers wrapped around his, her blood dripped down, splaying over the planes before meandering into the crevices, filling the space between them, obliterating it. He tucked his thumb into his palm, cutting it, sucking in a breath as her blood blended with his. She frowned up at him. "I so don't understand you."

"You don't need to understand me. Just obey me."

"That's not ever going to happen."

"Why not?"

"Remember me, Caleb? The woman who talks to voices in her head and doesn't listen worth a damn?"

Oh, he remembered. He remembered the gut-wrenching fear that he wouldn't get there in time when Dane had attacked her that first night. The horror that Dane would rape her, kill her before he could stop him. His complete fury that she had refused to run when he'd told her to. Her utterly insane decision to come back for him. Son of a bitch, he remembered.

Caleb brought their joined hands between them, bracing her chin on their linked fingers, making her look him in the eye. "When it comes to your safety, you will listen to me."

She canted her head to the side, her brown hair sliding through the muted glow from the overhead light, picking up reds and golds, highlighting her face in flickers of color. "Or what? You'll spank me? Oh, that will be effective."

Another roll of her eyes and a total lack of concern. He touched his thumb to the center of her mouth, shaking his head as a smile fought with his anger. "You, woman, have enough sass for two people."

"You like it."

That he did. He rubbed the smear of blood off her chin. "At times."

"But not now?"

He shook his head. "No."

"Why?"

This time when she tugged, he let her hand go. "You're my responsibility."

"Ouch. First I wasn't your choice, and now I'm a responsibility. On a scale of one to ten, you're at a negative three on the win-the-girl meter."

"That's neither here nor there. As long as you're safe, my work is done."

"And my being safe involves wearing a bra and panties, doing what you tell me, and not attracting the interest of other men?"

He gritted his teeth. "Yes."

She stared at him with those blue eyes that saw too much. And then she smiled, a totally inappropriate, completely Allie smile. "You don't have to be jealous, Caleb."

He notched his cock to her groin, annoyed she read him so easily, relieved she read him so easily. "You're mine."

Her smile blossomed to delight. Her bare foot rode up his denim-covered calf, her thigh dropping to the side, opening herself more to his thrust. "Tell me something—is it just me having sex with someone else that you're worried about, or is there more?"

He brushed her bangs off her face. Another woman would have been screaming at him. Another woman might have used his desire against him. Allie wanted to understand it. He didn't have anything else to offer her but what he felt in his gut. "You're mine."

He'd seen dying critters get less pitying looks than the one she gave him. "Caleb, you can't hold me unless I want to stay."

"Watch me."

The pat on the shoulder she gave him was beyond patronizing. "You're big, sexy, and intense, but unless you make this relationship worth my while, nothing will keep me here."

If she thought he would lose her, she had another thing coming. It would be easier if she just fell into step like a more biddable woman, but a more biddable type would likely bore him, so they'd both have to learn to take the good with the bad. Starting with him here, giving her what she needed. He hitched her a bit higher in his arms. Her legs came around his waist, squeezing tightly. "So what would it take for a man like me to start interesting a woman like you?"

He opened his hand over her spine, easing the spasm of pain that shot through her back. The hunger spasm that she was trying to hide from him.

"You could start by reminding me why I fantasized about you so much before all this happened."

He skimmed his hand under her T-shirt. "You fantasized about me?"

The heat of her blush belied the boldness of her "Yes."

He liked even more that she didn't use that shyness as a barrier. He lowered his head so his mouth brushed her ear. "About my mouth?"

Her nails dug into the edge of his hand. "Yes."

Her nipples bore into his chest in silent demand, her scent increasing in tempting waves, wrapping around him in a welcoming hug. He kept his voice to a whisper, so low she had to strain to hear, increasing the intimacy between them. The want. "Was it good?"

"Very good."

He lowered her feet to the floor. "And where was my mouth that made you feel so good?" He brushed his hand across her cheek. "Here?"

She shook her head. "No." Her lower lip slid between the edges of her teeth as he slit the side of her jeans with his nail. He bent his knees, nipping his way down the side of her neck, cutting material as he went, the rasp of tearing fabric a sultry accompaniment to his journey, pressing his mouth to the welcoming curve between her shoulder and neck. "Or maybe here?"

Again the shake of her head, this time accompanied by a little moan.

"But you like it here." He sucked lightly, laving the sensitive flesh, breathing deeply as her body made her pleasure known, accentuating the arch of her body into his, keeping her hands pinned over her head as he nibbled his way down her shirt. "Was it maybe . . . lower?"

"Yes."

He grazed the top of her right breast with his teeth, knowing the thin material was no barrier to the tantalizingly sharp edge. She lurched toward him, swearing when her trapped wrists snapped her back.

"Let me go, Caleb."

He shook his head. "Not yet."

He caught her nipple between his incisors, bearing down lightly around the turgid peak. Her gaze flashed to his, telegraphing fear and desire in equal parts. He teased with a shake of his head, keeping her wrists pinned to the wall, feeling her gasp all the way to the soles of his feet. Her hands yanked against his grip. He pressed their backs against the smooth wall. "Keep them there."

"There you go, bossing me again."

He spread her shirt so her nipple peeked out, admiring the view before dipping his mouth toward the tempting morsel. "Do you really object?"

She shook her head as each word drew the nipple tighter. The blood coursed closer to the surface of her skin. Embarrassment or excitement?

A shudder took her from head to toe as he lapped it delicately. She arched her back at the end of the brief caress, her hands firmly pressed to the wall, offering herself for more. Her "Not in the bedroom" was pure breathless anticipation.

Ah, excitement. He smiled and pressed the flat of his tongue against the eager point, heating it. "You're such an adventurous little soul."

Her hands strained his grip as she angled for more room to maneuver, standing on her tiptoes in an effort to rub her nipple against his lips. "Is that a complaint?"

"Hell no." Her head thunked against the wall as he gave her what she wanted, taking the hard nub between his lips, sucking gently, enjoying her response to the simple caress. She was so open and honest when she was with him. He liked that. He pulled back just enough to see the result of his care. Damn! She had pretty breasts. Small, taut, and pert, with nipples just the right size for nibbling or pinching. He cut a glance up at her face. All he could see was the underside of her chin and the way the muscles in her throat worked as she swallowed hard.

"Do I look a fool?" He blew across her right nipple before kissing it lightly in reward for its immediate response. With a slash of his talon he slit the other side of her jeans from hip to cuff. They slid to the floor, leaving nothing but satiny skin under his fingers. He cupped her hips in his hands.

Her hands dropped to his shoulders as he lifted. "No, but you still aren't in the right spot."

He angled his left shoulder under her thigh. She blossomed to his touch, thighs spreading, breath catching, bracing her shoulders back against the wall. He slid his right hand down her leg, narrowing his grip until his fingers circled her delicate ankle. He worked it back and up until she took over the chore for him, wrapping those sweet legs around his neck. "How do you do this to me?"

"I'm not the one with fantasies." He sifted his fingers through the tight curls, separating the plump outer lips. "Sweet."

Allie's hips lifted toward his hand. Her palms dropped to his shoulders. "You're so not going to let me live this down, are you?"

Caleb let his finger slide along the path she set, riding the swelling edges of the inner lips, smiling. He cocked an eyebrow at her as he worked his finger in deeper, past the outer folds to the inner moisture. "Not a chance."

"Oh God."

He wanted to drown in her scent, her desire, bind her to him in a thousand ways—none of them ethical, all of them effective—but he'd promised her a choice and he was a man of his word. "Is this where you dreamed of my mouth, Allie? On this beautiful pussy?"

"Oh God, yes."

He cupped her buttocks in his palms, squeezing and spreading the lush curves as he pulled her to him. His hat brim bumped her stomach. He reached up, only to find her hands there first, keeping it put. A glance revealed her lip between her teeth, a look of uncertainty on her face. And a devilish amount of hope.

"That was part of the fantasy, too."

The smile started deep inside. He settled his thumb on her center and rubbed lightly, calming her with his touch, working her past her embarrassment back into the fire. He definitely wanted her to burn. Allie on fire with desire was every man's dream. "I can work with that."

Her grin caught him on his weak side, sliding under his caution, tapping into the emotions that seemingly seethed at her command. She settled the hat back on his head, scooted her shoulders down, and angled her hips up. "Good."

❧ 12 ❧

"INTERESTING look."

Caleb stood in the doorway, one shoulder leaning against the jamb, his eyes assessing her from head to toe. No doubt looking for an injury. He was obsessed with the thought that something was going to happen to her.

Allie reached up to her head, fingering the three bright blue feathers she couldn't get rid of that stuck straight up, the embarrassing aftereffects of her failed attempt to shift into a blue jay. An attempt she'd made because she desperately needed to succeed at something. She forced her lips into a smile as fake as her confidence these days. "I thought so."

He pushed off the jamb and came toward her. The narrowing of his eyes belied the lazy roll to his gait. "I thought we agreed—no more experimenting with shifting until Slade figures out what's going on with you."

The closer he got, the more the mark on her finger burned. "Actually I think you were in a snit and laid down some sort of edict."

"Which you chose to disobey."

"Naturally." Rather than smiling as she had expected, Caleb's mouth tightened. She felt a ridiculous need to apologize. She reached up to the feathers, measured Caleb's frown, and dropped her hand back down. "Besides, you can't consider a few hair follicles a full shift."

He stopped two feet in front of her, his eyes locked on those feathers like they held the secret of life. His fingers twitched. "No, I suppose one can't."

She rubbed the mark on her finger, not buying his easy agreement in the least. "Did you have a good hunt?"

His gaze flicked to hers as his hands reached up toward her "display." "I've got supper if that's what you mean."

Ouch! The man was not happy if he was opting for bluntness. "I'm thinking it would be easier if you just hooked me up to an IV."

With a slight shake of his head, he touched the feathers. "But not nearly so much fun."

This close she couldn't miss the fatigue tightening the skin around his eyes and the slight pallor underlying the naturally dark color of his skin. He was exhausted. "I think my need has gone way past fun."

It was killing him, and Caleb didn't even have the survival instinct to save himself.

His hand skimmed the feathers back. It tickled. He took advantage of her flinch to cup his hand around the back of her neck. It rested heavily there for a second before he adjusted the weight, then it became a lingeringly soft caress of heat and security as he pulled her into his chest. His "You've got a hearty appetite, for sure" ruffled her bangs.

She tilted her head back for the descent of his mouth. The man was always touching her, kissing her. And damn—she closed her eyes as his lips moved over hers, brushing, probing, parting for the flick of his tongue that always sent a shot of pure lust through her—he was really good at it.

His breath puffed into her mouth. "Glad you think so."

She didn't even open her eyes at the comment, just tilted her head a fraction more. "Mmmm, was I projecting again?"

His tongue teased the corner of her mouth, the shudder that went through her inspired the smile she felt press into her cheek. "Yeah."

"I guess I'll have to work harder on getting that under control."

"Don't bother on my account." Shivers joined the shudder as he traced his way across the supple terrain of her lip, using the sensitive inner lining of her lower one as a guide, not stopping until he reached the other corner. He announced his arrival with another taunting flick of his tongue. Her knees buckled. He held her up with a hand at the back of her neck, keeping their lips in play with nothing more than the hunger for more. She kissed him back, standing on tiptoe to increase the pressure.

"Okay." She caught his lower lip between her teeth, let his shudder blend into her desire as she bit down gently, and spoke around it. "I'll keep my motivations strictly selfish."

Another laugh, another airy caress, and then the warmth of his hand down low on her back, sliding lower. "You do that."

Her body softened at the play while her mind sharpened, building to that point of hyperfocus that reduced her world to only him. After two weeks, she was getting used to this aspect of their interaction. She leaned her hips into his.

"Oh for Pete's sake!"

Allie jumped at the interruption. Caleb steadied her, pulling her close with the hand at the base of her spine, turning them so his big body shielded her from view as the brothers entered the room. Another set of footsteps heralded someone entering behind the Johnsons. Derek?

"They need to get a room," Jace added to Slade's exclamation.

"They've got a room, and if they don't start using it, I'm going to start thinking these displays are an invite," Derek drawled.

Caleb growled—a deep rumble that reverberated against her cheek. She shook her head, which in her current position resulted in little more than rubbing her cheek against his chest. Keeping her voice low, she said, "He's just yanking your chain again."

Her feathers ruffled as he bent his head and whispered back, "Then he can enjoy the consequences."

From the set of his jaw, consequences translated to a fistfight. Men were so predictable.

"Actually," Jared interjected, "I don't think he is."

Allie closed her eyes. Damn vampire hearing. No matter where she turned or what she did, someone was always watching or hearing her. It was getting on her nerves. "You shouldn't eavesdrop."

The stroke of Caleb's hand down her back didn't soothe her irritation.

"Let it go, Allie."

"No."

"I don't think any of us can afford to," Slade said, an abnormal tightness in his drawl.

Against her, Caleb stiffened. He lifted his head. Cool air wafted over her forehead where his cheek had rested. She sighed. The moment of intimacy was gone. She stepped back. As always there was that moment of resistance before Caleb let her go.

"What's on your mind?"

Jace's eyebrows went up, echoing the surprise on all the men's faces as her feathers came into view. "Feathers on your head?"

She had no reason to feel defensive. But she did. She also felt inadequate and the biggest burden a person could be. She folded her arms across her chest. "I was bored."

"And you thought feathers would liven up the day?" said Slade, whose keen eyes probably saw more than she wanted.

No way was she admitting she'd tried to shift and gotten stuck. "It was a start."

"Blue feathers?"

"They reflected my mood."

Caleb's gaze homed in on her, setting the mark to burning again. "You were blue?"

She rubbed her thumb over the irritation. "Why would I be depressed? I have a whole compound of men waiting at my beck and call, ready to fulfill my every need if I but deign to communicate it."

Derek closed his eyes for a second, his mouth settling in a decidedly sensual grin as he rocked his chair back on two legs. "Now there's a picture to carry a man."

The temptation to tip his chair the rest of the way back tugged at her foot. Caleb had no such reservations. With a heft of his boot, the were went back and over. Derek landed with a crash that made her jump but didn't even earn a glance from the other men. As one they stared at her, reading her face, probing at her mind, searching for the truth. Pain bloomed in her head. She pressed her fingers to her temple. "Stop it!"

Immediately, the probes backed off, but the brothers still stared. She glared at them. "What is it with you all? I can understand Caleb worrying, it's his nature, but the rest of you need to get lives. You're way too involved in our relationship."

"She's right."

Jared was the last one Allie would have thought would take her side.

"Which brings me to my previous point."

A glance at Slade's face told her more clearly than words that she wasn't going to like what he had to say. She reached out and Caleb caught her hand. She let him bring her into his side. From the look on the brothers' faces, she was going to need some bracing.

"Spit it out," Caleb ordered.

"Your relationship is affecting everyone."

"How so?"

"I wasn't sure at first, but as time goes on, it can't be ignored."

Caleb's deep breath pressed his ribs against her shoulder. "What can't be ignored?"

Slade, Derek, Jared, and Jace exchanged a look. The silence

stretched to a tense thread and then Jace sighed and said something so ugly, Allie had to ask him to repeat it. His green eyes, two shades lighter than Caleb's, met hers.

"We want you."

Caleb snarled and shoved her behind him, her stumbling compliance just part of the recoil from the announcement that left her reeling. They wanted her? The whisper just slipped out. "That doesn't make sense."

"No it doesn't," Jared pronounced flatly.

"No one wants to want her," Jace added.

The room suddenly felt too small. "Gee thanks." She took another step back, staring at Jace, feeling as though she'd never seen him before.

Caleb went with her, pinning her between the wall and his broad back. She didn't think he was aware of what he was doing. He was completely focused on the other men, the tension in his body signaling his readiness to fight.

"Speak for yourself," Derek interjected over her sarcasm. "I'm more than happy to want her. What I don't like is this building need to do something about it." He raised a brow at Caleb. "If I'd known sharing blood with you would have this kind of side effect, I would have passed."

For a second there was no sound in the room except the sound of controlled breathing and the creak of wood as men shifted in chairs. Finally, Caleb asked, "Are you all feeling this way?"

Allie buried her face between his shoulder blades, not wanting to know the answer to his question but helpless to resist the opportunity. She bunched Caleb's shirt in her fingers. "Don't tell me—they're all nodding, aren't they?"

"You just told me not to tell you."

"You know darn well that was a figure of speech."

"You've got a fancy way to dress up everything."

"Just answer the question."

"Yes."

She pressed her head into his spine. "This can't be good."

"No," Slade agreed. "It's not."

"Does this have anything to do with my increasing need to protect her?" Caleb asked.

"I think so."

"Any idea why?"

"I know it's tied into the mental energy we can all share at will, and it's obviously tied to instinct, but why it's spreading like fever, and why it's increasing proportionally to her blood intake, I can't say."

It just figured that the first time Slade had a theory on her difference it had to be one that scared her spitless. Allie stepped back against the wall. "The more I want blood, the more you all want me?"

A disconcerting emotion tickled her spine. She looked around the room, taking in the faces of the men, their hard expressions, feeling like she'd never seen them before. It took her a moment to figure out what it was. Fear. She was afraid of them. The shadows from their hat brims deepened the glitter in their eyes to a sinister cast. The width of their shoulders took on more meaning, the strength of their hands more threat.

She folded her arms across her chest. She wanted to take another step back, to run, but there was nowhere to go. Nowhere she could hide from this—from them. Nowhere she could hide from herself.

"Why is everything so different with me?"

Slade sighed. "You've tossed a stick in the spokes of what we know for sure."

Not a settling observation. Then again, nothing during the last month had been settling. She touched Caleb's back, needing him to move so she could leave. Beneath her fingertips, his muscles were stiff cuts of aggression. Pain and determination rolled off him in waves. If the brothers' statements felt like a betrayal to her, what must he be feeling? He'd cared for his brothers his entire life. With them, he shared a bond so close he had brought them with him into immortality rather than lose it. With Derek he shared a friendship close enough to make him all but a brother. Bonds like that had to work both ways. The Johnsons and Derek might doubt that, but she didn't, and someone had to do something to bring that fact to the fore before everything went to hell in a handbasket. Since they were in this predicament because of her, it was up to her to get them out.

She stepped around Caleb, dodging his grab. His eyes bored into her back as she took four shaky steps to the table. She pulled out a chair beside where Jared stood. He stiffened. Her heart skipped a beat. This close she couldn't get away if he went all primitive on her. Caleb growled. A glance up showed Jared's jaw muscles knotted and his gaze skirting his brothers'. Unease filled the room.

Allie jabbed her elbow in Jared's side. His brows snapped down along with his chin. She matched him glare for glare. She might not be able to do the slightest vampire thing, but she could handle men, and these five were going to be reasonable if she had to beat it into them.

"I don't care what voices are muttering in your head, Jared Johnson. You may be an arrogant ass, but you're Caleb's brother. There's nothing in this world that could make you betray him, so stop glaring at me like you're some sort of threat."

She grabbed the chair seat and tugged it forward. It caught on a floorboard, slipping out of her grip. Before she could tug again, it moved. A glance back showed Jared pushing it in.

"You sound damn sure."

For once, arrogance didn't lace his tone.

"I am." She accepted his help with the chair, sitting down with as much unconcern as she could muster.

"How?"

"It's a gut thing."

He blinked. That flicker of emotion that crossed his face could have been relief. She hoped it was. The fact that he took a seat at the other end of the table wasn't encouraging.

"Don't dismiss her gut instincts," Caleb said, coming up behind her. "They're what had her saving my ass while I was in wolf form."

Derek whistled. "Those are some instincts."

"And they tell you we're not a threat?" Jace asked.

No, they were telling her to run, but none of the men needed to hear that. "None of you would betray Caleb."

Caleb's hand came down on her shoulder and squeezed. "Thank you."

She placed her fingers over his. "You're welcome."

The chair to her left scraped across the floor as Caleb pulled it out. Under the table, she hooked her fingers around his pinky as the other brothers took seats as far away as they could. Derek sat on the right with the brothers. She doubted the symbolism of she and Caleb being on one side, while unintentional, was lost on anyone, least of all Caleb. There was definitely a symbolic "us against them" theme developing here. Completely unacceptable, in her opinion.

"This can't continue."

"That's for sure," Caleb said in a drawl so calm she could have kissed him. "Either you all get over this fascination with my wife or we'll leave, but this has to end."

Again with the wife thing. "I'm not your wife yet."

Slade's head snapped around. Jace shook his head, the ever-present smile missing from the corners of his wide mouth. "I'm thinking that would not be a point you want to be arguing right now."

Allie shifted in her seat, unease flitting through her. It wasn't their stares that bothered her, but that indefinable underlying tension she sensed. The hair on the back of her neck stirred. Caleb's hand enveloped hers. Tension hummed off him, too, but more lethal. More focused. She sighed. "Maybe not."

Caleb squeezed her knee. Comfort, or an order to shut up? "How long has this been going on?" he asked.

"Near as we can figure, it started the second day after she arrived."

Allie did the math. She glanced up at Caleb, who was studying the other men at the table as if he'd never seen them before. "That would make it after we—"

Another squeeze, harder this time. She shut up.

"And it's been building steadily?" he asked.

Jace ran his hand through his hair. "Pretty much every time you notice she needs more blood, we notice how much more appealing she's getting."

"Sexually." Caleb didn't pose it as a question and no one treated it as one.

Jared's flat, cold "Definitely" was more scary than a thousand words could ever be. The hair on the nape of her neck danced. Caleb's hand flipped on her thigh, lying there in an invite she didn't hesitate to accept. She took an easier breath when his fingers closed around hers. Some things, like being the focus of mass lust, were easier to take with a reminder that he was there if she needed him. "I swear, I haven't done anything differently."

Another of those cold realities that gave her the willies. This time from Slade. "We know."

"How bad is it?" None of the deadly emotion she could feel coiling within Caleb colored his drawl.

The twist of pain deep in her gut made her gasp. Hunger. How could she be hungry again so soon? As if in answer to her question, the tension started again. Along with the hunger came something else. A tickle of sensation, and then an alien whisper of sound so faint she wasn't even sure it was real and not a hiccup of her imagination.

Come.

She blinked slowly, looking around the table. Had anyone else heard the command? Given it? There was nothing to indicate either way. The men were all looking at Caleb. She waited. The whisper didn't repeat. The sensation didn't linger. Only the hunger remained, strong and growing stronger by the second. She pushed it aside as it began its claim. She couldn't deal with it right now. Especially knowing that others were privy to the struggle she thought was private. Another look around the table revealed every man present was looking at her with an expression of urgency and determination. "Good grief, I might as well be wearing a neon sign."

"It's true." Jared waved his hand at their interlaced fingers. "She gets an urge to put on the feed bag and we want to feed her. She has other . . . needs, and we want to fulfill them, too."

Other needs. She stood so fast her chair teetered and then balanced with a staccato rattle. He could not be talking about what she thought he was talking about.

"Sexual needs," Caleb reiterated, pulling her down onto his lap. "Exactly."

Allie shot Slade a glare. "You don't have to sound so excited about it. One of you is more than enough for me."

She was rather proud of the way she kept her voice steady, because in reality, the thought of every man in her vicinity wanting to stake a claim was terrifying. Heat seared her face at the images that might be going through their minds at that very minute. She cut off the imaginings and gritted her teeth against the tremendous, totally understandable urge to flee. She wasn't talking bookworms and geeks after all. Every man she'd seen for the last three weeks was a walking ad for muscular, testosterone-laden perfection. Which had been intimidating enough when she'd thought they saw her as part of the woodwork or as a duty to get through. Knowing they now saw her as some sort of sexual toy up for grabs sent chills chasing the hunger prowling through her being.

Slade shook his head and flicked a crumb from the edge of the table. "I'm excited about the clues being put together. I'm not excited about wanting my brother's woman."

She believed him. There couldn't be a worse hell for the brothers than an urge to turn on each other. Because of her. She didn't know what to say except, "I'm sorry."

Caleb pulled her back against the solid muscle of his abdomen. His hands cupped her shoulders, the fingers spreading down over her collarbone, moving back and forth with soothing regularity. "It's not your fault, Allie."

"You keep telling me that." She traced an old nick in the maple tabletop. The warmth of his touch did not reach the cold hollow deep inside. Who knew her talent for disaster would follow her into immortality? "But every time I turn around, I'm causing some upheaval in your existence."

"A little shaking up is good for us."

A little maybe, but this was ruining his life. She glanced up. Derek and Jace's gazes were locked on Caleb's fingers, their faces etched with an unsettling heat. She glanced down. The third button on her shirt had come unbuttoned, exposing the beginning of cleavage. She reached for it, watching their faces as she did so, noting the way their throats worked as they swallowed, watched as Derek's tongue dampened his lips and felt his lust as clearly as she felt Caleb's. Above her, Caleb's "Son of a bitch" grated through the heavy silence.

She fastened the button with fingers that shook, her mind racing a hundred miles an hour. This wasn't good. Couldn't be good. Couldn't end well. She scooted from under Caleb's grasp, getting to her feet, shaking her head when he would have pulled her to him, unable to ignore any longer the threat surrounding her, wanting nothing more than to go back one hour in time to when she'd had the bliss of ignorance.

"Allie."

She shook her head. "Not now, Caleb."

"No one's going to hurt you."

"I know." At least logically she did, but there was another part of her, one primitively feminine, that told her to get away, to hide. "I just need some privacy."

Jace's "For what?" ended in a grunt as Derek's elbow connected with his rib cage. The small violence chafed her restraint. Her senses, so much more acute than they used to be, fed that kernel of panic with the increased scent of male interest, the accelerated heartbeats, the deeper rasp of breaths drawn too fast. It caught them all and amplified them, a warning attached to every sensory trickle. *Run!*

She didn't run, but she did walk very steadily out of the room. When she hit the stairs, she let go, burning off the edge of adrenaline with a rapid ascent, forcing herself to slow when she reached the top, to avoid the board that squeaked in front of the first bedroom door, to sedately progress to the door where her and Caleb's bedroom was located. The Johnson brothers were not a threat and she wasn't going to let her crazy imagination make them into one.

"SHE'S not safe with us, Caleb."

"So it would appear." He just didn't believe it. The scent of Allie's panic lingered in the wake of her flight. Upstairs a door closed too slowly. As if the person closing it was making a point. Caleb wondered who was supposed to absorb it, Allie or himself. He looked over at Slade. "What I want to know is, what's changed?"

"I don't know."

"That wasn't the answer I was looking for."

Slade shrugged. "It's the only one I've got."

"You find anything out from that damn Internet?"

"Beyond the fact there are more myths surrounding vampires than fact? No."

"Dig deeper."

"There's only so deep I can go without rousing interest from parties like the D'Nallys."

"Shit."

"We could ask that bunch of loco weeds over on the other side of the mountain."

"About all they'd do is try to convert her to their religion." And he did not need Allie experimenting with that group's sort of altered reality.

"Heck, they're not even talking to us after Jared tossed that too-pretty wannabe out on his ass when he approached him for a special time."

"Still, they have a lot more contact with other vampires."

"Anyone ever see them with a converted female?" Caleb asked.

He hadn't seen any and wasn't surprised when his brothers shook their heads. He glanced at Derek. The were shrugged. "It's hard to say for sure because they get trigger happy when anyone gets near, but no were in these parts has ever seen a vampire female. Or if they have, have never mentioned it."

And they would have mentioned it. Of that Caleb was sure. He took a breath, scanning for Allie. She was in their room. Upset, hungry, and trying not to show either. "Then they have no more experience than we do. That being the case, there's no sense alerting them to Allie's presence."

Jared nodded. "I agree. Even if they are more prone to spit philosophy than bullets, we don't need to take chances. Especially if her effect is the same on all males."

Derek's chair creaked as he turned it and straddled it. "There's another possibility that might explain what's happening."

"What?"

He draped his arms across the back. "When a packmate gets . . . in the family way, instinct drives the mother to separate herself."

"Why?" Jace asked.

"A fertile female is a very valuable commodity. Worth any cost to steal."

"Again, why? If you can make as many weres as you want, why is pregnancy so special?"

"We can't."

"Can't what?"

"Make as many weres as we want. It's a rare human that can be converted, but most just die, poisoned by the bite rather than converted."

"Shit." Caleb hadn't known that. "But some can be converted?"

"Yeah."

"And to think we thought all we had to worry about was rabies."

Caleb cut Jace a glare before turning his attention back to Derek. "How do you know if a human can be converted?"

Derek shrugged. "Pretty much, it's just instinct."

"Anyone ever guessed wrong?" Jace asked.

The twist of Derek's mouth told the story. "Enough that anyone trying to convert a human these days faces execution."

"Which doesn't explain why pregnant females go into isolation," Slade pointed out.

"Weres mate for life and only mated pairs have a prayer of bearing offspring."

"Not following your point."

"Mating with a fertile female means pack position and power. Anyone wanting that power has to kill the original male and all his offspring to insure the propagation of his own line," Derek explained, the expression on his face not exactly reflecting happiness with the way things were.

"Son of a bitch!"

Caleb glanced at his younger brother. "Jace?"

Jace didn't seem to hear, his attention focused inward, his lips pressed into a flat line, his eyes swirling with angry lights. Caleb repeated his name. "Jace? You all right?"

Jace ran his hand through his hair. "I'm fine." He turned to Derek. "How long will a female stay in hiding?"

"As long as she has to."

"Hell!"

"Anything you want to share, Jace?" Damn, Caleb hoped Jace hadn't been messing with were women again. With everything else going on, they did not need an escalation of the war.

Jace met his gaze dead-on. "No."

Derek glanced over at Caleb, one eyebrow quirking upward. "Could Allie be pregnant?"

The question hit him like a fist in the gut, driving his breath out in a harsh grunt. Could she be pregnant? Did vampires even get pregnant? "I don't know."

"Don't know if she's pregnant or if she could get pregnant?"

"Either." He'd never even considered the possibility. He turned to Slade. "Can a male vampire get a female vampire pregnant?"

"How the hell should I know? Procreation hasn't been a subject that's ever come up before."

"You've been the one looking up all the lore."

"You know what I know. According to lore, which isn't exactly science, vampires are sterile."

Shit! Caleb ran his hand through his hair, resting his hand on the back of his neck, squeezing hard as what Slade said sank in. He'd been making love for centuries under the assumption—*the assumption*—that he couldn't get a woman pregnant. Goddamn it all to hell. Could Allie be pregnant?

"It would explain a lot of things," Jared said.

"For what it's worth, I've never heard of a vampire mating resulting in offspring," Derek offered.

Caleb ran his hand through his hair again, ripping through a snarl, frustration, elation, hope, and panic all combining in his gut. Maybe it wasn't possible for a female vampire to get pregnant, but he'd taken Allie as a human, part changed, granted, but part human still. Maybe human enough to conceive.

"A vampire baby?" He took a breath, struggling to contain the elation that soared. A child. He might have a child. He settled his hat back on his head, reaching for steady when all he wanted to do was shout with joy. Damn, a baby. Maybe even a little Allie. Wouldn't that be something? He hadn't been around a baby since Jace was born. They were tiny little things. Delicate. Helpless. Would a vampire baby be bigger? Grow faster? Sure enough it would still need its parents. It took everything he had to keep his drawl neutral. "What the hell would that even look like?"

"Like us."

The hoarse, angry whisper snapped into the room. Caleb turned. Allie stood in the doorway, feathers bobbing on her head, her fingers gripping the jamb until the knuckles showed white, and all the pain in the world glaring at him from her big blue eyes.

Shit.

❧ 13 ❧

"**H**OW long were you standing there?" Caleb asked.

Allie pushed away from the wall. Her hands clenching into fists at her side. "Long enough to know that beneath the vampire, men are still men."

He took a step toward her. "Allie girl . . ."

"Don't."

The wave of her hand was supposed to warn him off, but if she thought that was enough to keep him from her when she was hurting, she had another thing coming. As soon as he got within striking distance, she lashed out. He caught her wrist in his hand. Spinning her around was easy considering she'd put everything she had into that blow. He grabbed her other hand and crossed her arms over her torso, pulling her back against him, wincing when her heel connected with his shin.

"Let me go."

"No. You're hurting."

"You called our baby a freak."

Her head snapped back into his face, striking squarely on his chin. Stars exploded between his eyes. "Son of a bitch!"

Behind him, chairs scraped across the floor. Slade reached for her. "Allie—"

Caleb motioned him back, sinking to the floor, taking Allie with him. She didn't make it easy, fighting him all the way, her pain striking him harder than any blow could have. She thought he didn't want their baby. He braced his back against the wall, turning Allie in his arms as he sat, keeping her arms pinned to her torso with one arm as, with the other, he gripped her chin, bringing her gaze to his. Her mouth worked. "If you spit at me, I swear to God, Allie Johnson, I'll strip you right here and paddle that lush little ass of yours."

She didn't spit, but none of the mutiny left her face. "Sanders! It's Allie Sanders!"

"Call yourself whatever you want, it doesn't change the facts."

"Any more than any two-stepping you do now changes the fact that you don't want our baby."

Not want their baby? He shook his head. She couldn't be more wrong. "Open those ears, and hear me good. For over two hundred years I've lived with the thought that this is as good as it got, one day blending into another. No kids, no wife, and no hope. Just a future that plods on like a horse heading to the next stop."

"So?"

"So, you stubborn woman, *if*, and it's a mighty big if, you are somehow miraculously carrying my child, then I have a reason to go on. One that I never thought I'd get."

"Which means?"

"I want my Goddamn baby!"

"What if it looks like a freak?"

Son of a bitch, she was pushing him. He tilted her head back and his anger disappeared as if it had never existed, because beneath the challenge and anger, he saw the fear and hurt that tore her apart. The same hope and hurt that lodged in him when he looked into her face and she denied the permanence of their relationship.

A tear spilled down her cheek, her lips thinned, and her chin came up as if sheer force of will could dispel that moment of weakness. He stroked his thumb over her cheek, catching that tear on the pad, watching it spread as it hit the grooves. The next stroke smoothed the salty drop into her skin. Another tear hovered, ready to fall. "I want the child, Allie. Red, blue, or riddled with polka dots, I want my child. More than you can ever comprehend."

Doubt clung to her expression, but she wanted to believe him. He could feel it. He closed the small distance that stretched like a canyon between them, need and desire making up equal parts of a kiss initially more pressure than passion.

Allie had to believe him. Her lips were still under his, passively resisting his demand. His gut wrenched. Allie was never passive. He pulled back a millimeter, allowing just enough space that a breath of air could get through. He tightened his grip, pulling her deeper into his embrace, as if eliminating the physical distance between them could do something about the mental distance she was establishing.

His "You can believe me, baby" bridged the chasm, riding the lingering moisture and emotion, spreading across her mouth, slipping inside as her lips parted on a breath. He closed the gap, fitting his lips to hers, edge to edge, seam to seam. Delicately. Gently. Respectfully. Because, dear God, she deserved it. He tried to keep the passion out of the moment, tried to convey what she meant to him through the kiss because her mind was closed to him.

And she let him, just lying against him, allowing him to do what he wanted. As if it didn't matter—he didn't matter—and then, when desperation was at its peak and his vampire was howling at him to force her compliance, her lips moved. Tentatively at first, little more than a soft fluttering, but then they parted, relaxing all the way, inviting him in.

He didn't hesitate. He thrust his tongue into the dark warmth, claiming it as his, claiming her as his, dragging her closer, needing her to be closer, wanting to draw her so deeply inside him she wouldn't be able to hold herself separately again.

When he pulled back, she was looking at him with bruised lips and eyes that showed the bruise on her soul. He balanced her chin on his forefinger, sliding his thumb into the moisture lingering on the lower curve, pulling her lip down until the white edge of her teeth peeked at him. Another tear hovered, ready to fall. "These tears are unnecessary."

Her hand came up to circle his wrist. Her gaze clung to his with the same uncertainty. "I'm scared."

That soft confession gouged his soul. His indomitable Allie was afraid. "There's nothing to be scared of."

"If I'm pregnant there's a whole heck of a lot to terrify me."

"I'll take care of you."

"Unless you have a set of initials after your name that read OB/GYN, I don't think your care will do me much good."

He stroked his thumb along the edge of her lip. "I'm your husband."

"Lover."

She could split hairs all she wanted, it didn't change the facts. She was his future, and he was hers. "I'm all you have. Initials or not."

"That's not a comfort."

He knew that, too. "Comfort or not, it's what you've got."

Her eyes narrowed. Her grip on his wrist stayed firm, but something in her eyes softened, giving him hope.

"I won't fail you, Allie girl."

"You realize, of course, that I have absolutely no reason to believe, even if you mean it, that your promise is going to be enough."

"True."

Her gaze clung to his, the fringes of her mind stretching to enfold his. He felt her anger, her frustration, but mostly her hope. "So why in the hell do I believe you?"

"Because I don't lie."

She was shaking her head before he finished the sentence. "That's not it."

"Are you saying I lie?"

"I'm saying your honesty, or lack thereof, is not part of the equation."

"Then why do you think you believe me?"

No minute was ever longer than the one she subjected him to as she studied him, her lips pursing around his finger with the rhythm of her thoughts. She couldn't really believe him. Logic said he was the devil to her angel, the evil to her good, but as he sat there as each second passed, more and more of him wanted her belief. Her trust. Shit, he was as irrational as she was.

"I trust you for the same reason I came back for you after the wolf ripped your throat out." She touched the scar on her finger, permanent because he willed it so. "I trust you because my gut tells me to."

Caleb wrapped his arms around her, pulling her into his embrace, pressing her face to his chest, breathing in her scent, making it part of him, gratitude to whomever had given him this woman flowing out of him on a silent prayer of thanks. "Then you, Allie Johnson, are a damn fool."

SHE wasn't a fool. Her family thought her dead. Her vampirism made her into something she didn't recognize, she might be pregnant, and all she had to cling to was Caleb, but she wasn't a fool. She was a fish temporarily out of water, but even flopping around as she was, searching for her place, she could see the pluses and minuses of Caleb's logic. The major plus being the baby's father. There was nothing more solid than Caleb. No more cohesive a group than the Johnsons. However, a baby was going to change everything. Raise the stakes in whatever game the vampires and weres were playing. Raise them beyond petty back and forth or hostilities. Allie lifted her head from Caleb's chest, ignored the stares of the men around her, and looked up at Caleb. "You are not going to be enough."

"You've got my family, too."

She shook her head. "Who have just declared they're as big a threat as anything else."

"That's not true," said Jared.

"What's changed?" she asked.

"The possibility you might be pregnant."

"According to Derek, that will just make things uglier."

"Where we come from, family sticks together."

"You're talking pre-vampire days."

Jared folded his hands across his chest. "Vampire or not, kin is kin."

And that apparently was that as far as the Johnson brothers were concerned. She was beginning to appreciate their black-and-white view on some things. Her attempt to slide free of Caleb's embrace got her nowhere. She glanced pointedly at his arm around her waist. "Do you mind?"

He shook his head. "Your hunger is returning."

Like she didn't know that. "That's why I came back down here, to let you know."

"And instead you ended up hearing what you shouldn't have."

"I'd say I came back just in time to hear what I needed to." She pinched his arm, letting him know with her eyes that she could pinch harder if he didn't see reason. "Let me go."

"I'm feeling a bit protective right now, so you probably want to be humoring me."

"This millennium protective, or eighteen sixties protective?"

His hand dropped to her stomach, cupping the flat surface. As light as his touch was, it didn't diminish the depth of the emotion behind it.

"Definitely eighteen sixties."

"Well, hell." She let go of his arm. A pinch wasn't going to get her around that. A glance around showed all the brothers looking at her with the same protect-with-their-lives intensity. "You realize

I'm the same woman you were lusting after fifteen minutes ago, right? Nothing's changed."

The only satisfaction she got was an infinitesimal flick of their gazes from hers. A reflection of shame for the emotions they hadn't been able to avoid feeling. From everyone except Derek. He was still arrogant and still amused.

"Sweet thing, if you don't know that, for the brothers, everything's changed, then you don't know your men."

"Nothing's definite."

"Sometimes potential means as much as reality."

Again that subtle tension entered Caleb's muscles as he asked, "But not for you?"

Derek shrugged. "I don't have your upbringing. To me, her pregnancy just makes her more attractive."

Caleb set her aside. He came to his feet in a slow, deadly uncoiling of muscle and intent. "That kind of honesty will likely get you killed."

Derek's right eyebrow cocked up. "Or that kind of honesty could just make me a werewolf."

Caleb held out his hand. She took it. He pulled her to her feet and to his side. Derek continued to stare and the tension continued to build. Against her, Allie felt the rumble begin in Caleb's chest. Dead. The wolf was going to be dead. Caleb's talons pressed into her hand. Across the room, Derek sat and watched, no equivalent tension in him, which could only mean one thing. He was testing Caleb. For what? There were so many undercurrents here that she didn't understand, so many layers to the relationships to which she didn't have a clue. She didn't look away, just kept her eyes locked on Derek's. "Caleb?"

"What?"

"You're jealous for no reason. Derek would never betray a friend. He's just not the type."

"And you know this how?" It was Derek who asked, a barely detectable flicker in his lids betraying his surprise. Surprise at her direct action or for knowing what he was up to?

"The same way Caleb does once he gets past his first emotional response. Instinct."

"You think Caleb's emotional?" Jared asked, a level of amusement in his voice she recognized from dealing with her brothers. He was working up to harassing Caleb. She could put an end to it, but Caleb deserved harassing for a lot of things and payback could be a bitch.

"He has a tendency to lean that way."

"The hell I do."

"I think that growl just might count as exhibit A," Slade offered.

"I definitely think so," Jace tossed in.

"Never thought of it before, but he is prone to yelling."

"Jared, shut the hell up."

Derek caught her eye and gave a little nod, and then she understood. It wasn't Caleb he was testing, but her.

She shook her head. Another layer to add to the growing pile. "You are all nuts."

Caleb loosened his grip, his hand reaching up toward the feathers bouncing on top of her head. "Says the woman with feathers on her head."

She stepped quickly away, the sense of inadequacy coming back. "Feathers or not, we need to talk."

He smiled, a humor-the-little-woman smile. The one that set her teeth on edge.

"I'm going to have a hard time taking you seriously with those feathers waving about."

"Oh, I don't know," Slade interjected. "She looks a bit like a hurdy-gurdy girl from the good old days."

"Hurdy-gurdy girls?"

Caleb's expression went from amused to cautious in one blink. There could only be one reason for that. Allie put her hand on her hip and sashayed a step forward. "Did you like hurdy-gurdy girls, Caleb?"

"Like? Hell." Jace laughed. "He kept them in feathers."

She had a hard time picturing that. Allie simply could not see a man like Caleb having to pay for sex. "Really?"

"Jace is exaggerating." The glare Caleb shot Jace said the opposite.

Jace just shrugged. The grin tugging his lips lightening his expression, giving her a clue to how he must have been before the whole conversion happened. Bold, reckless, and a good time on two feet. "Big Red was always real happy to see you."

"The way I remember it," Jared cut in, crumbling the edge of a pastry, "Caleb was always paying her to stay off his lap."

"The woman weighed about three hundred pounds."

Allie dodged Caleb's hand again. The gleam in his eyes didn't bode well for her continued success. "You don't like big women?"

"Don't go there," Derek warned.

"Wasn't planning on it," Caleb drawled. She scooted past him to the stove, secretly disappointed when he didn't lunge, her heart beating as if he had.

"Seriously, if I get big as a barn, are you planning to push me off your lap?"

"If he does, I'll be there to catch you."

She gave Derek a sweet smile. "Thank you." She turned back to Caleb. "You didn't answer my question."

"Probably because it's not relevant." He folded his arms across his chest, the biceps bunching with the move. "Vampires don't get fat."

"You're always telling me what vampires can and cannot do, one thing being that vampires don't get pregnant." She spread her hands wide, jumping back a step when he straightened. "Yet, here I stand, potentially knocked-up, unwed, undead, and with no visible means of support." She shrugged. "Go figure."

Hands caught her from behind. Masculine laughter surrounded

her shriek. She had a glimpse of Jared's face before he passed her to Slade who then passed her to Jace who in turn passed her to Caleb, who accepted her weight with a very superior smile and a soft kiss. "You've got lots of support."

Allie relaxed into Caleb's hold, and glared at Jared. "That was so unfair."

"What Caleb wants, I tend to see he gets."

"That doesn't make it right."

"I'm not overly concerned with right."

She'd remember that for future reference. She tilted her head back to look at Caleb. He was looking at her, making no attempt to hide his smile. "And it's very uncool to gloat."

"I'll remember that."

He might remember it, but she didn't think he intended to do anything with it. Just like she didn't think he intended to put her down anytime soon. Which wasn't a good thing, as this close, she couldn't avoid the temptation of his scent.

Her stomach clenched and the familiar pain resumed its slow inner grind. Her ears hyperfocused on the slow beat of his heart, the whoosh of his blood through the valves, the steady in and out of his breath. Humor fled with the intrusion of reality. She was a vampire. She might be having a vampire child, and she was completely dependent on this man. And she had no idea what that meant. She needed answers. "Put me down."

"What's wrong?"

"I just remembered that I'm totally screwed."

Caleb shifted her weight, but he didn't put her down. "You're not screwed."

She shrugged, working her arm deeper against his side, seeking a bit of leverage. "That's a matter of opinion."

Her elbow anchored on his hip bone. With a push and a twist she threw herself out of his arms. Unfortunately, without the grace she would have preferred. She landed in a heap at his feet.

As one, the men swore, Caleb's "Son of a bitch" louder than the rest, or maybe just more audible to her ears. She'd noticed over the last week that her senses seemed to focus in on him. He was beside her in an instant, fingers pressing along her hips as he searched for breaks. "That was a damn stupid thing to do."

She waved his hand aside. "I'm fine. And it's not as stupid as tossing me about like a sack of grain."

He tipped her chin up and looked her in the eye. "The difference is I'd never drop you."

No he wouldn't. She touched his wrist, her finger on his pulse. "I know."

His boot scuffed the floor as he shifted position. "Do you hurt anywhere?"

She couldn't look away from his eyes. There was something different about the way he was watching her. "My pride's smarting."

"Want me to kiss it and make it better?"

"At the risk of ruining my chances with you, I'm going to agree with the Johnsons on this." Derek stood apart from the brothers. Just one step back, but it was an important foot. It marked him as an outsider. "That was dumb."

The hunger writhed within, diminishing her retort to a squeaky gasp. This time Caleb didn't bother with a hand. He grabbed her upper arm and hoisted her up. She twisted her arm free as soon as she found her feet. Her immediate stumble was a bit of a setback in her capable-woman moment, but she caught herself without any further need for assistance. Thank goodness. She might be a klutz, but she didn't want to prove it beyond a shadow of a doubt with five hunky men in the room. She was dead, but not that dead. "We need to stop fighting among ourselves."

Caleb folded his arms across his broad chest while he watched her like a hawk. "I wasn't aware we were."

She tried to cock an eyebrow at him like he did to her, but it didn't work. From the quirk of his lips, about all she'd accomplished was to contort her face into an amusing caricature. So much for that. She waved her hand, the gesture encompassing all the men in the room. "Everyone here is family, including Derek, and I think we need to keep that knowledge above the weird emotional stuff going on."

Caleb didn't immediately agree. Did he disagree with her statement or was his objection routed in her inclusion of Derek into the Johnson family circle? She folded her arms across her chest. "Whether it goes with your code or not, Caleb, Derek and all the weres that are here are family. You treat them like family. They treat you like family, so you might as well call them family."

Still no response. "I mean it, Caleb."

Caleb cocked up his hand, stopping her argument. "I'm not arguing with you."

"You're not agreeing either."

"Probably because the objections to Derek being family aren't mine."

Across the room, a board squeaked, the only indication Derek had moved. Allie couldn't believe it. But the answer was there on his face. "You're the one with issues?"

"Our friendship with the Johnsons has already put our pack on the fringe of ostracism. An allegiance would not be accepted."

"By whom?"

"Other weres."

"You socialize with other werewolves?"

"Yes."

"As in there's a hierarchy of werewolves, a network beyond the Circle J?"

"Of course."

A flicker of movement in her peripheral vision warned her. "Don't you dare tell him to shut up, Caleb."

He palmed her buttocks. The fingers lingered way past casual. "You're getting too big for your britches."

"Impossible. You just told me I couldn't get fat."

The fingers pressed. "Damn convenient time you picked to get literal."

She flashed him a smile, liking the way his eyes smiled back with that certain difference she couldn't quite place. "Just trying to follow the rules you set out."

The pressure grew and she took a step closer. Closer to that smile. Closer to that certain intriguing something.

"I'm thinking any sign of cooperation on your part is a reason for a man to start checking for ambush."

His right hand joined his left.

"Oh, puh-lease." She rubbed her stomach, pressing her knuckles against the spasms. "So if the werewolves have a hierarchy, do the vampires?"

Slade's "No" was way too quick. The way a man bent on hiding something would answer. She stared at Caleb, waiting. He cocked his eyebrow. She pressed harder on her stomach, suppressing the pain through sheer force of will.

"In a minute I'm going to start puking, and if you don't tell me what's going on, you're going to be the first to take the brunt of it."

His second eyebrow joined the first. His hand covered hers. "I've been puked on by the best. As threats go, you're going to have to do better."

As always, under his touch, the pain grew more manageable. "Is that a challenge?"

He moved her hand aside, sliding his beneath. She almost groaned with relief from the heat that radiated inward.

"Merely a statement of fact." She squeezed Caleb's fingers, holding on as she unleashed the fears eating her alive.

Fingers.

"I don't really have any threats."

"Then what do you have?" Slade asked, his eyes narrowing.

"A lot of fears and a need for answers. A lot of them."

"What's your main concern?" Derek asked.

"That if you don't make peace with the D'Nallys, form strong alliances with the others around you, that the something that's out there, whatever it is that controls the voices that invade my mind, is going to get in here. Get to my child." She took a breath. "That terrifies me."

Caleb swore. His arm around her tightened. She hated putting pressure on him, but at the same time, it couldn't be helped. This couldn't continue.

"That would terrify anyone," Jared agreed.

Caleb ran his hand through his hair. She felt bereft without both his hands around her. Damn, it couldn't be good the way she was coming to depend on him. "I'm not sure an alliance with the D'Nallys is possible."

Derek nodded. "They are pissed."

"Why?" Allie asked.

No one answered. Probably because no one knew. She sighed. "Then maybe that answer should be where you start."

Jace shifted in his seat. "I'll give talking to them a shot."

"I thought you were more interested in irritating them than talking to them," Caleb said.

Jace shrugged, staring out the window as if what he was searching for was just past the glass pane. "Allie's right. If we're going to start being family men, things need to change."

"We?" Caleb asked with an arch of his brow.

Jace cut Allie a glance. There was a pain in his eyes that made her want to reach out and offer comfort. "If you found a mate, it stands to reason there's hope for the rest of us."

"Hope." Derek rapped his fingers on the table once. "Welcome to the world of the werewolf."

"Except we're vampires," Slade pointed out with that infallible logic of his.

"As I've said before, not that anyone would notice."

Allie rubbed the mark on her finger. "Except for the people you bite."

"You don't think a were knows how to mark his mate?" Derek asked, amusement in his expression and his voice.

She rolled her eyes. "I'm sure they know all sorts of archaic chauvinistic things, none of which is pertinent to the situation at hand."

"And what would be pertinent?"

The words rushed to her throat, clogging on the last of her control. Control that was destroyed by the simple brush of Caleb's lips across her hair. "Say what you need to say, baby."

He wanted to hear it? She looked around to find them all watching her. They all wanted to hear it? Fine. They could hear it.

"Okay. How about this? My gut says I'm pregnant. As crazy as that sounds, as impossible as it sounds, I really think I am. When I get really sick, I hear voices calling me, demanding that I come, and I have a really strong need to go, but my gut tells me there's danger, but I don't know from where, I don't know from whom, and because all of you keep me so damn protected and in the dark, I'm pretty sure I'm about to do something stupid on the way to find out, because I simply can't live like this, afraid of every shadow because I don't know what's real and what's not."

That quick she was wrapped tight against Caleb, his chin brushed her head, his lips her ear. "Shit." She dug her nails into his arm, holding him to her because now that her fears were put into words, they had so much more force. "You all have that sum-it-up-in-one-word thing down pat, but right now I need explanations. Facts. Answers."

"We'll get your answers," Caleb promised.

"Though it'll take time," Derek warned.

"Because you're afraid who may be watching?"

"Pretty much."

"It's too easy these days for people to track inquiries."

"What people?"

"Any people."

This was getting worse by the minute. "You don't even have specific enemies?"

"Technology has allowed a lot of people to explore their fascina-
tions."

And vampires were fascinating to humans. "But who is speaking
in my head?"

"It has to be the Sanctuary," Jace said, leaning back in his chair.

"What's the Sanctuary?"

No one answered.

"If it is the Sanctuary, we've seriously underestimated them."
Slade drummed his fingers on the table. "They shouldn't be able to
lock on her at will."

"No shit." Caleb looked at Derek. "Any input?"

"The Sanctuary is a very large group of vamps, but no one's ever
found them to be dangerous."

"And?"

"Hell if I know." Derek shrugged. "They're a weird bunch. They
spend a lot of time chanting and studying. They've left you all
alone because you pretty much haven't been of interest, holed up as
you are here in your neck of the woods training horses and acting
human. But bringing in a woman, especially a pregnant one, would
catch their interest. They make a science of studying everything
vampire."

Allie couldn't believe it. There were other vampires out there
close enough to visit. Vampires who might have answers to the questions she needed. She glared at Caleb. "You've been holding out on
me."

He waved her accusation aside. "They're fanatics."

They could worship the color yellow and she didn't care as long
as they could shed some light on her current situation. "You mean a
bunch of fanatics who have made it their eternal life's mission to
understand their vampirism?"

"At least their version of it," Derek responded.

"At this point, anything is better than nothing. And nothing is
all you've got to offer me when it comes to information about what's
going on with my conversion."

Derek shook his head and blew out a skeptical breath. "As a source of information, I'd say they're questionable. Their beliefs are more than a little skewed."

"But they might have insight as to what's going on with me."

"Or they might just decide you're a sinner in need of redemption."

"Talking to them would be worth a shot."

Caleb's "No" was emphatic. She didn't care. "I need answers, Caleb. If a bunch of whacked-out religious fanatics have them, I'm all up for paying them a visit."

"I might be able to shed a little light on your situation," Slade interrupted.

"You have a theory?" Caleb asked.

Slade nodded and leaned forward over the table, elbows braced, fingers tented, excitement lighting his deep hazel eyes. "Every one of us changed when we converted. Whatever we had before got better. Stands to reason the same would have happened to Allie."

She blew her bangs off her forehead, touching her feathers self-consciously. It was embarrassing. "I don't think I got anything."

Caleb shook his head and pushed off the counter, taking her with him, tucking her into his side in a smooth move. "You're doing just fine, Allie. We just haven't discovered your secrets yet."

"I can't change even into the simplest thing, can't even feed like a normal vamp. How is that fine?"

This time when Caleb touched her chin, she tipped her face up, leaning into his side. She really needed to hear something good about herself right now.

"You, baby, can do something better."

"What's that?"

His mouth softened. He cupped the curve of her belly. Right on the extra five pounds she blamed completely on her pre-vampire addiction to chocolate. The only thing that kept her from flinching self-consciously away was that expression in his eyes.

"You can make miracles happen."

❧ 14 ❦

"**H**ER ability to make miracles might be the reason for her failures at other things," Slade continued. "For example, I can't think it would be healthy for the baby for a pregnant woman to shift."

"Oh God, did I hurt the baby?"

Slade shook his head. "That's my point. Your body's not letting you do anything that will hurt the baby."

Allie's fingertips rubbed nervously over the back of Caleb's hand. "Explain."

"Everything about vamps ties to blood. What if you can't feed from anyone but Caleb because it's meant to be that way?"

"I fed from Jared."

"Just that once and it might have been too early in the pregnancy for there to be a problem."

Jace frowned. "Hell, that was only the day after she got here."

"Exactly." Slade just sat there, eyebrows raised, waiting.

"How would that make a differ—" Jace looked at Caleb, understanding replacing confusion as he dropped his gaze to their linked hands and then back up. "And here I thought turning vampire had slowed you down."

One by one the men looked at her, then Caleb, and then back to her again. A blush seared from the inside out heating Allie's cheeks until they felt like they were on fire. "What?"

"Allie . . ."

She ignored Caleb's warning. There were times when a woman just had to brazen things out. "Are you going to stand there and say you don't have a sex life?"

Jace laughed. "Hardly."

Slade looked offended. "No."

Jared was to the point. "Sure as shit not."

He looked her over from head to toe. The last of the bear claw crumbled onto the table before him. The corner of his mouth twitched. "Though I can't say I ever indulged in the middle of a conversion."

She held her ground and tilted up her chin. "What makes you think I did?"

"Allie?"

She turned on Caleb. "There's no way he can know when . . ."

"Jared's gift is an ability to read minds."

She slapped his arm, mortification rising with nausea at the reminder. "Do *not* tell me he knows what we did."

Caleb looked at Jared, who shrugged. That didn't bode well. "It's likely."

She dug her nails into her stomach as the hunger dug deep, then twisted around in exasperation. "What part of 'do not tell me' slipped your notice?"

"The middle part." The back of his fingers brushed down her cheek in a featherlight caress, pausing when they reached her neck, rubbing twice before reversing course. "You need to feed, Allie."

"Not yet."

"Yet."

She shook her head. The feathers bounced, tickling her skin.

No wonder no one was listening to her. She still looked like a reject from the cuckoo nest. "I would like to get rid of these feathers first."

It was a little thing, but she needed to be in control of something.

"I thought you liked them?"

"Don't be an ass. You know damn well I just can't figure out how to get rid of them without risking another catastrophe."

Jared shook his head and pushed his chair back. "You, woman, are a menace."

"That is *so* rude."

Caleb caught her as the hunger bent her double. His hand slipped beneath hers to massage the tight muscles, his body served as a brace for hers. She panted through the pain, wincing as the feathers stabbed into her head as she pressed it against him. "How do birds wear these things?"

The world tilted and another pain stabbed deep as Caleb adjusted her in his lap. Immediately, his hands were there, soothing and warm. Caring for her. He was always caring for her and she did nothing in return.

"Allie?"

Caleb's deep drawl threaded through her concentration. The pain ebbed, flooding Caleb's determination. He wasn't happy with her right now. "What?"

"How long do you think I'm going to let your suffering continue?"

"Long enough for me to get rid of the feathers?"

A boot toe invaded her vision. It was scuffed, worn, and tough. Like its owner.

"I can help you with that," Jared offered.

He could if she was willing to let him into her mind. In light of everything that had been revealed this evening, she was a little leery of that. She rested her cheek against Caleb's shoulder and worked through the fear with logic. As tough as Jared was, he wasn't a match for Caleb. Jared burned with a restless edge, but Caleb wore his strength like others wore hats, with an easy confidence. That being the case, she really didn't have to be nervous of Jared's intent. But she was, though she knew Caleb would never let anyone hurt her. She'd never get used to having someone else poking around in her mind, but if she wanted the feathers gone, she'd have to allow it.

"Is there another way?"

Caleb's hand slid up beneath her hair to rub subtly at the tension in her neck. "You want them gone?"

She titled her head back. The smile lurking in his gaze snatched the sharpness out of her retort. "Don't you?"

The smile fanned out from the corner of his eyes in sexy creases, adding an intriguing maturity to his innate handsomeness. This was a man who'd lived before and after he'd been converted. This was a man who knew what he wanted and wasn't afraid to go after it. "I think they're kind of cute in a different sort of way."

This was the man who wanted her. The caressing fingers spread until the breadth of his palm settled behind her skull, not demanding, just resting there in an invitation, leaving it up to her whether to accept it or not. She didn't hesitate. She let him support her, understanding that, for him, the need to do so went much deeper than this moment.

He saw their relationship as a new beginning. For a man who'd lost everything, rebuilt his life, and then lost it all again, that was huge. "I'm different enough, thank you very much."

His thumb stroked her jawline, and the shake of his head negated her stab at humor. "There's not a damn thing wrong with you."

"Only you would say that."

The corner of his mouth lifted. The warmth of his touch spread deeper. "Only you would think that."

She shook her head. She was a perfectly normal woman. "Nuh-uh."

The other corner of his mouth joined the first. His lids lowered and the sexy grin shot straight to her core, adding the pang of desire to the hunger churning inside. His thumb came to rest on the pulse point just under her jaw. "How about we let Jared take care of those feathers, and then I'll take you upstairs and work on proving it."

The suggestion sucked her mouth dry.

"I'm willing to do my part." Jared squatted beside her. His calloused hand cupped her cheek, strong like Caleb's but without the heat. "Look at me, Allie."

She did for the simple reason that she couldn't do anything else beneath his compulsion. In his hazel irises the swirls gathered, took shape, highlighting the intriguing flecks of blue and green. The deeper she stared, the more she knew she should understand what she was seeing.

"Focus."

The order swirled around her in a hollow echo, tugging at her will from all directions. Jared's eyes flared with silver lights, so different from Caleb's. She reached up and grabbed for his wrist. She didn't like this.

Caleb caught her hand and folded her fingers in his. "Trust him, baby."

Easy for him to say. He wasn't the one feeling like his mind was being tossed out into a black ocean of nothingness.

"Not nothingness, Allie." The words skimmed the surface of her conscious.

"No." She fumbled along the waves blindly, swimming toward Caleb's voice. It wasn't nothingness.

"Find the pattern," Jared ordered, his voice resounding like thunder in her head.

Pattern? There was supposed to be a pattern in this? She didn't see any pattern, just an overwhelming darkness and disjointed waves of energy that threw her about, shoving her toward the center of the darkness that locked on her like a winch, pulling her in. Panic clawed at her mind. She didn't want to go there.

Breathe.

Caleb's strength flowed through the chaos, a solid ribbon of energy. She grabbed hold, clung to what she couldn't see, refused to let go, searched for that "something more" that waited just beyond her mind's eye. The foreign pull kicked up its power, endangering her grip. She fought it and fought Caleb's efforts to slip free. She didn't want to be alone in this.

Try.

She could feel him letting go. *No!*

It was too late. Caleb let go and she had no choice. She was on her own. Panic and determination warred for dominance. Determination won. She could do this. She would do this. She shoved at the curtain in her mind. There. In a corner of the impenetrable blackness, a fleck of gray. She dove toward it, focusing, pushing, fighting, gathering strength from the energy around her. With a suddenness that left her gasping, the blackness winked away. Once again she was in the kitchen, her fingers wrapped tightly around Caleb's. Jared's hands still cupped her face. His eyes, narrowed and serious, studied her face. His lips parted and one word breathed into the room. "Impressive."

"Very," Caleb agreed.

Slade asked the question she wanted to ask. "What?"

"She broke Jared's hold," Caleb explained.

"Damn!"

The awe in Jace's and Slade's "Damn" was freakier than the actual experience. If she hadn't already been pressed tightly to Caleb's chest she might have reached for him.

"Anyone ever done that before, Jared?" Caleb asked.

"No." Jared's gaze searched hers with a clinical assessment that only added to her nervousness.

"Are the feathers gone?" she asked.

She reached up to see. Jared's hand blocked hers, bringing it back to her side.

"Picture them gone, Allie," Caleb directed.

"I've already tried that." She sighed. Jared let go of her hand. "About a hundred times."

"Let's make it a hundred and one."

"Fine. But it's not going to make a difference." She was a total flop at this.

"Humor me."

Closing her eyes, she did as Caleb asked, not expecting anything, but there was a soft tingle and then . . . she knew. She kept her eyes closed and squeezed Caleb's hand, excitement building. "They're gone, aren't they?"

"Yes."

The joy burst inside. She opened her eyes. The first thing she saw was Caleb. She wrapped her arms around his neck and kissed him hard, running her tongue over his lips when his didn't immediately part, nibbling at the bottom until he gave in. With a groan, he took over, kissing her deep and hot, sharing her joy, giving it back to her along with passion and . . . desperation?

Frowning, she drew back. A glance around showed none of the men were smiling. All of them looked as if the grim reaper was knocking at the door. Of them all, Caleb looked the grimmest. His green eyes were dark, gold lights swirling slowly in the depths, belying the gentleness of his touch and the happiness of the moment.

His lids flickered. Anxiety gathered in her stomach, squelching the excitement, joining the roll of pain from her hunger. "Why don't you look happy? I did it right."

Jared put his hand on her shoulder, the way people do when imparting bad news. "Because we just figured out what your gift is."

This was so not going to be good. "What?"

Slade delivered the news. "You're an empath."

Caleb finished it. "Who drains energy."

SHE'D so been hoping for something with a bit more pizzazz. Something more interesting. Something sexier. "That's it? I'm a parasitic empath?"

Deep and low and even—too even—Caleb's drawl rolled over her. "Yes."

"Well, hell." She dropped back against his chest.

"There's nothing wrong with being empathetic."

"It's wussy and—"

"Womanly and sexy," Caleb finished for her.

She rolled her eyes. "I was hoping for something leaning more toward the Lara Croft end of the skill scale."

Jace snorted. "I don't think Caleb's heart could survive that."

She did her best to ignore the rising nausea and the needle of panic piercing her core. "How can feeling other people's emotions be dangerous?" It sounded about as boring as mud to her.

"Empathy is not dangerous, but the ability to drain the energy of the person feeling the emotion . . ." If Caleb's body language had echoed the calm in his drawl, she might have been able to still her growing sense of dread, but he held her too tightly, his body curved too protectively around hers.

"That's a whole different story, isn't it?"

"That might make you a weapon."

"Depending on?"

"Depending on whether there are limits to how much you can draw," Slade answered.

"So, someone might be stalking me because I'm female, because I'm fertile, or because I'm a potential weapon?"

"Pretty much."

She glared at Jared. "I hate when you say that."

"I'll keep it in mind."

"Do you think it's the other vamps?"

"Hell." Jared scooped the pile of crumbs that had been one of her bear claws into his hand. "No way would the high and mighty be up to something like that."

"Who are the high and mighty?"

He got up and dumped them in the trash can. "The Order of

Vampire. Members of the Sanctuary." The way he said "Sanctuary" contained more scorn than she reserved for big hairy spiders.

"Run by me again who they are?"

"A bunch of rule-mongering, think-too-highly-of-themselves vamps who got together and put themselves in charge of deciding what's right for vampires everywhere."

"Right in what sense?"

"Whatever sense they deem fit."

She slipped off Caleb's lap, restless energy and the growing hunger driving her to pace. "They sound charming."

"Oh, they are."

"Couple hundred years ago, they invited us into the fold," Caleb informed her as he watched her every move, no doubt cataloging every nuance of emotion she revealed.

She folded her arms across her chest. "You didn't appreciate the invitation?"

One short shake of his head said it all. "Not a group I want to hitch my team to."

She rubbed her arms against the chill that crept over her skin. "Why not?"

"Too much philosophy and too little sense."

"There was also that set-to Jace had with the head honcho's brother the one and only time we went calling," Slade interjected dryly.

"Hey, the guy took my smoke."

There had to be more to the story than that. "And?"

Slade leaned back in his chair. The protesting squeak added to the strange tension in the room. "At the time, Jace was real fond of his smokes."

"And?"

"They took offense."

This was like pulling teeth. "And?"

"There was a fight."

She could easily see that. Just the memory had Caleb flexing his fingers. "And you lost?"

"It'd take more than those pantywaists to kick the Johnson brothers' butts," Jace retorted.

She took a breath as a cramp seized her gut. "So you won?"

"Yup."

Pain strained her voice. "And your reward was?"

"Turns out that honcho was real touchy about his brother's pretty face getting rearranged." Caleb shrugged those broad shoulders in a way that clearly said the Sanctuary's reprisal didn't matter. "We got exiled."

The next cramp bent her double. "Now why doesn't that surprise me?" she gasped.

No one answered.

Which also didn't surprise her. The Johnson brothers had gone to war with an established society and won the battle, but lost the war, and didn't see that as a negative. Either the Johnsons were contrary beyond belief, or the members of the Sanctuary were too different to relate to.

She reached out. Caleb's hand encompassed hers, always there. His arm went around her waist, supporting her. His fingers stretched to cover as much as her abdomen as he could. Pain speared deep, stronger than she'd ever felt before, more violent. There was something about it she should question, a difference that disturbed her. Before she could center on the difference, another bolt of agony struck, driving up her spine, lodging in her skull. "Caleb!"

"Right here."

She clutched his hand, her talons digging in. Desperation commanded she hold on as tightly as she could. "I need you."

Her knees buckled. Curses peppered the growing haze around her, as violent as the foreign presence spreading inside. Malevolent, relentless, it prowled mental paths she didn't even know existed, riding the battering ram of pain deeper into her psyche. The scent of blood melded into the moment.

"Feed, Allie."

She shook her head. She didn't want food. She needed . . . "Jared?"

"What is it?"

She had to tell Jared. He was the telepath. He'd know what to do. The pain gathered in a knot in her throat, choking off her voice.

"Goddamn it, Allie, feed now, chat later," Caleb growled.

She shook her head, the pain intensifying as she struggled for coherence. "Something's wrong."

His hands stilled and all that muscle tightened to lethal preparedness. "What?"

"It's after me."

She had an impression of green eyes flaring with deadly anger, the brush of Caleb's mind over hers, and then a soft imperative, "Jared."

"Right here."

"Get in there."

Hard hands touched her, as irritating as Caleb's were comforting. She flinched away.

"Just focus on me, baby. I've got you."

"It's gross." The feeling of that presence was foul and slimy, as though a grub crawled through her mind. A tendril of pain snaked around her vocal cords, choking them closed, continuing to squeeze, taking her breath. Caleb stretched her neck, trying to open a path for air that wouldn't come.

"Help me." Had she managed to say it aloud?

A disoriented flash, like lightning but broader, more encompassing, shot through the darkness. Another presence joined the intruder. Angry, strong, and relentless, it tore through the edges of the inky tendril, shattering its hold. She took a shaky breath.

Caleb. The whisper was both mental and physical.

Come here, baby.

Calm in the midst of chaos. "Here" was a hollowed-out spot

deep within the shadows. A tiny beacon of light. The evil gathered around her, pulling her back.

I can't. She couldn't outrun the smothering evil. Nothing could. *Now.*

She shook her head. *Move.* Light shot out from the edge of the hollow. The blackness writhed and withdrew, pulling farther back, seething and gathering at the edges of the newly established boundary. The slimy blackness reared as two separate arms, waving in a silent scream. Between those foul extensions lay a narrow path.

Move it. The snarl whipped across her nerves. She jumped. The arms looked so ready to swat whatever was foolish enough to enter the path. She couldn't believe she was being this stupid. But she was. Because Caleb told her to. With a prayer, she shot forward, blindly running down the path, the salvation Caleb offered. Behind her, the darkness lurched. Pain—crippling, blinding, unnatural pain built, stealing her focus, sapping her concentration with single-minded purpose. She focused on the hollow. She was close. So close. She couldn't fail now. Her strength faltered. *Help me.*

Calm coated the panic. *A little more, Allie.*

She didn't have any more. The darkness was too strong. Stronger than anything she'd ever felt, and so determined. It wanted her, and it was going to get her. There was nothing anyone could do. Fighting just endangered them all. It was better that she just surrender. The brothers didn't need her. They were better off without her.

No. The brothers' united protests roared in her head.

Caleb's voice rose louder than all the rest. *Goddamn you, Allie girl, if you give up now I'll fucking paddle your ass!*

He was such a nag. She dug deeper. White light flashed. The blackness flickered. She gathered her will.

C'mon, Allie. Come here.

She went, giving one last desperate lunge, making it halfway before the sucking energy cut her off.

Caleb!

Another brilliant light shot out, wrapped around her, and yanked.

For a moment, she was suspended between the light and the darkness, caught in a tug-of-war while agony shattered her from the inside out. Jared's determination beat inexorably at her surrender. Caleb's unwavering strength gave her hope.

But the darkness seduced more subtly. Promising relief from the pain. Promising peace. Knowledge.

It doesn't have anything to offer you, Allie.

Yes it did. Understanding skittered along the edge of agony. If she could just hold on a moment longer, she'd see what it was. Learn.

She didn't get her moment. With a wrench that threatened to sever her psyche, she tumbled into the hollow Caleb had carved. As soon as she landed in the safe zone, three bolts of light separated from the hollow, lashing into the darkness with calculated fury, splintering it into fragments of nothingness. It vanished with a scream that reverberated in a cacophony of frustration. The echoes faded like the rumblings of a storm, passing grudgingly into the distance, taking the threat with them. For now.

She opened her eyes, dragging air into her lungs on hoarse breaths. Real. Oh God, it had seemed so real.

Arms came around her. She screamed and yanked away, to no avail. She slashed with her talons. Hands caught hers, twisted her around. A broad chest cushioned her back in a familiar embrace. The fight drained out of her in a shuddering sigh. "Caleb . . ."

"It's all right, Allie girl. I've got you. It's all right."

❧ 15 ❧

IT wasn't all right.

"I've been slimed."

Well and truly slimed. Deep inside she could still feel that oily, sinister, pervasive presence. Gross. Allie kept her eyes closed as she assimilated her surroundings. She was on a bed. The sheets were clean. She felt sated, yet still felt that she could nibble, which meant she'd fed probably a few hours ago. In the distance, muffled by walls and doors, she could hear men's voices, low murmurs that rose and fell in a deliberate hush. The house creaked with the wind that rustled the leaves in the trees. Energy drifted toward her. Intense. Impatient and concerned. Caleb. She'd recognize him anywhere. "Did you get the name of the entity that slimed me?"

"Am I supposed to make sense of that comment?"

She cracked one eye. Caleb stood beside the bed, skin glowing weirdly pale in her night vision. The lines beside his mouth were deeper shadows of the same gray, more carved than she remembered. He looked tired. "Guess you're not a fan of *Ghostbusters*."

He brushed the hair back from her eyes. His fingertips grazed her skin in a touch as insubstantial as the moonlight coming through the window, drifting down her cheek to her shoulder, delving into the hollow above her collarbone, coming to rest midway down. "No."

While his tone was conversational, his eyes never stopped roaming her face. Searching. She was afraid to ask why.

"Do you have any idea what *Ghostbusters* is?"

"I'm guessing a movie."

The blanket weighed like lead, pinning her arms to her chest. Why was she so weak? "A very funny movie," she corrected. "One that's full of demons, jokes, and paranormal activity." She cracked her other lid. "In other words, right up your alley."

"Uh-huh."

Her wisecrack didn't even earn a twitch of his lips. Damn, this must be serious. "Would that be an I'm-humoring-you-because-you're-at-death's-door uh-huh, or an I-don't-like-modern-movies uh-huh?"

"The latter. I'm more fond of reading."

She closed her eyes in relief, then immediately reopened them, because the persistent sense that something was very wrong wouldn't go away. From this angle, Caleb's shoulders seemed broader than ever, strong enough to handle anything. She smiled as she realized he was wearing her favorite shirt. The green flannel one that brought out his eyes when she could see color. She dropped her gaze lower. He was also wearing her favorite jeans. They were really faded and really worn, to the point they no longer just fit his body, but hugged it in a loving embrace, revealing every surge of muscle, every bulge of masculine flesh, in a mouthwatering display. The man was truly blessed.

"Could you turn on the light?" She really wanted to see his shirt, the color of his eyes.

"Why?"

"I don't like this night vision."

His reach for the lamp was more of an impression of movement than actual movement. Floorboards didn't squeak, air wasn't disturbed. He just glided to his destination.

"I have got to learn to do that."

"What?"

"That floaty thing." The light turned on. Color assaulted her senses—the rich brown of the floors, the washed burgundy of the walls, the deep green of Caleb's shirt, the deeper green of his eyes. She took a moment to absorb the familiarity. The utter normalcy of it. "Thank you."

In two gliding steps, he was back at her side. He adjusted the blankets over her shoulders, a smile ghosting his lips as his knuckles brushed her cheek. "You're welcome."

"You look good." And he did, despite the signs of fatigue, he looked very, very good. He always did, and just seeing him had a way of making things right in her world. His right eyebrow raised. It was such a blessedly familiar moment after the weirdness of before that she turned her head to kiss his forearm.

"Jared just got done telling me I look like hell."

Beyond a break in his next breath, Caleb didn't relax. That alone was enough to worry her. She puffed out a disgusted bit of air. "What does Jared know? If it isn't dressed in black, he can't relate."

"I'm glad to see you've got your sass back."

It was her turn to raise her eyebrows. "I lost it?"

He sat on the side of the bed. Her body followed the dip of the mattress, rolling until she came up against his hip. His hand braced on the mattress behind her left shoulder. The shadow of his body cocooned her in intimate darkness. Her night vision kicked in. The black and white emphasized the harshness of his facial structure, highlighted the character so deeply embedded in the planes and hollows. She remembered the horrible presence, the way it'd taken over, but mostly she remembered the way Caleb had gone after it, blazing light and fury, fearless and determined, no hesitation. She'd needed him and he'd been there. They'd all been there.

"You've been out for a day."

One whole day? "Good God!"

Caleb's mouth tightened to a thin line as he eased his hands under her shoulders. "God was nowhere near that mess."

"And just what exactly was that mess?"

He lifted her. "Someone, we think vampire, came calling."

"The Sanctuary people?"

The shake of his head was emphatic. "They'd be more likely to convert you than to attack you."

She felt as stiff and creaky as an old door as he slid behind her. Her joints protested the move, the bones grating with the effort. Her hand went to her stomach. "Our baby."

Caleb covered her hand with his as she eased back against him. "Everything's the same as it was as far as we can tell."

"What does that mean?"

Caleb sighed. Allie wanted to know for certain if she was pregnant, but he didn't have an answer. It wasn't like they could just stroll into town for a pregnancy test without raising eyebrows, and they certainly couldn't send blood out to a lab.

Beneath his hand, Allie's stomach fluttered with the conflicting emotions ricocheting inside her. He wished he could tell her if she was pregnant or not, but he didn't know. Son of a bitch, they didn't know anything they needed to know when it came to her. "If you were carrying, you still are, and if you weren't, you still aren't."

Her palm came over his. Soft, warm, she pressed his hand to her. To the place where maybe his child rested. The miracle of that possibility just bowled him over. Caleb slowed his breathing, staring into the shadows, old dreams coming back. Dreams he'd built for his brothers as well. Dreams he'd put away as useless when they'd turned vampire. Dreams that involved family and kids and making a place for themselves that was better than what they'd lost. And now, after all these years, it was dangling just out of his reach.

How the hell was a man supposed to adjust to that? How the hell was he supposed to deal with the morass of emotions that came with the resurrection? Rage at any that would threaten her. Joy at the gift she brought. Fear that she could be taken away. No way around it, Allie made him vulnerable, and that was going to take some getting used to.

She shifted in his arms. Adjusting his grip to accommodate her new position, he looked down. Allie's eyes were closed. "Tired?"

She shook her head, the rosemary scent of the shampoo with which he'd washed her hair teasing his nostrils. "Just pretending it's you and me here in the darkness. No bad guys, no freaky visiting entities, no uncertain future. Just you and me and possibility."

Caleb ran his index finger up the bridge of her nose, his own personal miracle, bracing his fingers against her forehead, easing her head against his shoulder. "I'd like that."

"Me, too."

There was a very un-Allie-like silence and then she took a breath. Caleb braced himself. She was going to tell him she wanted to leave. He'd always known she'd reach a point where things would become too overwhelming for her. Though he'd told himself he'd respect her decision if she asked to leave, he wasn't sure he could let her go. Not now. He liked to think he could, but about ninety percent of that thinking was pure bluff.

Eyes still closed, body relaxed against his, she exhaled. "I make a lot of jokes, you know."

"I know." It was how she coped with life's toll on her emotions and defended herself from the way the world sometimes beat up on that sensitive heart of hers.

"But I can be serious."

The seam of her lashes shimmered with the surge of tears. She blinked once, twice. He tucked her closer, resting his chin on her hair. On the third blink, she swallowed hard and found her voice. "And I really want there to be a baby."

A tear spilled to her cheek, a silver beacon for his attention. He let the moisture spread across his lips, a salty bridge between sadness and hope. "Me, too."

She held herself so still, as if she was afraid to move because to do so would be to shatter the possibility she hoped for so desperately. "I'd like a little boy with your eyes."

"I've got my heart set on a little girl with your spirit and smile."

"We're probably just kidding ourselves that vampires can get pregnant."

"Probably."

"What kind of parents would we be?"

He pulled her higher against him, opening his hand and pressing down, wanting. "The best we learned how to be."

"I'd make mistakes."

"Then I'd help fix them."

"And when you screwed up?"

His right eyebrow rose, and the easy smile he was getting reacquainted with since meeting her tugged at his mouth. "What makes you think I'd screw up?"

Allie leaned back, letting him catch her weight as she slid far enough to the side to see his face. The trust implicit in the move touched him.

"It's a given, Johnson. With you as a father and me as a mother, she's bound to have a wild side. Combine that with your penchant for wrapping the people around you in cotton wool, and there's going to be some clashes."

"Damn straight she'd be protected. I'm not having any weres or vamps sniffing around my little girl."

She looked at him with those big blue eyes and a slightly mocking smile. "The way you sniffed around theirs?"

Caleb shook his head and touched the corner of that smile. If their child was a girl, sure enough he was going to have his work cut out for him keeping the boys away. He ran his finger along her cheekbone. So much intrepid spirit contained within such a soft body. If her daughter had half her appeal he was going to need reinforcements. "Exactly."

"Which will just mean I'll have to run defense around you so she gets to have a life."

"I don't think so."

Her eyes narrowed. "Count on it. Girls are entitled to just as much freedom as boys."

"Little girls are vulnerable in ways boys aren't."

"Then we'll teach her karate."

"Karate won't give her a man's strength."

"I didn't need karate to save you."

He nodded. "True enough. Teaching her to shoot is definitely a plan."

But he was still not letting her out without protection. Ever.

Allie frowned up at him, her lips compressing. He might not have guarded that last thought as well as he'd thought.

"We are in the twenty-first century."

She was always tossing that at him as if time changed the basic instincts of males and females. "I noticed."

She didn't take her eyes off him, watching him like a hawk. "Before we have any children, you need to accept that."

"What makes you think I haven't?"

"Your archaic opinions on men and women."

"Time might change the way people talk to each other, but it doesn't change the impulses under the skin."

Her lip slid between her teeth. There was a long pause in which he counted the pulse in her throat. When he got to twelve, she blew out a breath. "We're so different"

"Not where it counts."

"Where would that be?"

"In what we value. Loyalty. Honesty. Courage."

She blinked. "We are alike there, aren't we?"

He brushed his lips across her brow, needing to connect. Although he held her in his arms, he had a feeling she was slipping away. "Like two peas in a pod."

Her teeth sank deeper into her lip. He could feel the resolution inside her strengthening in a steady push of energy against the intimacy he was building.

"What is it?"

Allie's palm rubbed the back of his hand, the one sheltering the possibility of their child.

"I just want you to know that if I'd had the opportunity to pick a father for my baby, it would have been someone like you."

Son of a bitch! She about cut his feet out from under him when she said things like that. He cupped her head, careful not to stress her muscles, tipped her chin up with his thumb. "You did pick me."

"Not completely."

"Completely." Utterly, with an instinctive understanding she didn't trust, but she'd chosen him. Caleb wouldn't let her forget that. He brought his mouth to hers. Carefully, so very carefully, feeling her surprise in the breath that puffed over his lips, the whisper of his name . . . A tilt of his head and her mouth was under his, soft and feminine, as giving as her soul, letting him linger where he wanted, caress as he needed, encouraging him to find the words he couldn't voice.

"Allie girl . . ."

Her hands came around his neck. "I know."

And even without touching minds, he knew she did. He didn't want to break the moment, but there were things she had to know. For her protection and maybe their child's, he had to warn her. He broke off the kiss, readying her for the seriousness of the conversation with a stroke of his thumb across her mouth.

She sighed and kissed the pad. "You're going to ruin the moment, aren't you?"

"Sorry."

Hitching herself higher she shook her head. "We are definitely going to have to work on your killjoy factor along with your chauvinistic tendencies."

"Uh-huh." He didn't let her leave his arms. The scare she'd given him was too recent for him to totally let her go.

When she settled herself in a semi-upright position, she waved her hand. "Spill it if you must."

There was no other way to say it but to be blunt. "Whatever came here wants you."

She didn't even blink, which told him she'd already figured that out. "For what?"

"I wish I knew."

"Are you sure it's not the Sanctuary people?"

"They've never shown the inclination or power before." But that didn't get them off the hook.

She blew her bangs off her head. "Rats."

"Slade's working on it. Derek and his pack, too."

"Really?"

"This last little visit gave us all a kick-in-the-pants scare."

Allie just bet it had. The Circle J had been invaded, by a mental enemy, but an enemy all the same. That had to shake everyone up. For her part, she couldn't remember anything beyond a slimy presence invading her soul, and she still shuddered. She'd had no illusion of safety or control whereas Caleb was on the opposite side of the spectrum, always assuming everything he saw was under his dominion.

"I'm glad it's all a blur for me."

The hand on her stomach contracted. "You don't remember anything?"

"Trust me, I'm doing my best to eradicate even the sensation of a memory."

Caleb turned her in his arms, draping her thighs across his, tilting her face up to his. Faint gold lights swirled behind his pupils as he said, "I'm afraid I can't let you do that."

Allie sighed. "I had a feeling you were going to say that."

"But I'm not going to ask you to remember right this minute."

"That is a relief."

Caleb touched the corner of her mouth. "You need to feed."

"I'm not hungry."

"Slade thinks that letting the hunger get too bad weakens your mental shields and creates an opportunity for trespassers."

"How so?"

"You're an empath, Allie girl. That means unless you close it, there's an open path from everyone around you to you."

She gripped her arms tighter, wishing she had the strength to lift her head. "You're not making my day."

His lips ruffled her hair. "I'm not exactly dancing a jig."

"Any chance I can exchange this gift?"

"I'm afraid not."

"First, you're a vampire. Next, you're a walking invitation to a freak-fest. I swear, Caleb, if you don't start waking me with better news, I'm dumping your ass."

He opened his shirt and sliced his nail through his skin. Blood flowed, scenting the air, drawing their passion around them in a cocoon as soft as the understanding in his voice. "I'll work on it."

APPARENTLY for Caleb, working on it meant keeping her blood intake high and her stimulation level low. Allie paced to the window, drew back the curtains, and stared into the moonlit yard. Men moved within the shadows, fading into one before moving on to the next. Powerful men. Weres called in to protect her. From something they didn't recognize. Something they couldn't see. Something that attacked mentally. Something that needed her. She wished she knew for what.

No matter how hard Allie tried to remember that night, the details remained buried behind a haze she couldn't penetrate. Lingering in her mind like a cancer, deadly and invisible, hiding the identity of the stalker who'd attacked her. But somewhere in the darkness beyond the window it lurked, getting stronger.

She dropped the curtain back in exasperation. She might not know what that thing was, but she knew damn well that waiting was wrong. That thing, that threat, had the edge, and if they didn't know what they needed soon, they were all dead. Convincing Caleb of that was the hard part. He didn't have as much faith in her gut as

she. Or it might be better to say he didn't care if her gut was right
or wrong. His first priority was her immediate safety, and that of
their possible baby. Her priorities were a little more broadscale.
She wanted a home to bring her baby to when it was born.

While Caleb and everyone else felt she needed to stay here, that
these walls somehow protected her, they were wrong. Way down
deep in her gut, she knew they were wrong. That much knowledge
had been gained from the visitor, which was an interesting twist on
the transmitter/receiver aspect of her empathic abilities. Apparently, when anything scanned her, she was also able to scan it. Some
ability seemed to be instinctive, but she'd discovered it definitely
got better with the daily practice-makes-perfect drill sessions Jared
and Caleb put her through.

The harder part was not letting the scanner know that she was
taking sneak peeks of her own. She wasn't so good at that. Which
was why she'd been so excited to see the invitation made out exclu-
sively to her that had arrived from the Sanctuary two days ago.
Talking with Sanctuary members might give her the vital information she needed to be able to protect herself.

Caleb hadn't shared her enthusiasm. Hypersensitive, on full alert
since the psychotic attack, he had wanted to burn the invitation
immediately. Jared had wanted to go in and wipe the place out for
the insult. In his opinion, overlooking Caleb's position as her mate
was a killable offense. Slade had been more sane. He thought they
should first analyze the invitation, find out how they'd known about
Allie, and then wipe the Sanctuary out for what to him was the
equivalent of propositioning his brother's wife.

Her logical suggestion of accepting the invitation and then having an equally logical discussion with people who had spent their
lives learning all they could about what they'd discovered about
vampirism hadn't even been considered. She'd gone off in a huff,
but something had made her take the invitation with her. And
something kept making her come back to it over and over. Instinct
said she needed to accept the invitation. Needed the missing piece

of the puzzle that was locked in her mind. If there was a chance the members of the Sanctuary could provide her with the skills she needed to solve the puzzle, she needed to go.

She peeked out the window again. To that end, tonight she was going to force a couple hands. She grabbed her pack off the bed and opened the window. Thanks to the greasing she'd given it earlier, it slid smoothly. Cool air rushed in. Along with it came a chill. She tugged her coat around her and funneled more energy into her mind shield as Caleb had taught her. She couldn't afford to be detected. She placed her pack on the roof and slid her leg over the sill. Doing her best to be quiet, she stepped out onto the roof. Her foot didn't slip and when she put her weight on it, didn't go through the shingles. So far so good.

She stood and stretched her spine, breathing deeply of the fresh air, the first she'd had in the last week. Since the last "visit" Caleb had assigned her a guard, and since he feared the accessibility of the outdoors, kept her inside.

Creeping down the roof wasn't as hard as she'd feared. Hopefully, evading the guards wouldn't be either. She glanced at her watch. She figured she had two hours before Caleb returned. A woman could go a good distance in two hours. Enough distance so he wouldn't be able to force her to go back before dawn for fear of her being caught in the sun. Enough distance that, hopefully, he'd be forced to cooperate.

Allie stopped at the edge of the roof, her toe on the edge of the gutter. A story up didn't sound like so much until she was actually looking down from that height. It was a long way to the ground, and the moonlight did nothing to soften the image of her body making impact with the hard surface. Might be time to rethink the descent. Instead of just stepping off and hoping she could float, she decided to do a "dangle and drop." With the backpack over her shoulder and the metal of the gutter cutting into her fingers, she closed her eyes and pictured herself floating down. When she had it solidly in her mind, she let go.

She hit the ground with bone-jarring force. Her teeth snapped together and her shins screamed. She crouched, rubbing at the sharp pain until it became manageable, then ducked behind a leafless bush as she waited to see if anyone came to investigate the disturbance. No one did. Oh yeah, she was safe with these guards.

She crept to the left, heading for the woods, unease flaring as the leaves rustled in the trees. To her overactive imagination they sounded like whispers tracing her path. Woman or vampire, she still didn't like the dark.

As soon as she reached the concealing brush at the edge of the woods, she tightened her right shoulder strap and settled into her pace, following the inner vibration she picked up from the invitation that drew her along the path of the moon. She didn't know where the Johnson property ended, but she assumed there would be an illusion at the road, as there had been before. She just hoped there wasn't another pack of killer D'Nally weres on the other side. The last two weeks had provided quite enough excitement in her life, thank you very much. She wasn't in need of more.

Nerves on edge, constantly scanning for wolves, goblins, or any other paranormal freakiness, she trudged on, grateful for at least one thing—vampirism had increased her endurance. A fox skidded out of the hedge to the left and she shrieked before she could contain it. Allie slapped her hands over her mouth, as if that would somehow take back the betraying noise. It was too late.

"Going somewhere?"

Caleb was beside her—no warning, no sensing him. Just there. Big, bad, and mad. It was enough to make her heart flutter. Stupid heart. She put her hands on her hips. "How do you do that?"

He didn't pretend to misunderstand. Just raised an eyebrow and folded his arms across his chest. "Practice."

He didn't look happy. Just the opposite, but that was just tough. She'd talked herself blue in the face trying to get him to see reason. Extreme stubbornness called for an extreme wake-up call.

"And for your information, I'm heading east."

"Then you're heading in the wrong direction."

Allie rolled her eyes. "Okay, north."

"Try again."

She pointed to the deepest part of the forest, where the tingling told her to go. "That way then."

"West."

She hitched the pack on her shoulder. "West. I'm heading west. Any more questions?"

He caught her arm before she could take a step. "Yes. Why?"

"Because you don't have the answers I need."

"And you think something out there does?"

"Not something . . . someone." She was sure of that.

"That thing is out there."

"So are, apparently, a whole lot of other vampires with, hopefully, a lot more study on the syndrome."

"There's nothing they can give you that I can't."

Oh, that was such a load a crap. She ignored his hand on her arm and folded her arms across her chest. "How about an answer on whether I'm pregnant or not?"

"Time will tell that."

"So would a pregnancy test if vampire bodies functioned like human ones."

"That's not necessarily true, according to Slade."

"Uh-huh." The pack dug into her shoulder. She moved it to a more comfortable position. "According to Slade, a lot of things are possible, but without the right equipment, he's pretty much stuck with theory."

"I'm working on it."

"I don't have time to wait."

His mouth set in that straight line that said she'd roused his stubborn side. "Time is about all we do have."

She wanted to kick him in the shins for that. They had the potential for a lot. A great relationship, a great future. Maybe even a family. "You know, if you keep looking for the negative, you're always going to find it."

"I'm not negative, I'm practical."

"Well, I'm adventurous."

"You're reckless."

"Get used to it."

"Not an option." The tug on her arm punctuated his conviction. "We need to head back."

"No."

His weight shifted to his heels and his grip on her arm loosened, but for all his nonchalance, she couldn't shake the feeling that he was just waiting to pounce. Her own big bad wolf.

"I could just throw you over my shoulder and take you back."

She ignored the laziness of his drawl and looked beneath it. "That is so eighteen sixties."

"But so true."

His tone mocked her, but his eyes said he was going beyond the moment, considering his options. Allie adjusted her backpack. "You realize, of course, that this time I arranged it so you could find me."

The edge of his mouth kicked up in a smile. "You think there'd be a time when I couldn't?"

"I think I could arrange it in the future so you couldn't find me in time." She let the knowledge seep between them. Saw the flare of anger in his eyes before it faded behind a wall of assessment.

"In time for what?"

"For you to be a part of whatever I planned."

❖ 16 ❖

"**I**F you say 'I told you so,' I'm going to scream."

Caleb leaned against the wrought iron gate and folded his arms across his chest. "Can I at least mention that my deciding to wait until tonight rather than showing up in the wee hours of this morning was a much better plan after all?"

"No."

Smug men were so annoying.

"You do know how to take the fun out of a man's day."

Who did he think he was kidding? Every three minutes the man found something about her that inspired a chuckle. If she didn't think he needed the laughter so much, she'd work up to offense. Allie pushed the intercom button again. There was a low hum as the bell rang inside the structure.

"You going with the philosophy that ten times is the charm?"

"No." She started punching the button in a funky rhythm. "I'm working on the theory that if you grate on someone's nerves enough, eventually they'll show up, if for no other reason than to tell you to knock it off."

"And once you get them here?"

"I intend to keep them here until I get inside the gate."

"Based on that annoyance factor?"

She cut him a glance. The amusement in his green eyes sliced through her frustration to tug an equally amused grin to her mouth. "I thought once I had them here, I'd go for the poor-pitiful-little-woman angle."

"You do look pretty pathetic bundled in those two coats."

"Gee, thanks."

"No need to get your feathers in a twist." He glanced at the top of her head. "You're also damn cute."

She was reaching for the top of her head before she realized there was no way the feathers could be back. Of course, Caleb noticed. She rolled her eyes. He chuckled.

She kicked the beat on the buzzer up to three-quarter time. "I hope whoever comes to the door is as old-fashioned as you."

"Why?"

"Because there's no way they'll be able to ignore a vampiress in distress. All that old-world chivalry will force him to comply with my wishes."

Caleb looked through the gates. "This would probably be a bad time to mention that old-world chivalry you keep harping on was more myth than fact."

She followed his gaze. "A very bad time."

The man coming toward them was the epitome of a horror novel revelation. He was dressed in a flowing white robe that just looked bizarre in combination with his monster fangs and beady eyes.

A soft whir and the gates, the only barrier between him and them, began to open. Caleb straightened. "Get behind me."

"Just because he looks—"

She never got a chance to finish the sentence. Caleb grabbed her arm and practically threw her back. She caught her balance just as the beast-man cleared the gates. Flew through them was more like it. Straight at Caleb.

"Stay down," Caleb snapped.

Did he think she was as nuts as him? The backpack with the gun was on the other side of beast-man. A glance around showed the well-manicured grounds clear of debris. Why on Earth was there never a stick around when she needed one?

She closed her eyes as beast-man collided with Caleb. She immediately forced them back open, pushing away her instinctive fear and reaching for her courage. Caleb was going to need her help. No way could he win against something that big. That ugly.

Caleb's answering growl rumbled as the two men's shadows blended, a low, deadly, yet somehow sane counterpoint to the beast's ferocious roar. She scrambled to the side, trying to see what was happening. She just needed an opportunity, an opening to help Caleb. Another thud and the sound of bones breaking snapped her gaze around. The men leapt into the air, spinning as they came together, falling as they pummeled each other. The ground shook as they hit again. The beast-man was on top. Anger surged, sending tingling darts of energy down her arms and out her fingers. If that thing hurt Caleb she was going to personally neuter it with a pair of rusty pliers. The men rolled and came to a stop. Caleb rose above the monster, his boot gouging into the monster's groin and his talons digging into the man's massive chest.

"You picked the wrong day to get on my bad side."

Such an innocuous statement to carry so much lethal intent. From the way beast-man's eyes were bugging, she got the impression he was too terrified to make a sound. She couldn't blame him. Caleb in full vampire snit was scary. A little too scary. She came up behind Caleb, trying not to focus on the image of his hand knuckle deep in the creature's rib cage. "I swear to God if you rip out his heart, I'm going to puke all over you."

That might just be a growl from his throat. "I told you to stay back."

"I thought you might need help with beast-man here."

The glance he cut her was disgusted. "You thought wrong."

Blood pooled around his fingertips. She quickly averted her eyes.

There were some things about vampires she would never get used to. "So shoot me."

"I'd rather paddle your ass."

"You have a real thing about my ass."

He never took his eyes off beast-man, but he still managed to put a sexy rumble in his voice. "Can't help it. It's a damn attractive ass."

At least one of them thought so. "What are you going to do with him?"

"I was thinking of ending his miserable life."

That's what she was afraid of. "But since you know that would be really uncivilized of you . . ."

Caleb lifted the man's torso off the ground, keeping him earth-bound with the boot in his groin. "My wife doesn't think I should kill you."

Beast-man spit the blood from his mouth. "You'll never get out of here if you do."

Caleb shook his head. "I'm thinking you were sent because you're expendable, which would make ending your sorry life an agreeable option."

That was so wrong. "No one is expendable, Caleb."

"Too bad for this guy that I don't share your philosophy."

He sounded so calm, so unphased by the prospect of taking a life, it made her uncomfortable. And the way the muscles in his wrist bulged like he was thinking about doing it any second worried her. He couldn't just kill the man. Vampire. Whatever it was. "Violence doesn't solve everything."

"It works for me."

"The lady has a point."

The very cultured voice slid across the violence like a balm. Allie turned to the speaker, taking a step backward as she did. Good God. It couldn't be. But it was. "Vincent?"

It wasn't the Vincent she remembered—the one who wore polo shirts and jeans and talked spreadsheets until she'd wanted to fall over in a coma. This Vincent was still very handsome in a suave, urbane sort of way, but the blond hair she remembered was so pale it almost glowed the same white as his flowing robes. He also radiated an aura of power and control she didn't remember, but at least he didn't present a threat. Which was good. She'd about had her fill of uncivilized violence. She mustered a smile past her amazement at his change. "Hi."

Vincent inclined his head. "It's good to see you again."

"You know this yahoo?" Caleb growled.

"We dated once or twice." Way back when in her unsuccessful straight-laced phase. She'd hired on as a temp at an investment firm. He'd been one of the boy wonders. The relationship had ended when she'd begun treating him like a human being rather than a god.

Another growl from Caleb, followed quickly by an order. "Come here, Allie."

She ignored Caleb's order and held out her hand to Vincent. "I didn't know you were the one who sent the invitation."

His smile was benign. "I wasn't sure how you'd take the revelation that I was a vampire."

"Well, at least it explains why you always insisted on late-night dinners." He returned her smile, but there was something wrong with his gaze. Or maybe it was his energy. "This is my friend—"

Beast-man hit the ground with a thud. Caleb stepped to her side and, with a bloody hand on her shoulder, put her none too gently behind him. "Husband."

Good God, Caleb was almost a caveman. She glanced over her shoulder. Beast-man was lying unnaturally still. Had Caleb killed him? "This is Caleb Johnson."

"Allie . . ."

The growl in Caleb's voice raised Vincent's eyebrows. The gesture was at least familiar.

"I've heard of the Johnson brothers. They're rather a local legend."

He didn't make it sound like a good thing. Even though she knew how irritating the brothers could be, it irritated her that Vincent felt so free to point it out to her with Caleb standing there.

"They're a bit eccentric, but they grow on you."

Caleb looked toward them, from whatever he was doing with beast-man. "You're pushing me, Allie."

She ignored his command to come to his side. She was not going to heel like a puppy. Especially in front of an acquaintance. "That's only fair. You're annoying me."

"I've heard it's not a good idea," Vincent offered.

Allie shrugged. "I've gotten used to his bite."

Vincent's gaze sharpened. "He's bitten you?"

"Why sound so shocked? It is a vampire thing after all."

"True. And one to which you seem to be adapting well." The dip of his head was a charming affectation she didn't remember. It was almost like he was two men. The one in her memory and the one before her. Of course, the man she'd met the year she'd lived in California might not have been who she thought he was, which bore remembering.

"Were you a vampire when I met you before?"

"Yes," Caleb said, coming up beside her. "He's a very old vampire."

She glanced up. "How do you know?"

Caleb caught her hand in his, keeping her put. "You can feel it in his energy. Which only begs the question, why was he sniffing around you?"

"Well, gee. Thanks for the vote of confidence."

Vincent's expression went haughty in the blink of an eye. That she did remember. "I was probably attracted to her for the same reason you were. Allie is a very attractive woman."

To vampires at least. Not a comforting thought. "Thank you, Vincent."

Caleb snorted. She ignored him. Vincent nodded to the beast-man moaning on the ground. "I'm sorry about your welcome.

We've had some trouble lately, and a few of the members have be-come very protective of our privacy."

"Which would explain your kill-and-don't-tell policy," Caleb drawled.

"It's not our policy, but I'm afraid Daniel had a bad experience with humans before."

Caleb bared his fangs. "I'm not human."

"I'm aware of that and can't apologize enough." A graceful wave of his hand indicated Allie's coat. "Are you well?"

"I'm fine, why do you ask?"

"Most vampires don't feel the cold."

Caleb tucked her into his side.

"My wife's not like most." There was a world of possession in the word "wife."

"I'm sure." Vincent motioned to the gate. "Won't you come in?"

Allie hugged her arms to her chest and eyed Caleb for any sud-den moves. "We would love to."

Beast-man grunted and propped himself up on his elbows. Caleb lifted his lip. Beast-man dropped back down.

"Behave," she whispered under her breath.

"I am."

"Well, do me a favor and try not to be so eighteen sixties once we get inside. We need answers, and we're not going to get them if you rip out the hearts of everyone we meet."

He shrugged, the golden swirls very prevalent in his eyes. "It's a habit."

"Oh for goodness sake." He was determined to be difficult.

Vincent took a step toward the gate. "Shall we go in where you can be warm while we talk?"

Her instinct wobbled between staying outside and going in. Caleb was no help. He just raised an eyebrow at her. Now he had to go all egalitarian?

She studied the gate and the compound beyond. Neither looked particularly impressive. She bet Caleb could clear the fence with the aid of that floaty thing he did, and beyond were just the dark shapes of normal-looking structures. There was nothing to cause the unease creeping under her skin. Forcing a smile she nodded to Vincent. "Absolutely."

Vincent waved them ahead, the gesture reestablishing the sense of familiarity. Still she was glad for Caleb's nearness. When she touched his hand, his fingers curled around hers, warm and strong. Allie held on tightly. There was an undercurrent to the place she didn't trust.

Caleb's energy stroked along her in a definite "I told you so."

"Was there a particular reason you decided to accept our invitation?" Vincent asked as they reached the gate.

At least she wasn't going to have to hunt for an opening to the subject she wanted to broach. "Yes. I have some questions about conversion."

Caleb released her hand as she stepped through.

"For yourself or someone you want to bless?"

She blinked. For someone she wanted to bless? "That's an interesting way to look at it."

"We here at Sanctuary feel vampirism is a richer way of life. One where the few select recipients are elevated to a higher plane through their gifts." He waved them through an archway ahead. "Not everyone can be converted, you know."

"No, I didn't know that."

"It's true. More die than live through it."

The same as with the werewolves. She glanced back over her shoulder. Caleb was a few steps behind, the gold swirls in his eyes still vivid. The shrug of his shoulders let her know this was news to him, too. "I guess I should consider myself fortunate."

"Oh, very. Especially if you were converted without advance knowledge."

She stopped dead two steps past the archway. All around her flowers and lights came together with rock arches and angles to create a glistening, beautiful wonderland that maximized the silver, gray, and white of her night vision. For the first time ever, she enjoyed that aspect of her vampirism. "This is stunning."

"Thank you. One of the things we found our members needed was that sense of harmony with nature that was lost when they lost sunlight. Harmony with nature is one of the prime foundations of our beliefs."

Beliefs? She glanced away from a shimmering, almost iridescent fern. The hairs on the back of her neck prickled. Most people didn't just drop a word like that into the conversation. Not without reason. "I can see where harmony would be important."

Vincent directed her down the path to the left where moonlight appeared whiter, amplified. It had to be a trick. She squinted into the darkness beyond. A hand touched her shoulder. She jumped and turned her head. Caleb stood just behind her. She usually felt his energy before she saw him, so how had he snuck up on her? "You startled me."

"Sorry." He studied everything around them, paying particular attention to the dark hole. It suddenly occurred to her that maybe he'd agreed to come for reasons that had nothing to do with her. She slowed her steps, letting Vincent get ahead and allowing Caleb to catch up. He rested his palm on her shoulder, his thumb on her nape. She leaned into his hand and spoke to him mentally, shielding as best she could. *This place is weird.*

I told you they were a few straws short of a bale.

Actually, I think you harped more on their arrogance.

They have that, too. Stay close.

I'll try.

His fingers tightened. *Succeed.*

Ahead, Vincent stopped and turned back, smiling as if just realizing she wasn't following. Something flickered in his eyes as he saw her with Caleb. Something her gut didn't like, but then it was gone and she was left wondering if it was just an illusion of the weird lighting.

"Is there a problem?"

"None whatsoever." Allie smiled, wondering if she'd seen what she'd thought she had, or if Caleb's suspicions were influencing her perceptions. She still hadn't quite managed this mind hook-up thing, and Caleb's emotions tended to bleed over.

"Caleb and I were discussing the complexity of this environment." It wasn't completely a lie. "How do you get the moonlight so bright in here?"

Vincent bent down, his hand very gentle on an eerily beautiful fern. He moved it aside. Behind it she could see a mirror. "We borrowed a bit of magic from the ancient Egyptians."

Bet he uses smoke and mirrors elsewhere, too.

Caleb's mental comment was almost indistinguishable from the hum of insects and the brush of night air across her cheek. Fatigue and her growing hunger must be affecting her perception. Or else the shields she had up against Vincent were bleeding over to Caleb. She rubbed her forehead. She wished she was better at mental speak.

Vincent straightened, the sigh of his silk clothing louder than any other sound. "Are you not feeling well?"

The soft squeeze of Caleb's hand warned her to silence.

"My wife is hungry."

She reached back and caught his wrist in her hand. The plan was for her to assess whether she wanted to proceed, and he'd follow her lead. "I'm fine."

"I'm sure we can find her something that will suit her taste."

That was an interesting way to phrase things. Maybe he didn't know she was converted. "Um, I am a vampire."

Vincent's expression didn't change. "And a very charming one, too. Whom we would be more than happy to provide for."

He rang a bell that was attached to a partition. Immediately, a man dressed in the same robes as Vincent came forward. "Our guests are hungry. Please arrange a meal for them."

He can't mean what I think he means.

The mental thought she sent to Caleb dead-ended at that annoying, buzzing sound she'd previously thought to be insects. She shook her head. She took a step closer to his side, taking comfort from the familiar touch. "That won't be necessary, but if you could spare us a few minutes of your time to answer some questions, that would be great."

Vincent shook his head before she finished. "I wouldn't hear of it. No one leaves Sanctuary hungry for any kind of sustenance."

If he brings me blood in a cup, I'm puking.

Again, no sign that her message got through to Caleb. The hollow sense of disconnection grew. She waved away Vincent's offer. "Really, I'll be fine."

"There's no need for sacrifice." He motioned to the path that diverged from the one they'd taken. "Our devoted are more than willing to serve."

Three men and three women, wearing flowing white robes that glowed with the same silver as the ferns, approached, hands folded in front of them, their heads down, perfect supplicants.

"Uh." She took a step back. She didn't know how to finish the thought. Caleb had no such problems.

"My wife feeds only from me."

For once she didn't correct him, glad for his support. She studied the humans. They definitely weren't right. "Are they drugged?"

Vincent looked shocked. "Of course not." And then, as if it explained everything, "They're hopefuls."

She blinked. "For what? Sanity?"

Vincent's smile became even gentler, more benevolent. Weirder. "There are many humans who would like to enrich their lives with the blessing of vampirism. We provide them with an opportunity for hope."

"So you're really just providing a service." And keeping a herd of whacked-out humans convenient and at the ready.

"Yes."

"That's real sweet of you, but I'm truly not that hungry."

She'd never be that hungry. She pressed back against Caleb so hard that she felt the bones of his ribs, even through both coats. What she didn't feel was their mental connection. In its place was that faint, annoying buzz.

Do you hear it?

No response. She took a breath, and then another and another, reaching for patience and calm with everything she had while her gut jangled like an old-fashioned alarm. The great vampire empire seemed to be little more than a cult with all the appropriate accoutrements, including brain-dead, self-sacrificing wannabes.

Hunger twisted harder as one of the men stepped forward, his face classically handsome, his aura dementedly peaceful, as if he truly believed serving himself up as an hors d'oeuvre was the road to salvation. "Mistress, it would be my pleasure to see to your needs tonight."

"No thanks."

Another stepped forward, the arch of his brow and the set of his mouth making clear that he was more interested in what came after the feeding than serving. "It is our pleasure to serve you in any way you require."

Before she could shake her head, a woman stepped forward, her long blonde hair floating about her like an inviting cloud, every move, every nuance laced with seductive invitation. "If the master would agree, I would be happy to submit to his pleasures."

Okay, there was gall, and then there was gall that demanded retribution. Allie ducked under Caleb's arm, the hair on her arms standing on end with the fury that grabbed her at the woman's blatant offering. She made it as far as his side before he pulled her up short. Her fangs itched with the need to rip into the woman. Not to feed, but to kill.

Caleb squeezed her arm in warning. He inclined his head toward the woman, his eyes glowing beneath the brim of his hat. With desire or suspicion. She couldn't tell, and that just drove her jealous fury higher.

"Not tonight, ma'am."

Allie clenched her fists. Not ever.

"I have been told that my services please." The woman's too-long lashes lifted slowly, suggestively.

Great. Blood and sex on order. Everything the discriminating vamp could ask for in a club, assuming they wanted membership. Which she didn't. But what she found distasteful, Caleb might like. Which meant he might just be interested in the little bimbette who probably invested more in artificial eyelashes than she spent on clothes, and had forgotten more about making a man's head spin than she had ever learned.

Caleb shifted his grip on her arm.

Allie raised her chin, even as her spirit sank. She had no claim on him. He was within his rights to accept whatever invitation he wanted.

"Allie."

She didn't look at him. He'd laugh at her. As if he sensed the emotion tearing at her, he turned her to him and pressed her cheek to his chest. Beneath her ear there was the steady beat of his heart. A little faster than normal, but steady, and in combination with the soothing rub of his fingers up and down the side of her arm, comforting.

"I've got the woman I want, thank you."

There was no doubt he meant it. Oh God, she was going to cry again. She wrapped her arms around his torso and pressed close, her relief way too great for the situation, but she needed the connection with him, especially in light of the absence of the mental link she'd come to rely on as part of their bond. On the next pass of his fingers, he overshot her shoulder, the backs grazing her cheek, catching the heat and reflecting it back.

She accepted it, letting it sink past her fear and insecurity to the bottom of her soul, cherishing the warmth, needing it inside this beautiful place that chilled her so. His fingers lingered, giving her more. He bent his head, the brim of his hat providing a modicum of privacy. His lips on her ear were as light as his touch. His knuckle pressed into the corner of her mouth. "When we get home, you can make that moment of doubt up to me."

The blush started in her toes and worked up and out. So did the excitement. "What makes you think I want to?" she whispered.

"What makes you think you don't?"

He had her there.

"For better or worse, baby."

"Saying it doesn't make it real."

He pushed her hair back. "Feeling it does."

"But whose feeling it, you or your vampire?"

She waited with breath suspended, but he didn't have an answer. "That's what I thought."

She stepped back, his frustration hitting her as hard as her own. Either the man wanted her with everything he had, or she wasn't hanging around.

The hopefuls shifted. She waved them away. "We're not interested."

"If you don't wish to partake at this time, might I suggest we go in where it's warm, and talk?" Vincent asked in his smooth, well-modulated tones.

Allie nodded. "Thank you."

"If you'll follow me?" Vincent turned. Like the Red Sea, the hopefuls parted, taking positions on either side of the path. Walking between them was an eerie experience. She could feel their hunger, not like hers for sustenance, but for something deeper. Acceptance.

At the end of the path, Caleb drew her up short, and frowned at the doorway in front of them. Try as she might, she couldn't see anything wrong with it beyond more ornamentation than good taste would accept. He shook his head. She strained, sensing he was speaking to her telepathically, but nothing came through. No matter how hard she tried, all she got was that annoying buzz and another twist of hunger. She tugged his hand, just wanting this over, so they could go home. "C'mon."

He shook his head. "Wait."

She didn't argue, just planted her feet, trusting his instincts above her own this time. Beyond the archway, Vincent waited. Nothing in his demeanor indicated impatience, which just made her more suspicious that Caleb had the right of it.

Something was definitely wrong here. No one was that serene. Especially around her. She would have stayed there forever, but with a force that bruised, something collided with her ribs, jettisoning her out of Caleb's arms into the room. Instantly, the archway flashed with light, then shimmered and hazed. She ran for it, hitting it hard. An electric shock went through her, ripping apart her nerve endings. She flopped on the floor like a landed fish, muscles spasming and contracting in the aftermath. A roar stuttered through the internal scream reverberating across her synapses. It took extraordinary concentration to turn her head. "Caleb!"

She meant it to be a shout. It came out a whisper. He hit the charged wall before she could warn him back. Sparks showered the spot where he struck, trailing behind him as the charge pounded him back. He flew ten feet before hitting the ground. His big, powerful body bounced awkwardly, coming to rest with his back arched over the pack. Unlike her, he didn't get up. Vincent caught her before she could charge the barrier again.

"Don't."

She yanked her arm, not taking her eyes from Caleb. *Move. Oh God, move.* "Let go of me."

"The shock will kill you."

Pain shot up her arm as his talons dug into her flesh through the coats. A sharp reminder of what he was. The doorway hazed, obscuring Caleb's image one particle at a time.

She could feel Vincent's stare, an outward extension of his will. She refused to look at him.

Caleb! Every particle of her being raged against the possibility that he could be dead. She wouldn't accept it. A two-faced scumbag like Vincent couldn't take out someone like Caleb. He might try, but Caleb was too contrary to cock up his toes so conveniently. Gathering the scattered bits of her energy, she focused her mental call to a scream.

"You need to forget about him." The statement struck her mind a second before it hit her ears. She shook her head to clear the disorientation. "No."

The archway blurred more. She strained to see through it. Was that a twitch of Caleb's fingers?

Vincent tugged her arm, dragging her away from the entryway. "He's no longer a part of your life."

He would always be a part of her. Shadows moved on the other side of the entryway, barely visible through the hazed edges creeping toward him. The hair on her arms and neck stood on end. *Wake up!* Caleb had to wake up. She turned on Vincent, biting and clawing with the need to get to Caleb. He defeated her efforts with only minimal exertion. His longer reach and greater strength subdued her wild attack. Smooth fingers grabbed her chin and forced her face around. His long robes wrapped around her legs as he stepped forward, pressing his body against hers. Peace and contentment flowed off him in a demented wave as he leaned in.

"I sensed your potential the minute I met you. You have a unique energy, my dear. Feminine yet filled with untapped strength. I think with time and training, you'll be quite useful to the Sanctuary." He smiled that unholy, peaceful smile. "Though you defeated my initial attempts to secure you, you were quite obliging this time."

"Fuck you."

He closed the two inches between them and kissed her cheek. "The goal, my dear, is for you to be fucked."

✳ 17 ✳

THERE was a reason girls didn't kiss on the first date, and that was it. Allie scrubbed at her cheek. Vincent's kiss had the same ick factor as a big hairy spider crawling across her skin. And just like when a spider crept across her skin, no matter how much she rubbed, she couldn't get rid of the disgusting feeling.

"You'll soon see things my way." Vincent didn't stop her rubbing and didn't get angry, just watched her with that unnervingly calm gaze. The buzzing in her head increased.

Vincent took a step back and relaxed his arm, until her feet touched the ground. His voice was all the more scary for the lack of emotion behind it. A glance through the archway showed a blurry image of Caleb still down and still surrounded. That really wasn't good.

"Resisting will only make things more difficult for you."

She cut him a glare. "I'm funny that way."

"You like pain?" He would have to smile on that question.

"No, but I have real trouble with the whole concept of forced cooperation."

It wasn't like she was letting out state secrets. Everyone learned that about her sooner rather than later.

"You'll soon adjust."

She backed up a step. "So everyone's always telling me."

"I'm very good at ensuring cooperation."

It was a threat. "Great."

Followed by the promise, "And I will have yours."

He braced his arm on the wall to the right of her head, blocking her view of the doorway. She bent her knees, sliding down. "I'm sure you'll give it your best shot."

Bastards like him always did. Caleb was still there. Figures were all around him. No one was moving.

Vincent again caught her chin in his grip, squeezing hard enough to bring on the burn of tears as he easily forced her back up onto her toes. "I will succeed."

The shake he gave her head snapped her gaze to his. Red swirls moved in the depths of his gray eyes. Emotion she didn't want to define moved right alongside. "I've been waiting too long for you. I won't fail."

Now there were words to give a woman pause. The man was practically salivating. Over her. Which absolutely made no sense. She wasn't a woman men anticipated meeting. "Any chance you need glasses?"

It took a minute for her reference to connect, but then he blinked and shook his head.

"Your value has nothing to do with your appearance."

"How . . . flattering." Through the thick haze she saw the figures converge on Caleb. Hopeless panic surged. She couldn't give in to it, couldn't collapse. She had to stay strong. Think. She took a breath, turning her focus inward, pushing that annoying buzz aside, channeling her panic to mental energy. There had to be a way out of this, an angle she could play. All she had to do was find it.

She made it as far as the count of six before the figures blended to a lump. A lump with flailing appendages, all driving downward to one point. Her inner vampire screamed in outrage. Her human soul vowed revenge. Amid the raging emotion, her brain started clicking, her thought processes riding the ensuing adrenaline, rushed toward higher function. Everything she'd heard from Caleb and the weres clicked through her brain, sorting through Vincent's comments until a picture began to take shape. A plan began to form.

She looked up at Vincent. He wasn't looking at her. His attention was on the scene beyond the archway. From the smile on his lips, Caleb's demise was obviously another thing for which he'd been waiting a long time. The last piece of the puzzle fell into place. "You can't let them kill him."

Vincent didn't even glance her way. "He's no longer your concern."

Another breath and she managed a reasonable semblance of calm. "If you need me alive, you need him alive."

Please let them need me alive.

His gray eyes deepened to a harsh slate color as he glanced down at her. The red swirls multiplied until they dominated the irises. "Why?"

"I can't accept blood from anyone but him."

"You're lying."

The lump of bodies on the other side of the haze shifted to an irregular shadow. She met his gaze directly. "No, I'm not."

His pupils narrowed and then expanded. She didn't even attempt to try and block his probe. Sometimes it was just easier to let people find out for themselves what was true. When he pulled back, she reinforced his deduction. "Without him, I die."

He frowned. She followed the direction of his gaze. The lump separated into six shadows. One still lay on the ground. *C'mon, Caleb. Move.*

No response from Caleb, but Vincent smirked. "You can't use your telepathy here."

"Why not?"

"Because I will not allow it."

"And who are you to tell me what I can or cannot do?"

"Your future husband, soon to be father of your children."

What was it with everyone wanting to marry her? He stared at the archway again. A sensation of mental energy stretched outward from him. The shadows moved, picking up Caleb. He exploded into action. Two of the shadows went down under his attack. For a brief second his silhouette stood out against the haze, broad-shouldered, proud, and deadly. The other four converged on him. The cry was instinctive. It came from her soul.

Fight!

He did. With a fury and skill that awed, but he couldn't win. Not with the numbers that came at him. So many shadows that they looked like one, only the occasional profile proving that he wasn't up against some huge, monstrous alien life-form. The ferocity of the attacker's retaliation didn't give her much hope. She whimpered when he went down again. It seemed an eternity before the shadows separated, stood.

They stretched out in a line, some forming individual silhouettes. The ones in the middle converged to one long shadow. The middle of that long shadow dipped and then straightened. The middle of that long shadow had to be Caleb. He wasn't moving. She bit her lip on the agony of what that might mean. As if sensing her thoughts, his head lifted. He was alive. But for how long? She clenched her hands into fists, one finger at a time, not looking away from the archway until Vincent forced her to.

"You will forget about him."

"I don't think so. He's my husband."

"That can be changed." He dragged her across the room, proceeding as if her struggles meant nothing.

"Not according to Caleb."

"Your cowboy, as you might have discovered, isn't exactly an authority on vampire reality."

She grabbed for the doorjamb, planted her feet, and held on. "And whose fault is that?"

"His."

With a jerk he wrenched her free. She hissed in pain as her talons ripped, but took a certain amount of satisfaction in the deep grooves left in the ornately carved wood. Vincent jerked her up against his chest, glancing over her shoulder at the damage and then back down. "You'll pay for that."

"And so will you."

"For what?"

"For every mark your cronies put on Caleb."

"That cowboy won't be in a position to do anything."

The way he sneered the word "cowboy" hit her last nerve wrong, breeding determination in the spot she'd thought reserved for fear. She used Vincent's grip on her arm as leverage and pushed her face closer to his. Caleb might be difficult, and she might not have known him long, but he was her damn cowboy, and no one got to threaten his life but her. "But I will be."

His scoffing laugh didn't surprise her or even offend her. People always underestimated her. She stood there, memorizing his expression, his energy, every line in his face. She wanted to remember him beyond anyone's ability to erase. She waited, letting the anger feed her determination. Remembered the horror when Caleb went down. Imagined his pain as they beat him at this man's command. Oh yes, Vincent would pay for that. For all of it.

She stared long after his burst of laughter faded to nothing. Vincent's lids flickered. An almost imperceptible betrayal of unease. It was enough. She pushed herself a fraction closer, keeping her voice as even and as calm as his. "And I never forget."

There was another telling hesitation before he said, with all the smooth nonchalance of before, "I'll take my chances."

She smiled, held his gaze, and flicked his energy with hers. "You do that."

And when her chance came, she would take it.

He snarled and yanked her forward. The hall he dragged her into was long and wide. Expensive pieces of art lined each side. Unfortunately, he kept her to the middle where she was unable to reach anything valuable. She bet ripping those canvases would really hit a hot button. Vincent seemed the type to put a lot of stock in his image and all the accoutrements that supported it.

"What exactly is the point of this society you're so proud of?"

"Quite simply, those of us with the power have banded together to create a world that meets our needs."

"You're kidding me, right? You actually found a way for a bunch of arrogant asses to coexist through eternity?"

"There is always unrest, but in the end, the strong triumph."

"And you are?"

"The strongest."

"In your opinion."

"As proven by time, conflict, and intellect."

"Over whom?" He yanked her through the next doorway too fast for her to make her mark. "The bimbettes you collect as a food source?"

"Over all vampires, weres, and humans. And, soon, my dear, you."

He dragged her over to a long spiral staircase. She grabbed the banister. "It's really too soon in our relationship for you to be obsessed with me."

She scanned for Caleb. There was no sign of his energy. She mentally called his name. Still nothing. Panic began to blend with hunger and anger, churning in a frustrated knot. She so did not do frustration well.

Vincent reached over and pressed a point on her wrist. Her fingers went numb. With another of those superior smiles, he lifted her hand free, locked both her wrists in his grip, and started up the stairs. Two tugs proved she was trapped. Why did vampire men have to be so strong?

"Because we were meant to be superior."

He honestly believed that. He really was loony tunes. "Smugness is such an unattractive quality in a man."

"Is it?"

She eyed the distance from her foot to his butt as he preceded her up the stairs. Too far. "Yes."

"I find that hard to believe, seeing as your former lover is one of the most unreasonably arrogant men ever born."

"To some, maybe."

He stopped, the smile on his lips a perverted twist that didn't bode well, talons growing, pressing into her skin with the promise of pain. "There's a difference between confidence and arrogance."

"Right."

"Something I fully intend to teach you." He delivered on the promise, extending his talons past her flesh into the muscle beneath, scraping the bone. There was no containing the scream. It hurt too much for pride. She dropped, striking out with her mind, hitting a solid wall. Oh God, she was helpless. He let her fall to her knees, keeping her wrists above her head, punctuating the lesson he wanted her to learn with a flex of his knuckles.

"It'll be up to you which way it goes, pleasure or pain."

He twisted her wrist, bringing her to the position he wanted, which was kneeling at his feet, looking up at him.

With his free hand he stroked her cheek, making the statement into a question. "Which will it be, Allie? Pleasure or pain?"

Her skin crawled at the parody of a caress. She closed her eyes, remembering Caleb's touch, how different it was. She might drive him nuts, but even at his most furious, he'd always had respect for her. Vincent did not. The truth just popped out along with her revulsion.

"You don't please me."

"It isn't your pleasure that matters."

"I know."

Tell me what you want, Allie girl.

Caleb or Vincent. Pleasure or pain. Heaven or hell. There was no comparison.

"You're nothing to me," she ground out through the agony.

She never saw him move, but suddenly he was squatting in front of her, his fingers a painful bruise on her chin, his face just inches from hers, his eyes writhing with red lights. "I'm God to you."

She swallowed, logic definitely called for retreat but everything in her responded to his aggression. "You're nothing."

The lights in his eyes burst into flame. Her head snapped to the side. The metallic taste of blood filled her mouth, and the right side of her face exploded in pain. It took her a good fifteen seconds to gather her addled wits and figure out what had happened. He'd hit her. The bastard had hit her. Through the buzzing in her brain, she heard a cry of rage. The roar swelled and grew, reverberating with anger, taking shape. Her name.

Allie!

Caleb. He was still alive. She shook her head to clear it of the buzzing. She glared up at Vincent. Wiping the blood off her cheek with her shoulder, feeling it smear more than absorb on the water-proof coat. She got to her feet. "And of course, that was a display of your superior intellect."

"Shut up."

Damn, she needed to shut up, but she couldn't. Shutting up meant giving up, and she wasn't going there. "You're just another egomaniac throwing a tantrum when the world sees him for what he is."

"Bitch."

"Well, duh!" She arched her eyebrows in her best Caleb imitation. "I've even got the T-shirt to prove it."

He leaned in, his face taking on that half-morphed vampire state she just hated. His lips thinned, parted. She caught the gleam of his fangs.

"I think I'll let your lover—"

"Husband."

He kept right on going, as if she hadn't interrupted. "Watch as I drink from you."

She leaned back as those teeth closed the distance between them. She turned her head aside. His breath hit her cheek.

"He's not into the whole threesome thing."

"I imagine he'll quite hate it."

He cut the tiny distance between them by half. She pulled as hard as she could, everything in her rebelling at the thought of any man but Caleb taking her blood. But especially this man. Desperation had her grasping at straws. "I thought you said you wanted him to watch."

"He is."

Mentally, he meant mentally. Did that mean the barriers were down? She called to Caleb. Nothing.

"Do you want to talk to him?" The words were a fetid breath against her skin. "I don't mind letting him hear you scream this time." He pulled her hands up, lifting her into the press of his tongue. Revulsion tore through her as he lapped at the corner of her mouth. "I enjoy it when a woman screams."

She didn't want to give him his wish, but the minute his mouth touched hers, the scream wrenched from her soul, a bone-deep protest. A totally unfair plea. For Caleb. To help her.

Caleb's snarl wound through her soul, his anger bled into hers, and in the middle, a strange flicker of energy, foreign and foul. Vincent. The doorway through which all this was happening. She clamped down on her bile. Focus. She needed to focus. She needed to remember this path. And hell, she also needed to shield. None of which were possible as Vincent pried her jaws apart with a squeeze of his fingers and thrust his tongue into her mouth. She couldn't bite, would not scream, and couldn't make him stop. There was only one thing left to do.

She vomited.

VINCENT flung her away. She spun and fell, his curses ringing in her ears. She stumbled down one step, caught herself on the railing, and continued to vomit. From the corner of her eye, she could see Vincent scrubbing at his mouth, a look of utter revulsion on his face.

That would teach him to attack a woman with a weak stomach. After the next violent heave, she probed for Caleb. Nothing. All she could feel was Vincent's total vulgarity that she'd vomited into his mouth. He was projecting so hard, she retched again in sympathy.

Projecting.

An idea nibbled at her mind. She hung over the stairs, pretending a level of nausea that didn't exist as she explored back along Vincent's energy, shielding as she went, probing until she found that thread of energy she'd marked. She tested. The shield around it was strong, but not solid. She knew Vincent wasn't weak, which meant he just didn't perceive her as a threat. She could use this. But not now. Now she needed to deal with the physical man who was advancing on her in full vamp morph, eyes completely red with rage, talons bared. Shit.

"What?" She wiped at her mouth. "You don't like the way I kiss?"

His snarl sent every reflex into full get-your-ass-out-of-here alert. She vaulted over the rail and hit the smooth tile floor running. She made it three steps before he was on her, his weight slamming her down. She brought up her knees, protecting her stomach. His weight hit her like a ton of bricks, crushing her knees into her ribs. His hand slapped the floor beside her head, setting off a ringing in her ear. His other fastened in her hair, yanking her head back.

"If you kill me you'll never get what you want," she gasped.

"I don't have to kill you to make you pay."

Damn, she wished he hadn't thought of that. "You realize, of course, people don't really say things like that outside of movies, right?"

"Really?" His weight left her body. Pain flared through her scalp as he yanked her up. He held her high, her feet barely touching the floor. Tears poured down her cheeks. She held on to her bravado because it was all she had left. Vincent shifted his grip to her throat.

"Then maybe you should just consider this your own personal movie set."

It was hard to breathe, let alone talk with his hand on her windpipe. "If this is my show, I want say over the script."

"No." His head cocked to the side. "I don't think so." He tightened his grip.

She couldn't breathe and couldn't escape. No matter how she kicked and clawed, he held on, choking the words from existence. Spots spun before her eyes. Blackness crept into the edges of her vision. In her mind she heard Caleb's howl and Vincent's laughter. Her world diminished to the voices in her head and the gleam of Vincent's fangs.

His lips moved with disjointed flashes of color over the white as he spoke words she couldn't hear. He turned and slammed her against the wall. Her head smacked into the sheetrock. More stars joined the first.

"You might as well give in. You can't win."

Against him. That's what he meant. She grabbed for his wrists. His flesh melted like butter under the rake of her talons, but not his intent. He didn't let go. The scent of blood filled her nostrils. Hunger twisted in her gut. Vincent's laugh filled the room. The buzzing disappeared.

Give him what he wants, Allie. Caleb's order came through strong and clear.

No! She'd never give him what he wanted.

Survive!

"Yes, Allie, survive." Vincent echoed the order in a seductive parody. He released her throat. He brought his wrist up. Blood, thick and rich, dripped onto her cheek, trailing inward, toward her mouth. She jerked her head to the left. He brought it back with a ruthless yank. "Feed."

A drop hit her tongue. Then another. Her stomach heaved.

Caleb!

She spat, but couldn't get rid of the vile taste. Her fangs retracted. Her knees drew up. The buzzing was back. She shook her head violently from side to side. Vincent simply put his forearm across her throat. *Caleb!*

"He can't hear you." He slashed his wrist with his thumbnail. "Now feed."

She struck out with her mind, hit that invisible wall again. Vincent laughed. Blood poured into her mouth in a torrent she couldn't avoid. It was either swallow or drown. Oh God, she'd rather drown but her survival instinct wasn't quite ready to give up. She swallowed. The foul blood hit her stomach. The cramps were immediate. Violent and vicious.

"If you puke on me, I'll let you drown in your own vomit."

He meant it. Her face felt cold and clammy. Her stomach writhed in a knot of wrenching pain. No way could she not vomit. No way could she drink more of his blood. It burned like acid inside. She swallowed back her gorge. Two more shallow, desperate breaths and she knew her options were coming to an end. She either had to surrender or die. She looked straight into Vincent's burning eyes, Caleb's order ringing in her memory, and went with the only option she could accept.

Right before she vomited, she groaned, "Fuck you."

✤ 18 ✤

THEY were taking her to see Caleb. Allie stood just ahead of
Vincent and her guards in the doorway of the room that had
been her prison for the last two days and kept her mind locked on
that fact. Held it as a talisman against the weakness that had her
swaying. She had to see Caleb. Had to know he was alive. Of all the
doubts that had plagued her since she'd last seen him, that had been
the worst. Wondering if Vincent had killed him. Wondering if the
kernels of hope Vincent handed out that Caleb was alive were just
more of his sick mind games. She didn't know how she'd missed it
during their dates, but the man was seriously warped.

He delighted in pain, gloried in inflicting mental torture. Not
just on her, on everyone around. Including the pathetic hopefuls
who thought conversion was theirs for the asking. His to deliver. If
they'd bothered to study up, they'd know Mother Nature didn't
work that way. She had her own plans, complete with checks and
balances.

"Get moving."

A hand landed in the middle of her back, sending her to her
knees. She didn't have to look to see who it was. One of the hope-

fuls. Vincent didn't like to get his hands dirty. He preferred to have others do it. It increased his delight to pull the strings that administered the pain. It added another layer of satisfaction to his need for power.

Sick bastard.

He especially liked torturing her. He'd wait until she was practically delirious with pain from the hunger, or violently sick from the blood they'd forced into her, and then he'd weave tales of what he'd supposedly done to Caleb. How he'd died. How he'd suffered. He might have succeeded in driving her crazy with the emotional torture, with the worry she had that the vile blood was hurting her baby, except every time he finished a tale, he'd end with, "I let the sun finish him off."

He didn't know Caleb could walk in sunlight. That was a good sign. She wrapped her arms around her chest, shuddering from the cold that was embedded so deeply in her soul that she knew she'd never get warm again, and stood in the doorway to her room, blinking against the light and the flood of color after the enforced darkness of the last fourteen hours.

With a rough jerk on her arm, Vincent pushed her forward. "Let's go."

She took a step, bracing her hand on the wall as dizziness rose. The white robe they'd put on her swished annoyingly against her bare legs. She hated the damn thing. It was too long, too white, and left her too vulnerable.

"If you don't keep up, I'll leave you where you drop," Vincent snapped impatiently.

"Bastard." She took another step. The distance between them widened. Allie bit her lip against the hunger tearing at her strength, pushing back the waves of nausea that built, swell upon swell. The hall seemed to stretch forever, too long to contemplate walking if she fixated on the end. By keeping her focus on Vincent's back and the mechanics of putting one foot in front of the other, she got herself moving.

The hunger blossoming inside magnified the sound of every heartbeat of the hopeful bimbettes lining the passage. One of the males stepped in front of her, hand out. He was just as perfect as the women. Perfect skin, perfect hair, perfect lashes. Perfectly handsome. She waved him aside. Walking was easier now that she had momentum, and she couldn't afford to falter. The man stepped aside with a small bow, the move sending his perfect blond hair sliding over his perfect broad shoulders. Had Vincent and his cronies physically altered the people or had they simply pasted an illusion around them, making them merely seem nauseatingly perfect? Next time Vincent interrogated her she'd ask. She needed new material to goad him with when he started on his perfect race mantra.

Allie hugged her middle. Holding on to her sanity with a scant thread, reaching for humor. Who knew bad guys could be so disgustingly pedantic? It wasn't like she was ever going to share his narcissistic dream of a genetically superior race. She would never feel for him what she felt for Caleb, and if she ever did, she'd slit her own throat.

She made it halfway down the corridor before pain writhed like a wild thing inside her, and for a moment she didn't have the strength to hold on. She braced her hands on her knees and landed back against the wall.

"Damn you, Caleb," she muttered to her knees. "You owe me for this."

She took a breath as the pain lessened, garnering strength in the void before the next assault. Despite his threat, Vincent waited, implacable and unconcerned. Obviously, he didn't see her as a danger.

That she could make work for her. Vincent absolutely believed she was no threat. Too unskilled, too . . . weak to be dangerous. But she had skills. Things she'd discovered in the hours he'd tortured her. And as long as he kept believing her to be nothing more than a loudmouthed blowhard with grandiose ideas of her own importance, she might have time to hone those skills. And escape.

But she wasn't going anywhere without Caleb. He might be

overbearingly protective and old-fashioned in his ideas, but he was honest, loyal, and caring. And he was hers. Besides, he was still the hottest thing she'd seen, and her hormones would shoot her if she just up and left him behind. Hormones could be very demanding things, she had discovered.

So could hearts.

She ignored that prompting from her emotional side. She wasn't going there right now.

Vincent checked his watch. The first sign of impatience she'd seen.

"I thought you were in a hurry to see that cowboy."

Bastard. She pushed off her knees, her bones aching with weariness and weakness, and went forward. Away from the sunlight. Deeper into the mountain. They passed doors left and right, but she did not hear the strong, steady heartbeat she was listening for.

She needed Caleb. Way down beneath the hunger, deep in the bottom of her soul. Right there on the level of gut instinct, she needed him. And he needed her. He was way too serious if left to his own devices, missing a lot of the fun around him. And as for how she needed him? She forced herself to continue walking. And sighed.

Quite simply, the man understood her. He didn't think less of her for the way she laughed even when something bad happened. He understood it was her coping mechanism. Sometimes, she thought he even appreciated it. Men could be strange beings, but until she had encountered a vampire male, she had never understood that there was a man who might just fit her. Who would take her humor in times of stress as an asset. That was a very endearing asset in a man.

They reached the end of the corridor. The only option was a sharp turn to the right. Vincent took it and she followed, moving with mechanical precision. The sense of leaving sunlight was stronger now. She wondered if this meant they were going underground.

The corridor ended at a big, impressive-looking door. On the right side perched a small panel of flashing lights, and the closer they got, the sturdier the door looked. Caleb must have put up a hell of a fight if they had decided he was dangerous enough for heavy steel doors and electronic bar locks. Allie strained for the sound of life, any sign of life, beyond the thick panel, but there was nothing.

It took excruciating seconds for Vincent to punch in the code. He didn't bother to hide it, which tossed a new ember of worry onto the pile she was collecting. Why wasn't he worried about her knowing the code?

The door slid open on an almost silent whisper. Inside, a row of fluorescent lights ran the length of the ceiling, reminding her of every science lab she'd ever seen in every horror movie she'd ever watched. Not comforting.

She took a step inside, driven by hope. There was no sign of Caleb. Behind her, the door hissed closed. She spun around, lunging for it, catching it halfway. It continued on its track with the same silent precision with which it had opened. Eventually, she had to jerk her fingers free or see them crushed. Why didn't she have vampire strength?

Vincent caught her arm and pulled her back. "You said you wanted to see the cowboy."

"Caleb's not here."

He motioned to a door at the other end of the room. "He's in there."

Why would Vincent have Caleb locked in a sci-fi-horror-movie-thriller-lab environment that was cold, sterile, and intimidating enough to put the fear of God even into her. "In that particular room? Now?"

"Go through and find out."

"Why do we have to play these little games?"

"Because it amuses me."

"And by all means the great Vincent, the most superior person in the world, must be amused."

He inclined his head. "Yes."

"I am so not impressed."

Her sarcasm just rolled off his confidence. And why shouldn't it? He knew he had the upper hand. He knew she would do anything, agree to anything, to see Caleb. The only positive was that he thought the reason she wanted to see Caleb was the horrible wrenching pain in her gut.

The reality was she had a plan. Not the best plan, but a good one. She just needed to find Caleb alive to set it in motion, while keeping the whole concept of a plan under Vincent's mental radar. Not so easy, since, not only was he a bastard, he was a nosy one. She accepted Vincent's invitation to go ahead of him. When she got within ten feet of the door, she felt it—a slow steady seep of energy through the portal. There was a restless edge to the energy. An intensity she recognized. Caleb. He had to be crazy with worry, wondering what had happened to her.

The locks turned with an impressive series of clicks and clunks. That, more than anything else, stated how dangerous they considered Caleb. Which might put a damper on her plan, except—she looked down at her unfettered hands—they still didn't see *her* as a threat. The element of surprise was going to have to be the edge she needed.

The door took its own sweet time sliding open. She tapped her toe, a scream of impatience echoing in her head. Adrenaline surged. When the door finally opened far enough, she practically leapt into the room.

Caleb was on a table in the center of the room. His big body strapped down with bands that shimmered on his wrists and ankles. There was no reaction to her entry into the room. No stirring of his fingers. No twitch of his toes. No increase in the energy. She stepped closer, the hunger clamoring at the knowledge that he was there.

She knew he wasn't dead, which meant something else, something more substantial than the steel, bound him. The farther she moved into the room, the more the flicker of the lights bothered her. The normal white light of the previous room faded, leaving her with the disorienting rhythm of this one. She reached for Caleb with her mind. She hit that same wall of buzzing sound. Instead of pulling away, she probed, using her eyes and her senses. Gradually a pattern emerged. The buzzing vibrated in tandem with the flicker of the light. Interesting.

She stepped up beside Caleb and touched the table. Her hand trembled. "Hi, sugar."

He didn't say a word. She looked over her shoulder at Vincent. "What did you do to him?"

"He's merely being contained."

"Contained?"

"Yes."

She touched the edge of his sleeve with her pinkie. She bet he'd kicked some major ass before they'd brought him here. "Scary when he's in a snit, isn't he?"

"He's strong."

There was an element of confusion in the statement, as if Vincent didn't understand how that could be. That was interesting. She had known Caleb was strong, but without a benchmark to use as a guide, she had just assumed he was normal for a vampire. But to Vincent, he was an unexpected threat. A very powerful, very young— she glanced at his face—very handsome threat. Every sophisticated, aging man's nightmare.

She took a breath. Caleb's scent invaded her senses, worming down to the burning pain, fanning the flames, driving them higher. She fell to her knees and gripped the edge of the table as agony buried everything else, panting as muscles wrenched in spasms. Vincent made no effort to help her. She cut him a glare.

"Apparently," she gasped, "chivalry went out the window with the new superiority."

She caught what might have been a surge of energy from Caleb. She strained, but it was gone as fast as she reached for it. Vincent, however, was giving off big-time energy. Nervous, anticipatory energy. He expected something to happen. But what? Just her feeding couldn't be the answer. What was he hoping to gain from getting her down here? She grabbed the edge of the table—the cold metal chilled her fingers to the bone. How had Caleb endured being imprisoned in this cold place?

It took everything she had to pull herself up, fighting the hunger, her weakness, and her weariness. Vincent laughed when she slipped. The bastard. He could laugh now, all he wanted, but one of these days he was going to be the one to suffer. And she was going to be the one to make it happen. She shifted her elbow onto the table and hauled herself up. Her fingers brushed the roughness of cotton. She grabbed hold. The thick, solid muscle of Caleb's arm felt alien and cold. So cold. She leaned over him, bracing her weight on his chest.

He was cold all over. Her Caleb who was always so warm. Who kept himself warmer than he would like because she had a tendency to chill, was colder than she'd ever dreamed of being. She glared at Vincent. "You are so going to pay for this."

"I'd probably be more impressed if either of you could stand upright on your own right now."

He probably would. She pushed up with her hands, bracing her elbows. She didn't know how she was going to do this. She had so little strength left. And the pain? Oh my God! The pain was absolutely unbearable this close to what she wanted. Allie opened her palm over Caleb's biceps. Even relaxed they were firm, the curve pressing into her hand, shaping her grip. He lay beneath her touch, unmoving. This was so wrong. She shifted her weight to her left hand. She touched his shoulder, too afraid of touching his cheek, afraid the lack of response would break her heart. Allie glared at Vincent. "I can't feed from him like this."

Vincent merely raised his eyebrows as if she were a recalcitrant child. "Yes, you can."

She took a breath as another spike of pain drove the air from her lungs. It took a moment to recover before she could continue. "Let me put it this way, I refuse to feed from him like his."

"I hardly think you're in a position to refuse anything."

"I don't see it that way."

"And I'm supposed to care about that?"

"If you want me to live past the next hour, yeah."

Vincent didn't move, just stared at her. She ignored him. He'd give in. He had to. He wanted her too badly to argue, and she wanted Caleb back too badly to give in. Allie slid her hand over Caleb's shoulder to the strong column of his neck, up to his chin. The rasp of his beard touched her fingertips, evoking memories of other times it'd touched her skin. It had been different then, the touch backed by the laughter and the heat of his desire. Neither of which was evident now. She pulled herself up and touched her mouth to his.

"I'm sorry," she whispered.

No response. Not even a flicker of an eyelash.

She traced the slight crease at the side of his face, the place where his smile would form if he could move and see her fussing over him. "Have you let him feed?"

"Not hardly."

She glanced at Vincent from the corner of her eye. "Then we have a problem." The table creaked as she shifted her weight back. "He won't have enough blood to replenish me."

"Then suck him dry."

She shook her head. "I won't do that."

"Think about how he stole your life. Took you away from your family, killed you, imprisoned you." His smile cut deep. "That should help."

So one would assume. The only thing that wounded was the mention of her family, but she hadn't given up on finding a way to make that work. She just needed more time. "I won't feed from him like this."

"I could make you."

She braced her hand over Caleb's restraint. "No. You can't."

The energy coming off it was familiar. Had a familiar pattern. And it, too, flickered with the same rhythm as the lights. Another clue, but to what? She closed her eyes, concentrating.

"You are incredibly stubborn."

"So I've been told." Her arm quivered with the effort of supporting herself.

"Would you really die rather than feed from him in his current state?"

"You really don't know me too well, do you?"

"You haven't provided me with much of an opportunity."

"Well, you've had clues." She brushed her bangs out of her eyes with her shoulder. "I do what I want, when I want, and how I want. And I'm not real inclined to settle for anything less."

"And you like your food moving?"

A glance over her shoulder showed Vincent staring at her with something almost approaching respect. "I like it at least conscious."

"You know, I really shouldn't humor you, but I find that we're so much alike, it's difficult not to indulge your moods."

She blinked. "Thank you."

When the pain hit this time, the room wove out of focus. She dug her nails into the band and the table. The band throbbed and glowed, responding rather than resisting. "I'm about to pass out."

Vincent cast her an enigmatic glance before walking over to the table. He slid between her and Caleb and opened a drawer. Inside were an assortment of tools. They all looked like instruments of torture to her. Vincent grabbed up a syringe loaded with a greenish mixture.

"What's that?"

"What you wanted."

He pressed the plunger, ejecting a bit of the suspicious-looking stuff.

"Step aside."

She stayed put. "What's in it?"

In answer, he shoved her back and plunged the needle down into Caleb's biceps. His thrill of excitement at the vicious act reached out to her. The hardest thing she'd ever done was to keep her voice calm and steady in the wake of the violence.

"How long before it takes effect?"

"Not long."

She wanted Caleb now. She reached for him with her mind.

"I'm not going to allow you to talk to him mentally."

She shrugged. "It was worth a try."

And worth the tiny bit of feedback on the trail she was building into the back door to his brain.

"As much as I appreciate the power you're going to bring me"— he put the syringe back in the drawer— "I never really appreciated how much enjoyment you're also going to provide."

The path to his mind snapped shut with the same quiet efficiency as the drawer.

A chill that had nothing to do with her hunger shot down her spine. She closed her mind, counted to five, and elbowed him out of her way. "There's a proverb about not counting your chickens until they're hatched."

She took her place at Caleb's side, breathing as if she'd just run five miles rather than merely moved two feet.

Vincent's stare was as heavy as a touch, loaded with nuances she didn't comprehend. "All my chickens are present and accounted for."

The color was returning to Caleb's face. Normal tension began to return to his muscles. "Then, I guess that makes today your day."

Caleb's fingers twitched and his eyes flicked behind his lids. "Caleb? Can you hear me?"

"He can hear you."

She wanted to scream at Vincent, tell him to shut up. She wanted to simply lose it. She wasn't hero material. She wasn't cut out for this. Touching Caleb's cheek with shaking fingers, she breathed a sigh of relief. He was alive and he was coming back to her. That's all she needed.

Caleb's eyes opened.

"See how easy things can go when you cooperate?" Vincent asked.

"Yes."

Her hand on Caleb's shoulder served as a warning. She slipped her other hand down to the manacle on his wrist. Nothing was more welcome than the touch of his gaze to hers.

"Are you okay?" His drawl was hoarse, slower than normal.

"I'm fine."

His green eyes dropped to her mouth where she knew the cut on her lip was evident. His eyes narrowed. The swirls flared to brilliant light. Every muscle in his body snapped rigid. The table vibrated with the tension. "I'll kill the son of a bitch."

"I kind of get the feeling there's a whole long line of people ahead of you wanting to do that very thing."

And her name topped the list.

Caleb didn't look at her, just at Vincent. "The others will have to wait their turn."

Allie slid her hand down his wrist until she could tuck it against his palm. His fingers immediately curled around hers. His gaze slid from her lip down her body and then over to Vincent.

"Are you sure you're okay?"

"He didn't rape me if that's what you're asking." She cut a glare at Vincent who had the gall to be amused by the private moment he was witnessing. "He doesn't have the stomach for it."

Caleb looked pointedly at the bruises on her neck and the cut on her lip. "I find that hard to believe."

"Well, it might be more correct to say that I didn't have the stomach for it. I puked on him when he tried."

He smiled. "You *are* full of surprises."

She leaned her weight on her elbow, her ability to fake strength rapidly failing. "Some of them are even pleasant."

His gaze narrowed then cut to Vincent. "She's weak."

"She refused my hospitality multiple times."

Another wrenching pain doubled her over. Her elbow collided with Caleb's stomach, knocking the wind from him. Her fingers slid off his shoulder. The metal table screamed a protest as her talons scratched over it. Her nose smashed into Caleb's shoulder as the scream built in her throat and reality faded.

Beneath her, Caleb shifted, straining against his bonds. "You need to feed, Allie."

"Yes she does."

"I can't."

"It's the only choice you have."

"No it's not." She held Caleb's gaze, reaching for him so he'd understand, but hitting that mental barrier instead.

"I could always just choose to die."

She was close as it was, and part of her was ready. A minuscule part generated by lack of sleep and escalating pain, but there. Enough to fake intent.

Caleb narrowed his gaze. Though she couldn't feel it, she knew he was reaching for her, too. Not to persuade her, but to command her. The muscle in his jaw jumped. His hand gripped hers hard enough that bone grated against bone. "No way in hell, Allie."

"You're hurting me." His grip lessened slightly.

"I'll do more than hurt you if you get stubborn about this."

"It would solve everything."

"If your death would solve anything, I'd probably just opt to let you die," Vincent interjected.

"You could." Shaking her bangs out of her eyes, she glared at him. "But you won't."

He nodded. "Not yet."

But he was running a tab, she knew. And when the bill came due, if she was still here, he'd make her pay. Just one more reason to make sure her plan worked. "Because we have a deal?"

He inclined his head. "And I am a man of my word."

"Like hell." Caleb jerked at the bonds, the scent of his blood reached her nostrils. Her stomach leapt and quivered. She raked the split in her lip with her fang. The spill of her own blood broke the spell.

"Be quiet, Caleb."

"Yes, do be quiet, Caleb. If not for your value as a food source, you'd be dead."

The buzz in her head grew to pounding. Lights skittered away from the center of her gaze.

"Vincent." She waited until he took his attention off Caleb. "Shut up."

His hand was a blur, but she felt the yank on her hair as he dragged her up until her face was inches from his. "You, woman, forget your place."

Her eyes watered from the sting in her scalp. Her bruised throat muscles ached from the strain, and her mind reeled from the black violence of his.

"We have a deal," she croaked.

"What deal?" Caleb asked.

She ignored Caleb. It was Vincent she needed to manage right now. "You aren't supposed to stick your nose in."

Caleb wasn't willing to let it go. "Allie . . ."

"We agreed that I get uninterrupted time with Caleb."

"I'm only going to give you so much rope, Allie," Vincent warned.

"That's so kind of you."

"Allie girl, that's enough." That order came from Caleb.

It probably was, but she had a hard time with limits. "He doesn't want to kill me, Caleb, just rape me, impregnate me, and raise a whole brood of genetically superior baby vampires with me."

"Then let him."

Shock stole her breath. Nothing in Caleb's face suggested he was kidding.

"Whatever you need to do, you do it."

"See, even your lover wants you in my bed." Vincent let her go with a push. She stumbled forward. The table edge caught under her ribs, giving her the split second she needed to catch her balance. She lay there panting for a brief moment doubting herself until Vincent extended his hand with one of those flourishes he was so fond of, and smiled smugly.

Sheer determination got her back on her feet. "It doesn't matter if the whole U.S. Senate shows up and votes on it." She glared at him. "It's not going to happen."

Fingers touched hers. She looked down, expecting to see anger, not understanding. "You do what you have to do."

He was giving her permission, alleviating her guilt. It was the most horrible, sweetest thing anyone had ever said to her. "That's an amazingly enlightened view for an eighteen sixties sort of guy."

"How touching."

It was her time to grit her teeth. "Vincent, one more time and our deal's off."

Caleb tapped her hand with his finger. "What was the deal?"

She stroked her fingertips over his wrist, lingering over the restraints that bound him, feeling that shivery energy bleeding into her palm. It was more familiar now. Energy, she was discovering, was a funny thing. A person couldn't give it without receiving it, but anyone could take it without leaving clues behind. Vincent had left her lots of clues.

"My cooperation in persuading you to cooperate."

"If part of the deal was that I'd drink from that son of a bitch, it was a bad deal."

"You need blood. So do I."

Caleb jerked his chin at Vincent. "They'll be putting me six feet under before I drink from him."

"You won't drink from him, but I'm supposed to sleep with him?"

"You're supposed to survive."

"So are you."

"I don't matter."

"Shut up."

He raised his eyebrow. "Would that be your way of declaring your intentions, Allie Sanders?"

She gritted her teeth, regretting it immediately when her head pounded as if it was about to explode. "I repeat, shut up."

"I hate to intrude in a private moment, but what Allie isn't telling you is that she has an aversion to you feeding from one of the female hopefuls."

"So bring on a male."

"You made quite an impression on them. None will volunteer."

The pounding in Allie's head increased to a steady pressure. "Our deal is so off, Vincent," she gasped.

"That's fine. I wasn't going to honor it anyway."

Then why had he brought her here?

"You still need to feed," Caleb said, the frown on his face letting her know she wasn't doing a good job disguising her distress. With a twist of his hand he pinched her thigh, the little pain an intimate connection summoning her attention.

She shook her head.

"Look at me, baby." She did. There wasn't an ounce of give in Caleb's expression. Even bound and pinned he was still a formidable man. "Vincent might not be able to make you feed, but you can bet that pretty little ass I can."

He was putting her in an impossible situation. She couldn't bear to watch him feed from another woman, and he refused to feed from Vincent. Vincent was her only out. "You can make the men let him feed from them."

"I could, but . . ." He shrugged. "There's that matter of your continued disrespect."

Inside, her vampire snarled. She would love to lash out at him, but she couldn't. Caleb still had her hand.

She glared at Vincent while yanking her hand. The man didn't flinch or apologize, just stood there in his white robes and asked, "What's it going to be?"

There was only one choice. Caleb would have to feed from one of the female hopefuls. She dug the talons of her free hand into her palm. "Bring on the bimbettes."

❧ 19 ❧

THE door slid shut behind Vincent.

"Interesting that he can't just summon the women here," Caleb murmured.

"I thought so, too."

He stared at the door, a frown on his face, eyes glowing as he concentrated. "He's using a combination of technology and psychic power to control this place."

She rubbed her arms. "Is he gone?"

He turned back. "Yeah." His gaze narrowed, and he frowned for a different reason. "How long did they have me out?"

"Two days."

His curse was harsh and to the point. His power radiated over her, looking for a connection. Another curse when he couldn't link with her. Caleb's gaze returned to her face and lingered on the dark circles she knew were under her eyes. "And he let you suffer?"

"I wasn't exactly cooperative."

His fingertips rubbed her thigh through the robe. His lips set in a straight line. "I'm sorry for getting you into this."

"I think I was the one who started it."

"But I'm the one who knew better."

She didn't want his guilt. "No one *knew* anything. That's been the problem all along."

She leaned against his side, letting him take more of her weight, absorbing his heat, rubbing her hands over those strange bonds. Just taking her time, thinking about things more important than the sharing that was about to commence. Like how to decode the energy in the bonds. Like how to forget Caleb would soon be feeding from another woman.

Caleb's whisper reached out to her with the softness of his touch; even without the mind link, he knew her well enough to recognize that she was worrying. "It's not the same, Allie. What's between mates is different."

"She'll be giving you something I can't."

"She's chow, nothing more personal than that. I can get what she gives me anywhere."

"You can get what you want from me anywhere, too." She rested her cheek against his chest, listened to the steady beat of his heart, closed her eyes against the tightening in her stomach. Before the pain came again she wanted a moment of peace. Just one.

"You know that's not true. When we put this behind us, remind me to paddle your ass for that bit of doubt, too."

She smiled, wanting to shake her head while she was at it, but the moment was too fragile to risk the disturbance. And she was too tired to exert the effort. "The way you're going, you'll be paddling my ass into the next century."

"There's a thought to keep a man hopeful."

She chuckled and rubbed her palm over the bond on his right wrist again, applying the subtlest of mental pressure. Was that a bit of give? A shot of agony broke her concentration. She bit down on her lip, trapping the cry in her throat as the hunger clawed for satisfaction.

The subterfuge was pointless. Even without the mental connection, Caleb knew what was happening. The hard edge of his chin pressed against her temple as he tucked his face to hers. His whisper barely reached her ears. "You can't keep this up, Allie."

There was a fluctuation in the buzz, a momentary increase in intensity. Vincent spying from afar? She mentally flipped him the bird. "The alternative isn't an option."

"It is for me."

Allie made her whisper as soft as Caleb's. "You're not the one who would have to live with it."

Frustrated power writhed around her at her denial of his wish. The buzzing increased, and the band under her fingers flickered. Interesting what happened when men couldn't have what they wanted. Caleb couldn't force her to submit to Vincent to save her life. Vincent couldn't force her to feed from him to control her life, and the bands couldn't withstand the psychic confusion to contain Caleb's life.

"Anything that needs sorting out in the aftermath, we'll sort."

"Then I guess we're both just going to have to live, but know this, Caleb. If you die, all promises are off."

She could just see him sacrificing himself for her.

"You have more than yourself to think about."

Damn him. "So do you."

She glanced over at the door. Vincent would be back soon. They didn't have much time. "So, that's our plan, we both live?"

She still didn't have the key to the bonds, and she couldn't test them too hard without alerting Vincent. She needed more.

The door hissed open. She didn't look up to see what was coming in. Couldn't.

"Come the rest of the way up here, Allie girl," Caleb murmured, his eyes on the being walking toward them.

"Why?"

"Because I told you to."

"You realize of course, it's now imperative that I don't?"

Again that little pinch on her thigh that somehow translated into the most intimate of hugs. "Do it."

That pinch was her undoing. She climbed up beside him. As each inch of her body blended into the hollows of his, all the horrifying changes in her life flashed before her. As each fragmented image surged forward, layering one over the other in a ruthless collage in her mind, her grasp on her composure slipped.

"Caleb?"

"What?"

"How much less will you think of me if I totally lose it?"

"Right now?"

She shook her head, burying her face in the hollow of his throat. "No. Not now."

The hunger roared with Caleb's scent. Her own private dinner bell. The pain raged through the barriers she'd built, swelling with the beat of her heart, the pounding of memories of her life. Her family. Of what had happened to them all. Even if she and Caleb got out of this, it was never going to be the same. Allie blinked back tears. Her emotions didn't care one bit that now was absolutely not the right time to crumble. Her control just methodically fell apart, one piece after another tumbling out of her reach into the black pit waiting below. "Maybe in about five seconds?"

"Shit."

His big body tensed and heaved, the powerful muscles flexing beneath her as he fought the bonds. She stroked his chest, trying to quiet him, opening her palm over his heart when he finally lay still, taking the rhythm of the beat and the reality of what he was into her.

Power and temptation. Promise and doom. Heaven and hell. He was all those things to her and more. And Vincent thought to use him, to hurt him, for a cause only he understood. Her tears dried. No way in hell was she allowing that. She looked up to find Caleb staring back at her, a frown on his face and worry in his eyes.

"Allie . . ."

Footsteps approached. By concentrating, she could make out three sets, two light and one almost nonexistent. Vincent had returned with two women, and from the hard pulse of his anger, he wasn't thrilled with what he saw. She concentrated harder on decoding the bonds.

"Free my hand," Caleb growled.

She jumped, thinking he meant her, but a quick glance up showed the bottom of that stubborn chin. He wasn't looking at her.

"Now why on Earth would I want to do that?" Vincent asked.

"Because if you do, I'll make your death quick rather than the painful one I've currently got planned."

"I don't think you're in a position to threaten anyone."

Caleb didn't move, but a deadly energy radiated off him. Cold. Black. Scary. "Thinking seems to be your weak point."

Vincent motioned the women forward. "High talk for a man strapped to a table."

"I won't feed without the use of my hand."

"Then starve."

"What can it hurt?" Allie asked. Nothing was going to hurt as much as watching Caleb seduce another woman with his mouth. Take pleasure from her body. She pulled in a breath. "He's confined with so many straps, freeing one of his hands can't possibly be a problem."

"It would make him happy."

And that ended that. The sadistic son of a bitch. Anger rose, so thick she thought she'd choke on it. The anger swelled within, growing to an unbearable tension, past the point she felt she could contain it, pressing outward. The rage grew like a wild thing, searching and seeking a target. Allie met Vincent's gaze across Caleb's chest. His eyelids flickered. So did the bond under her hand. She smiled inside, satisfaction joining the rage.

"Please, I'm begging you, I need him to hold me. Please free his hand."

Three steps and Vincent was at their side. She flinched when he touched her hair. Shuddered when he stroked his hand down the length. Beneath her, Caleb snarled.

Out of the corner of her eye she could see the obscenity of Vincent's smile.

"Ah, nothing's prettier than a begging woman, don't you agree?"

"Will agreeing get my hand free?" Caleb asked.

Vincent repeated the caress, but he wasn't looking at her. His focus was totally on taunting Caleb. "Try it and find out."

Caleb's jaw clenched. His drawl lacked its normal fluidity as he ground out, "There's nothing prettier than a begging woman."

"Now that wasn't so hard, was it?" With a magnanimous flourish, Vincent waved at the right restraint.

The bond under her hand heated, became hectic with tendrils of energy. Critical energy. Allie focused, absorbing all she could, cataloging the information. The electronic bond winked out. Too soon.

The steel cuff released with a clank. Caleb's arm came around her slowly, the muscles undoubtedly stiff from so long without moving.

"Thank you." The words escaped on a sigh as the weight of Caleb's arm settled around her. Solid and heavy. Blessedly familiar. His palm curved around her shoulder, tucking her tighter into the shelter of his embrace. Pure unadulterated agony cramped her belly. She was so hungry. Needed him so badly.

She felt his "Come here" as much as she heard it, wishing with all her heart he was talking to her, knowing he was talking to one of the honey blondes waiting with plump lips, anxious eyes, and full D-cup breasts. His pectorals flexed as he shifted his weight. She felt his hunger, not in her mind, but in the honing of his muscles, and that particular intensity that was uniquely his. There was a feminine gasp above her head that quickly became a sigh.

Anger, hot, searing, and primitive, shot through her as the woman's scent flooded the vicinity. She was offering herself to him.

Allie watched her talons extend from her fingertips, elongating along the curve of Caleb's shoulder, each deadly inch a reflection of the destructive hatred burning deep. The bitch moaned with pleasure. A snarl welled in her throat. Her muscles bunched. She'd kill her.

Caleb's hand clamped down on the side of her head, pressing her fangs into his flesh. Blood filled her mouth. She let it roll out, hunger a secondary concern to the woman rubbing against Caleb's side, seducing him with her perfect body, perfect blood, perfect willingness. She jerked her head around. Her face throbbed with a strange tension. Her fangs cut into her cheeks. The woman's expression sliced through Allie's confidence like a knife. Her smile was dreamy, replete, and so satisfied, it begged for retaliation.

On a growl that rumbled up from her toes, Allie slipped out of Caleb's hold and went for her. A hairsbreadth from sinking her talons into the woman's chest, she was yanked up short. Pain exploded through her scalp. She spun around. Pressure on her hair tightened her turn, spinning her into the curve of Caleb's wrist. His eyes glowed with gold lights, a smear of blood lingered by the corner of his mouth. She lashed out at him for the offense. He turned his head away from the slap. Her nails cut into his cheek just under his eye.

He took the blow, but when she pulled back her hand to swing again, he shook her, keeping her suspended above him with his grip on her hair. His "Stop it" picked up the internal litany ringing in her head. *Stop. Stop. Stop.*

Blood dripped down his cheek from the cuts of her nails, slowly pooling along his mouth, eventually reaching the other woman's mark. She watched as it seeped along the edges, bleeding into the stain, covering it. It wasn't enough. She needed him to bleed more, hurt more, enough so it wouldn't matter.

"It doesn't matter, Allie."

Caleb repeated the assurance again as he held Allie above him at arm's length. He didn't even think she was aware of her grip on his wrist or the way her talons pierced his skin. All she was aware of was his touch on another woman, her emotional pain brilliant in her blue eyes, the golden lights vivid glittering shards of betrayal.

Her vampire couldn't handle this. He should have known it couldn't, but she'd seemed so calm about it. Accepting. "Seemed" being the operative word. He didn't dare pull her as close as he wanted. All that pain made her unpredictable. Maybe even deadly.

If she wanted to kick his ass after this was over, that would be her option, but until she was safely back at the Circle J, she was going to have to keep her ass kicking in the fantasy realm. He shook her again, the hair spilling over his fist, the tendrils swaying with the violence between them.

"She means nothing." Her gaze dropped to his mouth, following the movement of his lips as if hypnotized. "Food, nothing more."

He waited, blood flowing down his cheek, for the words to sink in, wishing he could use the mental connection again, but the return of the buzzing meant Vincent had slammed the door shut as soon as he'd realized Allie had opened it.

Beside them, oblivious to the danger, the other woman stood panting, her breath coming in hungry gasps, the scent of her desire fouling the air. Blood gushed from her open wound. He had to do something about that. He snapped his fingers, locked his gaze to hers, and ordered, "Put your wrist in my left hand."

The woman reacted like a puppet on a string, her eyes clinging to his, her hips brushing against his fingers, rubbing in a clear invitation. He pressed his thumb on the artery he'd bitten into, suppressing the blood loss. If Allie's need wasn't reaching critical point, he'd send her away, but without blood Allie wouldn't be able to escape. And as much as he hated that she hurt, her survival was priority. Blood pumped, flowed, pooled, while he waited. At last, Allie's gaze lifted from his mouth, a question in her eyes.

"Hard choices, baby." There were so many hard choices in this life. He'd spare her as many as he could, but there were some she would have to deal with alone. Like this one.

Her mouth worked, but no sound came out. She closed her eyes. Her lips worked some more, shaping syllables he understood. Counting. She was counting, he realized. He relaxed. She was regaining her control. Her whisper when it finally came was as shaky as he'd ever heard it.

"You don't want her?"

"No." In the past he'd wanted his prey. Lust and bloodlust went together. He'd never indulged. Taking a woman who wasn't aware of what was going on amounted to rape in his book, but he'd felt the passion. He lowered Allie to rest against his chest again.

"Allie, either I close this artery or I feed."

"Why am I always the one making these decisions?"

Because she was the one they kept hurting. Damn, he wished he could change that, but he couldn't. No more than he could shelter her from the pain. All he could do was hold her and whisper truths that had to sound like empty promises. "My turn's coming round soon enough."

Because after this, he couldn't justify holding her. If she wanted to leave him, he'd let her go and take the emotional death that came with her departure as no more than he deserved.

Her leg drew up over his thigh. Her fangs raked his flesh with that feminine delicacy that always shot straight to his groin. That little hesitation was the most erotic thing he'd ever felt. And it didn't matter if they had witnesses. His body reacted like they were alone.

Her pleasure hummed against his skin. "I like that."

"What?"

"The way you come alive at my touch."

"That's good, because I don't have a choice."

Over the slight curve of her shoulder, he could see Vincent's impatient shift. He was letting this play out for reasons of his own. Reasons Caleb didn't think Allie was aware of, but the bastard wouldn't get his hands on her. Caleb would personally guarantee that. He just needed them both at full strength before he could get them out of there. Allie took advantage of his distraction to glance at the woman again. Her body went tight.

Caleb squeezed her shoulder. "I don't have to let her enjoy it."

Allie jerked. Her hands clenched, nails digging into his thigh and screeching down the metal table as she battled herself. Her "No" was hoarse, telling him how hard the battle had been between her human self and the purely selfish drive of the vampire. "Don't let her hurt."

It was the answer he'd expected. Still, he was amazed that she'd been able to make it with jealousy riding her so hard. He dropped a kiss on the top of her head before pressing her face into his chest. "Close your eyes and stay put."

For once she followed direction without argument, burying her face in his throat as the muscles in her back writhed under his hand with a fresh surge of hunger. Damn, after two days, the pain had to be unbearable. And he couldn't share it or bear part of it for her. This feeding needed to get done. Caleb held Allie's head against him as he caught the gaze of the hopeful. "Give me your wrist."

Beyond a shudder, Allie didn't move. He fed as fast and efficiently as possible, not handling the woman's lust like he might have, leaving it to Vincent to deal with. When he was done, he called the other girl over, almost identical to the first, same bust size, same ultrathick lashes, same hair color. The only difference was bone structure. But even that was very similar. While they were all someone's idea of perfection, it was a consolation that none of them looked like Allie.

The woman presented her arm. He bit gently, fed efficiently. As soon as he took as much as he could, he ordered the woman away.

"Done already?" Vincent asked.

"Yes."

Allie's head came up. Along with it her snarl. He thought she was going to hit him again. He'd let her if she needed to. Instead she fought the sleeve of her robe and scrubbed obsessively at his mouth. When his face felt raw and she still showed no sign of stopping, he wrapped his fingers in her hair and tugged. "Enough."

The wildness left her eyes to slowly be replaced by horror. She looked at her arm, and then at his mouth, which had to be reddened from the abrasion. Tears welled in her eyes again. "Oh my God, I'm so sorry."

"And here I was about to thank you for making me presentable."

She stared at him for a heartbeat, clutching her wrist in her hand. She blinked and then gasped. He didn't have to ask why. Her stomach muscles cramped so hard he had the impression she'd doubled over long before she actually had. "Shit."

She struggled to get off him. He held her in place.

"I think I'm going to be sick."

"Then get sick."

She shook her head. "Not on you."

"I'd prefer you hit the floor, but if it comes down to me holding you through it or you going through it alone, you go right ahead and heave up your toes all over me." Holding her was the only comfort he could offer her, and he wasn't going to withdraw it, not for love or money, or the threat of a mess.

She lay on her side on top of him, her body twisted into a fetal ball, riding out the pain he'd given her when he'd turned her, panting in short staccato breaths that didn't leave much room for speech. But she still managed a "Glutton."

He stroked her hair. "When it comes to you, always."

Across the room, Vincent stood straight, those pale eyes watching with a predatory gleam, a damn coyote waiting to steal the prize. Caleb flipped him the middle finger. He was never getting Allie.

Allie bucked on him, dry heaves racking her body. So violently he expected her bones to separate from her joints. He didn't know how she survived it. She felt so frail to him, though if he told her that, he had a feeling she'd spend an hour explaining to him the wrongness of his notion. The heaves finally ended, leaving her pale and shaking, barely conscious, so exhausted her breaths were whispery sighs rather than healthy inhalations.

"Enough of this." With two quick, heavy steps, Vincent approached the table, staying on Caleb's bound side. Too bad. Caleb would have taken great pleasure in wringing his neck. Vincent grabbed Allie's upper arm, yanking her up and around before shoving her face to Caleb's throat. She hung limp in his grasp, either incapable or unwilling to follow his order to feed.

Fury as he'd never known poured through Caleb. Fangs exploded back into his mouth. His talons extended to their full six inches. With a disgusted curse, Vincent dropped Allie. She sprawled atop Caleb like a broken doll.

Vincent poked her. She didn't move. "Fucking bitch left it too late."

It wasn't too late. He wouldn't let it be. Caleb cradled Allie's head in his palm, holding her mouth against his chest. He slipped his pinkie between her lips and his skin, angling it down, slicing deep. Blood pooled against his finger and spread to her lips. She didn't respond. Damn.

"C'mon baby. Just a little. For me."

Her eyes closed. He guessed he could take it as a no. Vincent shook her. Her head rolled back and forth. Caleb slashed Vincent's arm, snarling in satisfaction as blood sprayed in an arc. "Do that again and I'll cut your fucking arm off."

Vincent sealed the wound with his tongue, ignoring the crimson splash across his robe. "Your usefulness is about over, cowboy. Instead of making pointless threats, I'd suggest thinking about ways to keep me from killing you."

Talk about useless. That threat was about as viable as teats on a bull. "She's unconscious."

Blood pooled on his chest between them, chilling in the cool air. Caleb rubbed some on her tongue. Did her lashes flicker?

Vincent folded his arms across his chest. "Wake her up."

Caleb didn't spare him a glance. "Drop the barrier."

"You don't give the orders here."

"I'm giving this one, and if you want Allie to feed, you'll follow it."

The other man held his gaze, projecting his dominance with mind and stance. Caleb dismissed both. He'd kicked the asses of more impressive men while on a three-day bender. He pushed Allie's bangs off her face. She was so pale. Too pale. He brushed his lips over her hair. With an abruptness that resounded louder than a clanging bell, the buzzing disappeared. Vincent had given in. Caleb hid his elation against her cheek.

"Allie, if you don't wake up and feed right now, I'm going to trash that damn stove you're so fond of and sell it as scrap." He put his lips by her ear. "Just think, you'll never get that bear claw recipe perfected. Jared will forever be teasing you about your baked goods." Her eyelids definitely flickered then. "And before you give up, you might just want to remember how long a time forever is for us."

Her lips moved against his chest.

"What?"

"Bastard."

The smile pushed out from his soul. "That's my girl. Come out swinging."

"Can I feed now?"

"Yes."

She lapped at his skin. Her body moved against his side. Soft, sweet, and sexy. His. Everything he ever wanted. He massaged his fingers through her hair, giving her the time she needed, knowing how difficult it was going to be when it ended. He didn't think she'd thought that far down the road to what would happen when one hunger replaced another. But, seeing the expectation on Vincent's face, the eagerness betrayed by his tense muscles, Vincent had.

And that conversion of desire was the whole reason he'd brought Allie here. Vincent figured on taking the lust that followed blood-lust and using it to bind Allie to him. He planned on raping her.

Caleb lifted his lip in response to Vincent's smile. The son of a bitch would never touch her.

With a little sigh that shot straight to his groin, Allie centered her fangs. Every color in the spectrum of erotic delight shot through his system as her bite took him over the edge into pleasure. He loved the moment when she gave herself to him like this, trusting him to take care of her, *letting* him take care of her. She was such an independent soul, it didn't happen often. Not a wholehearted surrender. The moments when it did should be savored.

But this one wouldn't be. Just one more debt to lay at Vincent's feet. This time there was too much at stake. Allie's lips brushed his skin in velvet caresses as she fed, her breath a soft quavery invitation, breeding a deeper need. He let it rise, subtly gathering his strength behind the veil of the hunger, projecting his sexual response, distracting Vincent with the sensations, while in his mind he gathered the familiar voices. His brothers were coming.

It was hard to discern night from day this deep in the mountain, but the fact that his brothers' war cry shivered along his own battle instincts meant it was night. The Johnson brothers were on the warpath, and the Sanctuary was coming down. The Johnson brothers didn't kick shit fancy, but they did kick shit well.

Allie's tongue licked over his chest in little darts of flame, her hunger primitive and demanding, uncaring of an audience, uncaring of danger. Her body drew on his in long, slow contractions. His cock leapt. He pressed her mouth tighter to his chest as she did it again. Vincent stepped forward, reaching out. Caleb only had time to send one thought before the buzzing began again.

Get ready, Allie.

Caleb locked on the buzzing, linking his mind to the rhythm and the flickering light, moving between the patterns. Against them, Allie quivered and kissed his neck, her lush breasts rubbing against him. He countered her moves with his, feeling Vincent's confidence that he was too far gone to protest, using the distraction to sneak behind Vincent's mental barriers, looking for the loophole that would make everything possible. He found it, breached it, and then all hell broke loose.

❧ 20 ❧

VINCENT struck first.

A blinding flash of brilliant agony shot into Caleb's brain wrenching a scream from his psyche. He contained it as he grabbed hold of that betraying beam, following that energy back, knowing if he backed off now he'd never have the opportunity again. Knowing if he failed, Allie was gone.

Blood pooled red behind his eyes. Sparks shot inward from the perimeter of his mind's eye, and in the center of the mental confusion glowed the bright yellow light that was the power Vincent wielded with such skill. The control center for this whole compound. The barrier he needed to breach.

The mental calls of his brothers grew louder as he probed deeper, three of the hundreds of threads of energy making up the rays of light. With every call, they telegraphed to Vincent where they were, what they were planning, unwittingly giving their enemy all the information he needed to ambush them.

Caleb gritted his teeth. It wasn't going to happen. Vincent wasn't getting his wife and he was not killing his brothers. Not if he had any say about it. And he did. A lot.

Tapping into the threads, he pulled himself deeper, riding the tendrils of his brothers' energy, sheltering himself within the familiar, but they weren't a straight path. They looped and spun, forcing him to loop and spin with them. Every time he touched Vincent's power, thousands of synapses in his brain writhed in agony. And he betrayed his presence. He could feel Vincent searching for him. His brothers' tendrils swirled into the center becoming completely entangled in Vincent's. Hiding time was over.

As soon as he hit the wall, a bolt of energy flashed outward, hitting him square on. The world went black. Allie's scream ricocheted around him, hatred and violence blending with desperation and determination. His brothers' voices grew louder and more distinct. Their power brushed his. Too far away to help. He closed his eyes and fought on. He would have to; he couldn't let Vincent win.

And then he felt it. Another presence in his mind: soft, feminine, it came alongside, attached to his force before branching out along the light, surrounding it in pale pink ribbons of feminine power. Allie. Damn it! Once again, where she didn't belong. Putting herself in danger in an effort to save him.

Another raw burst of energy shot out from Vincent heading for Allie. Caleb pulled the energy into himself to keep it from striking, imprisoning it as blistering fire seared up his spinal cord, tearing along his nerves. His body spasmed. His talons dented the steel table as he arched his back and released the agony on a roar of rage. A whisper skated along the edge of his consciousness. *Hold on. Hold on.*

Allie didn't have to worry. He wasn't letting go until the son of a bitch was dead. Caleb tried to redirect the light, but it was too powerful, a breathtaking burn consuming his brain, one cell at a time, eating away at his strength. Debilitating shudders racked his frame as he took more of the assault into himself, giving Allie time, watching the little bits of feminine strength stretch like veins into the outpouring of energy, weaving through the pattern, finding key spots in the sequence, marking them with visible color. Every pink line that twined around that burning light was his woman, fighting with the same stubbornness and determination that had defeated the wolves. Vincent didn't stand a fucking chance.

Hurry, Allie!

Even as he said it, Caleb didn't know if she could. She was expending a tremendous amount of energy. He could feel her desperation. She sensed he was losing the battle. His brothers' curses grew louder, Vincent's mental blows stronger. Caleb deflected what he could, learning as he went the rules of a battle fought solely in the mind. And he held on. Held on to that violent, sickening pile of hatred, keeping it from lashing out, keeping it still so the sweetness of Allie could rip it apart. Who knew feminine strength could be so devastating?

The pattern of light wavered. Energy ebbed and flowed. Caleb tested his bonds, needing to be free, ready to take this war to the physical plane. Soon, it would be soon.

Beyond the mental battle he could hear his brothers' war cries, the staccato thunder of gunshots, the crash of glass, hoarse yells punctuated by the cold methodical feel of vengeance being wrought. The light wavered again. Trying to maintain his stronghold's defense was weakening Vincent's mental strength.

Lightning shot down the light Caleb held, knifing into his brain. His body bucked, his hold loosened. He heard Allie's scream as his strength faltered. Vincent's laugh echoed in his head.

You cannot win.

Watch me.

And from Allie, her own personal war cry. *Fuck you!*

That was his woman. Grit to the bone. Strong enough to weaken Vincent's hold. Strong enough to keep fighting no matter what.

Caleb felt Allie gathering strength. An incredible amount. More than was possible for her to have. More than she could spare if she unleashed it all at once. Instinct, vampire and human, said to drive her back, shelter her. Protect their baby.

A start of surprise rippled through Vincent's shield.

So she's breeding.

Caleb gritted his teeth. Shit. He knew. Adrenaline pumped. Rage hammered out the imperative, Vincent needed to die. Icy calm centered Caleb's purpose. He searched the pattern of Vincent's energy, found the center of the stream he held, and drove straight up the middle, striking at the heart of Vincent's mind, expecting his parry, slipping around it, looking for the spot behind, that tiny break that would flash. Catching it at it's widest point, he thrust through.

Vincent's howl echoed inside and outside his head. Caleb struck again and again, until his mental gash gushed energy. Then he changed targets and aimed for the pink markers Allie had left. Beneath each pink thread, the light spilled in a rushing stream. Caleb didn't know what Allie was doing, but whatever it was, it was working. Vincent was hemorrhaging faster than he could repair.

Caleb sent out a mental call. *Jared!*

This time there was an answer.

On our way.

Allie?

I feel her.

Get her out of here.

How badly are you hurt?

Bad enough.

Shit.

There was a pause.

You okay?

Another one of these wuss ass banditos.

Wuss ass?

The term fits.

How soon can you get here?

Keep talking and I'll let you know. The place is a labyrinth.

Work fast.

Light flashed in the perimeter of his mind's eye in a warning.

The energy blow that came at him was incredibly strong but wild. Caleb easily evaded it. Vincent was getting desperate.

Caleb wrenched at his bonds, the light surrounding the steel bands flickered and weakened. He yanked again, the bones in his right wrist broke, but the band broke. He absorbed the agony, freeing his feet with equally brutal yanks, swearing when Allie's attention immediately diverted to him, freeing Vincent.

He rolled off the table, dragging her with him as the other man struck with savage force. Steel groaned and rattled as Vincent's fist punched down. Caleb shoved Allie under the table. She glanced up. Her face turned paper white at the perfect outline of fist and talons above her head.

"Stay."

His fangs made the order a guttural exhalation.

Her gaze cut to Vincent. He no longer resembled the smooth, urbane gentleman they'd met at the gates. Fully morphed he was as ugly as his energy. The ridge of his brow thrust over his eyes, eyes that were no longer cold but burned with the fires of a man who knew he was on his last chance.

Allie's gaze cut back to him. Her eyelids flickered as she caught a glimpse of his face. Caleb knew he was fully changed and to her eyes must look as hideous as Vincent. He didn't have time to reassure her beyond a light touch on her cheek. His talons were obscene against the delicacy of her skin. "You did good."

She didn't respond with her usual humor, just a nod and a glimmer of something he didn't understand. Her blue eyes abruptly flew wide. A shadow passed over their surface. Shit! Caleb twisted and blocked Vincent's thrust, using the other man's speed to offset his balance.

Caleb leapt to his feet, stepping back. Vincent followed, swiping at his midsection. Caleb sprang back, away from Allie. Son of a bitch, he was fast. But not fast enough. Caleb bent over, clutching his midsection and waited. He had only one chance to make this right. He sent Allie a mental command.

Run.

Allie got to her knees. The door was only a few feet away. Slightly ajar, no doubt from the hopefuls' rapid departure. She'd make it. That left only Vincent to contend with. Caleb let his anger settle around him, draining his world of anything but the cold clarity that sharpened his senses.

Vincent was scared and determined. He wanted Allie. A breeder for the super race he thought his genetics would create. Caleb tackled him mid-lunge as the man made to cut off her escape. "No fucking way, you bastard."

"She's mine."

"Never."

"Yes!"

"Caleb!" Allie screamed in warning.

Burning agony ripped through his chest, back to front. Once, twice. Son of a bitch. He looked over his shoulder as he dropped to his knees. Four more vampires had entered the room.

RUN.

Caleb's order screamed in Allie's mind as he went down. The newcomers leapt onto his back with evil hisses of victory. She held her breath.

Get up, get up, get up!

The chant thundered in her pulse as she watched the battle. Blood suddenly spewed in a horrifying spray. Caleb's or one of the others'? One of the lesser vamps stumbled to the side.

She released her breath. Not Caleb. Caleb was alive and he was fighting. Making the ultimate sacrifice to buy time. For her.

She dug her nails into her palms as she got her feet under her. And it would be all for nothing, because no way in hell was she leaving him there, but what could she do? Even Lara Croft would be no match for that much muscle. She needed help. There was only one place she knew to look for it.

Slade? Nothing.

Jace? Still nothing. Damn. She took a breath.

Jared?

At first nothing, but the void wasn't as empty as it had been with the other brothers. There was a silence that was something more. Almost invisible static. Like maybe she wasn't quite tuned to where she needed to be. She screamed as one of the attacking vampires went flying, blood following from him in an arc. The cry died in her throat as the second vampire, a black-haired monster, landed a blow to Caleb's side. Adding more blood to his already covered torso. It didn't slow him down. He launched the other vampire to the left. Straight into Vincent. Oh God. She hadn't even seen him stalking her.

The order came again. *Run.*

She stared at Caleb helplessly. She couldn't leave him. He bared his fangs, no doubt trying to scare her. Like that was going to happen. Beneath the morphed form was a man ready to die for the chance that she and her child could have life. It was hard to be afraid of someone like that.

Allie refocused, summoning the memory of Jared's anger that first day, locking onto the determination she'd felt from him. *Jared!*

Calm smoothed over her panic. *Coming.*

She shoved back at his calm. *They're killing him.*

We're almost there.

Almost wasn't here. And Caleb didn't have any more time. There were only two other vampires and Vincent facing Caleb now. The other two were motionless, scattered across the room like so much bloody debris. But Caleb was still standing, battered and bloody, but he was standing, muscles tensed, head thrown back, an image worthy of a movie poster with all that rampant masculinity, power, and challenge. Her man. She stood up, took a step forward . . .

Get back.

She ignored Caleb's and Jared's combined order, frowning as the vampires converged on him again. His blood splattered the wall. The agony flowing from him to her unchecked a split second before he cut it off. The next blow Caleb took shattered something deep inside her, releasing something primitive and feral she didn't recognize. But welcomed.

The two vampires hauled Caleb up, imprisoning him between them, dangling him as a gift for Vincent. A growl erupted from within. Her face tingled and numbed.

"I'm going to enjoy this," Vincent gloated, squaring off against Caleb as he struggled between the two vamps.

The statement echoed around her as reality shifted. Vincent's image blurred behind a strange light. She saw Caleb's lips move, but she couldn't hear. Sound distorted. Time froze in a deadly tableau. Only she could move. Only she had control. She drifted through the fragmented spectacle, focusing on Vincent. She reached out. The light luminesced, flowing forward, toward the bright yellow light that was Vincent, finding the black tendrils perverting his energy that were so obvious now. So obvious.

Elation boosted her rage as she slipped into the flow of energy, ignoring the distraction of its discordance, focusing on the center pulse, pulling it into her. More and more. An endless amount, expecting the initial resistance but not the ease that followed. And it was easy, so easy to draw off his power. To drain him. And so damn satisfying. More. She had to take more until there was nothing left and Vincent was just an empty shell. A threat to no one.

"Allie!"

Caleb's voice slid along the edges of her consciousness, drawing her attention, drawing Vincent's. She held Vincent harder, too afraid to let go. If she let go, Caleb would die. That couldn't happen. Ever.

"I'm okay, Allie girl," Caleb said again, his mental touch stronger. "You've got to let go."

She shook her head, frowning as her hold weakened. Vincent had to die.

Caleb's whisper in her mind was as gentle as his touch. *But you don't have to be the one to do it.*

No. She couldn't kill.

"Let go, Allie."

Hands tugged at hers. She opened her eyes. And blinked. She could have sworn her eyes had been open before, but they hadn't been, because no way would she have forgotten the sight of her hands wrapped around Vincent's head, her talons sunk like tentacles into his skull. "Oh my God."

She leapt back into Caleb's chest, turning into his arms as she fought to erase the image of Vincent's lifeless body slumping to the floor, ten perfect punctures staring back at her in accusation.

Caleb's left arm came around her. "Shh, baby."

She shook her head, her cheek sliding in the blood covering his big form. Then she was saying "Oh my God" for another reason as she checked him head to toe for damage. She cradled his broken wrist in her hands. Tears dripped onto the red swathe, making clear circles in the crimson pool. "I'm so sorry."

His kiss landed on her head rather than her cheek.

"It wasn't supposed to happen like this," she whispered.

"No, it wasn't."

There was no accusation in his voice. She heard footsteps. Jared and Slade joined him. Both men's clothes were torn and spattered with blood and stuff she didn't want to identify. Slade knelt beside Caleb. He dropped a kit on the floor and pulled out an air splint. After probing the wound on Caleb's right side, Slade asked, "How many times have I told you not to drop your right hand?"

"I was distracted."

By her. Allie bit her lip. "When did you get here?"

Slade's smile was more a quirk of his lips. "About the time you started sucking the life out of Vincent."

"I didn't bite him." And the horror of that was greatest of all. Without biting a man, she'd killed him.

"He's not dead."

She could have kissed Caleb for his habit of reading her mind.

"Going to be in a minute though."

She quickly buried her face back in Caleb's chest as Jared jerked the man up. He hung limply in his grip, all sophistication gone. The scent that was uniquely Caleb's reached her through the stench of blood. She clung to it, riding the rapid rise and fall of his chest, slipping her arms up his back, taking more and more into her. Just needing something familiar to cling to.

"He's not going to kill him right now," Caleb said so easily, so at ease with the violence around them.

"Does it make me a failure as a vampire if I say 'good'?"

"No." His hand cupped her skull, his fingers curling into her hair. "It just makes you human."

She ignored the small tug that was an invitation to look at him. "But I'm not human anymore."

"Not strictly, but you're still the sweetest thing I've ever seen."

"That's an evasion, not an answer."

This time she couldn't ignore the tug on her hair. She tilted her head back. Caleb, the human, looked back at her. She touched his cheek. "Your face is back to normal."

Beneath her thumb, his lips tugged into a wry grin. "No longer a monster, eh?"

His beard pricked her palm. "You're not a monster."

"I am what I am. No sense dressing it up."

"I hate it when you do that."

"What?"

"Try to make me dislike you."

"Baby, that's not even logical." He pulled her into his lap.

"I know. You should work on it."

A commotion on the other side of the room drew her attention. Before she could turn, Caleb's arms locked down, immobilizing her, keeping her from seeing any of it. Hearing a stuttered gurgle, she bit her lip and understood why he blocked her view. "I don't like this."

He looked over her head, nodding to someone she couldn't see. "No reason you should."

"All done."

She recognized Slade's voice.

She clutched Caleb's shoulders as he leaned forward and then back, rising smoothly to his feet. "Time to go."

"I can walk."

"I know."

She raised her eyebrow at him. "Then why am I not standing?"

"Because I'm having a hard time getting rid of the image of you walking up to three vampires after I told you to run."

"I knew what I was doing." It was only a small lie. Part of her had known exactly what she was doing. She just hadn't made the acquaintance of that part of herself at the time.

"Bullshit." The air crackled around them. Caleb turned sideways to get them through the door. "It was reckless, impulsive, and fool-hardy."

The brothers fell into step beside them. Armed and ready, they were an impressive escort.

"You left out successful," Jace said, coming up alongside.

She countered Caleb's "Shut up" with a smile. "Thank you."

She craned her neck until she could check the condition of the men around them. They were all there, in various stages of worse-for-wear, but there. "How did you find us?"

"Once Caleb sent word you'd set out, we followed along in case your welcome wasn't as warm as you were hoping."

"You could have stepped it up," Caleb growled. His grip tightened. He was still angry.

"Had a bit of trouble with the D'Nallys," Jace growled.

"Not to mention that barricade." Slade stepped over the body of a dead hopeful. Allie felt a twinge of pity for the misguided soul until Slade bent down and picked up the gun a couple feet away. "Our friend Vincent might have been nuttier than a cow on loco-weed, but he was brilliant when it came to weapons."

He fired the weapon. The wall exploded. "Laser mixed with light in the spectrum of sunlight. Silent but deadly to weres and vamps alike."

Slade nodded. He threw the weapon over his shoulder. "Except to our Caleb here."

"Why in hell would someone invent a weapon like that?"

"Only one reason I can think of," Jace offered, checking the next hall. He stepped in, reappearing a second later, motioning them on. "Someone's readying for a war."

"The question is, against who?"

Caleb stepped through the door. "My guess would lean toward everyone who doesn't fit their genetic ideal."

Allie shook her head. "It's bigger than just Vincent."

The men glanced at her. "What do you mean?"

"I mean, when I was connected to Vincent, I felt a connection to more entities, widespread but connected." She shook her head. "I don't think killing Vincent put an end to this."

The men glanced at each other and then around the high-tech room. Jared summed up the brothers' thoughts in one word, "Shit."

Caleb shifted his rifle in his grip. "In that case, we'd better get going."

Jared fell into position ahead of them, clearing a path. A mean, angry man looking for an excuse to vent. She felt sorry for anyone who got in his way.

Caleb fell into step behind them, still carrying her. Under his guise of strength she could feel how weak he really was. "Let me walk."

"No."

"Yes."

She frowned up at him. "Don't make me go all vampiress on you."

The flash of amusement in his eyes soothed a bit of the fear inside. "You can throw anything you want at me, baby."

The "It's not going to scare me" was implied. She patted his cheek and tugged his head down so she could whisper in his ear, "Put me down before you fall down."

He grimaced. "You weren't supposed to notice."

"Don't worry. I still think you're macho."

"Ouch."

"What? You notice everything about me, why can't I notice a thing or two about you?"

"Because it's hard on a man's pride," Jace said, coming up beside them. "I can take her."

"I can walk."

No one paid her any attention. Caleb handed her over. She would have wiggled in protest, but her legs and arms had the substance of Jell-O.

Since she had no choice, she relaxed against Jace and asked, "Is Caleb really going to be all right?"

"What did Slade say?"

"He said he would."

"Then he will be. Slade is never wrong."

She rested her head on Jace's shoulder. It wasn't comfortable like Caleb's, but it was okay. "It's really not fair. You all turn vampire and become supermen. I turn vampire and remain a wuss."

All she could see of Jace's smile was the slight crease where his chin met his cheek. "I wouldn't exactly call you a wuss."

Caleb's "hardly" was dry. He caught the gun Jared threw him. It took him about three seconds to figure out the mechanism. He tossed it in his hands, testing its weight. Guns were obviously a guy thing, because it looked damn natural in his hands. "Let's move."

He gave her a smile. She tried to smile back, but in reality, reaction was setting in and her composure was a bit limp at the corners. Caleb frowned, obviously not buying her act. Well, hell, she used to be better at this.

"Don't feel bad. He does that to all of us," Jace said.

"What?"

"Sees more than we want him to."

"Who says I'm hiding something?"

"That big grin on your face, when anyone can see how hard you're shaking."

"Damn."

Caleb came over and brushed her cheek with his thumb. There was blood on the back of his hand and a lethal energy about him. He was almost a stranger except for the crook of his grin and the emotion in his touch. Gentleness in both at a time when he'd never looked more savage.

"We'll have you home soon."

Home. Back to the ranch that was a strange mix of paranormal beings, modern science, and antiquity. Who would have thought it could sound so good? "Thank you."

His finger stroked the curve of her lips in a familiar caress, rubbing at the corner. Spit or blood? She almost asked which and then stopped herself. She really didn't want to know. "I look a mess, huh?"

"You look beautiful."

The glance Caleb cut Jace from under his brow was dead serious. "No matter what, you keep her safe."

"You've got it."

One tap of his finger on her lips, which had them plumping and firming for a kiss that didn't come, and she was looking at his back. His broad, injured, determined back. "Does he ever believe he can't win?"

Jace shifted her weight in his arms. She clutched his coat until she was sure he wasn't going to drop her. "No."

"Why not?"

As soon as Jared gave the "all clear" they went to the next corridor, toward . . . She took a moment to orient herself. The night. It was night. Thank God.

"Are we going to have time to get back?"

"Yes."

Jace stopped at another door, dropped into a crouch, and set her beside him. The sounds of combat came at them from the other side. "Stay."

She tucked her feet under her, ready to move. "I'm not a dog."

"If you were, we could just slap a leash on you when you got difficult."

"Charming."

He slipped his gun off his shoulder. "I try." His attention was clearly ahead and not on her. She'd rather *he* be ahead, with Caleb, who didn't seem to understand his injuries made him vulnerable. "I really don't mind if you join in the fun." Whatever was happening on the other side of the door was definitely a more-the-merrier situation.

"You're stuck with me."

"The bad guys are ahead of us. I'll be fine if you"—the wall shook as something slammed into it— "want to even the odds."

"There's only about a dozen in there."

Which meant the odds were three to one. She inched away from the wall, expecting to see something unpalatable burst through it at any moment. "I realize, back in your day, it was cool to pretend the impossible was possible, but these days we just ask for help."

He had the gall to look surprised. "You really don't know Caleb that well, do you?"

"No."

He grinned. "Trust me, with the odds three to one, the only ones you have to feel sorry for are those on the other side."

Another . . . something hit the wall. Jace smiled when she flinched. Asshole.

She eyed the knife in his belt. "At precisely what point should I be concerned?"

"When someone tells you to run."

"Uh-huh." In her experience that was usually too late. "I'm not good at running."

He considered that for an instant, taking his gaze from the door before turning it on her. For once there was no laughter, just seriousness as he studied her from beneath the brim of his hat. "So I've heard."

She drew her chin up. She might feel like a bowl of quivering Jell-O because of what had happened in that room, but she wasn't afraid. The wall shook again and she jumped. Well, not much anyway. Jace kept staring and she kept glaring. He nodded as if something had been settled. He pulled the knife out and handed it to her, hilt first. "If you need to use this, don't hesitate. Thrust first and ask questions later."

The knife felt good in her hands—comfortable. "You know, I think you might just become my favorite brother-in-law."

He fired three times in rapid succession with the sunlight gun as a body came through the doorway. The vampire didn't get up, likely due to the huge, gaping hole through his chest. Smoke rose from his unnaturally still body. Jace glanced at her. "Do me a favor and don't tell Caleb that."

"Why not?"

"When it comes to you, the man has a short fuse, and he's still sputtering over our introduction."

She shifted the knife in her grip, hilt up. "Come to think of it, so am I."

He looked at the knife and the implication. Unbelievably he laughed. "I bet you give Caleb fits."

"As often as I can."

Three sharp whistles and he relaxed. "Looks like things are cleaned up."

The room was carnage. Absolute, amazingly bloodless carnage. Apparently, laser guns cauterized as they destroyed. Allie was pretty sure just to the left of her was an arm, all alone, lying there as if waiting for the body it was supposed to be attached to show up. Her stomach heaved. She swallowed hard. Immediately, Caleb's gaze swung her way. She smiled, hoping she didn't look as appalled as she felt. It'd be nice if he could be proud of her for a change.

He came toward her, big and mean, stepping over the bodies as if they didn't matter, as if what he'd done didn't matter. Which logically she knew it didn't, but she wasn't used to this kind of life, and killing, even if it was necessary, just wasn't that easy to adjust to. His hand closed around hers. Warm and strong, pulling her to her feet. Some of the coldness and uncertainty inside left. She rubbed his forearm. "Were you hurt?"

"Nah. How about you?"

"I'm fine."

"I can see that."

He pulled her into his side. She pretended it was the way he held her that forced her face into his chest and not the horror of the room. The other brothers were rummaging through the bodies, taking and discarding stuff as they went. Some of the items they kept caused a flare of excitement that reached across the room. Men, give them a gadget and they were all the same. "How much farther?"

"We're almost there."

There was a certain tension in his voice that made her ask, "We'll be more vulnerable when we're outside, won't we?"

"Don't worry, I've got you."

She did push back then. "I'm not some fragile flower you have to protect. I can help."

He shoved her face back into his chest as they headed toward another doorway. "I'll call on you if you're needed."

"Don't think I don't hear that silent 'And that'll be when they're making snowballs in hell' attached to that statement."

"The day comes that I can't take care of my own will be the day you can start fighting my battles for me."

"We have seriously got to talk about your he-man issues."

"Uh-huh." He started walking, taking her with him.

She inched forward with her left foot, pushing against his side. She might as well have pushed a concrete wall. "It really sucks that I didn't get any vampire muscle."

He kept moving, slowly and steadily. "Even if you had, you'd be no match for a male vampire."

"You don't know that."

His reply was a grunt. It was a small victory, but at this point she was taking them where she could get them. Her foot tangled with his leg. He handled the stumble by lifting her up until she caught her balance.

"This will go a lot easier if you'd let me see where I'm heading."

"In a minute."

She wrestled a peek down and immediately wished she hadn't. The sight of a decapitated body was vividly close. She pressed her face into his ribs hard enough that she was in danger of leaving a permanent imprint. "Oh God."

"I told you not to look."

"No, you didn't. You said 'in a minute.' That's not the same thing at all."

"It is to me."

She swallowed back her gorge. Her throat was tight in the aftermath. "I'm adding communication issues to the stuff we need to work on."

"I communicate just fine. The way I see it, your listening is off."

"Uh-huh." She stumbled, unthinkingly reaching out and grabbing his bad arm. He didn't say a word, just gave a short grunt of pain and an equally short grunt in response to her apology.

"Seriously, this is not comfortable, so if what's ahead of us has an ick factor under five, I'd appreciate you letting me go."

A pause. "I'd say we're looking at ten and up."

"Great."

His response was to bend his knees, slide down her body, and lift her up. His shoulder dug into her stomach. Up became down. She braced her hands on his butt, locking her elbows, shaking her hair out of her eyes, but keeping them shut. "Okay. This is too caveman even for me."

"Would you rather wade through a puddle of blood?"

The image was too graphic. "I suppose I can suffer it for a bit."

"I thought so."

She stuck her tongue out at his back. She tried to gauge the distance they traveled by counting his steps, but math had never been her best subject and the dread of a psychotic hopeful or a demented vampire leaping out of the shadows and clawing her unprotected back wore on her concentration. Finally the suspense got to be too much for her. A quick peek behind revealed nothing revolting. They'd moved into another corridor. This one, thankfully, free of new death decor.

"Caleb?"

He didn't slow. "What?"

"Thanks for coming with me." That wasn't what she really wanted to thank him for, but she didn't know how to thank him for enduring the agony Vincent had inflicted on him, for holding on because she'd needed him, for being there for her through the hell she'd gotten them into.

"I didn't exactly have a choice."

Yes he did. And seeing as how he had, she could admit something else. "You were right about the other, too."

"What other?"

"You know."

"No I don't."

Two more steps and then a rhythmic jostling that took her a minute to comprehend. They were climbing the stairs. Which meant they were almost outside. God knows what awaited her there. Her throat closed. She had to take a careful breath through her nose, holding it to the count of ten before she could find her voice through her terror. "It was really stupid of me to insist on coming here."

"You disregarded my gut instincts."

"I was wrong."

"You can make it up to me later."

"I'm not sure I was that wrong."

Something hard and metal rapped against her butt. The gun? "You will be."

"What?"

"Sure."

"What makes you think that?"

The barrel tapped her butt again, not so gently this time. "Because I intend to paddle your ass until you are."

❋ 21 ❋

THE trip back to the Circle J had been anticlimactic. So much so, that Allie really didn't know how to cope with the tension that held her. She'd been braced to fight something, anything, but they'd encountered nothing but the dark of night and the uneasy sensation that they were being watched every step of the way. Despite their clean getaway, she didn't believe this was over. Neither did anyone else. The sounds of preparations were everywhere as the Circle J prepared for war. The only question was who would they be battling, the Sanctuary or the D'Nallys, too?

She'd prefer they didn't fight anyone. Maybe the Sanctuary would be impossible to talk down to peace, but she was sure there was a shot with the D'Nallys. Allie rubbed harder at the moisture in her hair, and plopped on the bed. Someone should try rather than just assume it was impossible. But, of course, no one listened to her. She was just the reasonable one on a ranch full of out-of-control males.

Oh hell. She blew her bangs off her forehead. She was driving herself nuts with this, and she was too tired to deal with much of anything. She pressed against her stomach as it rumbled. Tired and hungry.

"Hungry again?"

She looked up. Caleb stood in the doorway, leaning against the jamb, looking so damn masculine she couldn't fault her pulse for kicking it up a notch. He tipped his head back, revealing his own hunger as his gaze dipped to the gaping front of her robe. He was wearing his hat, which meant he was planning on going out. "I'm sorry."

He pushed away from the wall, his fingers going to his shirt. "Why? Part of my he-man charm is I like providing for you."

"You were going out."

He smiled. "Staying in looks much more interesting."

Two steps and he was beside her. His hat landed on the nearest bedpost as his shirt fell open, revealing the hard curve of his pectorals and the washboard temptation of his flat abdomen. The mattress dipped under the press of his knee. She leaned back against the headboard, letting his laugh flow over her like the softest of blankets, sliding her hands up his chest as he came down, her head dropping naturally into the cradle of his palm.

Caleb's lips touched her ear, her throat. Soft, breathless little cherishings so contradictory to the violent emotion she could feel pulsing under his skin.

"What are you doing?"

Laughter buffed her skin. "You can't tell?"

She shivered as he traced the curve of her ear with his tongue. "You're angry."

"Uh-huh."

"You're not acting angry."

The bed dipped as he braced himself over her. Amusement dented the right corner of his mouth. "How do you want me to act?" Allie shrugged. "Like a mad man?"

A press of his fingers and her face turned to his. Desire and anger merged in the lines there, carving an image into her mind of his power, his intensity, which only served to remind how much she enjoyed those qualities of his when they were in bed.

"I think we've played with madmen enough today."

She slid her hands over his shoulders, and gave a little tug. "Ugh! That pun was so lame."

"Hmm." He lowered his head. "Blame it on my being distracted."

Glancing between them, she saw her robe had completely slid off the right side of her chest. His face blurred as he came closer, coming between her and the light. Her night vision kicked in, taking the color from his face and leaving it in austere black and white, highlighting the confidence and strength he wore so easily. So different from her, leaving her to again wrestle with the same question she'd had since meeting him: What did he see in her?

The answer wasn't in his eyes. There, she could see only the iridescent swirls in his gaze. He knew everything she was thinking, and she couldn't even figure out if he was angry or passionate. "We are so not right for each other."

His lips aligned with hers, top to bottom, edge to edge, in the barest of contact that somehow felt like everything. "You feel pretty right to me."

She shivered as the delicate friction of his statement wove to her center. She wiggled in his grip, not realizing how betraying the gesture was until he laughed softly, seductively. "Open your mouth, Allie girl."

Suddenly, she didn't want to. There was something about him this time. Something determined. Something that said this was more than sex.

The stroke of his thumbs at the corner of her lips had them opening despite her reluctance. "It's always been more."

The words breathed into her mouth, over her tongue. She took them deeper with her next inhalation, feeling them flow through her being, lodging with certainty in areas they had no business being. Not in any woman born in the twentieth century anyway.

"You're taking over."

Caleb accepted the accusation with the same calm assurance that he accepted responsibility for her weight, scooting her down, lowering her to the mattress slowly, gradually, following her down, covering her in the same slow process. He propped himself above her on one elbow and pushed her bangs away from her face. "There can only be one boss in any outfit."

She slipped her arms around his shoulders as her head hit the pillow. "Why can't it be me?"

His shoulders blocked out the last of the light. "Because you prefer it to be me."

Yes, she did. At least when it came to the bedroom. Especially when he tilted his head just that way, fitted their mouths together the same way he fitted inside her soul. One millimeter at a time, one breathless moment at a time, blending anticipation with expectation, hope with promise, until with a thrust of his tongue, delivered both. Her whimper matched his groan, as if he, too, felt the power of the moment, the welding that wouldn't be denied. His fingers curled in her hair, tipping her head back, opening her mouth for more. More of his kiss, his possession.

And she accepted it, welcomed it even. As different as they were, she'd waited her whole life for a moment like this, a man like this. Passion welled out of lust, emotion out of passion. She didn't name it, wouldn't name it, but she felt it. From the tips of her toes to the depth of her heart, but if she whispered it, she'd be lost. Given over to another lifestyle, a future she wasn't sure she wanted. Given over to a man who thought so much differently than she did. A man who had continually threatened to spank her.

Caleb drew his lips from hers. "What's going on in that brain of yours, Allie?"

Oh sure, the one time his snooping would be useful, he chose to respect her wishes. She kissed the peak of his upper lip, that slight, totally masculine curve that always intrigued her. "What makes you think I can think of anything when you're kissing me?"

"You're not kissing me back with your usual enthusiasm."

She made a note to work on her multitasking. "I'm just wondering how serious you are about what you said before."

It could not be coincidence that his hand opened on her back and slid down her spine. "About what?"

"You know."

"What if I don't?"

His fingers eased over the curve of her butt. He so knew. "You do."

"You in a hurry to get to your paddling?"

"You're not?"

"Not particularly."

She curled her fingers into his hair. She loved the way the thick strands felt against her hands. Straight and cool as silk to the ends, and then just the hint of curl, just enough to catch on her fingers. "Then I guess we can just forget the whole spanking thing."

Allie caught the glimmer of his teeth before he captured her lower lip. He bit down, just enough to let her feel the sharp edge, just taking the seductive pleasure to the edge of pain. Her back arched instinctively at his taunt, presenting herself for more, blatantly tempting him to give her more. Caleb leaned back, tugging her lip erotically before letting it go. She sucked it into her mouth, soothing the sting with her tongue, savoring his lingering taste.

Allie had a lot to learn about him, Caleb decided. He watched her tongue slide over her lip, gathering the flavor of his kiss, watched her nostrils flare as his taste melted through her mouth. Watched as her cheeks worked and her spine drew taut and arched. Watched and suffered the agony of his desire. Never sated, still humming from the frustration of earlier. It would be so easy to forget about her disobedience. So easy, but it would be a mistake.

Reaching out with his finger, he lengthened his talon and sliced through the tie on her robe, baring the shallow valley between her pert breasts. They shivered with her indrawn breath. Her big blue eyes widened suspiciously and excitedly at once. The edge of violence that surrounded their lovemaking excited her. The robe's lapels parted before his hand's descent, baring the white flesh of her stomach. An intriguing trail of goose bumps sprang up in the wake of his touch.

He bent. She gasped again. A fine sheen of sweat appeared on her skin, tantalizingly sweet and lightly musky, a prelude to the deeper scent he knew awaited him, lower. He lapped the first bead of sweat from the delicate valley. "It would be a mistake, baby, to think I don't always mean what I say."

He had her flipped and pinned with an arm across her back before the meaning sank beneath the sensual haze. Her legs dangled over the edge of the bed, giving her no leverage but plenty to him. The full curves of her rear pressed up and out against the soft cotton of her robe. Allie had a very pretty ass. He stroked the full curve or her right cheek, patting it lightly, smiling when she jumped as if he'd landed a blow, her screech loud enough to wake the dead, assuming they weren't already wandering about.

"Don't you dare, Caleb Johnson."

He held back a smile and shook his head as tension shot up her spine. He was mad as hell at her, but she could still make him smile. "Baby, I dare about anything."

"Not this."

Her muscles quivered with the strain of pushing in vain against his grip. She really had been shortchanged in the muscle department. A squeeze to her butt had her squeaking and jumping again. "Yes, even this."

He hooked a talon on the neck of her robe. A woman sometimes had to test a man's strength to trust in it. "Next time I tell you to stay put, you'll stay."

"Is that an order?"

"Yes."

"Then for sure you're out of luck."

There was another screech as his talon tickled her nape. "This is my only robe!"

Her ass waved as she tried to get away, too much lush temptation for a red-blooded man to resist. He gave it a tweak. "Good."

He didn't like her wearing clothes that showed the full curve of her hips, and the soft fullness of her thighs, and the thin robe did both. Even over pajamas. She was too pretty, and with her vampire allure, too tempting. "I don't feel like spending my days beating men off you with a stick."

She stopped struggling. Her hair fanned out as she looked over her shoulder, then settled around her face in a silent cloud. "You think I'm that sexy?"

How could she doubt it? "Oh yeah. And as soon as I get done paddling this sweet ass, I'll prove it to you."

Her head whipped around, her body shaking with the strain of holding the position. There wasn't an ounce of worry in her expression. "You wouldn't hurt me to save your life."

He did love the way her eyes glittered with shards of deeper blue when her emotions were aroused. And the light flush on her cheeks only served to enhance the effect. "Are you sure?"

He sliced through the rest of the robe. It parted in two falls of white, revealing her skin in a slow slide revealing her neck, the delicate line of her spine, the nipped-in curve of her waist, the flare of her hips, the swell of her buttocks . . . He replaced the material with his palm, raising his body temperature so she felt it more.

"If you keep cutting up my clothes, I'm going to have nothing to wear."

"Naked does have its appeal."

"I thought you were threatening me?"

He was. He never wanted to repeat the moment when she'd been separated from him, not knowing what they intended, unable to protect her from whatever was about to happen, not knowing if she'd survived. He brought his hand up. "Brace yourself."

She relaxed completely. The scent of soap and arousal rose with his hand. He brought his arm down with every intention of blistering her ass, but at the last minute he found himself pulling back the force, until all he delivered to the smooth white flesh was a light pat. She laughed, and then hummed under her breath. "This could be fun."

He shook his head, keeping his hand where it was, tucking it around the lush curve, slipping the fingertips into the crease between the plump cheeks, holding her still. "Does nothing put the fear of God into you?"

"The thought of losing you."

It was one of those spontaneous admissions that could tear out a man's heart. Or make him crazy with joy.

He patted her butt again. His granddaddy would turn over in his grave at Allie's willful nature, but Caleb didn't really want her any other way. "Now you did it."

She wiggled. "Did what?"

"Unleashed the beast."

Another wiggle. "I like the beast."

Yes, she did. And so did he. He slid his hand under her stomach, turning her over. Her hands opened in surrender. He caught them in his, pressing them into the mattress beside her head as he braced himself on his forearms above her. "You don't leave a man much ammunition, Allie girl."

"It's a natural talent."

He kissed her cheek. She wrinkled her nose. "Yeah, but now I'm feeling a little cheated."

"Why?"

"In my day, if a woman put herself at risk, a man got to have his eighteen sixties moment, fair and square."

"At the risk of repeating myself, it's no longer 'your day.'"

"Uh-huh." He kissed her other cheek, lingering for a bit. "But it did have its moments."

"Charming ones, I'm sure," she said with a dry bit of sarcasm.

"It was, actually."

Roles had been very clearly defined in his day. A woman waited on her man, deferred to his wishes, at least in public, and pretty much let him run the show. And men, well, at least the men he knew, cherished the women who filled their lives with love, comfort, and all the other softness so devoid from the land around them.

"I've read about how charming it was. Men owned women and treated their 'possessions' any way they wanted. Beat them, abused them, cheated on them, and basically behaved as complete asses if they wanted, without anyone having a say. Least of all the poor women involved."

He shook his head. She'd read about it. Hard to believe what was vividly real to him was dry history for her. She'd kept saying they thought differently, but until this moment he'd never wrapped his mind around the depth of the chasm between them. "I imagine each century has its share of assholes, but in the majority of households, life was a partnership. It had to be. You depended on each other for survival."

The doubt on her face didn't lighten. He rested his forehead against hers, timing his breaths so he breathed in as she breathed out, the tiny culmination of taking her breath into his lungs, holding it safe until she needed the next one before breathing out and giving it to her, calmed him. "Underneath all the rules, a woman trusted her man to take care of her."

"And if he didn't?"

"I don't know about back east, but where I come from, women were more precious than gold. Any man caught abusing one would soon be short his woman and probably his life."

She rolled her eyes. "Hard to believe, considering your constant threats to beat me."

"That's more a figure of speech than a real threat, and you know it."

He kissed her lips, smiling as they parted immediately. "You can't keep doing what you want all the time, Allie."

She tilted her head to the side "Why not? It works for me."

"Your doing what you wanted almost got you killed today."

"It seemed like a good idea at the time."

"But it wasn't."

Her lips flattened and then pursed. The fight left her body in a drawn-out breath. "No, it wasn't."

Thank God, she could admit to mistakes. He touched her nose to his. "So maybe when it comes to those situations, you could follow my orders?"

Her nose pressed back as she wrinkled it. "Orders aren't my thing."

"Seeing you raped or killed isn't mine." Dark anger surged through him as he remembered the moment before all had gone black when Vincent had allowed him to see Allie struggling for air as he'd slowly strangled her, cutting off the connection before he'd known if she'd live or die. "So we've got to come up with a better system."

He had to wait three seconds before Allie presented her compromise. "How about I promise to try?"

Knowing how impulsive she was, he figured that was about as good as he was going to get. "I'll take it."

"But no more threats of spanking."

"I promise, unless you're hot for it, no spankings." He tipped her head back, letting desire thrum along the residual anger simmering in his blood, drowning it in the fire of lust. "But now we've got a problem."

She swallowed, tipping her head back farther as he brushed his mouth along her jawline. "We do?"

He took the lobe of her ear between his lips. "My brothers are very eighteen sixties."

She tilted her head into the caress. "So?"

"If they don't hear some screams soon, I'm going to go way down in their estimation as a man who can't handle his woman."

"And that matters to me how?" Her fingers wrapped around his forearms, tickling along the hairs there, sensitizing his skin.

"A man low on confidence isn't much good in the bedroom."

The smile he loved showed in her eyes as her ankle curved behind his knee. Despite the invitation in her body, he felt resistance, almost a reluctance, that worried him. "We can't have that."

He pressed his lips against her neck to the accelerated beat of her pulse. Her body's hunger and need summoned his. It vibrated on the same level as his own. Separate yet the same. He slipped his thigh between hers, bringing her softness closer to his hardness. So different from him, but so perfect for him. His wife. His mate. "I thought you'd understand."

Caleb propped himself up on his elbow, still keeping her in place with his hand behind her head. Allie's smile broadened. Her lips parted. She was all seduction and humor. Everything he'd ever wanted, and while he was admiring the opulent display of her curves, she tilted her head back. Offered her throat, her breasts, her body. Her deep blues eyes shimmered with gold lights that beckoned his beast. Her smile reached deep into his body, to the depth of his soul, caught on his lust, and dragged it forward as she took a deep breath and held it, held him until . . .

She screamed. Loud and long. Screamed as if Vincent had just shown up for a rematch, as if snakes had appeared in her bed, as if everything vile she'd ever dreaded had just landed between them. Son of a bitch. Caleb slapped his hand over her mouth, cutting off the horrendous noise. Above the ridge of his palm, her eyes sparkled with the light of amusement. He cautiously removed his hand.

"Was that good enough?"

The door burst open. His brothers spilled into the room, guns drawn and at the ready. He shifted his body, blocking her nakedness from their view. "I think it covered the job." And then some. He felt each of his brother's stares—Jared's censure, Jace's amusement, Slade's speculation.

"Jesus, Caleb." Jared sounded totally disgusted.

Jace laughed. "Teaching the little woman her place?"

Unbelievably, heat crept up his neck. "Something like that."

He felt Allie's chuckle more than heard it.

"Well, could you do it a little more quietly? Some of us are trying to have a discussion."

"I'll give it a try."

"Before you do, make her feed."

He cut Slade a glance. His serious face was set in sterner lines than usual. "Her hunger makes us uncomfortable."

"He'd better just be talking about my stomach rumbling."

Since Allie couldn't see the slight shake of Slade's head, Caleb didn't disillusion her. "More than likely." He jerked his chin in the direction of the door. "If you could all excuse us?"

"I, for one, am sure as shit not making promises, but I'll give it a try," Jared grumbled as the brothers walked out, grabbing the doorknob and closing it on his brothers' backs and the curious faces of the weres.

As the latch clicked, Allie wiggled beneath him. "I seriously think Jared needs a girlfriend."

"What makes you say that?" He tucked his hand under her left thigh, coaxing it up and out with gliding pressure. She caught on quickly enough, hooking her ankle around his hip as her hands came around his shoulder. "He's way too grumpy. He needs someone to focus all that intensity on."

"Other than you?"

"I am getting tired of his disapproving stares."

"You'll get used to him."

"That's a bleak thought."

He chuckled. "I guess, to you, it would be."

Her hands slid through his hair, gentle, yet demanding, pulling his mouth toward hers. "Was he always that intense?"

Images of Jared as he was before—strong, reliable, focused on what needed to be done, but with a sense of humor he could touch when he took himself too seriously—filtered through his mind. "He had his moments."

Her tongue flirted with the corner of his mouth, tickling the nerves there in dainty flicks that shot like fire down his spine. Coaxing him around. "He needs to have a few more."

Yes, he did. He missed Jared's laughter more than he missed the feeling of exhilaration that came with battle, the challenge of surviving against the odds. Immortality had its downside. Suddenly, Allie didn't look so interested in the proximity of his body as she had a second ago. It didn't take much to know the two small pleats between her brows weren't caused by lustful thoughts. He'd seen that same look on too many matchmaking mommas to mistake it for anything but what it was. "You're not compiling a list of past acquaintances to introduce him to, are you?"

She had the grace to look guilty. "What makes you think that?"

"The gleam in your eye for one."

"Well, it was just speculation anyway. I can't really contact anyone."

"But you were thinking of ways."

Her nose wrinkled up. "I've got to work on my poker face."

"Kind of a waste of time with me."

The pleats deepened to a frown. "I'm going to work on a mental poker face, too."

She could work all she wanted. He'd never let her hide from him again. "You do that."

Her hands eased up over his shoulders, cupping the top, squeezing gently. Testing his strength? She didn't have to worry. He was strong enough to take care of her.

"I will learn to block you."

"Why do you want to?"

He felt that feminine brush, the impression of banked power before she pulled away. "Because it's annoying that you can read my mind whenever you want, but I can't read yours if you don't let me."

"Are you sure about that?"

"Aren't you?"

"Baby, I've seen you in action. I'm thinking there's nothing you can't do if you set your mind to it."

All expression in her face disappeared. Her lower lip sucked between her teeth. "Yeah. About that."

"What about it?" Fear flickered across her face followed quickly by an insecurity he'd never seen before. Instead of fading away, both emotions settled into the planes he thought solely reserved for laughter. For life. The sheets rustled as she unhooked her leg from his thigh.

"Aren't you afraid of me now? Afraid I'll suck the life from you?"

That was the reason she'd been so different since they got back? Not because of his failure to protect her, but because she thought he'd be afraid? Of her? He took her leg and hooked it purposely back around his thigh. "No."

She stiffened. Her hands pressed his chest. "Well why not? I'm a Goddamn psychic vampire! I sucked the life out of a guy with nothing more than my touch."

"You won't hurt me."

Her eyes flared with bright blue light underlaid with silver. "You can't know that."

"And yet here I sit completely unconcerned."

"How?"

"You're my wife." She wouldn't hurt him, any more than he'd hurt her.

Her hands fastened on either side of his face, hard and angry, her talons pressing into his skin, almost but not quite breaking through. "That might just make it worse." He felt her power come at him, strike deep, draw hard. "I could kill you so easily."

"Yes." He extended his own talons, the point of his index finger pressing precisely at the base of her skull. One thrust and her brain would be punctured. She froze. He let the understanding sink in. "We're all deadly, Allie girl, in our own way. It's what we choose to do with it that matters."

"That's the problem." Her talons retracted as her stress increased. The bitter taint of fear blended with the aroma of womanly arousal. "I don't exactly have a choice. What happened with Vincent, just . . . happened. I don't know how it started, and I sure don't know how to turn it off. He was hurting you, and I just knew he needed to stop. I was completely out of control."

"And I'm thankful for it."

"But," her legs dropped free, "what if it happens again? When I'm out of control for another reason? What if I can't stop and I hurt someone?" The stroke of her thumbs over his cheeks as her tears welled clued him in to her real worry.

"By any chance, are you afraid you're going to kill me between the sheets?"

"It's a distinct possibility. You make me pretty wild."

He stood, angling her hips up into his until his shaft nestled against all that moist, feminine warmth. When he was snug and tight against her, he bent down, arching her spine so her shoulders took her weight and her breasts stretched up for the descent of his mouth. The pretty pink nipples were tight and eager, rising and falling with each of her short breaths. "Then maybe we ought to check it out and see what happens."

Cotton ripped as her talons tore at the sheets. His cock throbbed as her pussy clenched around his shaft. More arousal, more fear scented the air.

"You can't be serious," she gasped

"Never been more serious in my life." He leaned in, teasing the puckered bud of her nipple with his breath, holding her gaze as he opened his mouth and reached with his tongue. Her hot little whimper went through him like a bolt of lightning a second before he touched the tip of his tongue to the tip of her breast. "Let me see just how wild you can be."

❖ 22 ❖

SHE didn't come to him wild. She came to him like the first breath of spring, cool and hesitant, a hint of warmth heralding the arrival of better times. The only problem with that was he didn't want her hesitant. He wanted her wild, confident, teasing him with her body and wit.

He wanted the Allie that he'd always known. Caleb curled his tongue around her nipple. She gasped and arched toward him. He welcomed her, opening his mouth wider, taking her flesh deeper. With his hands at the base of her spine he encouraged her closer. And she came to him, a breathless little cry punctuating the move. He released her nipple with a little pop. "That's it, baby. Let me see, feel, and hear what you're feeling."

Her response was a shake of her head and a tightening in her body and mind. She thought to resist him. He smiled against the side of her breast. She was welcome to try. "Is that a challenge?"

"No."

"A dare?"

"No."

"A request?"

"Can't it just be a denial of what you have planned?"

"Uh-uh."

"Why not?"

"Because I'm not in the mood to indulge you that way."

"Now, I *am* disappointed."

"Not for long."

Never for long. He nuzzled his way along the undercurve of her breast, sliding his tongue along the crease. "Have I mentioned how much I enjoy your breasts?"

Her laugh held a jagged edge. "There's not much to enjoy."

"Ah, but there's pleasure in every perfect inch."

"Perfect?"

He might have been short on female company the last two hundred fifty years, but before that, he'd never had his bed empty. He knew women, and more importantly, he was coming to know this woman. "More than perfect." He snuggled the assurance into the valley between her breasts. "Pure pleasure."

Allie's hands crept up his arms. "I bet you were quite the ladies' man in your day."

"Uh-huh." He grazed the slope to his right with his teeth. "But now I'm your man."

Her hands reached his shoulders, the nails pricking erotically into the muscle. "Maybe. If I decide to keep you."

Propping his chin on her chest, he found her looking down at him. "Now that, wife, was a challenge."

The third finger on her left hand wiggled in his face. The scar he'd placed there catching his eye. His own personal brand.

"No ring. No wife."

He kissed his way down the slight indentation of her abdomen. She was a persistent little thing. "You'll get your Goddamn ring."

Her fingers slid in his hair, tangling in the snarls, lingering as they caught. "A ring's not enough."

Lowering her hips, he dropped to his knees, finding her navel with his tongue, smiling as she shivered when he traced the small indentation. "Preacher, vows, and ring. You'll get it all."

Whatever she needed, whatever it took. He'd bind her to him in so many ways it'd take all of their forevers for her to untangle the knots.

"It won't work if you don't make me want it."

"You'll want it."

The downy softness of her pubic hair tickled his chin.

"I wouldn't be so sure."

For all her big words, she wasn't pushing him away. The lady wanted to be convinced. He cocked her hips up to his mouth and dipped his tongue through the nest of curls to the soft pink flesh beneath. "I'm sure."

He shifted his knees apart, adjusting his angle. She was as pretty there as she was everywhere else. Red brown curls highlighted the softest of flesh, moist and fragrant, addictively beautiful, calling to him. He had to taste her. At the first touch of his tongue she almost came off the bed.

"Caleb!"

The second had her freezing, every muscle, every nerve ending anticipating the third. He made her wait for it, made her speculate on the pleasure, doubt her senses, doubt his abilities, before he parted her folds with his thumbs, leaving her vulnerable for whatever he wanted to do. He glanced up her body, over the small curve of her abdomen, between her small, plump breasts, to her face. Her lip was caught between her teeth, her brow creased with concentration, her eyes swirling with golden lights beneath the deep blue irises. "Right here."

"It's not safe."

But she wanted it. With everything male in him, he knew how much she wanted this. Needed this. The same way he needed to stake his claim, she needed to be claimed. The episode with Vincent had shaken them both. "I've never been known for playing it safe."

"I could lose control."

"I'm counting on it."

Her chin worked as her teeth worried her lip. "I'd die if I hurt you."

"Baby, you couldn't hurt a fly."

"You make me sound like such a wuss."

He shook his head, sliding his fingers down the deep red channel to the depths beyond. "You're soft and gentle and fiercely protective of life. All life." He caught her gaze. "The way a woman should be."

"According to your criteria."

He cocked an eyebrow at her. "Does anyone else's matter?"

Her "No" was slow coming.

"That's what I thought."

She opened her mouth, no doubt to argue the politics of a man appreciating a woman's softness. Caleb forestalled it by simply leaning forward and taking her into his mouth. Her hips bucked and the argument was swallowed up by the passion that spiked between them, leapfrogging along her skin, dancing from pressure point to pressure point, landing in his mind.

The sensation of her pleasure mellowed with the transference through the link, but it was still incredibly arousing to know the touch of his tongue to her was a cut of pleasure, a gentle lap, a baptism of fire. To know the depth of joy when he pressed just so, just there. To hear her cry of ecstasy as he tasted her pleasure, felt her desire. Son of a bitch, it was almost too much. He nursed her through the aftermath of her climax, lapping and suckling gently, keeping her on edge, letting her down easy, but not letting her all the way down.

"You're holding back."

She looked at him over her heaving stomach like he'd lost his mind. "I don't think so."

"I know so."

Her head flopped back on the mattress. "Lord, just take me now."

"Trust me." He crawled back up her body, his cock so hard and full he thought he'd die with the agony of holding back. He settled his hips into the cradle of hers. "This is not the time you want to be saved."

She cracked an eyelid. "I don't?"

He slid his shaft along her crease, dragging the length along her ultrasensitive clit. "Definitely not."

Allie jerked and shuddered. Her hands clenched on his waist, talons digging in, pulling him closer. "Maybe not."

He did it again slower, longer, dragging the sensation out, delighting in her response, her pleasure. "Ah, baby, you burn me up."

"Good, because I'm damn close to ash."

The third pass had her arching and making demands. "Stop teasing me."

"But I like teasing you. Your face gets all flushed, you're eyes sparkle, and you get so deliciously wet."

"You forgot something."

Both eyes opened to slits. "What?"

"I also get distinctly . . ." Another tantalizing stroke. "Ah . . ." She gasped. "Homicidal."

Unbelievably, he laughed. His balls full to bursting, needing her so badly that it felt like he was about to explode out of his skin, and she had him laughing. "I'll keep it in mind."

His fangs extended fully into his mouth as her heels drummed on his thighs. Damn, she was sweet. "Are you ready for me, Allie?"

She nodded and then thrust up her breasts as she sucked in a hard breath that left no doubt. Her fangs dug against her lips. She was definitely losing control, but she wasn't there yet. Caleb cupped her buttocks in his palms, squeezing the firm flesh, separating the soft globes, smiling at her whimper and glare, and then inched his hand down her thigh, dragging his nails ever so lightly on her skin, thrusting gently along her slick crease as he tickled the back of her knee.

"Darn it, Caleb."

Her leg jerked back, creating a niche he moved into as he continued to tease, squeezing her calf, cupping her heel, then wrapping his fingers around her ankle and then lifting it up over his shoulder as he took a step back. As natural as breathing, his cock snuggled into the tiny well that awaited him. A bit of pressure and Allie's eyes widened as her tendons stretched right along with her body.

"Relax. You're going to like this."

He pressed in. There was an initial moment of resistance and then those brilliant blue eyes closed as she moaned. "That's it." He leaned forward, giving her that first breath-stealing inch. "Just like that."

He paused, granting her a moment to adjust, checking for any signs of pain. There weren't any. From the tight set of her face to the desperate fluttering of her inner muscles, she was a woman on the edge of climax.

"Pretty, pretty Allie," he whispered as he bent, taking possession of her body and her blissful cry as he sank deep, giving the latter back to her in his own groan as the blisteringly hot softness accepted him. All of him, hugging him with desperate entreaty. Too much to resist.

"Ah, damn." His forehead dropped to hers. Magic. She was magic.

She opened her eyes. This close, it was too hard to focus, but there was no mistaking her tension for anything other than it was. He held perfectly still. He didn't want to come yet. Not yet. This was too perfect. She was too perfect.

And this lesson was too important. If there was one thing he could give her, it was his own faith in her. "Hold still."

A shake of her head. "I don't want to."

The sexy airiness of her high-pitched denial took the intensity one notch higher.

"I want to make this good."

"It is good," she moaned. "Very good."

Yes it was. "But not good enough."

Her mouth met his, her tongue flicking along his lips, her fangs scraping gently. He opened his mouth. The growl that purred between them was definitely wild. As wild as her kiss. Lust flared. Caleb tucked his thumb between them, finding the swollen flange of flesh that screamed for attention.

He took over the kiss, pressing her into the mattress, pinning her with his kiss, his body, his cock, as she writhed beneath him. Her claws sank into his shoulders. Her teeth found the artery in his neck. Her "Yes" was a primal scream in his mind as she bit down.

His own satisfaction exploded right alongside hers as she drank his blood, his energy, his passion. And he didn't fight, letting her take what she needed, unable in that moment to deny her anything. She was his mate. Her survival was most important. He sank into her energy, the bliss of climax, holding her through the storm, steadying her as she fought with her need, lust, and love. And as he held her in that deepest level, he felt something else. Something wonderful. Something that brought every inch of his primitive instincts to the fore in a primal roar. The tiny flutter of new life.

"WE'VE got trouble."

Caleb slid into the shadows of the clearing alongside Derek. Below, shadowy figures haunted the edges of the clearing. Sanctuary vamps. "How many?"

"Just two. So far."

"Shit."

Derek looked over his shoulder. "They're scouting the area."

"Yeah."

"Word from the D'Nallys is there's a gathering of activity south of here."

"For attack?"

"Maybe. And there's a lot of new blood joining the fray."

"Why?"

"Apparently there's a hefty reward for whoever brings Allie to the Sanctuary compound."

"And here I was hoping that killing Vincent would be the end of it."

"That would have been too easy."

Derek sighted his rifle on the two wolves hunkered down in the brush. "There's only one reason why they'd push so hard for her."

Caleb filled in the blank. "They suspect she's pregnant."

"Hate to burst your bubble, but this much activity would indicate they know."

"How?"

"Could have been the way you broadcasted the news when you found out for sure."

Caleb winced. He didn't know what had come over him in that moment, but he hadn't been able to resist it. Part challenge, part victory, he'd opened his mind and shouted his impending fatherhood to all who could hear. "I was kind of hoping the news would stay local."

"Apparently not."

"Apparently."

He studied the energy coming off the two wolves. Vamp, not were. That at least was a blessing. For a second he'd feared it would be the D'Nallys. "Where do the D'Nallys stand on this?"

"Best I can tell, they're pissed intruders are trespassing on their territory."

Derek reset the safety on the gun as four wolves stalked the two intruders from below. A scan revealed them as were. Derek rested the rifle butt back on the ground.

"They've been taking them out as fast as they appear."

"So they haven't joined them yet?"

"And it's doubtful they will. The D'Nallys might hate your brother with a passion, but they're damn clannish. They fight where they want, when they want, with no loyalty to any cause but their own."

The four wolves took out the vamp wolves with silent, lethal efficiency. Blood dripped from the lead wolf's jaws as he looked directly at Caleb, eyes glowing yellow within his black mask in the faint moonlight, his ruff standing on end, a challenge in the set of his shoulders.

"Let's hope they stay unattached. That is not a clan we need fighting against us en masse."

"You can say that again. It's been tough enough with the feud we have."

Caleb jerked his chin at the wolf, returning the challenge, meeting strength for strength. The wolf yipped at his companions, and then loped away. Caleb didn't get the impression they'd gotten anything settled with the exchange beyond the fact that if either of them picked a fight, the other was willing to settle it. "Damn!"

"Kind of wish Jace hadn't alienated them," Derek muttered. "It'd be good to have them on our side."

If wishes were horses they'd all take a ride. But they weren't, and they were stuck with what they had. "For sure a fight's coming?"

"Yup."

"With the prize being Allie?"

"Yup."

He cut him a wry glance. "I would've been a lot happier if you'd just answered that last one no."

"I'll work on my dishonesty."

"Don't bother."

Derek was one of the most trustworthy men he knew. If he told a body they'd live, they did, and if he told them they'd die, they died. Either from his hand or whatever ailed them. The rest of his pack possessed the same unwavering loyalty and honesty. "Have I mentioned lately how glad I am you're on our side?"

Derek stood with a ripple of muscle that reminded Caleb how tough the big man really was. The kind a man wanted guarding his back in tight quarters.

"You could show your appreciation by having Allie whip up some more of those bear claws."

He shook his head. "That might be more than I can finagle. You're still on her shit list."

"Don't tell her they're for me."

"I could do that."

They'd been together too long for Derek to miss the slight emphasis on "could." He slung the rifle over his shoulder. "But what?"

"But I need something from you first."

"Which would be?"

"I need you to talk to the D'Nallys." Caleb adjusted his hat on his head. "We need this feud settled."

"Hell, the only reason we're still on speaking terms is because we don't speak of you all."

And because the McClaren weres didn't involve themselves in the Johnson–D'Nally feud. Caleb understood that.

"It's time to break with tradition."

Derek glanced in the direction the wolves had gone. "This could put them over the edge."

"It could also get them to spill why they're so dead set against my brothers and me."

Derek's expression closed. "They have their reasons."

"Which none of you will share."

"It doesn't concern you."

"So you keep telling me, but it feels damn personal whenever one of them tries to sink their teeth into me."

Derek smiled, his canines gleaming faintly. "I bet it does."

Caleb pushed his hat back and followed the direction of Derek's gaze. "I know it's a lot to ask, but with Allie being pregnant, there's more at risk here than pride."

Derek rubbed his chin. "We might be able to work the angle of her pregnancy. With wolf births down to almost nil, it's a safe bet a vamp getting pregnant is going to raise interest."

"Because vamps don't get pregnant?"

"So everyone used to believe, but Allie's sure put a kink in that."

He rubbed his chin again. "They're going to want something in return."

"Anything."

"Even if it's Allie or your brother?"

Damn! "Anything short of that."

"You don't ask much."

"YOU don't ask much."

Allie stood by the old stove, testing the heat with her hand.

"He's a good man."

"The jury is still out on that."

"He loves your cooking."

"That's one point in his favor with about forty still against."

"He's saved my life twice."

She cast a knowing glance at him from under her eyebrows. "And you've saved his a time or two, I understand, which makes you about even."

Caleb forced a sigh, pretending an exasperation he didn't feel, the same way Allie was pretending an aversion she didn't have. The instant he'd reminded her about Derek saving his life she'd caved, inside where it mattered. The display now was nothing more than pride. "He's my friend, Allie."

The heavy oven door closed with a thunk. She dropped the oven mitt to the counter. "And that means what to me?"

"It means if he wants bear claws, you could bake them for him."

She untied her apron. "And what will you give me in return?"

The seductive sway of her hips as she took a step toward him clued him in to which direction her thoughts had traveled. He took a step closer, meeting her halfway. Her next step brought her into his arms where she belonged. He tugged her head back, catching her smile with his lips in a hard kiss. She smelled of woman, hunger, and sweet dough. "How about a kiss?"

"Getting there."

"How about I play with your pretty breasts?"

She stood on tiptoe sliding her body up his in one long caress. His cock twitched as her lips brushed his ear. "If I tell you I'm not wearing any panties, does that give you an idea?"

The knowledge froze him in place. Ten minutes ago the kitchen had been full of weres and his brothers and she'd been running around in that short skirt of hers that showed way too much of her legs, and nothing beneath?

She yelped. "Watch the claws."

"Sorry." He slid his hand over her hip, tucking his fingers under the hem, pulling it up as he searched for the material he expected to find, discovering nothing but bare, warm flesh. "Son of a bitch, you're not wearing any!"

She had the gall to look smug and raise her eyebrows while her hips cuddled the leap of his cock. "What part of 'I'm not wearing any' did you not understand?"

"The part that said you weren't teasing." All that lush femininity had only been a flip of that nonexistent skirt away all night? The knowledge skipped along his veins like wildfire in front of a dry wind.

"Hmm." She unbuttoned the top button of his shirt. "I prefer to think of myself as accessible."

"To whom?"

She touched her tongue to the center of his chest. His heart stuttered and then took off doing its best to break free. The growl burned from within as her scent drifted up to him. She was aroused, vulnerable, and eager.

Her "Who do you think?" revealed sass and humor, but not one wit of caution. He was really going to have to work on his intimidation when it came to her. "Unbutton my pants."

"I thought you'd never ask."

The five little brushes of her knuckles as she worked him free stroked his cock with the hottest of touches. Her hand slipped inside the opening as he took the two steps to the chair.

"Now you're getting the idea."

Amusement rode double with pure, unadulterated lust as he shook his head and sat. The chair creaked a protest. He paid it no mind. "You keep a man on his toes, Allie girl."

"Good." Her hand was hot and warm as it surrounded his hard flesh. Very careful as he worked it free. "Oh."

"What?"

Her smile was smug, her gaze greedy. "You're very hard."

"Knowing that little ass is only a toss of a skirt away has that effect on me."

She pumped him through her hand, the whisper-light touch driving an agony of pleasure straight to his balls. "I have that effect on you?"

"Oh, yeah."

She straddled his hips, pumping her hand up and down his shaft, drawing his pike-hard cock away from his body with each long stroke. He could feel her heat and moisture just a breeze away. She went up on her toes, teetered, and then steadied as he caught her hips in his hand. Her muscles flexed as she lowered herself, fitting him to the sweet well. Her grip switched to his shoulders as her head dropped back. "Hmm, you feel good."

Good didn't half cover it. "Not as good as you feel to me."

He arched his hips up, spreading her that first tiny bit.

"Ah!"

In the next instant, he felt the edge of her talons cutting through his shirt. "You liked that."

"What's not to like?"

"Not a darned thing." A hand on her hips kept her poised for the next inch, which he fed to her one increment at a time. She was too damn tight for much else. He moved his right hand in, dipping his thumb between the hot, wet folds begging for his touch, seeking and finding that sensitive little nub. Her head snapped forward, her forehead hitting his collarbone with a muted thud.

"More."

Caleb pulled back, ignoring Allie's whine and gently thrust back in, rubbing his thumb in slow circles as he did. "There you go." She took a bit more this time, but not any easier.

"Stop teasing me, Caleb."

"I'm just warming you up."

Her laugh a low, husky rasp rubbed along his lust, coaxing it higher. "In case it's escaped your notice, I'm trying to have a quickie here."

"I'm getting there."

She bounced in his hands, impaling herself in tiny increments on his cock.

"Quickie means fast."

"I prefer thorough."

Her fangs grazed his chest, snapping his entire being to attention. "But I want quick."

He rubbed again, his breath suspending in an agony of anticipation of the bite. "You're too delicate for quick."

"Trust me . . ." She stood on her toes on the inhale and then dropped down on the exhale. Her frustrated mewl when he caught her thighs threaded through her words. "There's nothing delicate about me."

On that they were never going to agree. Everything about her was delicate and fragile. Infinitely feminine, infinitely sexy, but very delicate. Even if she couldn't see her own vulnerability, he was well aware of it. Her lips slid up his chest, her tongue lapping at the sweat on his skin in burning flicks of impatience. "I could prove it to you."

"How?"

She nuzzled her face into the hollow of his throat, her fangs pinpricks of erotic promise on his skin. "You could let go of my hips and let me call the shots."

He tilted his head to the side, granting her access to the spot she needed. "Too dangerous."

"Afraid I'll screw your brains out and put paid to your delicate notions?"

"More like I'm afraid you'll hurt yourself in your impatience."

"You're big, baby, but not that big."

In truth, he was getting bigger every minute, part because of his response to her challenge despite his efforts to remain calm. His vampire side swelled at the challenge, eager to pick up the gauntlet. "Dangerous words."

To prove his point, he pressed a little deeper, letting her feel the changes happening. Her breath sucked in on a gasp.

A glance at her eyes didn't reveal the caution that should be there, rather a greedy anticipation that found an equally greedy "Yes" inside him.

"Let me go, Caleb."

His vampire side didn't want to do anything else. His human side held on tight.

"I want to feel you in me, Caleb." Her tongue flicked over her lips. "Hard and deep. Don't you want that?"

"Eventually."

She raked him with her teeth, her talons, the tight grip of her velvety walls. "I want it now."

She bit down, ecstasy shot through him with debilitating force. His shout echoed around them as his grip loosened. Her laugh followed his shout; airy sweet and confident, it ended on a groan as she dropped onto his length.

"Jesus, Allie."

He grabbed for her, sanity returning too late. She'd taken him all, her body shook, her inner muscles rippled around him. He dug his fingers into her buttocks, which quivered against him. Fear ate like acid at his desire. "I told you, nice and easy."

Her fisted hands opened on his shoulders. The right one slapped at his muscle.

"Caleb?"

The wall between their minds dropped, and he was assaulted with a powerful projection of feminine power mixed with uncertainty and determination. And an incredible amount of frustrated desire.

"Shut up and make love to me."

Caleb took a breath, lifting her. Immediately, delight and passion thrust to the center of his being, different than his male lust, less centered, more mental. Sweeter. At least to him.

He held her suspended on his length for one heartbeat, savoring the sensation and her pure enjoyment of his possession. When Allie shuddered and dropped her head back, he lowered her again. Slowly, feeling her pleasure at the overstretching. The almost pain that made her breathless. He took her passion as his, and sent his own back along the connection, amplifying the pleasure he found in her heat, the ecstasy he felt when her muscles contracted around him. Her eyes flew wide and locked on his.

"Yes," he groaned with the remaining fragment of his voice. "That's good."

Arms shaking, legs braced, he lifted her again, the erotic slide of flesh on flesh bringing him close to the peak. He ground his teeth, resisting. She wasn't there yet. This time when he lowered her, it was easier, her body adjusting. He let her linger on the descent, tilted her hips the inch forward necessary to bring the thrust of her clit in contact with his pubic bone. Allie gasped that way he liked, and rocked against him. Pressing down with his hands, arching up with his hips, he brought her that much closer to the delight that had her inner muscles milking him in a prelude to release. "That's it, baby. Take what you want."

He lifted her, Allie's "No" barely past her lips before he dropped her back down. Her grunt came hot on the heels of his. The spike of her lust burned through the tattered thread of his control.

"Now that was a sweet little sound. Let's see if you can give me some more sexy little noise." Threading his arms under her calves, he lifted her legs up, grasping her waist, doubling her forward, leaving her stretched. Open. Helpless. He pressed down with his hands, forcing her to take more. She did, with a groan and a whimper that couldn't be confused with anything other than a plea for more. More of his cock. More of his passion. More of him. Wild and primitive, the vampire rose to comply. He lifted. She rapped his shoulder as her eyes closed on a shiver of joy and her head dropped back.

"That's it, Allie girl. Take what I can give you." He lowered her. "All of it." His cock throbbed and swelled as it struggled to satisfy her craving. "Every inch."

This time when her rear met his thighs, her breath caught for another reason. He lifted her again, man surrendering to vampire as he took her harder, faster, not letting her control the pace, not letting her do anything but accept the passion he forced between them. Faster and harder, his grunts blending with her cries, his shouts with her screams as she gripped him in a stranglehold. Her muscles made intimate demands of their own, squeezing him so hard he thought his head would explode, before releasing him, only to contract in rhythmic flutters that caused a different explosion. He slammed her hips down one last time, grinding her against him as the agony detonated in an orgasm so powerful he lost thought, lost control, lost a sense of anything except the need to fill her with his seed, his love, everything. She was his. His.

"Caleb."

Her whisper reached out to him. He threaded his hands into her hair, his breath sawing in and out of his lungs. "Are you all right?"

Her head dropped into the support of his hand. Her lids dipped over her eyes. She looked sleepy, sated, and hungry. "Very pleasantly bruised."

He'd hurt her. "Shit."

Soft hands on his wrists stopped his instinctive withdrawal. "Stay in me."

"I'm too much."

Now that passion had faded he could feel the intimate discomfort that edged on her satisfaction. He let her legs drop to the floor.

"You're perfect." Her mouth grazed his chest. "I'm hungry."

His cock, which should have been spent, jerked in interest. Allie's laugh breathed across his ultrasensitive skin, setting his cock to dancing within her again. Caleb pressed her face to his pectorals, trying to ignore his body's renewed interest. "Feed."

"You don't have enough."

She was his mate, she carried his child within her, he would always have enough. "I'll feed later."

"You're sure?"

He'd never been more sure of anything. "Yes."

Her bite was a leisurely exploration. Her lingering feeding reflected the sated state of her body. Hot, slow, and as arousing as hell. His cock swelled and throbbed. Her hips rocked on his. "Jesus, Allie."

She withdrew her fangs from his chest long enough to whisper, "Like this."

She rocked her hips on his, massaging him gently, delivering pleasure with her body, inside and out. "Come for me like this, slow and sweet while I feed."

Her teeth sank back into his chest, and he sank into the sensuality of the moment, giving her control, letting her take them both over the edge with the tenderness that was so much a part of her, anchoring himself on the emotion pouring out of her, out of them. Coming on a sigh as she shuddered around him, filling her anew with his seed as she closed the wound on his chest with her tongue, giving her more when she cupped his face in her hands, giving her every last bit of him as her subconscious reached out to him in a delicate truth he knew she didn't want him to know.

I love you.

❧ 23 ❧

THE door to the kitchen swung open. Allie leapt off his lap with a screech, yanking at her skirt. He got to his feet more slowly, scanning with his senses for the only thing that would have had Derek breaking into the kitchen despite his orders to keep out. He didn't find anything he didn't expect. Derek's gaze dropped to his open pants. The right side of his mouth quirked up. "Sorry."

Across the room Allie had her skirt down and her legs pressed tightly together, looking embarrassed and furious. With him, the were, or herself, he didn't know. Derek pointed to the window with the end of his rifle. "We've got company."

Caleb finished buttoning his pants. "How many?"

"At least forty."

"Have they breached the defenses?"

"Like they were butter."

"Then they're not were."

"No. I think it's safe to say Vincent's entourage has arrived."

"Shit."

Allie's gasp drew his eyes. Her spine was straight and her hands were fisted at her side, chin up and ready to take on anything. She was going to need every bit of that spirit. They were badly out-numbered.

"Least the battle will be short."

Caleb snorted. Derek did have a way with words. "It's going to be hell between now and daylight."

But if they lasted until daylight they had surprises of their own they could throw into the mix.

"How many men do we have?"

Derek tipped his hat at Allie. "I think your buns are burning, ma'am." As soon as Allie dove for the stove, he murmured, "Twenty-five," too low for Allie to hear,

He hid his surprise. Twenty-five meant Derek's entire pack was fighting on the Johnson side, which meant a lot of weres were go-ing to die tonight. He appreciated the thought, but it was a hell of a sacrifice for a pack leader to make. "This isn't your fight."

"It became ours the minute Vincent's gang chose to ignore pack protection." Derek crossed to the window and pulled the shade back. "Pack protection is held very dear by my kind."

"Friendship is held dear by mine."

Derek smiled. "Maybe not your kind, but you and your brothers are damn near wolf in your devotion to friends. We're thinking that line of belief should be preserved."

Caleb wished he could turn down the offer, but he couldn't. A year ago the brothers would have welcomed a fight to the death, but times had changed. Life had changed. He glanced over at Allie who had her back to them, working on something at the counter. He had a future, and if he did, his brothers could, too. "We appreci-ate it."

"You can owe me."

"Anything you need. Any time."

Derek nodded. An explosion echoed in the distance.

"Does Slade have any of those sun guns made up yet?" Caleb asked.

"Ten."

Damn. He'd been hoping for more. "Pass them out to the weres."

He didn't want any more of his friends to die.

"Slade already handled that."

He should have expected it. The one thing the Johnsons knew was how to plan a battle. "Good."

He looked at the high-powered rifle in Derek's hands and at the shotgun slung over his shoulder. "You didn't take one?"

"Nah. Sun guns are for sissies."

Allie turned from the counter, a tray of bear claws stacked two high, dripping with white icing. She walked toward them, her eyes unnaturally bright in her pale face. She walked straight up to Derek and shoved the bonanza at him. "They're not burnt."

The were's eyebrows rose.

She licked her lips, glanced at the window and then his gun. "Thank you for staying."

He slung his rifle over his shoulder and took the offering. "Shoot, no need for thanks. It's been decades since we've had a good fight."

Allie opened her mouth, glanced at Derek's face, shook her head, and bit her lip. Derek's face softened as he saw the stress on hers. "We won't let them break up your marriage."

"We're not married."

Derek's dark gold gaze cut to Caleb. "Hate to be contrary—"

"You live to be contrary," Allie interrupted.

Derek shrugged. "Be that as it may, there's no one on this compound who considers you single, and seeing how easily you were caught, you probably ought to be grateful for it."

The wild rush of color over Allie's face would have been amusing if not for the howling that commenced in the dark beyond the window.

Derek set the tray on the table. "Looks like we're on."

Caleb grabbed Allie's arm. "Yup."

Derek ducked his left shoulder. The shotgun dropped to his hand. He tossed it to Caleb. Another quick shrug had a belt of shells coming right behind. Caleb caught both. "This should hold you until you get her settled."

"Thanks." The gun felt good in his hands. Natural. He let the feeling spread, welcoming the cold, blank, calculating anger and internal stillness that always took him before a battle.

"With any luck, I'll be adding the cost of it to your bill." Derek disappeared through the door, two bear claws in hand.

They needed to get going, too. Caleb took Allie's hand. "C'mon."

"Where are we going?"

"To get you safe." No matter what happened tonight, Allie and his child would be safe.

He pulled Allie into the hall. To the left he saw Derek clearing the bottom of the stairs. Allie headed after him. "No. This way."

She frowned but didn't argue, just followed. Slowly. Too slow. The sounds of battle grew stronger. Caleb dragged Allie in his wake. When she stumbled, he yanked her up against him, tucking her under his arm and racing down the stairs. Above them, glass shattered. He spun, tossing Allie into the corner, hoping she had the reflexes to save herself. He cocked the shotgun, dropping onto his back as the creature screamed a bone-chilling war cry, landing on the stair above, jumping back as Caleb brought the barrel up.

Allie's scream blended with the attackers as he pulled the trigger. Blood sprayed in all directions. The creature flew back from the force of the blast and his own momentum. Caleb sprang after him, ripping his talons through the man's neck, severing tendons and vertebrae as he went, decapitating him.

"Oh, God."

Allie was staring at him, horror in her eyes. He knew he looked like the monster he was. Vampire and outlaw in one. He didn't have time for soft words. He leapt over the broken glass, landing by her side. Pulling her hands away from her mouth, too late seeing the blood on his own. "We've got to go."

She swallowed hard, and nodded, either unable or unwilling to take her eyes off the dead vamp.

"He was so young."

"He was trying to kill us."

She nodded again. One foot moving in the direction he wanted, still looking over her shoulder. "You took off his head."

"Just guaranteeing he doesn't get up again."

Another hard swallow followed by another of those nods indicating an understanding he knew didn't exist. Her free hand went to her stomach. "If you're going to get sick, you'll have to do it on the run."

Her chin came up under the lash of his tone. "I won't get sick."

"Good." He opened the bedroom door at the end of the hall and pulled her through before closing it behind him. Outside, howls blended with preternatural war cries and above it all, the Johnson brothers' battle cry. The house shook as something exploded nearby again. A scuff of feet on the wood floor in the hall said they had company.

Get in the closet, get down, and shield yourself, he hissed in a mental sotto voice.

Allie's confusion was palpable. Caleb didn't have time to explain. He just opened the door and shoved her in before closing it quietly and turning to face what came through the door.

These weren't like the young, too-eager vamps that first attacked. Experienced, they slammed the door against the wall with nothing but a lethal spray of bullets. Caleb dove to the side an instant before they punctured the wall where he had been standing. He rolled and came to his feet. A split second later, three intruders hurtled into the room.

He caught the first by the sleeve, sending him into the wall, kicking out with his boot, into the midsection of the second, missing as the man flipped, following the kick through on a low spin

that took him under the other's counterattack, loading a chamber in
the shotgun as he came down in a crouch. The enemy were just as
fast, finding their feet and flanking him. They spread out in a deliberate threat. One blond, one brunette. Both butt ugly. He waited,
shotgun primed. He just needed an opportunity.

"Where's the woman?"

"Go to hell."

"You, my friend, are the one who'll be going there. There's a
new day dawning for vampires, and you and your kind won't be
part of it."

"Then neither will my mate."

"Oh, she will. She's the key. Whoever holds her holds the
power."

"For what?"

"To rule, my ignorant hick. To rule."

"Who the hell would find a thrill in ruling a bunch of jackasses
like you?" He slid to the right. The second vamp moved with him,
stepping in front of the closet door.

Stay quiet, Allie.

"Just because you and those like you—"

"There are more like me?"

The blond vamp didn't appear to appreciate the interruption.
His thin lip curled in a sneer, revealing his fangs and the traces of
blood on them. Blood from one of Caleb's people. Ice-cold rage
filled Caleb. The son of a bitch was going to die twice as nasty for
that.

"As in any society, there's wheat and chaff."

"Naturally, you're the wheat."

"Of course."

The man's smugness begged a set down. "But not the leader."

"Not yet."

Naturally, he had aspirations. "Not ever. The way I see it, if they
sent you after me, they must see you as expendable."

Out of the corner of his eye, he saw the second man move. He swiveled the muzzle in his direction. He really hoped the asshole figured his reflexes could outmatch a bullet. The blond's eyes flicked over his shoulder. The other man inclined his head. The slight hiss was the only warning he had.

Caleb dropped as an arrow imbedded in the wall across the room. He blocked the brown-haired vamp's attack with his arm, going down under the force of the hit. Claws dug into his ribs. Fangs slashed for his throat. A shadow deeper than the twilight of the room flashed overhead. He jerked to the side. Talons embedded in the floor by his ear.

"Shit!"

He planted his boot in the stomach of the guy on top of him, and heaved just as the blond vamp cried, "Stand back!"

The two vamps leapt away. The hammer of a gun cocked. He had one second to make a decision. He didn't even need half that. He gathered all his energy and sent a private message to Allie, imprinting in her mind the secret passage, and the path to the safe cave a second before the gun went off.

The explosion was deafening in the small room. Caleb jumped to the side, knowing it was too late even as he emptied the shotgun in the direction of the shot. The agony never came. The expected bullet never hit. The man to his left went down in a gurgling scream. He stood there trying to figure out how he was still standing. And then he looked up. The closet door was open. On the other side of it, Allie stood, terror and anger twin companions in her expression. Her fingers gripped the doorknob like it was the last train out of hell. On the other side, the blond vamp got up from where she'd knocked him with the heavy door, swearing as he brought his gun around.

"Close the door!"

Allie didn't move. Caleb was on the vamp before he could fire, driving his talons straight into the blond's stomach. The soft tissue offered no more resistance than the vamp's throat as Caleb bit deep, tearing hard, trapping his scream there for all time. Blood filled his mouth, his vision.

The other men came at him like hell on fire. There was no time for finesse. Only survival. He went down between their combined weights, the gun sliding across the floor. He didn't go quietly. He slashed and bit, putting all his muscle and determination into buying Allie the precious time she needed to escape.

Run.

Again, he sent her the image of the passage and the safe home. Again, he felt her resistance.

Go!

A blow to his chest drove the air from his lungs. Blood spewed in a red arc. Allie's angry scream sent fresh adrenaline pumping through his body. He threw the men off, snarling as he found his feet, placing himself between the closet and the bleeding vampires. They snarled, baring their fangs, but they didn't charge. The likely reason why didn't give him a snuggly feeling. More must be coming.

He backed into the door, closing it with his weight as he gathered his reserves. He hit resistance before it clicked shut.

"Caleb?"

"Damn it, Allie. Get our baby to safety."

"I can't leave you like this." Her hand pressed into his back.

"You will or we all die."

"I want better choices."

There weren't any. "Go, baby."

"Promise me you won't die."

Even she had to know he couldn't promise that.

"Allie . . ."

"Promise me, damn it, or I'm going to stage a sit-in right here in this pool of blood."

Son of a bitch, she would. "I promise."

A brief squeeze of her fingers, a softly whispered "I'm holding you to that," and the closet door closed. The locking mechanism whirred and settled with a satisfying thunk. Too late, the vamps realized the closet wasn't a trap, but an escape. He smiled as the two men snarled their fury.

"Looks like it's just you and me, gentlemen."

ALLIE touched the cool wood as the door closed. On the other side, Caleb, wounded and bloody, battled to buy her time. Her other hand went to her stomach. He wanted her and their baby to live. She wanted him to live. Somehow, that all had to work out. She absolutely refused to go through this much hell to end up with nothing on the other side.

Behind her, the passage stretched dark and threatening. Nothing but stale air and gloom barred her path to freedom. There was no telling what was on the other side. According to the information Caleb sent her, the tunnel dropped her off in the middle of D'Nally territory. She shuddered. The D'Nallys were not the people she wanted to meet up with today.

So little light illuminated the space, her night vision was almost useless. She bit her lip and stared a second at the gray void. It felt so wrong to leave Caleb there. So wrong to run.

If you love me, run.

There had been a mental emphasis on "if" as he'd glanced over her shoulder. Morphed, and bloody, standing big and strong, fighting because it was the right thing. Because his vamp side needed her. But not because of any admitted love for her.

How dare he have doubts when she couldn't do anything about them. She turned from the door, keeping her fingers on the wood for as long as possible, maintaining that fragile connection until the last second, and then she ran. As fast as she could into the darkness, grateful for the extra speed being a vampire gave her, keeping one hand on the wall for balance, following the tunnel down and then up, her breath straining to keep up with the demands she put on her muscles. Even with her enhanced endurance, she didn't like up. Too taxing. By the time she came to the rock that blocked the entrance, she was winded. She pressed her nose against the crevice and breathed the cool night air deeply.

She really did need to get in shape. She allowed herself a minute to recover, and then she pushed at the rock. It didn't budge. She tried again, harder this time. The damn thing stood solid. The escape route had been made for vampires with vampire muscles, not a woman who'd gotten shortchanged in the conversion.

"Damn, damn, damn!" She couldn't go forward, couldn't go back. She felt along the floor, images of spiders creeping toward her as she sought something to use as a lever. Hell, at this point, she'd even settle for a bone from the skeleton that would be sitting by the cave entrance if this were a horror movie. It wasn't a horror movie, however. It was real life, and real life was turning out to be damn difficult. She sat back in the dirt, empty-handed and out of options.

A snuffling and then a low growl on the other side of the rock froze her in place. A bear? Instinct had her heart in her throat before intellect had a chance to speak up. She pictured a bear with its massive arms. A bear could move the rock. A bear could also eat her alive. She dismissed the latter. If she could mentally influence a bear to move a rock, she could also influence it to believe that she was nothing more than a hearty case of indigestion. She sent forth a mental image, feeling along the creature's energy to carve a path. A barrier she hadn't been expecting blocked her.

Damn.

She sent the mental image again, hoping. The snuffling increased, stopped. Rock scraped against rock. She scrambled back as clods of dirt fell. Silvery moonlight flooded the cave as the barrier between her and the animal collapsed. Sharp human intelligence met her mental probe.

Oh shit. Not a bear. Allie lunged back to avoid the hand that snaked in almost too fast even for her vampire eyes to follow, hit her head on the ceiling, and sat down hard. Fingers like steel manacled themselves to her wrist. With a strength she envied, the same hands that moved the rock yanked her out.

Oh, this wasn't good. She and the man holding her were surrounded by wolves. Big, nasty, we-want-to-feast-on-your-bones wolves. Ah hell, her day only needed this. She looked up at the naked giant who'd attached his hand to her wrist. She'd seen those golden eyes before. Images of the black-masked wolf who'd herded her car through the woods flashed into her mind. Those eyes had the same glow, the same intelligence. The same mocking amusement. "The D'Nally clan, I presume?"

His right eyebrow went up in a dark flag of surprise. "The Johnson bitch, I presume?"

The man was extremely handsome with dark hair, dark skin, and an animal magnetism that surrounded him like the seductive scent of a fine cologne. Not to mention those incredible, dark gold eyes. He was also very well put together from his very broad shoulders to his well-shaped feet, a fact she couldn't miss in his current, naked state. Her gaze skated his groin. Impressive all over.

"At your service."

His other brow went up. "An interesting way of putting it."

She really had to watch her sarcasm. The wolves milled. She eyed them warily. "Trust me, I'm not that interesting."

"I think you underestimate your appeal." His gaze dropped to her stomach. "We find some aspects of your existence extremely interesting."

That look in his eyes wasn't anger. She tugged at her wrist. "Pervert."

Behind her, one of the wolves lunged. A sharp pain in her buttock had her reacting before she thought. She kicked out, catching the wolf under the chin. She turned as far as she could, keeping the tan-coated SOB in her sight, holding his gaze as he backed up. "Keep your damn teeth to yourself."

"I believe his intent was to teach you manners," the naked man explained, amusement and something she couldn't define in his voice. The way the other wolf's tail dipped a fraction under her glare satisfied a bit of her rage.

"Then he'd better learn some first."

The leader's smile was a surprise. "Apparently." He inclined his head. "I'm Ian D'Nally."

"Allie Sanders." Another wolf approached, bigger than the first. Older, if the gray on its black muzzle was any indication. She turned, facing it, shoulders back, meeting the wolf glare for glare. "If it's expecting me to conveniently faint, it's wasting its time."

"No one expects an alpha bitch to faint."

"That's the second time you've called me a bitch." She wasn't sitting still for a third.

"It wasn't meant as an insult." Ian stared at the wolves. The black wolf blinked. With a twitch of its tail it dropped back. The others followed suit, forming a loose circle, creating the illusion of privacy.

"Weres are telepathic?"

"Some of us."

She was having a hard time keeping her gaze above Ian's waist. Not that she wanted to see that part of him, but there was no missing it while she kept her eyes on the wolves behind him. "Are you morally opposed to wearing clothes or is this," she waved her hand at his naked state, "some sort of statement?"

"Neither. It's merely a convenience."

"Great." She took a breath and said, "I'm sure you've got places to go, people to see, so if you could just step aside, I'll be on my way."

He didn't move, but his eyes narrowed and his manner grew intense. "The eldest Johnson must be desperate to send you out alone."

She didn't pretend not to understand. "He's a worrier."

"Does he live still?"

"Yes." She ignored the image of how she'd last seen him.

"The wolves that run with him asked for our help."

"The fact that you're hiding out here instead of fighting must mean you didn't give it."

"It's not our battle."

"It will be."

"So McClaren said."

"And you didn't believe him?"

"There was not universal acceptance."

She looked around the ring of wolves. "Brains must not run too deep in your clan."

Growls rumbled out of the shadows. She bit her tongue on a "Fuck you." Desperation was fast eating at her control. Caleb needed help. She needed help, and all that was available was this backward band of wolves. She had to hold it together long enough to get them to see reason.

"She wolves do not talk to their mates that way."

It was a warning. She waved it aside. "Seeing as I'm neither wolf nor mated to one, that rule doesn't apply to me."

The next words were for her ears only. "While in Rome . . ."

Do as the Romans do. The thought finished in her head. Was the naked were an ally? Dear God, let him be an ally.

She bowed her head. "My apologies."

"McClaren said you'd met these vamps."

"Yes."

"And how would you describe them?"

"Arrogant, brutal, and convinced anything that doesn't fit their plan for the future must be annihilated."

She glanced at Ian and then the other wolves. "If you think being wolves will protect you, you are so wrong. I linked with their leader."

"The one you killed."

"I didn't kill him." But she'd come too close for comfort. That horrible moment flashed in her mind. Her stomach rolled and she blinked slowly to dispense the memory. The hand on her arm surprised her. It was almost gentle. She kept her gaze locked on the leader's chest as she fought back the lingering nausea.

"But you tried."

"Yes. They're a really sick bunch. Any vampires who don't agree with their we-are-gods philosophy, they plan to exterminate."

Her words made no visible impression on the wolves, they just stared at her. Ian looked at her expectantly. What did he want from her? What did they need to hear? She racked her brain, sifting through fragments of conversation until she came upon something Derek had said. Something she might use. "They don't have any use for you. 'Furred vermin' I believe was the term Vincent used when he was convincing me to join up."

The snarl that curved Ian's lip rippled through the pack. She pounced on the moment.

"I would be worried, if I were you. They only want a few of your females. The rest they intend to exterminate."

Ian straightened. All warrior. All deadly intent. It wouldn't do him any good. "They cannot defeat the pack."

She waved off the boast. "Flash all that testosterone you want. The reality is, they're united and organized and everyone else is scattered and segmented. They're not going to have any more trouble with you than they're having with the McClarens and Johnsons. They'll just come in with their greater technology and greater numbers and obliterate every one of you, only keeping the women who can bear children. And . . ."

She closed her eyes, the reality of what was happening back at the compound pushing past her denial. They were being killed, one by one. Caleb, Jared, Slade, Jace, Derek, and all the others. People who'd fought to protect her. People she'd thought of as friends. The sob welled from despair, lodging in her voice, choking off her words.

Ian's hand on her arm was meant to be sympathetic, but the squeeze he gave just reminded her how powerless she was to stop any of it. She swallowed. "Next time, though, it won't be me running in the woods, hoping they won't find me, hoping I can stay alive long enough to give my baby a chance. It'll be your wives, your children they'll be hunting."

She reached for Caleb with her mind, finding nothing, just a void that doubled her over. "And they'll find them, too, and use them, because that's all they want. The power that will come from the children they'll force on your people." The anger burned hot. "Your women."

Women just like her, who only wanted a peaceful life with the men they loved.

A big gray wolf stepped closer, hackles raised. She sprang at him, releasing the pent-up anger that expanded inside. Another wolf hit her mid-leap, taking her down in a surprisingly gentle maneuver. She glared up into his dark brown eyes. All her frustration and anger fired the words from her throat, each syllable burning with the reality. "But you won't be around to hear their screams. You won't be around to do anything. The D'Nally clan will be dead. Annihilated by scum whose only advantage is they understand the rules of war and can band together to apply them."

The wolf's tongue touched her cheek. She scrubbed the spot. "I don't need your damn sympathy. I need your help."

There was another silence. She had a feeling they talked among themselves. The wolf pinning her stepped back. Ian bent down and extended his hand. She took it. In a smooth, oddly gallant move he drew her to her feet. His thumb stroked over the back of her hand. One of the wolves stepped toward the tunnel. She leapt in front of him, landing precisely where she wanted for once, blocking his way as if she did such athletic feats every day. "No."

His lips pulled back from some impressive fangs in what could have been a grin. He took another step forward. She stretched her talons to the limit and bared her fangs right back. Caleb had enough on his plate. She wasn't allowing a sneak attack.

"Be easy."

She didn't take her eyes off the wolves gathering. "I'll be easy when you get the hell out of here."

"You asked for our help."

"I've decided I don't need it."

"Your mate also asked for our help."

Surprise jerked her gaze off the gray wolf. "I didn't know that."

"It was a hard decision to make, to aid an enemy."

"Especially for a hotheaded bunch like you." No sooner had the retort left her mouth than she realized what he'd said. "What swayed the decision?"

"Pack members were attacked today. The men were killed, the mother and daughter stolen."

Exactly like she'd predicted. Too much alike. Were they really going to help, or were the D'Nallys just looking to attack while the attacking was good and get rid of the Johnsons once and for all?

The gray wolf in the back was definitely glaring at her, and if she wasn't mistaken, he looked a lot like the one she'd shot off her car.

"This is a rather sudden change of heart toward the Johnsons, isn't it?"

"We have reasons for our anger."

"And I have a reason for mine." She glared at the gray male.

"Enough reason to see your mate die?"

Well, hell. She met his gaze. "You touch him and I'll kill you. I might not look like much, but I'm capable of some very creepy stuff."

"It does not surprise me that the leader of the Johnson pack has an equally strong mate."

"We're not married."

"You are unattached?"

Remembering what Derek had said about fertile females, she quickly amended the statement. "No, just not married."

"A private issue between the two of you?"

"You might say that."

"Enough so that you no longer wish the elder Johnson's claim?"

"No."

His hands on her shoulders lifted her as if she weighed nothing. "Then step aside, woman. The D'Nallys have come to fight."

❧ 24 ❧

H E wasn't kidding. With the exception of Caleb himself, she'd never seen men, beings, creatures move with such methodical precision. After Ian transformed into a wolf, a startling enough process in itself, they'd bolted down the corridor in a flowing mass of fur, moving almost as one, creating the illusion of continuity. She'd run in their wake, only able to keep up because she knew the way and didn't have to slow to find the twists and turns of the tunnel.

When they reached the heavy door, they waited. Violence and anticipation radiated off the pack in seething waves. A path separated for her. She ran through it, breath sawing in and out of her lungs, panic an equal companion to hope. Were they in time?

Fighting still continued on the other side of the door as evidenced by the muffled sounds coming through, but try as she might, she couldn't feel any of Caleb's energy. Considering her last sight of him was a brief glimpse as he'd turned, bloody and injured, to meet whatever had come crashing through the opposite door, it was hard to hold on to hope. But she would because the alternative was unthinkable.

She dialed the combination with fingers that shook so badly she couldn't be sure which number she'd stopped on. She turned the handle. Nothing happened. Damn! She tried again. Same results. Nothing.

Damn! Damn! Damn! She forced herself to slow down, took a deep breath, released it, vividly aware that while she fumbled on this side of the door, people she loved were dying on the other.

"Third time's the charm," she muttered. This time she dialed slower. The lock gave with a barely audible click. She turned it in an agony of dread, felt the slight thunk, and shuddered with relief. She carefully slid the bolt and tugged at the heavy door. Hands fastened on her shoulders. Her scream died in her throat as another hand slapped over her mouth.

"Your mate sent you to safety," Ian whispered sotto voce in her ear. "And safe you will stay."

She shook her head. Caleb might need her.

Ian pressed her back against the wall, against the sturdy hinges. "Lock the door behind us."

The pack spilled into the void between her and the door. With a warning glance, Ian shifted again, man blurring and animal emerging until all she recognized were the golden eyes staring at her from his black-masked face. He touched his muzzle to the shoulder of the equally big wolf beside him. A subtle tension rippled through the pack. Hackles raised, a silent snarl on his lip, Ian eased the door open with his nose. The sounds of fighting increased, grunts and shouts, the grate of metal striking something hard, a shot, something softer hitting the floor . . .

The gap widened farther as another wolf pressed forward and then another. On a howl that sent chills up her spine, the lethal mass sprang into the room. There was a scream that ended in that familiar horrible gurgle and then the D'Nallys added their deadly snarls to the cacophony. Allie took a step toward the door, even had her palms flat on the wooden surface to push it closed, when she felt it. A whisper of sensation in her mind.

Caleb?

The whisper came again. Weak. Like she'd felt before. Fingers clutching the edge of the door, she opened her mind farther.

Help me.

Suspicion leapt before she could act on her first instinct to reach for him. That wasn't Caleb. Caleb would die before he invited her to walk into danger. She threw her mental shield up, probing along the edge of the energy pouring to her, practicing everything she'd learned from Jared and Caleb, but more importantly, from that sneaky bastard Vincent. At first touch, the voice sounded like Caleb, felt like Caleb, but as she explored there was something majorly missing. Whoever was faking being Caleb obviously didn't have a grasp of the man's personality. She closed the door and turned the bolt, jumping when something heavy hit the other side, feeling the vibrations up her arms. The force of the collision only served to prove one thing. As much as she wanted to help, she simply was not equipped to fight the supernatural on this level.

The whisper came again, this time loaded with pain and desperation. Oh, the guy was good. Very, very good. So good, even knowing it really wasn't Caleb calling to her, anxiety swelled. She let just a little of that anxiety out. A diversion to amuse the peeping Tom while she did a bit of peeping on her own. She turned her back against the door and slid down it, focusing on that stream of emotion, reaching back along its route to its source, going deeper than before but still keeping her touch light. She might not have the muscle to fight a full-out invasion, but she was equipped to fight this. Curling her hands into fists, she braced them on her thighs, breathed in five slow, steady breaths as she turned her energy more and more inward, tuning out the here and now and stretching herself into the mental void to find the enemy she didn't know.

Two things became immediately apparent. He wasn't close. And he was definitely male. It was very masculine energy she was following. Whoever, he was working from far away, tapping into her mental energy, experimenting with the tags everyone had that were like mental P.O. boxes. Her response to what she now recognized as a broad scope probe had given him her address. Caleb was not going to be happy about that.

The foreign energy flared and probed. There was a familiar pattern to his search. It was like Vincent's, but different. More sophisticated. Stronger, without the fanatical hyperactivity that had blurred the edges of Vincent's probes.

Allie smoothed her energy as she felt a push from the stranger, faking neutrality, keeping herself hidden behind normalcy. At least she hoped it was normal. So much adrenaline was flooding her system, she wasn't sure of anything. The probe came again, scattered. Whoever it was suspected she was there, but couldn't pinpoint her enough for a direct hit.

The bolt on the closet door rattled. She gasped and jerked. The start shattered her concentration. Bright light flooded her mind, heralding the invasion of that mental presence. She clapped her hands over her ears to squeeze it out as she scrambled away from the door that was opening. More light flooded her mind, obscuring normal vision. She blinked, but all she could see was that white light. It flickered with images of the door opening. Hinges murmured a protest beyond her ability to see. Oh God, she needed to see. She pressed her palms into her skull. "Get out of my head."

She felt the presence start, felt it gather as if for battle. She stabbed at it with something, she hoped it was negative energy, and she hoped it hurt. The effect she was hoping for didn't materialize. The light stayed as bright as ever.

She was lost. She didn't know what she should do, what she could do. Everywhere around her was disaster, and in her mind there was only white light and confusion.

The door continued to open, the hinges continued to protest as she struggled with her breathing, trying to quiet the rasping breaths, battling the adrenaline surging in her system, which increased the beat of her heart, the rhythm of her breath. Betraying sounds she couldn't afford to emit. The door hit her toes, and she quickly crawled back, staying a fraction ahead of it until her heels tucked against her hips. The door kept coming. She tucked herself into a ball, but eventually there was no place left to go.

The door hit resistance. The person on the other side pushed harder. Her knees collided with her chest. She stopped breathing altogether. The odors of blood, wet fur, sweat, and violence slipped into the stale passage, crippling the hope within. Until a split second later, another scent wafted over the stench of battle. This scent she recognized.

Caleb?

She still couldn't see. The light consumed her mind, the masculine presence taking over her brain, manipulating neurons she didn't know she had, working to ready her. For what? This time she said it out loud, "Caleb?"

"Allie girl?" No one said her name with just that combination of reprimand, softness, and emotion. No one but Caleb.

Oh God, it was Caleb.

She launched herself in the direction of his voice, trusting him to catch her. Hard hands locked around her waist, pulling her into the familiar solidity of his chest. The tattered edges of his shirt scraped her cheek. Smears of blood eased the glide of her hands around his neck, but she didn't care. He was alive. Alive and holding her. The presence in her head stopped its probing. Foreign satisfaction gilded her joy. A sting of light demanded her attention, and then five words flashed across her mind's eye in mental bold print.

Tell him he's not alone.

As if that opportunity was all the man had been waiting for, the light vanished and her reality once again consisted only of corridor, the only light breaking the darkness that came from the open door, and the only thing she could see was Caleb frowning down at her.

His hand behind her head was a relief, his thumb under her chin giving her the support she dearly needed. "Are you all right?"

She didn't get a chance to answer before his hands were all over her, one under her hips slowly working her back to where he needed her, pressing her against him. His thoughts bled into hers. She felt his need to hold her, mark her, claim her as his.

Her need was no less urgent. She locked her arms around his neck, her legs around his waist. She couldn't get close enough to obliterate the fear of losing him.

Images of the battles he'd just fought flashed from him to her. She clung tighter. She'd come so close to losing him so many times tonight and there was nothing on this Earth scarier than that. In the short time they'd been together, he'd become everything to her. The sun, the moon, the stars. Laughter and light. All this from a vampire, supposedly a creature of darkness and night. She cupped his cheeks in her hands. "I thought you were dead."

"I'm too ornery to die."

"Too ornery and too arrogant."

He smiled, dropping his forehead against hers. "Yup."

More footsteps approached the door and she stiffened. Caleb held her to him. "It's all right, baby. It's just friends checking to be sure you're okay."

As if to prove him right, Jace asked, "Is she okay?"

Caleb tucked her face into his neck, apparently no more eager to be separated from her than she was to be separated from him. "Cold, tired, and a little startled from all the fuss, but she's fine."

"In that case," Jared said, his voice easily recognizable by its flat timbre, "the leader of the D'Nallys wants to talk to you."

"Tell the son of a bitch to wait."

Allie tucked her head under Caleb's chin, relaxing into the caress he couldn't seem to end, understanding the pride that kept him from speaking the emotions that put that fine tremor in his hand. She would have liked the words, but she could settle for just knowing he cared. "You can't call the man who just saved your butt a son of a bitch."

Caleb's chin slid across her skull, the point of pressure telling her he was staring at the door. "The man doesn't look like he objects to being called a son of a bitch."

"Not in the least."

The mocking amusement in Ian's voice brought her head up. He was standing on the other side of the opening, naked as the day he was born, throwing invisible challenges at Caleb who seemed to be picking them up as fast as they were tossed.

"Do you ever wear clothes?"

The firm line of Ian's mouth softened as he glanced at her. "They get in the way."

She guessed they would. She laid her head back onto Caleb's chest, squeezing him around the waist as she gloried in his continued existence. "Thank you."

"For not wearing clothes?"

"For saving Caleb."

Caleb's grip loosened slightly. She could feel his annoyance. "If there is any thanking to be done, I'll handle it for the Johnsons."

She waved her hand. "Go right ahead then. I'm finished."

Instead of the reprimand she expected, the lightest of kisses ruffled her hair. "You still angling for that spanking?"

"I thought we already went over that."

"Apparently not enough," Caleb said dryly.

"She does lack respect."

Allie shot Ian a glare. "Just because I don't worship at the altar of your dangling bits does not mean I don't respect what needs respecting."

Masculine guffaws erupted from the other side of the door. She ignored it, the same way she ignored the were's amusement.

She tilted her head back to see Caleb's face. "Are the bad guys dead?"

"They've had a change of heart."

She took that to mean they'd beaten a strategic retreat. "Good."

The door creaked. Wolves slid into the opening, deadly shadows disappearing one by one down the tunnel. Ian glanced at the silent exodus. "We will be leaving now."

"You ever need help, give a holler," Caleb said in that steady drawl that backed whatever promise he made with the force of his personality.

Ian nodded. His head lifted, as if listening to a voice only he could hear. "The feud with the Johnsons is suspended."

Allie had never heard better news. "It's about time."

Ian cut her a sharp glance, his golden eyes flaring with light. "Not ended, suspended."

"And?" There'd better be an otherwise or she'd choke on the hope bursting through her.

"Allie . . ." She ignored Caleb's warning, not taking her eyes from Ian's.

His lips quirked. "The 'and' is not for discussion with a female."

Her elbow in Caleb's gut cut off his chuckle. "That is so backward."

Ian shrugged. "But our way."

She had to grab with her thighs as Caleb let go of her hip to hold out his hand. "Watch your back."

Ian glanced down at her before smiling at Caleb and taking the extended hand in his. "And you watch yours."

Before she could come up with a retort to the implication she was trouble, Ian changed and was gone in a flow of shadow. The only thing he left behind was the humor of his parting comment.

Jared stepped farther into the corridor. "You know, if he wasn't so dead set on killing us, I could probably get to like him."

Caleb stared into the room beyond the door, his jaw set as he viewed the carnage, and then followed the wolves' progress down the tunnel. "Like it or not, I'm just glad they landed on our side. How many did we lose?"

"Only two, but there are a lot of injuries." Jared's gaze followed Caleb's. "Without the D'Nallys it would have been a lot worse."

"Yup." Caleb rested his chin back on her head. "Never did see anyone retreat so fast as those Sanctuary types when they realized the odds had just evened up."

Jared's agreement was a twitch of his lips as he touched blood trickling down his chin. "Of course, one of those D'Nallys is worth two of them in a fight, so maybe it wasn't so much cowardice as brains that had them turning tail."

Caleb brushed the dirt off her jeans. "Next time it won't be easy."

Allie tried not to think of that. "So the D'Nallys know how to clean out a room."

Jared wiped at his cut lip with his shirtsleeve. "That they do."

Caleb glanced through the door again. "Too bad they leave such a mess."

Both men looked at her. Allie shook her head. "Don't look at me to clean it up. I'm in a delicate way."

Unbelievably, Jared's hard eyes softened with humor and, good grief, respect? "I haven't noticed it slowing you down to date."

She slumped against Caleb, mustering her most fragile feminine air. "It just kicked in."

A smile flashed across his stern features. "I bet it did."

She stroked Caleb's chest, feeling his joy at the victory, his satisfaction at defending his home. It didn't seem fair to burst his bubble right now, but he deserved to know.

The sigh as he set her on her feet told her that he knew something was bothering her. She turned in the curve of his arm as he looked down at her. "I'm feeling pretty good right now, Allie girl."

"I know."

He pushed her bangs off her face. "Real good. As a matter of fact, I'm thinking there's a victory cigar and a neat whiskey with my name on it waiting on me in the kitchen."

She bit her lip. She was really getting tired of the one bringing the bad news. "I know."

His thumb tugged her lip from between her teeth. "But you're not going to let me enjoy either, are you?"

"It can wait." Maybe.

He frowned, his eyes studying her face. And then sighed. "The news won't get any better for dragging it out."

She gripped her hands in front of her. "I know, but I just hate always being the bearer of bad news."

"You haven't borne anything yet." Leave it to Slade to point out the logical.

"What are you trying to tell us?"

She met Caleb's gaze, guilt blending with dread. He didn't need this. "It's really good that you're learning to make friends."

"Why?"

She squeezed her fingers harder. "Because I don't think Vincent and company were the only voices in my head."

❋ 25 ❋

ALLIE was going to develop a twitch if she didn't learn to relax. Caleb took another drag on his cigar, and leaned back in his chair. He still had half a shot of whiskey to enjoy, and as determined as Allie was to hop to the next challenge, he was just as determined to celebrate overcoming today's. The woman hadn't been around long enough to know there was always another battle, that the only real peace to be found was in the moments in between, but he had, and the way he saw it, tomorrow was soon enough to deal with preparing for the next Sanctuary attack, to find out who sent the telepathic message that he wasn't alone, and to square things once and for all with the D'Nallys. But right now there was peace, and he just wanted to enjoy his cigar, his whiskey, and his woman.

The cigar ash hung precariously. Caleb tapped it off in the black onyx ashtray he kept for just such occasions. "You really need to learn to slow down."

Allie jumped. The pan she was washing clattered on the counter. She cast him one quick, startled glance and then a blush rose on her cheeks. "I'm working on it."

He smiled around his cigar. Nice to know the woman's mind

was on lovemaking as much as his. "There, too, but I was talking about life in general."

The pan hit the drying rack with a thunk. She turned, hands on hips, and glared at him. Gold sparks fired off in the depths of her eyes, making them appear even bluer as she stood there in that barely-there red knit dress challenging him. "You did not just tell me you have a gripe about my lovemaking."

He stubbed the cigar out. He really didn't like the things, but the one memory he had of his father was of him lighting up a cigar at the end of a good day and sitting on the small porch of their house with his feet propped up, enjoying the satisfaction of a job well done. The scent of cigar smoke still meant contentment to him. The whiskey had been his own addition to the ritual. He picked up the glass. "What if I did?"

With short aggressive jerks, Allie wiped her hands on a blue checked towel. "I think I'd have to kill you."

He grinned, dropped his chair back to four legs, and grabbed her hand. Two tugs and he had her stiff and unyielding in his lap, that sexy dress riding obligingly up her thighs. He nuzzled his way through her hair until he found the outer curve of her ear. She had very sensitive ears. "You know damn well you burn me up in bed."

She didn't soften. "I know your vampire appreciates me there."

He took the lobe between his teeth, ignoring her swat, and focused on her shiver as he bit down gently. She smelled of lemon dish soap and warm, willing woman. "Aren't you the one who keeps telling me that me and my vampire are one and the same?"

"Aren't you the one who keeps telling me they're not?"

There was a tremor in that flat question that had him pulling back. The view he had of the top of her head didn't tell him a thing, but the tense way she held her head did. He gathered her hair in his hand, enjoying its silky feel against the roughness of his skin as he tugged it back so he could see her face. The annoyance he expected was there, along with the tension that came from lingering adrenaline, but there was something unexpected, too. An aching vulnerability that squeezed his heart. Damn. "And you've chosen now to start taking me at face value?"

She shrugged and looked down at the towel wadded into a bunch in her hands. "It doesn't matter what I believe."

Yes, it did. The whole paranormal world knew he was ass over bandbox for the woman, but this woman, his woman, was uncertain as to whether he felt the same way about her as she did about him. How had he managed to screw this up so badly?

He hooked his finger under that stubborn chin and lifted. It took more than the usual amount of effort to get her face up. As soon as he got a glimpse of her expression, he knew why. There were times in everyone's life when they just wanted something too much to even hope it could be. He smoothed his thumb over her lower lip. "Ah, Allie girl, I'm sorry."

She blinked rapidly and the wobbliest smile he'd ever seen stretched the skin under his fingers. "It's not like it's something you can control."

"No, it's not." What he felt for her was wild and uncontrollable. Deep, hot, and permanent. She sniffed and her eyes watered, but all the while she battled tears, that smile firmed up under the sheer force of will she applied to it. One lone drop escaped her control to hover on her lashes. He caught it on his thumb before it could spill. "You want me to go get Ian back here so he can kick my butt from here to Sunday?"

"Why?"

"Because I'm an ass for not telling you how I feel."

"How you feel, or your vampire feels?"

She was going to beat that dead horse into the ground, he could tell. "When it comes to loving you, it's one in the same."

"You don't have to say that."

"Obviously, there's a whole lot I should have said before now." He sighed and smoothed the tear into her cheek until nothing was left to mark its existence. "In all the time I've known you, you've never held back. You give with every bit of emotion in you—"

"I've always been a bit impulsive."

The little squirm that punctuated that statement was a clear indicator of how uncomfortable with that part of her personality she was. She had nothing to worry about. He pushed the bangs off her face. "I've developed a real taste for impulsive."

Her eyebrows rose, but a little of that anxiety left her expression and no new tears got in line behind the first. He took the towel out of her hand and dropped it on the floor. He lifted her up. "Put your legs over mine."

"Why?"

He smiled. She knew damn well why. "Because I like the way you feel against me."

Her thigh slid across his as her arms came around his neck. "You do, huh?"

He pulled her groin to his. She wiggled them into better alignment, notching his cock into her heat.

"Oh yeah."

Her head tipped back. "What else do you like about me?"

"Fishing?"

"Blatantly."

He chuckled and linked his hands in the small of her back, with his fingertips pulling up the material bunched there so he could rest his fingers on the top of her rear. "I love the way you lead with your heart."

"You think that's a plus?"

"I think it's a big plus."

Her smile flowed more naturally. "What else?"

He pressed her in, arching her back so her breasts thrust up and out. Beneath the material of her dress, her nipples peaked. "I love the way you keep your head in a crisis." He kissed her forehead. "The way you can make me laugh when I'm feeling my worst." He let his lips linger on her eyelids before seeking the softness of her cheek. "I love the way your eyes crinkle when you're amused, the way you bite your lip when you worry." The corner of her mouth beckoned next. "I love the way you curl your toes when you're about to tell a joke, and the way you blink to hide tears." Her lips pursed against his, asking for the kiss he'd give her in a heartbeat. He'd give her a thousand kisses. He skimmed his fingertips up her back, over her shoulders. "I love the fact that you're not afraid to cry, to laugh, to kick up a fuss." He cupped her face in his hands. Her blue eyes were shining again, but the emotion behind the tears couldn't be mistaken for anything but happiness. "I love you, Allie Sanders, to hell and back."

He caught the tear that fell with his lips, the salty flavor spicing his tongue with the reality of how much he really did. "And if you don't agree to throw your lot in with mine, lock, stock, and barrel, I'm going to—"

"What?" she interrupted, sitting up straight, all sass and irrepressible humor. "You're going to what?"

Ah, a challenge. He mated his lips to hers, upper to lower, edge to edge. "I'm going to keep you in bed until you agree to whatever I want."

Her eyebrows rose. Her tongue wet her lips, touching his, lingering in a tiny tease before she pulled a fraction away. "And that's my incentive to agree?"

"Uh-huh."

"Sounds like more of a reason to resist."

He shook his head. "Nah, I'm at my most inventive when I'm happy."

"Now that boggles the mind."

Her kiss didn't indicate a boggled state. It was passionate, intense, and singed his short hairs. But when he would have increased the depth, she pulled back, slowly separating her mouth from his, her mind from his. He let her get as far as his hand, his fingers naturally conforming to the shape of her head as he held her in place. "No more hiding. Whatever it is, we deal with it."

She bit her lip and grew serious. Her hands dropped between them, cradling her stomach. "Keeping me around is going to complicate things. There are people still after me. People who won't mind hurting your family and friends to get what they want."

She still thought of herself as an outsider. "You still thinking you're somehow not family?"

"It's not the same."

No. It wasn't. What he felt for her was stronger. Deeper.

He cupped his palm over hers. "Baby, whether you choose to stay or leave, one thing is for sure. No one gets to you without going through me."

"If the baby is healthy, it might be hunted, too."

He couldn't do anything about her fears as to the baby's health but share them. Her other fear he could address. "They can try all they want, but they won't succeed. The Johnsons protect what's theirs."

"You're sure?"

He slapped her exposed buttock, absorbing her start at the hot little sting, smiling when she arched her back as the warmth settled into her center. He placed his fingers deliberately over the spot. She jumped as if he'd spanked her again; the flicker of disappointment in her eyes when she realized he was just going to hold her nudged his libido up a notch. "I'm sure."

The worry faded from her expression. Her head canted to the side as mischief filled the void. Her palms slid up his chest, their heat searing through the cotton of his shirt. "So, pretty much, you're saying I'm stuck with you either way."

"Pretty much."

Buttons came undone under her nimble fingers. "Forever?"

"Oh, yeah." A cross of her arms, a wiggle that had him dodging her elbows, and her dress went flying across the room, a red flag of warning to anyone who thought to repress that wild spirit. "I like the sound of that."

He stared at her breasts, fascinated as pink color flushed the plump mounds. "So do I."

She spread his shirt wide. "Know what I like the sound of even better?"

"What?" He closed his fingers around her right breast as he ran his tongue just inside the edge of her lip, teasing the lining, absorbing her shudder in his palm as she pressed closer.

She caught her breath on a sweet moan. "Allie Johnson."

"Hmm." He pretended to consider it as he nibbled her lower lip. "I kind of like this living in sin thing. Adds a certain spice to the relationship."

"Really?" She tucked her breasts into his caress and wiggled that delightful ass as she sat back. "I thought things had gotten a bit monotonous."

"Then I guess I'll have to liven it up."

"With what?"

He reached into his back pocket and felt the small circle of gold he'd taken from his dresser earlier. His mother's ring. Another bit of his past. Not much to look at, just a simple band carved with care, but imbued with all the love and hope of his parents. Hope for the future that had set them journeying across this country with little more than the clothes on their backs. Hope they'd passed on to their children. Hope he'd carried in his heart for two hundred fifty years despite the logic that said it was impossible. Hope that Allie, with her irrepressible humor and belief, had brought into the light and made shine again. He took the ring out, keeping it tucked into his palm as he took her left hand in his. She bit her lip and met his gaze, the blue of her eyes deepening, her expression softening.

"I love you, Caleb."

There weren't words to express what hearing those words meant to him, what she meant to him. And that just made what he was doing more right.

They couldn't be more committed to each other, and the words of a preacher weren't going to make them any more bonded, but Allie was right in her insistence on the traditions that married past with present. Keeping them alive kept everything in perspective. He slid the ring on her finger, smiling when she just had to help him get it over the knuckle even though he wasn't experiencing difficulty. Not because it was too small, not because she didn't believe he couldn't do it, but because she needed to be an active part of things. It was who she was. A big part.

The ring settled into place. He rubbed his finger over the gold, a smile tugging at his mouth as she realized what she'd done, looking unnecessarily embarrassed when he wouldn't have her any other way. Caleb squeezed her fingers before easing her back into his embrace as he brought her closer to his kiss, to his heart. His lips brushed hers. They parted on a sigh. A soft feminine welcome that he took into his soul, letting it bond with the bone-deep desire welling out of soul-deep contentment. This was his woman. The other half to his soul. The missing part he never thought he'd find. He tilted her head a fraction to the right with a touch of his thumb, giving her his kiss and his heart as he breathed, "Marry me, Allie."

Sarah McCarty has traveled extensively, living in other cultures, sometimes in areas where electricity was a concept awaiting fruition and a book was an extreme luxury. While she could easily adjust to the lack of electricity, living without the comfort of a good book was intolerable. To fill the void, she bought pencil and paper and sketched out her own stories. In the process, Sarah discovered the joy of writing.

Sarah writes what she loves to read—fast-paced stories with vivid dialogue, intense emotion, and well-developed characters. Her attention to detail in her stories has earned her multiple awards and reserved her novels a spot on keeper shelves everywhere.

Sarah writes for Ellora's Cave, Harlequin Spice, Berkley Heat, and Berkley Sensation. Visit her website at www.sarahmccarty.net.